Light of Logan

Regina Smeltzer

Light of Logan
COPYRIGHT 2018 by Regina Smeltzer

Contact Information: titleadmin@pelicanbookgroup.com

All scripture quotations, unless otherwise indicated, are taken from the Holy Bible, New International Version(R), NIV(R), Copyright 1973, 1978, 1984, 2011 by Biblica, Inc.™ Used by permission of Zondervan. All rights reserved worldwide. www.zondervan.com

Cover Art by *Nicola Martinez*

Harbourlight Books, a division of Pelican Ventures, LLC
www.pelicanbookgroup.com PO Box 1738 *Aztec, NM * 87410

Harbourlight Books sail and mast logo is a trademark of Pelican Ventures, LLC

Publishing History
First Harbourlight Edition, 2018
Paperback Edition ISBN 978-1-5223-0140-0
Electronic Edition ISBN 978-1-5223-0138-7
Published in the United States of America

Dedication

Light of Logan is dedicated to my parents, Dallas and Jean Baker, who gave me life and provided the light for my Christian growth. I love you both.

What People are Saying

In The Light of Logan, Regina Smelzer provides gripping suspense with a surprising blend of the practical and the supernatural. Beautifully written. ~ author Donn Taylor

1

Wednesday, May 8

Mr. Charlie tapped the end of his white cane against the first of five steps leading up to the Logan County Courthouse. Groping for the metal railing already hot in the South Carolina sun, he lowered himself onto the third step and shifted his body to the right until he touched the coolness of the grass. Now, anyone with business in the large stone building could pass him.

He settled in to wait, just as he had for the past two years. But today his breaths were shallow. Tension stiffened his spine. They were gathering; time was short. He hoped he had prepared her enough.

~*~

A single crow sat in the tall dogwood and cocked its head as Ruth Cleveland exited the door at the Anthony Dunlap Law Office. With the workday over, Ruth headed toward the center of town. The snapping sound of her worn sandals hitting the back of her feet mingled with the rumble of passing cars.

He would be there; she knew it.

Historic houses, now converted to professional offices, flanked both sides of Main Street. A passing bus spewed oily smoke into the air, and she held her breath, hoping the evening's breeze would drag away the noxious fumes. She slowed, savoring the shade provided by the canopy of a live oak, then pushed herself back into a fast-paced stride as rivulets of sweat ran down her back. She was unsure why she felt a need to rush when she never had before. He would be there–and yet a strange unease disturbed her usual peace.

Five minutes later, the two lanes of Main Street widened into four. The smell of melted asphalt rose in twisted wisps as she passed City Bank. Ahead of her, built one against the other, stood Reiss Pharmacy, Hazel's Cut and Curl, Nola's Diner, and Spencer and Sons Hardware, with three abandoned storefronts set among them. By the time she reached the distant corner and spied the county courthouse–seven stories of gray, unimaginative block–she was almost running.

Professionals, laborers and secretaries joined Ruth on the sidewalk, cellphones pressed to their ears and one thought pounding in their brains: If they beat the traffic light, they could reach the parking lot thirty seconds sooner. Ruth wasn't headed to a parked car like the rest of them. She stood and waited with the crowd for the walk sign to signal go.

He was there, sitting on the courthouse steps just as he'd always been, Monday through Friday, for the past two years. His gnarled hands were wrapped around the white cane, and he seemed focused on the nothingness that drew him to the same spot each day. The sentinel of the county courthouse: that's what she liked to call him. Ruth had no idea why he kept this routine, and she never questioned him about it. They had forged a bond, she and Mr. Charlie, a friendship built on the simplicity of both of their lives. Ruth could be mistaken, but she might be his only friend; she knew he was hers.

Mr. Charlie's mouth widened into a welcome; scattered teeth standing proudly along his gums, his ebony skin shiny with sweat. Cloudy eyes drifted left of her face.

A wave of nausea and dizziness swept over Ruth and passed a moment later. Everything around her remained the same, yet something had changed. Ruth's stomach tightened against the unknown threat.

"You're five minutes late." His voice scratched as if from disuse. "That boss give you trouble?"

Long ago, Ruth gave up challenging the blind man. Somehow, in his darkness, he just knew things–like when she was close by or how she was late when he didn't wear a watch. "Attorney Dunlap never gives me trouble; I was just busy." Ruth smoothed the back of her blue skirt and settled on the sunbaked step beside him.

"You need to quit that dead-end job and find yourself a better one. You can do more with your life."

Ruth sighed. How many times had he given her the same advice?

"A bright thing like you, young and full o' life. You must be what, twenty?"

"Twenty-three."

The light on the corner turned green, and cars accelerated.

Ruth hated the smell of exhaust. A pickup truck raced by—diesel engine from the sound of it. She covered her nose with her hand. A man in a gray suit unwrapped a piece of gum, folded the soft stick into his mouth and tossed the paper to the street where it fluttered like a discarded leaf before settling against the curb.

"Twenty-three. Time to work for yourself." Mr. Charlie wouldn't stop until he had his say. Ruth listened, knowing he would soon run out of words. "There must be people who need papers typed. With your speed, you can crank out work faster'n they can get it to you."

That's what she feared—nothing stashed in the in-box. She had to prove she could live on her own and make good decisions in spite of her mother's lack of confidence–and the times she had proven her mother correct. Now distance separated her and her mom, and luck had helped her land a position at Attorney Dunlap's. Although the job was boring, she had no reason to leave. She had no reason to return to Atlanta where she would be forced to keep hidden why she left in the first place. Mr. Charlie tried to push her beyond her level of comfort, to make her believe she was more than she was.

"You find the work, Mr. Charlie, and I'll quit my job." A tired laugh rose from her throat only to become lost in the rumble of tires and the blare of rap music from a passing car, the base so high it vibrated the cement beneath her feet. Ruth rubbed her arms against the tingle on her skin. "Do you think it's going to rain?"

Mr. Charlie turned toward her and pinched his eyes together. If she didn't know better, she would think he was looking into her soul, assessing her hidden strengths and weaknesses, preparing her future resume. "It's not the rain that we need to worry about." He lifted his face toward the sky.

"I almost forgot to tell you," Ruth said, more to change the subject than anything else. "Mr. Dunlap is taking his receptionist, Kathleen Martin, to the State House tomorrow, and he invited me to go along."

"What's the occasion?"

"I guess there's some vote that Mr. Dunlap wants to watch."

"Hmm." Mr. Charlie rubbed one gnarled hand with the other. "Just be careful Light of Logan." He often called her the light of Logan. All was fair.

She pulled a sandwich bag out of her purse and handed him several slices of apple. "Red Delicious today."

The sun dipped behind the courthouse at her back, and a blanketing shadow began its slow march across the street and up the deep yard on the other side. The stately brick church with its wide porch and towering front pillars occupied a whole block of valuable real estate in downtown Logan. But then, this was the Bible belt.

"The crows are gatherin," the old man murmured, pulling a bit of apple peel from between his teeth.

Half a dozen dark specks circled in lazy patterns high above. "OK, how do you know that? You really can see, can't you?" She knew better, and she knew he knew. When had their minds become entwined?

"Yesterday there were only two."

"Don't birds roost at night? Maybe they're headed to their favorite tree before it gets too crowded." She folded the plastic bag and slipped it back into her purse.

"Something's gonna happen. It's not rain that's coming. You wait and see." He leaned toward her. "The crows are gatherin'. Nothing good'll come of it. Be watchful, little one."

The black specks continued to glide in a circle,

round and round, going nowhere, just like her life. A hot sigh escaped her lips. "I need to head on home." After a lingering look at her friend, Ruth stood and brushed off the back of her skirt.

Someone bumped against her. She stumbled and an arm caught her at the waist.

"Sorry." His voice was deep. "Are you all right?"

Looking up, she stiffened and pulled away.

Confusion spread across the man's face. "Sorry," he said again.

"Ruth?" Mr. Charlie's voice sounded tight.

Her face reddened. "I'm fine." Actually, she was far from fine. The stranger looked so much like Joe: the robin's egg blue eyes and sun-streaked blond hair. Figures, a reminder of Joe on a day when her skin already crawled with a strange anxiety.

With her heart hitting against her ribs, she took a deep breath. She reached for the chain around her neck as she stared at the man's back.

He bolted up the walk to the courthouse. At the door he called over his shoulder, "I really am sorry."

Mr. Charlie chuckled. "You've met Nate Bishop."

"He about knocked me down."

He gave a crackled laugh. "Knocked you right off your feet, did he?"

She bristled. "You know what I mean." This day needed to be over. She laid a hand on Mr. Charlie's shoulder. "I'll see you later."

Ruth walked a block beyond the courthouse before turning right onto Smith Road. A crow lighted on the branch of a crepe myrtle and cocked its shimmering head. Blunted by surrounding feathers, a thin pink scar ran from its right eye along the side of its head, only to be lost at the edge of its wing. Tiny round eyes peered her way. Ruth clutched her purse to her chest. Mr. Charlie said the crows were gathering, whatever that meant.

The sense of being watched sent a shiver up her spine. As she half-ran toward home, the feeling deepened. But she knew if she looked, no one would be there.

2

Thursday, May 9

With the unsettled feeling of the previous day forgotten, Ruth scooted to the edge of the wooden seat in the gallery's front row, her mouth stretched into a grin. Excitement over seeing her favorite legislator in his own world made it impossible to sit still. She felt like a grade-school girl at a circus. The noise and energy that ricocheted between the walls fed her high spirits.

Ruth itched to touch the gold embossing on red wallpaper that extended from the lower chamber to the balcony where she sat. Instead, she forced herself back into the seat, folded her hands in her lap, and thought about the morning's drive.

From the back of the car, she had stroked the leather upholstery as the sound of the engine purred around her. Her boss's luxury sedan shared little with the cracked plastic and ear-splitting roar from the defective muffler on her over-the-hill clunker, now-deceased. She clutched the iced tea Mr. Dunlap bought her with both hands, terrified lest she spill even a single drop.

The three of them arrived in Columbia an hour and a half before the start of the House session. The gallery was almost full with reporters, notebooks in hand, anxious for the vote.

Attorney Dunlap managed to find seats for them.

He leaned toward the women. "This is one of the most important issues these folks will ever vote on." He gestured toward the chamber below. "History is in the making, ladies." He smiled and settled back to wait.

The first time she had ever seen Attorney Dunlap was when her car ran out of gas on her way back to Atlanta. She walked two miles to Logan, hoping to spend a day or two earning gas money to get her home. The first business she came to belonged to Attorney Anthony Dunlap. The two level, red brick building occupied the far-left corner, and beyond it stood old Victorian houses turned into offices. The reception area at Attorney Dunlap's was full of men standing in groups of two or three. Their muffled conversations formed layers of tension trapped in the small space. Sitting behind a polished desk against the back wall, the receptionist's hand hovered above the jangling phone, never quite reaching the receiver.

As Ruth tried to decide to stay or leave, a door on the back wall opened. She caught a glimpse of a long hall before she focused on the strange looking man who filled the doorway.

He stood well over six feet tall, with gangly arms that seemed to stretch on forever. Wispy salt and pepper hair on top of his head was cut short and in disarray while the remainder of his hair was pulled back with a rubber band. The goatee framing his chin needed trimming. He wore a white shirt and a navy tie. She remembered because she had on a white t-shirt and blue jeans. The room quieted as the tall man scanned the faces. He stopped on Ruth and frowned.

Her knees knocked. She wanted to run out the door, but she had nowhere to go. "I can type." The squeaky words scraped their way across the now-silent room. "I just need to earn enough money to put gas in my car. If you don't like my work, you don't have to pay me."

The hippy-scarecrow man–she found out later it was Attorney Dunlap himself–continued to stare at her, his expression guarded. "I have some meeting minutes," he finally said. "Do a good job, and we'll talk." He turned to the receptionist and mumbled instructions.

At the end of the day, Mr. Dunlap offered her a part-time job. Over the next six months, her hours had increased, and now she was a full-time handy-person: running errands, cleaning, filing, doing computer research, and even filling in for Kathleen at the front desk on occasion.

She had rented a cheap apartment—the bottom of an old house—and by living frugally, she managed.

Now, here she was at the State House in Columbia. She leaned back in the balcony seat, a smirk of satisfaction etched on her face.

The legislators began to enter the chamber. Conversation in the balcony turned to whispers as spectators shifted half their attention to the scene below.

Ruth scrutinized the backs of each head, watching for her congressman, Representative Stewart Gleason. The room was filling and still he hadn't appeared. Ruth turned to Mr. Dunlap. "Where is he?" she whispered.

Her boss shrugged his shoulders. "It may be better if he doesn't show."

~*~

Stewart Gleason inhaled the scent of furniture

polish and worn books as the memory of past legislators–tough men and women who stood for what was right even during tough times–swirled around him like old ghosts. He considered staying in the State House Library for the next couple of hours. Better yet, he could slip by his colleagues and forego the opportunity to be part of the biggest legislative debacle in history. Without voting, no one could lay the blame on him when, some day in the future, the dream shattered. The resulting anarchy would be more disastrous than the crisis the legislators were hoping to prevent.

He fingered an antacid tablet, blue this time, and shoved the remaining pack in his suit pocket. When the vote was over, perhaps guilt would stop eating his gut like maggots in a rotting possum. Support for the landmark legislation was expected to be strong. His opposing vote would be needed. Sighing, he rose from the wide leather chair.

In the lobby, dozens of school children, some in green and white uniforms, others in jeans and t-shirts, were herded in small groups, their giddy voices drifting upward toward the rotunda. Tight-faced adults walked among the children. Too many kids; too few teachers. The vote would help. That was the prevailing thought, anyway.

At the double-doors to the House of Representatives, assistants, dressed in navy suits, buzzed in and out like bees seeking the last bit of nectar before the sunset.

Representative Dennis Welch approached. "You ready for the vote?"

Stewart tipped his chin upward in the fashion familiar to southern men.

An aide, juggling a stack of binders, broke between the two men. "Sorry, sorry," she mumbled as she pressed forward, the scent of a floral cologne lingering in her wake.

Inside the chamber, Stewart walked down the right aisle. Filtered air sucked the moisture from his face. Conversations streamed, the words indistinct by sheer numbers and the cavernous space. However, one voice broke free, and Stewart cringed.

Young and tall, Joseph Ackerman puffed out his broad chest. "As you know, this bill has been called landmark legislation because we have chosen to take a stand against inequity. We"—he indicated those around him—"have carved our place in history."

Stewart Gleason grimaced. The smug first-termer had leaped to power because of his name, not by his accomplishments. Some of the congressmen hung on the young man's words, as though the greenhorn's opinion was more valid than anyone else's. It all came down to social power. Joseph Ackerman came from wealth, and he made sure everyone knew it. His family could buy South Carolina if they wanted. They already owned Georgia.

Todd Myers, representative from Darlington County, slid into the seat beside Stewart. He pulled a folder from his briefcase and tossed the green file onto the table. "Did you see the crows outside? Man, they're everywhere. Huge boogers. Must be a hundred of them on the lawn."

Stewart had seen the crows, and they gave him the willies because the birds didn't act like crows. Crows made noise, they ate anything they could get their beaks on, and they definitely did not sit in the grass and stare silently. Something was wrong with those birds.

~*~

Ruth scooted closer to the railing; Representative Gleason looked just as he did at the public meetings at the library. She never actually attended, but he always seemed sincere as she passed by. The congressman sat with his back straight. Such confidence! Ruth beamed with pride. She would never be able to stand in front of people as he did, sharing thoughts and swaying opinions. Thinking about it made her shudder.

A few straggling legislators entered the chamber. Some joined small groups engaged in conversation while others strode with determination directly to their assigned seats, dropping expensive-looking briefcases to the floor with as much regard as she gave her lunch sack.

While Ruth tried to absorb all the activity below, her gaze kept returning to a group of legislators who seemed spellbound by the man in the center. Chins were rubbed and heads bobbed up and down, but no one interrupted the speaker. Shifting for a better view, she still couldn't see who held their attention. Her pulse quickened as she thought of what it would be like to command such respect. The group broke apart and as she stared, the man in the center looked up into the gallery.

Ruth gasped. She pushed herself back into the seat, hoping to melt into the wood and metal framework. As his glance met hers, sourness burned the back of her throat. She had known that eventually she would see him again, but not like this: not serving as a member of the South Carolina House of

Representatives.

Below, the gavel sounded, and the man took his seat but not before Ruth saw the smirk. Even from the distance, he looked directly at her and winked. Her surprise turned to rage. Thankfully, anger bound her to the chair because she wanted to stand and scream at him in front of his friends, to ruin his life as his selfishness had ruined hers. Her clenched jaws hurt and she tried to pry her teeth apart. As she stared at his broad shoulders and flaxen hair, she blinked. For just a breath of a second, he had looked very much like a crow.

Why was he here? His family lived in Georgia, not South Carolina. She breathed in and out, trying to control her raging emotions, the landmark vote forgotten as her mind whisked back almost four years.

His family house in Atlanta looked like a castle made of towering white brick, manicured lawns, and orderly flowerbeds. Ruth's mother cleaned house for the Ackermans three days a week. Ruth had hitched a ride to the rich side of town with her boyfriend, Morgan, when he set out to test-drive a car brought into his dad's garage for repairs.

"This is where you want dropped off?" Morgan asked. His eyes bugged. "Who do you know who lives here?" His remark wasn't sarcastic, just realistic. The tired apartment Ruth and her mom rented was a world away from the Ackermans' three-floor mammoth.

"My mom cleans for them. Thought I'd surprise her. She hates the bus ride home, and I saved a trip on my pass today, thanks to you." She got out of the car and waved good-bye.

He roared the engine in response. Even though his dad owned a garage, Morgan's financial situation wasn't that much better than hers. Any profit his dad made went back into the struggling business. But Morgan treated her well, and she envisioned a future with him. Morgan represented strength. He knew exactly what he wanted to do while she still floundered. It was May. Their senior year of high school was almost over. Because his dad needed him at the garage, Morgan planned to attend the community college.

She would bypass college and find a full-time job, maybe clerical, since she could type more words-per-minute than anyone else in the school. Not her dream, but then, this was life.

The day was hot, and sweat coated her face. The neighborhood seemed strangely quiet, and after a minute of contemplation, she realized the difference. This part of town lacked the smelly busses and exhaust-spewing semis that traversed her streets. A bird twittered, and she smiled, even though she couldn't spot the gleeful noisemaker among the young trees.

As she stood on the sidewalk staring up at the house, the front door opened, revealing the most handsome man she had ever seen. Her knees melted.

He'd been dressed in shorts and a polo shirt and held himself with an air that said money. His short, blond hair had been swept perfectly to one side. His chin was square and lifted just enough that his opinion of himself was instantly clear. "You need something?" he asked, a friendly smile curving perfect lips.

Embarrassment flushed her face as she tried to find her tongue now lost in her gaping mouth. "I'm waiting for my mom. Sorry if I bothered you." There was no law against standing on the sidewalk, yet she felt a need to acknowledge her place.

"Your mom?" He leaned against the doorframe, his tanned skin highlighted against the white trim.

"She's cleaning your house." *Please don't let me die of heart failure.*

He pushed the door open wider. "Come on in; no need to stand outside in the heat."

She'd stumbled backward. Her foot rolled on the edge of the sidewalk and she landed in grass softer than the mattress on her bed. Mortified, she jumped up. "Really, I'll just wait here."

"I insist." Was there humor playing on his face?

She found herself not only in the house, but on the back porch with iced tea in a real glass, as though she were a princess. But his house had not been a castle and what happened within had not been a dream come true.

And the source of her nightmare now stood on the House of Representatives' floor.

~*~

Stewart Gleason gathered his folders.

The vote was over. The solemn chamber erupted into a cacophony of shuffling feet, jangling keys, and pleasant voices. Representatives shook hands with colleagues they wouldn't miss during the off-season. As a body, the representatives moved toward the door at the back of the chamber, eager to escape from elected responsibilities until the next session. Always, there would be a next. Life was nothing more than a cycle of behavior, people running round and round like a hamster on a wheel, feeling pompous for the activity, but simply repeating history, over and over.

"Thought you might need a cup of coffee before you head back to Logan," Dennis Welch said.

"Sure." Stewart lacked the energy to say no. He counted Dennis among his friends, and right now, friends were in short supply.

The State House Coffee Shop was deserted, a rarity during sessions. Tile floors, streaked with black scuffs, would be buffed to a tough gloss before congress reconvened. A pink plastic carnation in a milk-glass vase sat on each of the thirty-or-so empty tables. The decoration was probably someone's attempt to infuse softness into a space where conversations swirled harsh and bitter.

The scent of hot grease and burnt meat lingered. The grill along the back wall guarded against anything healthy. One vending machine displayed stale-looking sandwiches behind glass doors while another held chips and candy, ready for the desperate. Stewart brought apples to Columbia with him, bags full, that he shared with anyone who needed a healthy break. Tonight, there would be no late-night workers rushing in for an apple from Stewart or sustenance from the Coffee Shop. The building breathed a heavy silence.

The two congressmen filled their cups from the large coffeemaker that held hot brew after-hours. They chose a table that flanked the hallway windows, a popular spot during the busy days.

Stewart sipped and grimaced. The coffee had evaporated into a thick sludge. Even so, it was hot; steam swirled from its surface and the cup offered warmth to his hands.

Dennis cleared his throat. "I know you aren't happy about the vote."

Stewart glanced around him: white Formica

tabletops and chairs with red vinyl seats. Normally, a heavyset woman sat on the stool behind the cash register, her kinky hair escaping the green hairnet as she scanned customers' food items and collected the money due. She was gone now.

The steam from his coffee rose and disappeared. He breathed in and out, calming his nerves while arranging his thoughts. "It passed," Stewart finally said. "I hoped it wouldn't."

"It may not be as bad as you think. Projections show—"

"It's immoral to bankrupt churches." The caustic words came before he knew he would say them. Rancid coffee and pent-up anger ignited in his stomach, and he reached into his pocket for an antacid. The legislators were idiots. No, not idiots, just smart people looking to fix a system that couldn't be fixed. Thanks to Joseph Ackerman, they had latched onto the one thing that would generate revenue for the struggling state. How long had it taken the man to figure it out? Ackerman didn't seem all that sharp; he must have had help.

"The state is in a bad way," Dennis said. "We struggle every year to keep the budget in the black. If we had money, the vote never would have happened." His eyes lit with energy. "You know as well as I do that our small towns are dying."

How many times had Dennis given his "cities are dying; we are here to save them" speech? His words sounded rehearsed.

Four children ran up the hall, their laughter and footsteps echoing in the tomblike silence. Were they a part of a lingering school group? Where was the teacher?

Dennis nodded toward the hall. "The average classroom in South Carolina has thirty-five students like those two, up from twenty-four just five years ago. Teachers can't provide the attention they used to. Our kids are falling behind; State Proficiency Tests prove it. Scores in math and science have dropped in spite of the new curriculum."

Dennis took a swallow of coffee and shoved the cup toward the center of the table. "Nasty stuff." He wiped his mouth with the back of his hand. "You're worried about our kids? Let's give them an education that will jump-start their futures." Dennis leaned back in his chair and a faint smile shaped his lips. "You can't disagree with that."

"I disagree with the source of the money."

Stewart wanted to shake the smug look from his friend's face, wishing for the time not-so-long-ago when manly disagreements were settled by a good brawl. Some legislature probably voted a fist-to-the-jaw as unacceptable. "Non-profits have always been exempt from paying real estate taxes," Stewart said. "Now, after today's vote, they have to pay, and they have to meet the first six months' debt in thirty days. Churches don't have that kind of money."

Dennis rested his forearms on the table. "Each municipality has the choice to implement the tax. Besides, we both know churches tuck money away for a rainy day."

Stewart leaned back in his chair. "Do you go to church?" His words barely rose above a whisper.

"I am a member of—"

"But how often do you actually go? Every Sunday? Once a month? On Easter and Christmas? Do you serve on a committee like the budget or missions?"

Dennis's eyes narrowed. "What's your point?"

"Do you tithe?"

Dennis pushed himself from the table. "Come on, Stewart. Look at the numbers. In a recent poll, 93% of South Carolina's adults claimed to be a member of a Christian church. We have almost four million adults in the state, so that gives an average of, what, nine hundred thousand, wage-earners who are church members? The churches have money."

"In my church," Stewart said, "we have a membership of about 500. On an average Sunday morning, the attendance is around 180. Of those who come regularly, about a third tithe. The others toss a dollar in the plate—maybe. On a good year, we collect eighty percent of our projected budget."

"Maybe you need a new minister."

"It's not the minister. He preaches the Word. Look at the statistics, Dennis, and you'll find attendance down in the churches nationally and financial giving right along with it. That huge savings you alluded to, it doesn't exist; and if it did, the money was spent long ago."

"So what are you saying?"

"Churches won't be able to pay this tax."

"Come on. The big income folks will bail them out."

"It won't happen. And if, by chance, some good person does donate the money for the taxes this June, what happens in January, and the next June, and the year after that? The tax will erode the church's effectiveness." He tried to soften his expression, forcing his lips into a fight between scowl and anger.

Dennis waved his hand in dismissal as he stood to leave. "Next session we'll talk again. It's going to work, buddy. It's going to work."

Stewart sat alone in the silent coffee shop. The issue wasn't about paying bills. The real issue was saving souls. Steward reached for the roll of antacids in his pocket, only to find the wrapper empty.

~*~

The roots released with little effort from the sandy soil. Ruth gripped the dandelion just below the yellow flower, imagining Joe's neck between her hands. The small vegetable garden usually served as therapy. She had been digging in the dirt for an hour, and the plot of tomatoes, peppers, lettuce and herbs stood camera-ready. But tension still squeezed her muscles. She rose and stretched her neck and back, feeling the tight kinks and aches that had started earlier in the day.

Seeing Joe had shaken her more than she thought possible. After almost four years, she had expected his greeting to be more civil. But to smirk at her! His haughty attitude bit into her fragile pride. His glance into the gallery and his recognition of her with such surety had not been coincidental. He must have spotted her earlier, when she'd focused her attention elsewhere.

As she picked soil from under her nails, she glanced around the backyard. Not much to look at, but it met her needs. Encircled on three sides by a rusty fence that wouldn't keep out stray cats or strangers, none-the-less it gave a sense of boundaries. The metal shed in the far left housed the garden tools and yard-sale lawn mower she had accumulated after moving in. The ancient gas mower refused to start half the time. Not that she could ask her neighbors for help. Most of them turned surly faces toward her when she was out, or else they shied away, as though afraid she might identify them in a police lineup.

The tomatoes were beginning to ripen, showing a blush of red across the green skin. In a week, she could pick the first of her crop. Already the cilantro stood tall and full. She plucked a leaf and popped it into her mouth. All the fixings for salsa, right here in her garden.

As the sun dropped below the tip of the trees, the mosquitoes ventured from wherever they spent the heat of the day. Swatting at the flying nuisances, she carried the rake and hoe to the shed and locked the sliding metal doors.

As hard as she tried, she couldn't stop thinking of Joe. The bad memories she had stored away in a cupboard of her mind had suddenly opened, one drawer at a time. But now the anticipated meeting was over, and she really could forget him. There was no reason she should ever see Joseph Ackerman again.

3

Friday, May 10

Nate pounded the roofing nail gun across the line of shingles, securing the brown strips to the black tar paper and plywood beneath. Sweat dripped into his eyes as the breathless May air trapped heat as efficiently as a cocoon made of plastic wrap. And the days would only get worse. Summer in South Carolina amounted to heat and humidity in massive doses.

Worse than the heat, more distracting than the sound of his friend Chet singing off-key from the other side of the roof, was the annoying memory of the woman's face from three days ago. It was just a quick, last-minute trip to the courthouse; something he had managed dozens of times for the boss. Only this time he'd stumbled over a girl. Oh, he had moved on and finished the boss's work, but the girl remained trapped in his thoughts.

Wiping the sweat from his face, he sat back on his heels. Even though his portion of the roof in the back baked in the sun, a large oak shaded Chet's front side of the house, and a mature magnolia, at least twenty-five feet tall, hugged the road.

He silently blessed the owners of this Miller Street property for insisting the trees be saved. Most of the construction sites lately were in new, logged-out developments on the edge of town. What a waste of nature–and what irony. He built houses for a living, yet he stressed over losing a few trees. Still, there had to be better ways of meeting the public's demand than stripping the land bare.

He lifted the tail of his t-shirt and dried the handle of the nail gun. He told the crew repeatedly that if the tool slipped in their hands, they'd as likely put a nail through their foot as through the roof. So far this season, there had been no accidents.

Something fell into his hair. It dripped onto his face. He swiped a hand across his forehead and stared at the white slime on his palm.

"Blasted birds." Crows, like a thick cloud of summer gnats, stretched across the sky. As a black undulating mass, they drifted high overhead, shifting, streaming down, and then effortlessly, rising back up.

Nate jerked a rag from his back pocket and wiped his hand and then scrubbed the rag across his face and hair. Sighing, he looked at his side of the roof. He only had three rows of shingles laid. It was just so hot.

On the other side of the roof, the sound of Chet's hammering continued.

As Nate shoved the soiled cloth back into his jeans, he pushed the nail gun out of the way with the toe of his work boot. "Ready for a break?" he called over his shoulder.

The pounding on the opposite side of the roof stopped as Nate backed down the ladder and headed around the house toward the shade of the live oak. An orange cooler rested on the open tailgate of his blue pickup truck. A hundred thousand miles on it when he bought it a year ago and it still purred like new, thanks to its diesel engine. He slid his hand across the top of the bed before filling a paper cup and pouring the icy water over his head.

"Looks like the birds found you, too." A grin the size of Texas spread across Chet's face as he jumped from the third rung of the ladder. He strode across the rutted yard and pointed to the telltale smear on the shoulder of his sweat-drenched t-shirt.

"I thought crows stayed in the fields and ate the farmer's corn. What're they doing in town?" Nate shielded his eyes and stared upward where birds still flew lazy circles above the trees. "We'll never finish the roof at this rate." He poured another cup of water and downed it in quick gulps, his mood blacker than the ebony feather that landed beside his foot. He gave it a kick with his boot.

"We'll never finish the roof if you don't get your mind back on the job," Chet said. "What's with you, anyway?"

Nate angled himself on the tailgate, and the weathered springs groaned. He lifted his nose to the air. "The Johnsons must have spread manure again."

"Come on, buddy. Forget the birds. Forget the cows. I've known you too long." Chet raised his eyebrows. "It's a girl, isn't it?"

Nate poured another cup of water and took a swallow.

"I knew it! It's a girl." Chet leaned against the truck. "So tell all, my friend. You haven't been interested in anyone since Kathy, and that was, what, four years ago?"

Nate narrowed his eyes. "There's no girl."

"Ha! You can't lie to me. I've known you since you were in third grade and still wet the bed."

Nate hissed through his teeth. How could he explain what he didn't understand? Yes, he was distracted, but he didn't know why. He had barely brushed against her. If she hadn't been bone-thin, it wouldn't have mattered. As it was, he about knocked her down the stairs. But what bothered him the most wasn't the fact he could have hurt her; it was her expression. Big brown eyes full of shock, as though he was her worst nightmare. He wasn't movie-star gorgeous, but his mug had never scared anyone before.

Gravel crunched beneath the tires of a white club cab, shiny and new. "The big boss's here," Chet mumbled.

A door clicked shut. "Am I paying you guys to sit around like little boys?"

Harold Evans had been Nate's employer for the past four years, since Nate graduated from the University of South Carolina with a business degree. Little good the degree did him when he worked as someone else's hired hand while he dreamed of owning his own business. "Hey, Mr. Evans," Nate said. "Just came down for some water and a bath. Those stupid crows–"

"I need this place under roof by the end of the week. The plumbers are scheduled to start Monday. Time is money." For all his talk, Harold Evans treated his workers well.

If Nate couldn't have his own business, working for Evans Construction was a close second. In the early years, the older man took the time to teach him new skills, and over the years, Mr. Evans had entrusted him with increasing responsibility, sometimes manning his own crew.

Chet walked back toward the house as Nate slid off the tailgate and stretched. Joints popped and crackled. Last night's restlessness had left his body groaning like an old granny.

A thump. A cry of pain.

Nate turned toward the sound, dread filling his gut. Accidents happened in construction–too many of them serious.

Chet lay at the bottom of the ladder, his left leg bent awkwardly beneath him; his ashen face spoke of the pain he wouldn't voice.

Nate ran and squatted beside his friend. One glance at Chet's odd-angled left foot and Nate's stomach clenched. He could never be a paramedic.

Mr. Evans palmed his cellphone. "A squad's on the way." He rubbed his chin; worry lines etched his forehead.

"Stupid crows," Chet mumbled through pale lips. "Slipped on some of their droppings." His fingers dug into the dirt as pain gripped his face.

"Don't talk, buddy. Help's coming."

Chet groaned. "Man, lousy timing. Sorry, Nate."

Nate attempted to take a deep breath, but his tight chest made him feel like the victim of a boa constrictor that hadn't eaten in six months. He needed to help Chet, but he didn't know what to do. When had he last been so worthless in an emergency? He gulped, remembering the girl. He didn't do anything to help her. But he had been in a hurry to get the building permit before the courthouse closed. When he came back out fifteen minutes later, she and the old man were both gone.

A siren sounded, and Nate jumped to his feet, almost stumbling over Chet's extended leg.

A crow landed on the roof of his truck.

Life was spinning out of control.

4

Saturday, May 11

Ruth walked with hurried steps. The unfamiliar county road cut a swath through pines and cyprus, the swampy ground beneath the trees hidden by a thick tangle of vines, ferns, and grasses. A strip of azure sky provided just enough light to melt both the visible and the hidden into a miasma of 'what if's.' Gnats buzzed around her face, making the hot trek more miserable. Why hadn't she brought a bottle of water?

Garage sale shopping provided the bulk of her weekend entertainment, but most of the trips kept her closer to home. She normally wouldn't have gone this far, but today, anger over Joe's behavior smothered her good sense.

She shifted the plastic grocery sack to her opposite hand, reminding herself the trip was worthwhile. Inside the bag lay three shirts she had purchased for a quarter each. She could remake them into something really nice.

Now past noon, her feet ached, the strap of her purse bit into her shoulder, and nothing sounded better than her own shady front stoop. Well, maybe a glass of iced tea.

She glanced around again, wondering about the lack of crows. All morning she hadn't seen one, which was strange, when most days, it was hard not to practically trip over them. Even the crow with the scar, that always seemed to be around, hadn't made an appearance. Maybe the crows didn't like the swamp; she wasn't too fond of it herself.

A car whizzed by, stinging her legs with loose gravel. She sighed, wondering where courtesy had disappeared to. The rude driver made her think of Joe, and then her mind wandered to that instant in the State House when she'd thought he looked like one of the huge, feathered birds. A husky laugh escaped her throat. Such an imagination.

Sprigs of dark-green among the light-colored grasses caught her attention. Tiny pine trees poked their heads above the slender blades. Ruth stared at the sturdy tops and smiled. They were just what she needed to screen the back of her yard. True, it would take several years before the pines provided much privacy, but she wasn't going anywhere, even though she just rented the place.

She stepped into the grass and stopped. Would taking the trees be stealing? Unsure what to do, she looked around and spotted a county truck and two mowers along the edge of the trees about a city block away.

As she approached, she saw two men sitting on the tailgate, a paper lunch sack and an old metal lunch pail stretched between them. Dressed in jeans and t-shirts with orange vests, they looked like the workers they seemed to be. Mr. Charlie's words came back to her: "Be careful." "Foolhardy," her mother would say, "to speak to strange men on a deserted road." A shiver of anxiety, like a chill without a cause, gripped her. From the pavement, such as it was, she called to them.

"Do you know who owns the sides of the road?"

The shorter of the two men ran the palm of his hand across his mouth. "Don't know for sure. The county maintains the strip along the roads. Not sure who owns the land behind it." He smoothed down his grizzled beard.

The younger man got up and poured water from a large red and white thermos into a paper cup. "You look like you could use a drink." He walked toward her.

Ruth hesitantly reached for the water.

"You shouldn't be walking on this road alone." He moved a couple of steps away as she drained the cup.

"I was wondering about the little pine trees–if I can dig them up. Your mower will chop them down…"

The young man laughed. "You want the pine trees? Help yourself, would be my guess."

Ruth stared at the muscles that bulged beneath the sleeves of his shirt. She backed up another step, still gripping the paper cup in her tense hand. "I need to go home and get my shovel."

"How long will it take you?"

Ruth looked down the dusty road. "I can be back within an hour."

"I hope to be on my way home by then."

"Where are these trees?" the bearded man called out. He reached behind him into the bed of the truck and pulled out a shovel. "Lead the way."

Keeping the man with the shovel in front of her, Ruth retraced her footsteps and pointed out the sprouts of dark green. The older county worker stomped through the grass, creating a path as he moved toward the saplings. The younger man lingered beside her. She sent her companion nervous glances, but he seemed intent on watching the older man.

"These sure are little things," the bearded man called over his shoulder. "Not much more than twigs. It'll take forever for them to grown big." He separated a patch of grass with his boot and bit the end of the shovel into the earth. When three sprig-like trees hung from his fist, he walked back to the edge of the road where Ruth stood. "What do you plan to put them in?" he asked, wiping his brow with his arm.

She hadn't thought about that. She stuffed the newly purchased shirts into her purse and held out the empty bag.

The grizzled worker shook sand off the dangling roots and slid the three gangly saplings into the bag. Ruth took it from his hands. "Thanks so much!"

"Want some more water?" the young man asked as they reached the truck.

"I've been enough of a nuisance. But thanks again for the help."

"Happy planting." The older man lifted the shovel above his head in a wave.

A smile crept across Ruth's face. She had been right to stop. One couldn't live in fear of every unknown. She thought of her dad—his murderer never found. A random shooting the police had said. His death had changed her mother. Overnight, she turned jittery, always looking over a shoulder, re-locking doors that were already locked, demanding Ruth stay inside even when her friends were playing in the small yard in front of the apartment.

No wonder Ruth tended to jump at every shadow. Clutching the bag of trees, she felt a renewed spring in her step. Yes, some people were worth trusting.

The road crew disappeared at the bend of the

road. Soon the swamp would be replaced with the edge of town and its modest houses. And then she would be close to home.

A white sedan shot past her, slowed, and backed up. The driver's window lowered. "You need a ride?"

"I'm fine, thanks." Ruth kept walking.

"It's too hot to walk. Come on. I'll give you a lift." The driver edged the car forward, keeping pace with her.

"No, really. I'm almost home." Her skin prickled as she tightened her grip on the bag of trees. She regretted her decision not to buy a cellphone. At least she should have purchased some mace. It couldn't cost too much, could it?

The car door opened.

Primal instinct fueled her tired legs as she ran, the stranger's feet pounding close behind her. The ground turned to mush and she slipped, falling to her knees, losing her grip on the bag and her purse. She clawed at the muck, trying to regain her feet.

A hard hand grabbed her upper arm and yanked her upright, wrenching her shoulder.

"Back off!" she screamed.

His hand connected to the left side of her face, snapping her head backward.

She fought back the tears, unwilling to show her weakness.

"I said I'd give you a ride," the man hissed through clenched teeth. "This is your lucky day."

She pulled and twisted, but his fingers dug deeper into the flesh of her arm. She drove the palm of her hand toward his nose, but he grabbed her wrist mid-strike.

"Full of energy, are you?" He wagged his

eyebrows.

She wanted to throw up. He was so much stronger. Trying to fight through the hysteria, she pushed to remember the self-defense techniques she learned years ago—lessons she'd never needed until today. She jammed her knee into his leg, trying to hit his kneecap.

The man groaned. He released her wrist and drew back his fist.

She threw her body to the right, wrenching her shoulder but avoiding his punch. Using her free hand, she dug her nails deep into his arm and twisted.

He wrapped his arms around her chest. With her back pressed against his abdomen, she put all her body weight on him. She leaned over his arms and drew both feet upward. Tender tissue yielded under her heels and the man screamed and dropped her. She struggled to her feet.

The man remained doubled over.

The sound of a speeding vehicle approached.

"You need help?" the grizzled driver of the county truck called out the window. The younger worker sprinted around the truck toward Ruth.

An engine roared, and the Taurus skidded down the road.

The older worker jumped from the truck and walked toward Ruth, cellphone in hand. "Called the police," he said. "You OK, kiddo? Thought we were coming to your rescue, but you did OK without us." He grinned. "You're some tough girl, but those trees didn't fare so well."

Her plastic bag, ripped and torn, lay on the ground, the trees crushed and splintered. Nearby, her purse dangled from a gangly shrub.

"I really need to sit down."

Two sets of arms grabbed her as her knees finally let go.

5

Tuesday, May 14

Nate avoided hospitals on the basis of what happened there. People were cut and chopped on, and then they died. This wasn't a rational reaction to places of mercy, but Grandpa Bishop had broken a hip and survived surgery, only to die the next day with a blood clot to his lung. It could happen to anyone, but Nate still shivered when he drove past the place. Now his best buddy had been locked in the Logan Community Chop Shop for four days.

During Chet's surgery, Nate bravely sat with Betsy, Chet's wife, in the waiting room. The smell of stale french fries, old coffee, and body odor nearly put him under the table, and he spent more time with his nose up his sleeve than not. The stench didn't seem to bother Betsy. But then, she had dealt with dirty diapers recently.

The lady at the reception desk smiled as he walked by, her pale eyes twinkling in recognition, the turquoise smock hanging loose around her stooped shoulders.

"Hey, Mrs. Murphy." Nate tried to keep on the good side of the grandmother-type.

"Are you here to see Chet again?"

"Yep."

"You were here last night."

"Yep."

He almost expected her to pull out a plate of freshly baked cookies, but instead she waved him on.

He rounded the wall to the elevators.

Two men in white lab coats with stethoscopes draped around their necks glanced at Nate then resumed their conversation.

The elevator doors slid open.

Nate pushed the five-button.

One of the men paused the discussion about the benefits of laparoscopic versus incisional exploration long enough to press eight.

The smell of antiseptic solutions greeted him as he exited the elevator. His stomach rolled. He hated hospitals, but he forced a bounce to his step as he strode into Chet's room and squeezed his friend's shoulder. "How you feeling, buddy?"

As usual, Betsy sat on the vinyl recliner alongside the bed, her legs drawn beneath her, and another hospital-issued white blanket draped over her lap.

Nate bent and kissed her cheek. "You ever want to dump this man for someone new, come my way." The words, spoken in jest, held a hint of sincerity. Nate dreamed of finding a woman as wonderful as Betsy.

"I think I'll keep him awhile yet." Betsy patted her husband's arm and gifted him with a smile that could speed global warming.

"Those crazy crows still out there?"

"You ask me that every evening, and yes, the crows are still here. Nasty things."

"Mrs. Rhonda told me the mayor is planning to trap them," Betsy said.

"Good luck with that." Chet's grin spread across his face.

"They don't act like normal crows." Nate glanced toward the window. He wouldn't have been surprised to see a black form sitting on the ledge or a group of birds flying by, brushing the glass with their wings. Somehow, he knew the mayor would be unsuccessful. These crows were smart, too smart. "People are starting to get freaked out, and the birds just keep coming."

"Do you think I should keep Chip inside?" Betsy glanced at Nate. "I haven't heard of anyone being attacked, but you never know. Maybe just until the mayor gets control of them?"

"They just seem to be here. That sounds stupid, but those beady eyes look as though they're watching us." Nate gave a shaky laugh and wagged his fingers in the air. "Here I am, all superstitious suddenly."

"I was hoping the birds would be gone by the time I went home. The surgeon's already written my release for tomorrow."

Nate lowered himself into a molded plastic chair. "You're doing OK, then?" He glanced at his friend's left leg encased in plaster, signatures scrolled over its white surface. Surgery to insert two pins would have kept Nate whining for weeks, but not Chet. "Sure you don't want to wait until you can chase the nurses around the bed before you leave?"

"I wonder where they're coming from?" Betsy mumbled.

Nate grinned. "The nurses? Want me to go ask for addresses?"

Betsy curled her nose at Nate, and then she turned to her husband. "Sorry, buddy, but no running for you for a while."

"I can get addresses for later…"

Betsy stared at Nate in mock-anger. "Doc told Chet he can go home if he stays off his leg for another week before putting any weight on it."

Chet didn't like to lie around. He didn't like to ask for help, either. The next seven days would be a battle of wills: husband versus wife.

Nate grinned. His bet was on Betsy.

"After a week, the doc will re-X-ray the bones, and then he can start walking a little bit at a time. But for now, its crutches."

Chet's head sank into his pillows. "You want her now?"

Nate held up his hands. "I think you need her more."

"Knock, knock." A chipper voice sounded from the door. "Supper's here." A woman dressed in a coral-colored uniform and sporting a white hairnet entered carrying a brown plastic tray.

Betsy rose from the recliner and took the tray from the lady's hands. "I can help him."

"Appreciate it, love. I got twenty more to deliver. Just let me know if you need anything, ya hear?" She disappeared out the door.

"Let's see what you get tonight or if I'll have to make another hamburger run." She lifted the insulated lid. "Looks like pot roast."

Nate's stomach growled. "Smells good, bro." Sad when hospital food smelled better than what was in his cupboards at home.

Betsy liberated a salad from the plastic wrap, took the paper lid off the iced tea, and buttered the roll.

"Lucky thing you have a servant-wife. I don't see any fair maidens in my future dropping grapes into my mouth."

A sugar packet flew past Nate's head and hit the wall. "Wait until I get home," Chet said. "I'll have to beg for help. She'll be too busy taking care of Chip to remember she has a helpless husband on the couch."

Nate picked the packet off the floor and pitched it under his arm toward the bed. Chet intercepted and returned it, sending the packet back to the floor, where it was retrieved by Betsy and tossed into the trash.

"Really, boys." She washed her hands at the sink across the room.

"Speaking of Chip, where is he?" Nate liked the boy. Mostly he avoided three-year-olds, but Chip was different. The kid was smart. One night, he had watched Chip make Lego dinosaurs that looked real enough to roar.

"He's with my mom," Betsy said.

"I miss the kid." Nate glanced at Chet, knowing his friend missed the boy even more. Though adopted, everyone said Chip looked just like Chet, a fact that made Chet puff with pride. Someday, Nate would like to have a family, but that meant meeting the right girl. A face appeared in his mind–the girl at the courthouse. He shook the memory off. Definitely not the right one.

A middle-aged man dressed in khakis and a blue shirt entered the room. "Looks like I got here at suppertime."

Chet held out his hand. "Hey, Carl, come on in."

Carl shook Chet's hand and then turned. "How you been doing, Nate? The new paint on the teen's Sunday school room looks nice, by the way."

"Thanks. I plan to hose off the front porch before Sunday. The crows have made a mess of it." He grimaced. "And I would be doing better at work if Chet would get off his lazy behind and come back."

Carl turned to Betsy. "Linda told me to ask if you need anything. The girls can sit with Chip once they get home from school if you need them."

"Thanks. My mom's got Chip."

"Word has it you're going home tomorrow." Carl raised his eyebrows. "Ladies of the church are planning on bringing a few meals."

"Thanks, Carl," Betsy murmured.

"Chet, you probably won't make it to church on Sunday."

"He isn't going out of the house until he sees the doctor in a week."

"I don't need to ask you." Carl turned to Nate. "When's the last time you missed a Sunday?"

Chet laughed. "I think he lives there."

"I don't–"

"Just glad you're a godly man." Carl stepped toward the door. "Linda probably has supper waiting." He waved. "You be sure to call if you need anything."

Nate got out of the molded chair. "I'm headed home, too." He had planned to drive by the courthouse after leaving the hospital and see if the girl and blind man were still on the steps, but it was almost six; they were probably gone by now. Leaving the hospital with its recycled oxygen, Nate took a deep breath of good ol' fresh air, replete with the scent of fast food. A semi rounded the corner, adding diesel fumes to his olfactory pleasure.

Reaching the parking lot and his truck, he stopped and groaned. White drippings lay splattered across the windshield. He shook a fist toward the sky. As irrational as it seemed, he knew the birds targeted his truck. Several crows watched him from the tops of parked cars. He never saw the birds eat. They never crowed. He never saw them do anything except get in his way.

Overwhelmed at work with his main help lying in the hospital, preoccupied because of a girl he didn't even know, and crows that, quite honestly, creeped him out; life felt out of control.

6

Monday, May 20

From his place on the courthouse steps, it seemed to Charlie as though the world was ending. He rubbed his hands on his pant-legs while sirens sounded from all directions. Fragments of conversations from passersby reached him: angry words laced with confusion. His dry tongue worked back and forth in the gap between his teeth.

He had been right; the crows were the first clue. The black-winged creatures had gathered to watch. Now, more than ten days since he had sensed their arrival, grains of sand lay thin at the top of the proverbial hour-glass. The countdown was ending. He turned sightless eyes toward the direction Ruth would come, but it wasn't time for her. Not yet. Urgency gripped him. Soon, his time with her would be over. He would have done all he could to help her, and this knowledge frightened him.

She had been excited for her trip to Columbia, but when he asked her about it afterward, her answers were evasive. For the past ten days, she had seemed edgy, not her usual high-spirited self. He pulled his brow together as he thought of her, so innocent yet head-strong. Strange how a southern girl could reach out to an old loner like him but be so insecure around others.

The sound of angry voices shot across the four lanes of asphalt. Footsteps on the sidewalk in front of him hesitated and stopped—a female most likely. Thin heels. Cars slowed. Muffled conversations drifted from across the street, from the old church. Chains? He tipped his head, straining to hear through the noise. Increased angry voices. Scuffling feet. Sirens. Doors slamming. More voices; more anger.

He lowered his head into his palms as the last grain of sand fell. The show was beginning, whether Ruth was prepared or not.

~*~

"I need you to go pick up supplies." Harold Evans, leaning against his truck at the Miller Street site, worked his hand in and out of his pants pocket.

Nate waited, sensing the man had more to say.

The older man raised his chin toward the house. "Nice job finishing that roof, by the way." Usually Mr. Evans spoke his mind, but today the boss seemed distracted.

Nate stifled a yawn. Eventually, dreams of the girl would stop, and he would wake rested again.

A stream of cursing rolled from the house.

Nate looked toward the opening that would soon hold insulated windows. "Probably O'Reilly hit his thumb again. Sounds like his voice."

Mr. Evans rubbed his jaw. "I don't like the cussing. Calm the man down, or he may find himself without a job."

Nate shifted his feet in the sandy soil. "Everyone's a bit edgy today. Don't see a storm coming; air's heavy, though." The sun stood west of midpoint in a cerulean blue sky. "The men feel it when the barometric pressure's dropping."

"There's nothing wrong with the weather. Just some heavy air passing through."

There might be nothing wrong with the weather, but something pressed against his shoulders like cement blocks loaded too heavy.

O'Reilly was a nice enough guy. He had a wife, a mortgage, and two kids. Came in drunk about once a month; nothing Nate couldn't work around. He had already talked to O'Reilly about his drinking and temper. It would be a shame to lose a good worker because of habits.

Nate heaved a sigh. "I'll talk to him about it again, boss."

"Good. Good." Mr. Evans continued to work his hand in and out of his pants pocket. It had been a long time since Nate had seen the man this antsy. Either something was up, or the boss felt the effects of the heavy air more than Nate and the men. Evans stared at the house. "With plumbers and electricians still working, there's no sense in you starting the drywall. Most likely, you'll just be in the way."

Nate wiped the sweat off his forehead. Only the end of May and already it was blazing hot. How did the crows do it, sitting out in the sun hour after hour with those black feathers, not moving, not seeking shade? Just waiting. But waiting for what?

Mr. Evans cleared his throat. "Let's be honest, Nate. I know you want a business of your own." The boss gazed at the field beyond the house, seeming to look everywhere except at Nate. "You don't need to be working for me. There's a good head sitting atop your shoulders, and I think you could make a go of it. More than that, you have ethics."

Nate managed a series of tight breaths. Was he being fired? His tongue stuck to the roof of his mouth–he couldn't even ask. Had the boss been softening the blow by praising him for finishing the roof? Man, he needed this job. Nate pushed damp hair off his forehead. He had worked hard for Evans Construction–for this?

"Just think about it. I don't need an answer today."

What, Evans was giving him a choice over being fired? Nate's face reddened as he stifled the sharp words that filled his mouth.

"I'm thinking of retiring and selling the business. I can't think of anyone I would rather turn it over to than you."

Nate's jaw fell slack as he stared.

Mr. Evans finally looked his way. "I'll give you a good deal, but it'll still cost you some money. I have over a hundred thousand in equipment alone."

Nate choked out a throaty laugh. "How much money do you think I'll need?" His mind raced. He had never considered buying out Mr. Evans. Most of his thoughts, while mowing grass at the church, or doing some other mindless job, centered on having to compete for customers with a man who had been a mentor to him. But now…could he do this? He had a small savings and a few matured bonds stashed in the dresser at home.

"We can talk about money later. I'm not ready to quote you a price, but check with the banks and see if you qualify for a business loan. I can provide a letter if they want." Mr. Evans cleared his throat and spit on the sandy ground. "Glad to know you're interested. Go on now; get at the list I gave you."

Loose gravel spun as Nate pulled from the temporary driveway onto the paved road. He put a hand to his chest, willing his racing heart to stay put behind his ribs. His own business! But first, the errands Mr. Evans had given him: pick up a vanity and toilet, match the brick sample with the stone mason, and get a building permit for the Hill Avenue project. His mind leaped back to Mr. Evan's news and euphoria bubbled again. His cheeks hurt from the stretch of his smile. Should he go to the bank first? Mr. Evans expected him to check on a loan during work time, didn't he?

Jittery fingers thrummed on the steering wheel. Maybe pick up the building permit first, while he was somewhat clean. He'd be grimy before he left the stone mason's, so he'd hit the bank while he was in town. The mystery woman wouldn't be at the courthouse yet. He hadn't been able to see her since the first unexpected meeting, but he couldn't wait for her today.

Cars crawled along Main Street and Nate scowled over the delay. Heat shimmered off the blacktop. By mid-June the stickiness of the tar seeping from the pavement would cling to his shoes, flip onto the backs of his legs, and coat the bumper of his truck. In front of the courthouse people loitered in tight bunches on the sidewalk. Several media trucks sat empty. There must be a big case being tried today. He never listened to the news; too depressing. Two blocks further he found a parking spot. He jogged back to the courthouse.

The old man sat in his usual spot. "Afternoon," Nate said as he gripped the man's shoulder in passing.

"Wait. Please."

Nate stopped. Impatient fingers tapped against his

leg. "Something I can do for you?"

"Tell me. How many crows do you see?"

Nate groaned. He wanted to leave the man and his wandering mind, but civility held him in place. Any other time, and he would have asked the blind man about the girl who'd sat with him on the steps, but the urgency of his task pushed him forward. "I don't know. Dozens. Maybe close to a hundred." He took a step toward the building.

"More than yesterday?"

Crows lined the tops of most of the buildings and perched on the ornate fretwork and gabled balusters that had been nailed in place a century earlier. Electrical wires bowed under feathered weight. Greenish-white streaks marred Main Street's brick buildings. Now that Nate thought about it, the town smelled odd. Moldy. "Yeah, I guess there're more birds today."

The man's lips tightened. "Look across the street."

First Street Church, Nate's church, occupied the block opposite the courthouse. In times past, Main Street had been called First; the street had been renamed, following the trend of the day. The church had not bowed to tradition.

Nate widened his eyes. Then he squinted. A chain hung between the handles of the church's two front doors, the end links secured with a padlock. Media personnel sporting cameras and microphones dotted the church's grass like ravenous wolves ready for the feed. Nate's heart lurched as he saw Pastor Clark, hands cuffed behind his back, being led toward one of the cruisers parked at the curb.

"What do you see?" Impatience edged the blind man's voice.

"I see trouble!"

Nate bolted toward the street with the sound of blood roaring through his head. Weaving across four lanes of cars, he kept his gaze fixed on Pastor Clark. "Stop! Wait!" Reaching the opposite sidewalk, Nate glared at the two officers as breath huffed in tight streams from his mouth. "What are you doing?"

"Don't interfere with police business, Nate." The officer's voice was low and angry. "Just get out of the way and let me do my job." The badge on the man's shirt identified him as Officer Turner, but to Nate, the officer was just Zachary, a kid a year ahead of him in high school and who played basketball, but mostly sat on the bench. The uniform gave Zach the respect he never earned on the court. Officer Zachary Turner had his hand on a gun—or was it a taser?

Either way, Nate took a step back. "Pastor?"

"It's a misunderstanding," Greg said.

Pastor Clark had served at the First Street Church for the last ten years, and Nate had never seen the man look more beaten. His drooping mouth and quiet voice caused Nate's muscles to tighten even more. Pastor Clark had baptized Nate and most of his buddies. As Nate watched, Zachary put a beefy hand on Pastor Clark's head and guided the pastor into the backseat of the car. The cruiser pulled away from the curb. Pastor Clark focused straight ahead as media crews scrambled for a better angle.

Nate stared until all that was left was the wailing of the fading siren that mimicked the angst inside his own body.

"You must know the priest."

Startled, Nate turned to find a woman dressed in a navy skirt and white silk blouse. A younger man stood behind her, his long hair pulled back at the base of his head. Sweat stained the underarms of his flannel shirt—obviously dressed wrong for the weather. The man shifted a camera to his shoulder as the woman thrust a microphone toward Nate's face. "Do you know what's happening here? What can you tell me about the arrest of the priest?"

"He's not a priest," Nate said through clenched teeth. "He's our minister." Nate felt like he was one of the colored chips inside a kaleidoscope, and someone was turning the handle, changing the shapes. None of this made sense. The church locked? His pastor hauled away by Zach? Nate stared hard into the woman's eyes. Brown, and thickly lined in black. Green eye shadow. "Get out of my face before I say something I'll regret."

Breathing heavily, hands balled into fists, he turned toward the church, his gaze pulled to the chained doors. The whole scene felt unimaginable, like a script from a movie, or something that would happen in the Middle East. This was America, for goodness sake.

Two policemen rounded the side of the church building. Nate darted up the cement walkway and grabbed one of the officers by the arm. "Can you tell me--"

In less time than it took to blink, Nate found himself on the ground jerking in pain, a gun pointed at his head, and four cameras, lights blinking, recording what would become that night's news.

~*~

Nate hobbled past the blind man the second time

in an hour. This time he didn't stop to speak nor to touch the man's shoulder in civil greeting. Fire raged through Nate's body, igniting a depth of anger he never knew possible. He reached the mayor's suite.

"You can't go in there–"

Nate ignored Mayor Bloom's secretary, Lydia. She went to his church. She should understand–if she even knew. The half-door slammed against the counter as he stomped toward the mayor's closed office.

"Nate, stop!" Lydia jumped from her chair.

Nate shoved open the mayor's door. Eight men seated around an oval table stared in surprise. Worn brown carpet muffled Nate's footsteps as he stomped toward the table. His lips were pinched; his eyes narrowed. The pain from being tasered lingered in his muscles. "Of all the low-minded, devil-driven things to do." The words hissed through clenched teeth.

Eight men pushed their backs against the hard chairs.

"I never expected this of you, of all people," Nate continued

Mayor Carson Bloom had run on an independent ticket, beating the incumbent Democrat, Jeff Arnez, and Republican opponent, Nick George. The sincerity of Bloom's platform: keep budgets under control, focus on critical services, and strive for community integrity won him the vote.

Lydia stood in the open doorway. "Sir?"

At the far end of the table, Mayor Bloom rose. "Do you know you just interrupted a very important meeting?"

"You padlocked my church!"

The mayor worked his jaw.

The beam of light coming from the second-floor

window wavered, creating patterns on the table that had not been there before. A crow sat on the ledge. Feathers shimmered blue, almost iridescent, in the afternoon sun. The bird stood with its pointed talons gripping the chipped cement, its head cocked toward the room.

"Someone get that bird away from the window." The mayor's voice warbled, like the strangled call of a drowning man.

Bill Stafford, the chief of police, tapped on the glass. "Go on there. Move off." The bird stared.

Lydia reappeared, clutching paper and tape. She and the chief covered the lower portion of the window. The stream of light broke at the next window. The crow had moved. As easy as that, the bird out-witted the smartest people in town.

For once, Nate cheered the bird. "What about my church?"

"Young man–"

"Name's Nate Bishop. I'm a member of the First Street Church. I was told the order to chain our doors came from you."

The police chief placed his forearms on the table. "My officers locked your building and half a dozen others today." He kept his steel-gray eyes fixed on Nate.

Nate stared back, his face hard with anger.

"My job," the chief continued, "is to uphold the law. Your church had time to pay the tax. Your pastor refused, and the church was closed. Simple cause and effect. This shouldn't have come as a surprise to you or anyone else in the community."

Nate bristled. Did they think he was a fool? "What law allows you to close churches? This is America, last

I knew."

"We're not targeting churches, son, and we didn't pick yours at random." The chief leaned back in his chair and crossed hairy arms over his abdomen.

"The state law was just passed," the mayor said. "The Salvation Law. It'll get Logan out of debt, help us fix our roads, purchase much needed emergency equipment, beef up our teacher's pay–"

"The Salvation Law," Nate spit the words out.

"Mr. Bishop," the mayor said, "if you will schedule a meeting with my secretary, I'll be glad to talk to you about this. Right now, I am in the middle of a very important meeting."

Nate stared around the room. Eight people and one bird stared back. No one seemed to harbor guilt over closing his church. Not one face showed embarrassment, discomfort, or even sympathy for his plight. Eight faces: all anxious for him to leave, all wanting to get back to whatever business was more important than his church; one bird at the window, momentarily forgotten.

"Either leave, or you'll force me to call upon the chief, here, to do his duty." Mayor Bloom remained standing, the large oak table and seven men formed a secure barrier against any advance Nate might make. A king with his knights.

Not bothering to close the door behind him, Nate bypassed the elevator and ran down the steps. Someone had to know what was going on, and he knew just whom to ask.

~*~

"Put his iced tea in a plastic cup, Betsy," Chet yelled across the room. "Don't give him real glass; the mood he's in, he'll break it."

"Hush!" Betsy poked her head into the living room. "You'll wake Chip from his nap."

Chet grinned. "As if I could. That kid sleeps like the dead. Nothing wakes him until he's ready to get up."

Nate mumbled a response and headed to the sofa while Chet hobbled toward the recliner. The Ross's two storied 1950's home had become Nate's haven. He always ended up in their living room when he felt out-of-sorts or just needed company. Now the late afternoon sun slanted through the beveled windows, sending rainbows across the hardwood floor. He and Chet had been best buds since elementary school, and now Betsy fit right in.

"See you got your walking cast." Nate needed time to breathe, to allow his churning emotions to congeal into something recognizable. Maybe then he could find a pattern in the mayhem that gripped his town.

Ice rattled in the kitchen. Soon Betsy handed each man a large cup filled with iced tea.

Nate placed the cup to his forehead; the cool plastic soothed his hot skin. As Betsy headed back to the kitchen, Nate called to her. "Hey, Bets, you can stay. In fact, I would like you to hear this."

She settled on the floor beside Chet's recliner.

Chet turned to Nate. "So, OK, Joe Sunshine, what's wrong?"

A crooked smile crept onto Nate's face. "Been a long time since we've used that expression."

"Secret code or something?" Betsy asked.

"No, just a joke between Nate and me. Nate had a cousin named Joe who was a royal pain in the neck.

The kid was a real downer." Chet turned to Nate. "What ever happened to him, anyway?"

Nate shrugged his shoulders. "Last I knew, he was attending graduate school at some Ivy-League college." Nate squeezed his eyes tight then opened them and looked at his friends. "Pastor Clark's been arrested."

"What?" Betsy gripped Chet's thigh.

"When?" Chet asked.

"An hour ago. Do you know anything about a new law that taxes churches?"

Betsy twisted around to look at Chet. Her calm face darkened. Obviously, Betsy knew something Nate didn't. He steeled himself for the bad news, but what could be worse than having their pastor arrested and their church taken from them?

Chet's words came slow. "Haven't you read the paper?"

"I never read the paper. You know that."

"Maybe you should." Chet settled the cup between his knees. "We talked about this a couple months ago, remember? The bill to include churches in property tax? It was in the Legislative Update."

"Yeah, yeah. Sounds familiar."

"At the close of the session last month, the bill passed. Come on, buddy. You know this."

Betsy frowned. "The pastor talked about it. He said to trust God for the solution."

Had Pastor Clark mentioned it? Nate remembered rumblings, but honestly, he must not have paid enough attention to the announcements. That's why he came to Chet. If anyone had an analytical brain, it was Chet. The man was a mental trap for information.

Nate should trust God, but under the

circumstances, it seemed God might need human help to solve a human problem. "Our church was just locked by the police who then dragged our pastor away in handcuffs. I was there. I saw it happen."

"Talk to me, bro." The recliner squeaked as Chet leaned forward.

Nate wet his lips, wondering where to start. "Mr. Evans sent me to town." He described the crowd, the chained doors. He told them about Pastor Clark being taken away in a cruiser. "I tried to find out what was going on, and got myself tasered in the process."

"You were tasered?" Betsy's mouth hung open. "You poor thing!"

Nate pulled fingers through his hair. Chet and Betsy were missing the point. "I went across the street to the mayor's office, and all I found out was that the church didn't pay some sort of tax. Can they do that, just lock the church?" Even though Chet was the analytical one of the group, Nate was the practical one, the problem-solver, the one with the solutions. Now here he was, sitting on his friend's sofa, drooling all over himself in ineptness.

"I'm surprised the mayor had time to see you," Betsy said.

"I crashed his meeting."

Chet gripped the back of his neck "The best I know, at the beginning of this year's session, the legislature made a promise to fix the state's economic issues. The only place they could find money was the untaxed real estate of non-profits."

"Including churches?"

"Including churches. So the Senate, then the House, passed the bill. Each municipality is allowed to decide whether to enact the tax on the churches. The governor already approved the bill. The Logan City Council voted to enact the law. Do you remember, Bets, the amount of money the new tax is supposed to bring in?"

"I read it in the paper but I don't remember. It was huge. Apparently, twelve percent of Logan's property is owned by nonprofits."

"I can't believe this." Nate rose to his feet and paced the length of the living room. "So why lock the church?"

"The article said that if the tax wasn't paid or good-will established, the property would be secured."

Nate bent and rubbed the sore spot on his thigh from the taser. He might as well be living in some third-world country. Logan's administration now controlled his church, and it had happened right under his nose. He never read the newspaper, but there were plenty of people who did. Why didn't they sound the alarm, rally the troops? He would have helped to organize a good old-fashioned picket at the State House, held television interviews–something. He sank back onto the couch.

"Nate, it's been in the news for months," Chet said. "No one took it seriously; at least, not at first."

"We didn't think the bill would pass," Betsy added.

No right-minded person would tax a church. But if Chet was right, then Nate should have known, and he should have done something to stop it. He had allowed his complacency to lull him into non-action. "So what now? We meet in the yard or under the picnic shelter until this mess gets straightened out?" Nate stood again, his muscles slow to respond to movement. "Thanks for the tea, Betsy. I need time to think all this though." He placed his cup in the kitchen sink and let himself out the back door.

Crows peppered the grass. Hopping on spindly legs, the birds moved as he passed, following him to his car. Once inside, and with the doors locked, Nate heaved a sigh.

If he was a lesser man, he would take up O'Reilly's habits.

7

Friday, May 24

The week had dragged, but finally Friday arrived. Arriving home from work, Ruth tossed her purse on the couch and plopped into an over-stuffed chair. After her mishap last weekend, Ruth decided not to do any wandering around town this Saturday, leaving the next two days free. Used to being alone, she didn't mind the lack of companionship. Raised by a mother who was always at work, leaving her to occupy herself alone in the small apartment, she felt awkward around people.

She rubbed her arms, working out the tightness. Mr. Charlie's strange behavior bothered her enough that she hadn't told him about her attack last weekend. He had been edgy since the church got locked. Today, he actually stopped talking in the middle of a sentence. He looked toward the sky, his jaw slack, a piece of half-chewed apple still on his tongue. Where did he go when he wandered off like that?

Sunbeams spilled through the living room window. She stretched out her legs and played with the light, creating dancing shadows across the beige walls. A thin smile pulled at her lips. She loved her apartment. It had been a derelict-space the first time she saw it. The landlord put enough money into the first floor of the old house to pass safety codes, and that was it. The second level remained untouched. But she felt lucky to get anything, based on her meager wage. With a lot of hard work and creativity, the place now looked and felt homey.

If only her mother could see the apartment. Neither one of them could afford a phone–she should look into one of those free emergency phones over the weekend–but her boss allowed her to use the work phone and she called her mom at the Ackerman house during their lunch once a month. It had been two weeks since they'd last talked, but then, even when she lived with her mother, they seldom chatted. Too tired, her mom always said when Ruth tried to describe the day's events.

Ruth dangled her legs in the light, thinking about the last time they had spoken to each other. "Mom, you should see my coffee table. Remember I told you I wanted to build one? Well, I found a couple of crates that were perfect to hold the cabinet door I've been saving."

"Do you really need a coffee table?" A drawn-out sigh had followed.

The stinging comment had brought to mind the day she had rescued an old wooden chair from the trash. It became her eleventh-grade art project. After being rebuilt and covered with decoupage, her teacher, Mrs. Grant, declared the chair the best in the class. One Sunday, while her mom was at her second job at the nursing home, Ruth had re-arranged the living room furniture and added the wooden chair. She danced around the room, readjusting a pillow, shifting the end table, as she waited for her mom to get home. When her mom finally arrived, the woman gazed from one side of the room to the other. Ruth then returned the room to how it was and carried the chair to her bedroom.

Ruth had squeezed her eyelids closed. "The table cost me less than five dollars and it looks nice. It really brightens the room." She paused, unsure why she felt a need to justify the expense to her mom. "I can use it when company comes. You know, to set snacks on or something."

"Do you have guests?" Her mom's voice brightened.

"Not yet...but I will." On top of the criticism about how she spent her money, Ruth couldn't bear the lecture she knew was coming: her lack of social life. How she needed to make friends; how it wasn't healthy to be alone so much. Ruth ended the call ten minutes early. She wondered, given different circumstances, if her mom would be the social darling that she wanted her daughter to be. Ruth couldn't think of a single person her mom called friend.

Now, as the fading beam of evening sun lay across the butter-yellow coffee table, Ruth's thoughts wandered to her dad. His features had grown fuzzy over the years, but his memory still enveloped her in love. She hugged a pillow to her chest. Life had changed so much when he'd died. She'd been eight.

Her mom had to get a job. They no longer enjoyed the Friday night trips to the movies. There had been no money for new dresses or haircuts at the corner beauty shop. Rice and beans became staples: poor people food. But while others flocked to the food banks and sought outside help, her mom never did. What Mom couldn't provide, they didn't need.

No one had earned Ruth's respect more than her mother, but all those hours as her mom worked while she stayed home alone came with a cost: their relationship. In spite of the lack of closeness, she loved her mom and feared disappointing her. Ruth had her own life now, and she had her own dreams.

But there was one thing her mother must never know. Ruth touched the chain around her neck. Its revelation would unravel the thread of any relationship they maintained.

Ruth wandered from the living room, through the dining room that was now converted to a bedroom, and into the house's original kitchen. Standing at the old porcelain sink, she spread peanut butter on a slice of bread and poured herself a glass of unsweetened iced tea. Sugar cost money, and she rationed it by the grain. With her last raise, she had enough cash to allow a few extras, but she chose to live without sugar. Instead she bought paint and fabric and thread, food for her creativity.

A noise came from the living room. She stiffened. No one should be in the house with her. The sound changed from nails-on-a-chalkboard to a soft reverberation. Her sandwich lay on the counter, forgotten.

Had she locked the front door when she'd gotten home, a lesson she had learned in Atlanta and rarely forgot? But her mind had been on Mr. Charlie. She looked for a weapon and grabbed the broom. The living room now lay in silence, whoever had entered had taken pause somewhere. She tiptoed across the kitchen.

From the kitchen doorway she could see straight through the bedroom and into the living room. The three pillows on the couch remained propped as she'd left them. None of the furniture appeared out of place.

No dusty footprints marred the wood floor. The front door was closed, but did that mean anything?

Ruth sneaked through the kitchen into the bedroom, holding the broom in front of her with both hands. Her heart pounded. Stay calm…stay calm…

Thoughts of the man in the car leaped into her mind. Had he found where she lived, and now sought revenge for her victory?

The bedroom held only a double bed pushed against the outside wall. She examined the small space. The quilt on her bed hung to the floor. Hadn't the last noise sounded as though someone slid under the bed? She licked dry lips, gaze glued to the edge of the quilt. She should turn and run out the kitchen door. Have a neighbor call the police. Instead she inched toward the bed, one slow step at a time. With one swift motion, she jerked the cover off the bed and jumped back, broom at the ready.

Beads of sweat coated her hairline. After several seconds of heart-pounding nothingness, she looked under the bed. Dust bunnies and empty boxes remained undisturbed.

Wanting to give the intruder time to escape out the front door, she walked with heavy footsteps across the bedroom. She entered the living room. No one darted from behind the couch. The thin beam of light from the window now flowed over the chair, as it should. Everything seemed normal, and yet her gut screamed otherwise.

The hair on her arms stood straight—she wasn't alone!

An airy sound. Something stroked her face. With her heart in overdrive, she swung the broom and ducked, just as a crow flew past her. The orange beak, only inches from her face, looked massive. She swiped the broom again, hitting air. "Get out of here!" she screamed, swinging the broom back and forth in front of her.

The crow's wings thumped as it swooped around the room. With its beak open and talons spread like massive fingers, the bird dove toward her.

She dropped the broom and raced for the front door.

~*~

Work over for the day, Nate drove with abandon. The sun had touched the top of the pines west of town, just as it did every day at this time. Strange, how things remained the same even when his life lay in chaos. The church, a sacred institution of the nation, no longer proved to be so. At least, not in Logan. Moving somewhere else wasn't an option. Logan was his family home for generations. He still lived on part of his great-grandfather's land, the bulk of it sold off years ago. But the ranch house that had belonged to his grandparents, and the fifteen-acre tract, ten of it woods, bound him to Logan as surely as the chains that secured his church.

Nate had wandered into one of the neighborhoods known for its crime. Just as the awareness hit him, a woman ran from a front door, her arms covering her head. Nate stiffened. Most likely she was protecting herself from the fists of a boyfriend. He pulled to the opposite curb and glanced at the house, ready to protect the woman, but no one followed her.

Even on the sidewalk, the woman's legs kept moving up and down as though running with nowhere to go.

"Hey, you all right?" Nate called from the window of his truck.

She turned and Nate's eyes widened. There stood the woman from the courthouse.

Her dancing stopped as she stared wide-eyed at Nate.

He got out of the truck and walked toward her. "Is something wrong? Can I help you?"

Still staring, she pointed toward the house. "Inside. A b-bird!" Her voice sounded tight, with none of the angry lilt he remembered.

A crow with a strange looking scar stood on the sidewalk and cocked its head toward them. More birds perched on electrical wires, porch railings, and tree limbs. So many crows, more than he had seen in any one place before. "One of the crows got into your house?"

She nodded, her eyes wide with fear.

"Stay here. I'll chase it out." A smile sneaked across his face. What were the chances of meeting the girl he had been trying to see for two weeks here on the street? Entering the house, he stared in surprise, the crow momentarily forgotten.

~*~

With arms wrapped tight to her chest, Ruth focused on the open front door. Mr. Charlie had told her, just today, to be careful. He had said to go home and stay there, not to go wandering around at night. As though she wandered. Where would she go? But Mr. Charlie's concern gave her the jitters. She had been sharing apples with him for almost two years, and he had never been as distracted as he had become since the crows showed up. He kept pushing her to be her own person, whatever that meant. His strange admonitions had heightened after the church was locked.

Mr. Charlie. Most likely his edginess is why she overreacted when the crow flew across the living room. She pushed out a shaky laugh. Scared of a crow. She had confronted worse horrors than feathers and flesh.

A car drove by and the driver whistled.

She ignored him and kept her gaze on the house. Nate, wasn't that his name? He looked so much like Joe. She bit at a ragged edge of her fingernail. The doorway remained empty. Where had her mind been, to allow some strange man to go into her home alone? He could be doing anything, looking at anything. What if he found…no, surely, he wouldn't look there. Now, with her fear gone, she should chase the bird out herself. She stepped forward.

A crow swooped from the magnolia tree and landed three feet in front of her. Standing on spindly legs, the bird cocked its head. Round eyes stared. A spark of life, a hint of intelligence, flickered within its dark depth. A scar ran down the side of its head.

Shivers ran up Ruth's spine as she stared back.

~*~

Nate stopped as soon as he entered Ruth's apartment. He couldn't have been more surprised if he had found himself inside a mansion. He gazed around the living room, the crow forgotten. In one of the poorer sections of town, and as a rental, he had expected the inside of the house to match the outside: tired and worn. This living room could have belonged to Chet and Betsy, the décor was so similar. Betsy called it country chic, or something like that.

A sofa rested beneath the front window, two chairs covered with yellow fabric stood opposite, flanking a fireplace. A short table made of crates and an old cupboard door sat in the center of the room. About half of the old wood floor lay hidden under a rag rug.

A black feather on the sofa reminded him of why he was in the house. Nate found the crow perched on the headboard of the bed, as though waiting for him. The bird took flight, one wing brushing against his face as it flew directly to the open door, Nate following.

Ruth stood where he had left her, arms still clutched tightly around her skinny body, eyes bigger than they should be in her too-pale face.

"It's gone," he said, feeling awkward but not sure why. He held out the feather from the couch. "Souvenir, if you want it."

"No, thanks."

He dropped the feather and watched it float to the grass.

"I appreciate you stopping. Silly of me to be afraid of a bird." A spot of pink colored her cheeks.

"Hey, anything that shows up where it isn't supposed to be makes a nasty surprise." He hoped his smile didn't look as awkward as it felt.

"I'm not sure how the bird got in."

Nate rubbed the spot where the crow's feathers had brushed against his cheek. "Do you have the damper closed on your fireplace?"

She stared at him blankly.

"OK. If you want, I can check. If the damper's open, the crow could have fallen through the chimney."

They entered the house together, and Nate looked into the dark maw of the chimney. He grappled blindly for the metal lever he knew should be to the right of the opening. The lever, stuck in place, finally let loose, dumping soot onto his head. Coughing, he brushed off what dirt he could before standing. "The damper was open," Nate said with a sheepish grin.

Ruth giggled. He had never heard her laugh, and the sound reminded him of warm sun on a spring afternoon. Her hand flew to her lips. "I'm sorry; I shouldn't laugh."

He wiped a hand across his cheek and felt the grit slide on his skin. "I imagine I just made it worse."

"Let me get you a washcloth."

She led him into the kitchen, where a small bathroom had been built along the inside wall. He emerged a few minutes later, soot-free and smelling like lilacs. Alone in the kitchen, he looked around. A sink, the porcelain worn off on the left corner, held the place of honor below the window on the side wall opposite him. Not much of a view: the neighbor's house. A cheap gas stove flanked the bedroom wall, and the refrigerator stood against the back wall. A folding card table with two metal chairs rested along the bathroom wall. Red gingham curtains hung at the windows over the sink and on the door. Yellow canisters brightened the worn countertop. The few white cupboards looked freshly painted. A cup was in the sink, the tea bag still draped across the top. On the counter, a drying peanut butter sandwich completed the tour.

As he entered the living room, Ruth stood by the fireplace, rag and bucket in hand, the floor wet but clean. "Thank you, again," she said. "You must have been on your way somewhere…"

"Actually, I was deep in thought, driving mindlessly without a single destination or purpose." Amazing how cool that sounded when, actually, his thoughts had been tearing him apart.

Pale lashes covered her eyes. "Sorry to interrupt your thinking time."

He chuckled. "The distraction was just what I needed."

"Would you like some iced tea? Sorry, but it's unsweetened. I'm Ruth, by the way." And then the smile again—faint, but there—as if she had almost forgotten how.

He rubbed his chin. It had been a disastrous week, and this was Friday night, after all. Should he chance it? It wouldn't be a date. Not really. "I haven't had supper yet. Would you like to grab a bite to eat with me?"

Her jaw tightened.

"Just a burger and some fries, my treat. We can go down to Jerry's Diner around the corner if you want. We can walk." He watched the indecision in her face. It felt important that she say yes. Maybe he wanted to be with her; maybe he didn't want to be alone with his thoughts. Either way, he stared at her, pleading with his eyes.

That smile again. "Sure," she said.

After double-checking the locked door, they headed toward town, stepping over the cracks in the sidewalk: slabs of concrete reshaped by tree roots. Grayness of early evening muted the colors, and shadows provided an illusion of privacy. Most of the crows had moved to the trees, leaving the branches heavy as the sun finally slept.

Nate's heart pounded crazily.

8

Friday, May 31

Why had she allowed herself to be talked into coming to a church picnic at his house? And who knew he lived so far out in the country? Nate had stopped at her place twice since removing the bird a week ago. The first time was to ask if she had any more crow problems, the second to invite her to the picnic. The time alone with him in the truck had passed easily enough, but now, standing among all the people, her awkwardness surfaced.

Nate spread out the hot coals around the campfire and streaks of light flew skyward. "OK, who's ready for a hot dog?" he yelled.

About sixty people stood in groups in the backyard. Saw horses and long planks of wood had been covered with colorful cloths. Now, the makeshift tables were heaped with platters of fried chicken, trays of pimento cheese sandwiches, dishes of steaming macaroni and cheese, slices of watermelon, and bags of chips. Children chased each other across the rough grass.

Nate had said he expected around two-hundred members from various locked churches to show up for the meeting.

The area pastors wanted to hold a combined church meeting, and Nate volunteered his home. Five acres of grass, mostly weeds, provided plenty of space to spread out, for the kids to play, and to allow the adults to talk.

Ruth stayed close to Nate. He introduced her to Pastor Clark, who told her the story of his arrest and his release later that same day, a misunderstanding, apparently. Nate introduced her to the others as they arrived. And they came—laughing and happy—the furthest thing from the attitude of anger she had expected when, according to Nate, closing the churches was nothing short of a cataclysmic event. There were a few faces Ruth knew from around town or from Attorney Dunlap's office. She smiled at a woman whose yard sale she had attended.

"Hey there, young lady!"

Ruth recognized the voice and turned.

Dressed in jeans and a t-shirt, a ball cap on his salt and pepper hair, the only part of the bearded worker that looked familiar was his eyes. They still sparkled with life, just as when he had grabbed a shovel and followed her to the pine saplings. A grin stretched across his weathered face. "Not wandering around alone anymore, are you?"

"You know each other?" Nate asked.

"He works for the county."

He man stretched out a hand to Nate. "Jeb Hawthorn. I attend Creek Side Methodist." With a wink at Ruth, he moved toward the food table.

"Mr. Nate! Mr. Nate!" Two small girls wearing flowered sundresses wrapped arms around Nate's legs.

"And what do you two princesses need?"

"You promised to cook us a hot dog," one of the girls said.

"Yes, I did." He turned to Ruth. "Don't go anywhere."

Ruth remembered fires with her daddy. He always burned the fall leaves. She loved the smell. After her father was gone, neighbors still burned the leaves from the huge oak trees outside the apartment building. The smoke would find its way into the narrow space between the brick structures and finger through her bedroom window. She would lie awake at night surrounded by the scent of smoke and memories.

Another SUV pulled into the gravel drive and parked in the yard beside the other vehicles. Two teen boys unfolded lanky bodies from the back. The driver, apparently the father, handed each a grocery sack.

Ruth couldn't believe so many people were concerned about a church building.

But then, it seemed that everyone believed, by using embossed letterhead and threatening words, a lawyer could either remove chains or bind them tighter, depending on the point of view. That first Monday, the documents needing processed had doubled. Now she could barely keep up. The whole church-closing thing felt like a three-ring circus with so much happening at the same time that one only got half of the show, no matter how hard one tried.

Nate turned from the fire and grinned, his cheeks red from the heat.

She forced a nervous smile. He seemed like a great guy, so she wasn't sure why he was giving her so much attention. Surely, he didn't feel guilty about the incident at the courthouse. Regardless, coming to the picnic was pushing her comfort level. She fixed a plastic smile on her face while her nerves jangled like a rock stuck in a hubcap.

Handing the girls their hotdogs, Nate turned to Ruth. "Want a hot dog?" He anchored two wieners onto the end of a stick. "I come from a long line of food-burners, so beware." He squatted and held the meat over the hot coals.

"I'd love one." A young woman in a strapless summer dress swayed back and forth.

Nate turned his face upward. "Oh, hi, Sarah. I didn't know you were here."

"I just got off work." She gave Nate a coy smile dripping with southern charm before glancing at Ruth.

A sudden possessiveness took hold of Ruth. She couldn't let this Sarah person take over—take over what, she wasn't sure—but she couldn't let her. She forced her brightest smile. "Hi. I'm Ruth."

"Sorry," Nate said, struggling to stand. "Ruth, this is Sarah Gardener. We went to high school together. Sarah, this is Ruth…?"

"Ruth Cleveland," she said, filling in the embarrassing pause. So much for convincing Sarah there might be another woman in Nate's life. As if she could compete with this glamorous person.

"Hey, man, did you think we wouldn't make it?" A lanky man with his foot in a walking cast and a petite woman ambled toward Nate. A wooden picnic basket with daisies painted on the lid swung from the man's right hand while the woman gripped the arm of a little boy, about three, who pulled to be let free.

Ruth felt sure she had seen the woman somewhere before.

"See you later, Nate." Sarah waved a hand as she sashayed toward the picnic table.

"About time you two showed up." Nate propped the hotdogs over the fire and then ruffled the boy's hair. "Hey there, my man. What've you been up to today? Pestering your poor mama?"

The boy grinned. "I found a feather." He held up a long black plume.

Nate raised his eyebrows.

"Couldn't convince him to leave it at home," the man said. "Plenty more of those around, but somehow, he thinks this one is special."

"Uncle Nate." The little boy's eye widened. "Look!" He pointed a tiny finger toward the fire.

"Ah, man!" Nate dragged the burning hotdogs off the stick and dropped them onto the coals.

"Hi, I'm Betsy," the woman said to Ruth.

"Sorry, again. I must have left my manners at work." Nate licked his greasy fingers.

"No chance of that," Chet murmured with a grin.

"Ruth, this outspoken man is Chet Ross and his wife, Betsy, and—"

"I'm Chip," the boy said. He gave another tug on his mom's hand.

Betsy released the boy, and he sprinted on gangly-thin legs toward a group of children chasing each other around the yard.

Betsy's stare made Ruth uncomfortable, but soon, the woman chuckled. "I know where I've seen you before: Donner's Drug Store."

"I go there. And your name is Betsy…"

"Ross," the woman said.

Ruth glanced at Nate.

Betsy laughed. "You got it right. Betsy Ross." She placed a hand on her husband's arm. "I had to think long and hard before I agreed to marry this man and end up with that name."

"But my charm won out." Chet grinned.

"Nice to meet you, Ruth, and I hope we can talk later. But right now, I better get this food on the table." Betsy moved toward the laden tables.

A dozen people surrounded the fire with sticks in hand. Most were men. A few children hunched over the fire, supervised by wary adults. The scent of mosquito repellent mingled pleasantly with the smell of burning wood and roasted hotdogs.

"Hey, this here the place for the church picnic?" An older man carried a box covered with a red-checkered dishtowel. "Kind of late to have a picnic, isn't it?"

"We had to wait until some of the guys got off work."

"It's gonna get dark on you. Skeeters'll eat you to death."

"I have lots of spray if you need some. We'll do our best to get the meeting over with as quickly as we can. I'm Nate Bishop. This is my place. Make yourself at home."

"I'm Harry, and this is Lottie, my better half." The man nodded to a woman standing beside him who was as short as she was round. In her cotton dress and a necklace made of buttons, the woman reminded Ruth of the lady who had lived across the hall from her in Atlanta.

"Make yourself at home." Nate nodded to the tables. "The meeting will start once everyone's eaten."

"Hey, Harry, good to see you." One of the men clapped Harry on the back. "Let me help you with that box. I want first dibs on whatever Lottie put inside."

"Everyone seems to know each other," Ruth said, as Nate speared a couple hot dogs.

"Logan's a small place."

At the table, they filled paper plates with deviled eggs, slaw, macaroni and cheese, chips, and cookies.

"Time for marshmallows!" Kids ran toward the table where Betsy manned the treats. Older teens with sticks stood by the fire, ready to cook or supervise as needed. Someone had organized this.

Ruth wondered if it had been Nate, or maybe Betsy.

After eating, Nate led Ruth to a lawn chair at the side of the house where she settled into the webbing, content to be alone with her thoughts. To the west, the sun drifted below the top of the pines. Night creatures began their symphony. An occasional frog croaked, its solo accompanied by the higher pitched crickets and the clicking of katydids. A bat squealed as it passed overhead. She closed her eyes and listened to the chorus as it melted with the sound of voices. A full stomach, a comfortable chair, and content to observe.

Nate moved through the groups, herding the adults toward the side of the house where lawn chairs and blankets waited in the newly mowed field.

"Need anything?" Nate asked as he circled back her way. "More iced tea or maybe a marshmallow?"

Ruth put a hand on her stomach. "I'm stuffed, thanks." As Nate settled in the grass beside her, she relaxed and enjoyed his closeness. There would be so many stories to share with Mr. Charlie on Monday. And she could hear her mom's excitement when she told her that she had gone out with someone, even if it was to a church picnic. As dusk deepened, she imagined what it would feel like to actually belong to this active, lively crowd.

Nate's pastor, Greg Clark, walked toward them, his face drawn in concern. But his eyes held Ruth's attention: soft eyes of an honest man. Nate had told her that Pastor Clark was raised in Haiti by missionary parents.

"Kind of discouraged by the turnout," Pastor Clark said. "With most of Logan's churches closed, I thought there would be more people here."

"We still have a crowd, over a hundred, I'm guessing." Nate glanced toward the fire. His shoulders were slumped. He was disappointed, too.

Greg Clark signaled to a couple of men to walk to the front of the crowd where someone had placed over-sized lawn chairs. As the ministers of Logan's churches took their positions, the talk settled. The laughter of the children and the occasional crack of the fire seemed louder in the silence.

Against the side of the house, Ruth stayed in her chair with Nate beside her.

Faces among the adults tightened; smiles disappeared.

The mood Ruth had anticipated finally arrived.

A gust of wind sent a paper plate skittering across the yard.

Nate struggled to rise from the ground and gave chase, shoving the soiled plate into a trash bag. He walked along the table, closing a chip bag, covering dishes with tin foil or plastic wrap, and swatting flies.

Standing with the other pastors, Greg Clark cleared his throat. Muffled conversations quieted. "First off, thank you for the e-mails and phone calls over the past couple of weeks. As you know, I had the pleasure of being the only minister in Logan to spend time in our city jail for disorderly conduct. Not an experience I would recommend, by the way, even though our 'city's finest' treated me with courtesy."

Pastor Clark gave a shaky laugh before his expression turned serious. "By now, all of you know we have been barred from our church buildings until we pay the tax for the first half of the year."

Voices murmured. Lawn chairs creaked as bodies shifted.

Nate slumped to the ground beside Ruth, his gaze locked on the pastor.

"I take responsibility for the premature locking of First Street Church," Pastor Clark said. "I made what was to be a respectful call on the mayor. Things got angry, and I took offense when perhaps I shouldn't have. The bottom line, I threw the letter describing the tax on his desk and informed him that First Street Church would not pay one dollar until we had a chance to appeal the state's decision."

Scattered applause broke out.

Pastor Clark held up his hands. "Hold on. The mayor took my comment as lack of goodwill, and had the church locked." He gazed toward the sky and then looked back at the faces staring his way. "My impulsivity cost us our church, and I apologize."

"Greg," the tall African American pastor beside him said, "we're all in this together now. No need to apologize for defending your church. We can't let the government control us like we're rats in a cage."

A murmur of assent came from a couple of the men.

Gravel crunched on the road as a sheriff's cruiser slowed and moved on.

"What is the reason for the tax if I may ask?" The old woman's first name was Hannah. Ruth couldn't remember the last name, but Miss Hannah looked to be at least ninety. She sat on a chair in the middle of a blanket, surrounded by her elderly daughter and half a dozen younger kin.

"I can answer the question about the reason for the tax."

Heads turned.

Stewart Gleason walked across the field toward the crowd.

Ruth beamed, but when he got closer, her chest tightened. Representative Gleason's hair had grayed, and his distinguished character-wrinkles grew into chasms.

Nate jumped up and motioned toward a vacant chair, but Mr. Stewart remained standing in the back.

"To answer the lady's question, the intent of the tax is good," Stewart said. As angry voices began, he held up his hand. "I didn't say I agreed with the law, just that the intent was good. I voted against it, but the bill was heavily promoted and gained acceptance quickly." Senator Gleason leaned on the back of a vacant chair. "South Carolina's been struggling with a slumping economy; we've cut critical services from the budget each year."

Ruth had heard all of this before: during the car ride to Columbia and later in the office. But budgets were always problems. No matter how much money one had, one wanted more. She thought of Joe and his family, always buying a bigger boat, a newer car. Never satisfied.

"Logan took a huge blow with the closing of Wilson Lumber Mill. The tax money from the mill was equal to the salaries of our entire fire department. With that revenue gone, cuts were made in the city budget to offset the shortage. It hurts. It hurts all of us. I can't blame the mayor for grabbing at a solution. I've met with the mayor, and the decision to tax churches came after considerable thought. The mayor knew there would be ramifications, but he hoped the churches would be able to find enough money within their congregations to meet the need."

"Just how did he think we were gonna do that?" Gilbert Henderson asked.

He had been the subject of one of the letters Ruth had typed, but she couldn't remember what it was about. So many documents passed by her, she rarely noticed specifics anymore. The hot dog churned in her stomach as the tension jumped.

"Some of us lost our jobs when the mill closed. We can hardly feed our families, let alone shove money into some bureaucrat's pocket," Gil Henderson continued, his arms stiff at his sides.

"I understand that; I really do. I wish I could say that's why I voted against the bill, but it isn't."

"Share with them what you told me, Stewart." Greg Clark's voice remained steady. "Tell the folks what we discussed around my kitchen table a week ago."

The crowd grew silent as they gave attention to the man elected to represent them.

"The tax will provide raises for teachers." Mr. Gleason's voice was soft. "We can provide more teachers per school, reducing the size of the classrooms from thirty-five to twenty. Streets will be repaired."

"I about lost my car in the crater on Third Street," someone said.

"No doubt, our roads need work," Mr. Gleason said. "We can off-set the deficit from the loss of Wilson Lumber Mill and pay to get career advisors in here to help the folks who lost their jobs. I can go on, but you get the picture. The money is needed and can be used for good."

"Then why did you vote against it?" a woman asked.

"Our tithes aren't given to pave roads. We're in the business of saving souls." Mr. Gleason rubbed the back of his neck. "There is precious little Godly influence in our world as it is. Shut down the churches and there's nothing left." He stared at the ground. "This is my worst nightmare."

"Look," an elderly male voice warbled, "just 'cause the church building is closed doesn't mean we can't meet. We'll gather in the yards. All our churches have grass, don't they? Or parking lots? Shucks, that could be a great testimony to the town."

"We can't use the property, or any of the buildings on the property," Pastor Clark said.

As one, faces rotated to the front. These people took their churches seriously, and they'd been robbed of something important.

"You mean we can't use our gym? What about the kids' basketball team I coach?"

"Basketball will have to be cancelled for now."

The big man pinched the top of his nose. "But the gym isn't the church."

"But it's on church property," Pastor Clark said.

"The law has not been tested by the South Carolina Supreme Court," Congressman Gleason said. "I plan to take the case forward as quickly as I can. Even so, it may be years before our appeal is heard."

"So what do we do in the meantime?" The woman moved the infant to her shoulder. A pacifier fell to her lap and she handed it to the man beside her. "Do we stop going to church until this is settled?" Wistfulness colored the woman's voice.

Ruth thought of the weekends she had spent alone while her mother worked at the nursing home to supplement the housecleaning wage. Time with her mom was a luxury, and she would not have wasted any of it sitting in church.

Nate waved his hand. "What if we all meet together for a while? No need for all the churches to make their own plans."

"I'm not gonna go to some strange church," Gilbert Henderson said.

"We can't go to a church, Gilbert. That's the point." Miss Hannah's tone admonished. Mothers must be the same everywhere. "We're all Christians. We ought to be able to worship God together."

Gilbert pushed out of the chair. "Well, I ain't going to be mixin' with strangers." He jutted a chin toward his wife, who, staring at her toes, stood and followed him across the grass.

"Dan, Devin, get over here," Gilbert yelled as he stomped toward the fire.

A boy and a girl ran toward Gilbert.

"I don't want to go yet," the boy said, his voice thin and whiney.

"I said we're going." Gilbert grabbed the boy's arm and pulled him toward the car.

Tension stalled over the crowd like the smoke from the fire, as it floated to the lowest tree branches and remained. Glances were guarded as folks stared at the ground, at the trees, toward the children who ran and laughed, unaware of the discomfort that choked the life from the adults.

"We can meet here if you want," Nate said. "There's plenty of room outside. I don't have much space in the house, but if the weather turns bad, we can make it work."

"How about if we build a picnic shelter: something simple, just poles and a roof?" Adam said. "It would get us out of the sun and the rain. I can donate shingles if you aren't fussy about the color."

"What do you think?" Pastor Clark scanned the crowd that sat in growing darkness. "Do you want to meet here on Sunday? You'll have to bring chairs and sunscreen."

The lady passed the sleeping infant to the man beside her. "I'll bring ice water and some paper cups."

Screams came from the children in the distance. In the fading light it was hard to tell the cause of their terror.

Being the closest, Ruth saw and gasped.

Crows, perhaps a dozen of them, swooped over the children, flying, diving, and flying again. Beaks reflected gold in the light of the dying fire.

Ruth stood paralyzed.

Above their screams came the terrifying sound of thumping wings.

The small boy, Chip, stood as though mesmerized by the acrobatics around him.

Ruth sprinted toward the child. She threw her arms around his slight body and tucked his head under her chin.

Men batted the crows as women pulled hysterical children toward the safety of the cars.

"Thank you. Thank you," Betsy said, her voice husky as she reached for her son. "I couldn't get here fast enough." The woman's eyes misted as she grabbed her son and disappeared across the yard.

As quickly as the birds came, they returned to the

darkness of the woods.

Soon Ruth stood alone in the yard, her heart still pumping wildly, abandoned bug jars blinking in the grass as families huddled in their cars. Nate's voice came from a distance, but she wasn't sure where he was. Mr. Charlie had told her, but she had laughed at him. In the side yard she stared at the overturned chairs and paper plates tossed from laps in haste. Her throat tightened.

This was the first time the crows had attacked people. None of the children were hurt. It seemed the intent was to frighten. Crows roosted when it grew dark. What made them fly around Nate's yard?

Ruth wrapped her arms around herself and stared at the tree line.

Dark trunks and underbrush blurred together. Nothing moved.

Men gradually slid from their vehicles, wary eyes scanning the back of the house. Quickly, picnic supplies and chairs were gathered and stowed, and one after another, the families left.

"Want help to clean up before we go?" Chet's voice broke the deafening silence.

Nate ran a hand over the top of his head. Had he been beside her all along? "What just happened here?" Wide eyes shadowed his tight mouth.

"I don't know, buddy. Something isn't right."

"Take Betsy and Chip home," Nate said.

"I'll help clean up." Ruth glanced toward the woods. But one crow, just one, and she would bolt.

9

Saturday, June 1

Ruth bounced out of bed early the next morning. Saturday was her favorite day—garage sale shopping! Her bad experience from a few weeks ago had faded, and she was eager for the hunt. Garage sales started early in Logan, some at 6:00 AM. There really wasn't a need for her to be first to shop since most people passed on items she wanted, but still, she rushed to dress and gobbled a piece of toast.

She listened for the lock to click as she turned the key in the front door. She thought of the cellphone again, and the mace, but shrugged her shoulders. She would stay in town. The sun hadn't breached the horizon, but tinges of orange and coral pushed to be born. She lifted her face to the dawn and allowed the moment to seep into her being: the twitter of birds awakening, the lingering hint of dew, and the air fresh from the night. A faint breeze brushed against her cheeks and tugged at the edges of her hair.

Every Friday she took the newspaper home from the office. She scanned the pages for garage sales within walking distance. Today's hunt included finding parts for a suspended pot rack for the kitchen. The house had few cabinets, and she owned even fewer pots, but she needed a dangling rack to dry flowers and herbs.

Passing Jerry's Diner, already open for the early breakfast crowd, Ruth's step lightened. Her supper with Nate Bishop a week earlier, and then the picnic last night, in spite of the birds, had been amazing. She felt like Cinderella at the ball. Other than the beginning awkwardness, she had really enjoyed herself. Nate told her stories about his childhood in Logan. At one time, his grandfather had owned cows and hired Nate and Chet to clean the barn. One accidental toss of a pitchfork of wet manure led to another, and soon both boys were covered. When his grandfather came to check their progress, the boys were sent to the creek to bathe before they washed down the barn walls. Tears of laughter ran down her face as he told the story. Last night, she had anticipated a kiss, but he squeezed her hand instead. The warmth of his touch felt personal in a sensual way—a promise of more in time.

Ruth tucked her memories away to be pulled out again later. Over the next two hours, she snagged a rusty wheel from an old bike, a half-empty can of purple paint, and three yards of red satin ribbon, all for less than a dollar.

Back home, she poured herself a glass of iced tea and headed to the front stoop. Closing her eyes and leaning her head against the door, she dreamed of a real porch and a house that didn't belong to someone else.

Vehicles rumbled past, each motor distinct; voices drifted into a melody. Bass thumped from a car. Is this how life was for Mr. Charlie: all sound and vibrations?

Opening her eyes, she saw several large crows sitting in the yard, mostly gathered under the limbs of the large magnolia that shaded the front. The crows seemed different today, almost evil. Overall, she saw herself as brave, seldom a victim of fits of terror. When a bat got inside a house, she was the one the neighbors asked for help. She never saw ghosts, and had given up a night light before her second birthday. Things that went bang in the dark didn't frighten her. But after last night…

Swallowing the last of the tea, she returned to the kitchen. Coins and a couple dollar bills left from garage sale shopping bulged in her pocket—enough money to buy toothpaste. Maybe Betsy Ross would be working at the drug store today. She chuckled, adding the woman's unusual name to the list of things she planned to share with Mr. Charlie on Monday.

As she grabbed her purse, something tickled on her arm and she smacked at it. A small red ant fell onto the countertop. And there were more. A trail of tiny creatures marched single-file from the wall behind the cupboard to the spot where her purse had been sitting. She grimaced and dumped the contents of her purse onto the counter. Picking up an ant-covered roll of candy with two fingers, she threw the disgusting object into the yard before tackling the ants in the kitchen.

As she pounded the hard surface with the flat of her hand, the release of pent-up anger felt good. Her thoughts moved from ants to crows to Joe and his deception. The faster her mind worked, the harder her hands pounded until her muscles hurt and tears of frustration flowed down her cheeks.

If she could just avoid Joe—her hand pounded the ants—now known as Congressman Joseph Ackerman—she pounded again—maybe, just maybe— there was a chance to develop a relationship with Nate. Eventually she would need to tell Nate the truth about her relationship with Joe—her palm fell hard and the glass in the sink rattled against the porcelain—but not now.

Nate didn't even know the man. How could he begin to understand?

Exhausted and holding her gooey hand away from her body, she slid to the floor. Avoid Joe. That's all she had to do. That and buy toothpaste…and ant spray.

~*~

As soon as Ruth entered the pharmacy, Betsy ran from behind the counter and wrapped her in a tight hug. "Thank you so much! I am so grateful to you."

Ruth's cheeks colored from the unexpected affection.

"I about died a hundred deaths when I saw those birds. And Chet and I were so far away. We couldn't get to Chip fast enough. What if those crows pecked his eyes out?" Betsy shivered. "I know I sound melodramatic, but honestly, that's all that went through my mind. And then you grabbed him, and the crows flew off." She pulled a tissue from her tunic pocket and dabbed her reddened eyes. "I don't know what would have happened to him if you hadn't gotten there so quickly."

It had been impulse that had sent Ruth racing to the boy. She was no hero. "No one was hurt."

Betsy's warm gaze stayed on Ruth. "I keep thinking you remind me of someone, but I can't figure out who it is. You look familiar somehow."

A woman approached, taking short steps on stacked heels.

Betsy retreated behind the counter, obviously disappointed their time had been interrupted.

Not that Ruth sought praise, but the connection she felt with Betsy warmed her. It had been a long time since she'd had a girlfriend. Heaving a sigh, Ruth walked down the far aisle and shivered against the cold radiating from the row of refrigerated units holding milk, soda pop, and bottled water. Not bound by brand, she divided cost by ounce and grabbed the winning tube of toothpaste. She turned the corner to the next aisle, hunting for bug spray.

Nate was staring at the display in front of him.

Quickly she retreated but then stopped. Why did she always avoid people, even those she knew? With a surge of bravery, she walked back up the aisle. "Hi, there."

"Hey. Hi, Ruth."

Her heart fluttered as his gaze lingered on face.

"Doing your shopping?"

"Yeah. Toothpaste." She held up the red and white tube.

"I can't figure this out," Nate said. "I shave every day. You would think I would know which blades to buy." He nodded at the rack. "One blade or six? Disposable or reusable? Easy grip or traditional? Do I want black or green or blue?"

"I like these." Ruth pulled a pack from the rack. "Two blades work better than one, but more than two are a waste." Blushing, she turned.

"Thanks. How about I buy you a cup of coffee?"

"No need." She didn't want him to feel obligated to entertain her each time they met.

"Seriously, how about a cup of coffee?"

"I am thirsty," she murmured, "but I don't like coffee."

"Beverage of your choice." He gave her a thumbs-up. "I'll even toss in lunch if you'll permit me."

"Hey, you two." Betsy grinned as they approached the counter.

Paying for their purchases, Ruth and Nate headed toward the door. "Off to get something to eat, Bets," Nate said. "See you tomorrow."

~*~

They snatched one of the café tables on the sidewalk. Nate held her chair. The blue umbrella shaded the table, but the metal seat felt hot against her legs. Ruth unwrapped her club sandwich, the intricacies of the task absorbing her attention. She had to quit avoiding people, assuming they didn't like her. Mr. Charlie tried to tell her that. He was right. Lifting her head, she smiled at Nate.

A man and woman walked by, chattering in a foreign language, maybe German.

"I've always wanted to travel," Ruth said wistfully.

"Why don't you? The world's an amazing place."

"People don't make a lot of money in Logan."

He laughed. "Isn't that the truth? Where would you go if you suddenly inherited a million dollars?"

She twirled the straw in her sweet tea. "Scotland. That's where my mom's family is from. I used to imagine that I owned one of the old castles there."

"I've seen pictures," he said with a chuckle. "You don't want one."

"I suppose not."

A pair of bike riders zipped along the edge of the road, leaving a hot breeze in their wake. Cars passed. Chattering voices surrounded them. Saturday was social time in town. The door to the deli opened, and the scent of baked bread wafted out. Three teen girls dressed in blue jeans and cropped tops pushed their way out, carrying large beverages. They stared at Nate as they passed, the second girl running into the back of the first.

Ruth hid a smile behind a bite of sandwich, enjoying their envy.

"Well isn't this a pretty scene. My cousin and my best girl sitting together."

The air punched from Ruth's lungs. Her worst nightmare had just walked down the sidewalk and now hovered over her. The man she planned to avoid was here in Logan. "Not your girlfriend, Joe," Ruth squeezed the words from her tight throat. "Not ever."

Nate wiped his mouth. "Joe, it's been a long time. Mom didn't tell me you were in town." He stared hard into the man's face.

Joseph Ackerman pulled an empty chair from the next table and slid it beside Ruth. His blond hair, the color of Nate's, remained firmly in place while Nate's shifted in the moving air. Blue eyes, identical in color to Nate's, stared at her. But Joe's eyes lacked the warmth she found in Nate's.

"So you two have met?" Joe placed a hand on Ruth's arm.

She pulled away.

"Bet you didn't know ol' Natie and I were cousins."

Wishing she could shrivel up and disappear, Ruth gazed straight ahead, avoiding the eyes of both Nate and Joe. Cousins. The first guy she was interested in since Joe, and they're cousins. She needed to throw up.

"What are you doing in town?" Nate shifted his

chair slightly toward Ruth.

"Your mayor wants advice on a budget issue. And here I am."

"I wasn't aware we had a budget issue."

"Some new money coming into the coffers."

"Don't we have a treasurer who handles our money?"

Joe picked at his fingernail. "Apparently, your mayor wanted a financial expert. My name came up."

Shrieks bit into the air. Metal chairs scraped against concrete.

"I can clean it up," a male voice said. "It's just crow droppings. Sit back down. It's OK."

"I hate those birds!" A female voice one notch below hysteria screamed.

"Exciting times here in Logan," Joe said. "I always did enjoy my visits."

Ruth balled the remainder of her sandwich in the wrapper. "I need to go. I'm meeting some friends in a few minutes. I don't want to be late."

"Let me walk you home." Nate rose from his chair, the scowl on his face deep enough to swallow the Grand Canyon.

"I can manage." She needed to get away, to think.

Joe stood. "It has been my pleasure, Miss Ruth Cleveland." He doffed a pretend hat. "I hope to see you again. Perhaps we can pick up where we left off."

Her cheeks burned. No way in God's world would she ever befriend Joseph Ackerman.

"Let me walk you home," Nate repeated. The lines around his mouth were tight.

"No. I'm fine."

"Watch out for crows." Joe's voice teased as she headed down the sidewalk.

~*~

Ruth snatched the homemade blanket from the end of the bed and clutched it to her chest. With too much built-up adrenalin coursing through her body but unwilling to leave the safety of her locked doors, she paced. Back and forth through the bedroom, to the living room and then the kitchen, only to repeat the path again as she fingered the ring that hung from a chain around her neck.

The nerve of him!

She collapsed onto the living room chair. Anger flared. She continued to roam across the floor. Hadn't Joe done enough harm? Now he was back—and for what? When life finally provided a bit of satisfaction, fate turned on her. She grabbed the quilt and brought the knotted-squares to her face, inhaling the scent. The warm covering, made from clothing no longer needed, was one of the few reminders of her past that she had kept. As her heartbeat slowed, she tried to separate emotions from facts.

Seeing Joe had been a shock, but worse was having him claim her as his possession. She wanted to claw his eyes out. She stared through the front window, seeing nothing but his mocking grin. What must Nate be thinking of her? It was a lifetime ago, but her sin followed her.

She walked to the bedroom and shoved her hand under the mattress. For a second, she felt nothing but the hard flatness of the plywood that supported her bed. Her heart did a flip. Probing with her fingers, she finally touched the thick envelope. She thought of the day Joe had given her the money. Sliding to the floor by the bed, she opened the envelope and counted the hundred-dollar bills. Twelve of them. Blood money, all of it.

Someone knocked on the door. The tap came again. Nate's rap.

Shoving the money back under the mattress, Ruth clung to the blanket as she crawled onto the edge of the bed.

"Ruth, are you in there?" He rapped again.

She chewed the edge of her lower lip. They were cousins, Nate and Joe. Blood ran thick among kin in the south. Nate seemed like such a nice guy, but what did she know about men? For the first time in a good while, she ached to have her mom tell her what to do; to have someone give her the well-thought-out decision she felt incapable of making.

"Ruth, I know you weren't meeting friends. Please talk to me."

She walked to the door and leaned against it.

"Ruth, please…"

She opened the door and motioned for him to enter.

"You're bleeding," he said.

Ruth licked the chewed edge of her lip.

"Are you all right?" he asked. "You ran off like you were being chased by the devil himself."

Nate reached for her, but she moved away toward the chair where she had tossed the blanket. She sat down, squeezing the blanket to her chest. "I didn't know Joe was your cousin."

Nate lowered himself onto the couch, never moving his gaze from her face. If the coffee table had not been between them, their knees might have touched. His voice softened. "I had no idea you knew him."

He was trying to calm her, but Ruth didn't know if she appreciated or resented the effort. Everything felt confused and jumbled. "We met the summer I graduated from high school," Ruth said. "My mom cleans house for his family in Atlanta." She paused. "I'm not his girlfriend."

"I wondered."

"I don't know why he said that. I haven't seen him for almost five years until my boss took me to the State House." She wouldn't share the shock or her anger at Joe's mocking glance from the floor of the chamber.

"It's been longer than that for me," Nate said. "Our families used to get together a couple times a year when we were kids. Eventually, it became too much of a hassle to get our schedules lined up. Everyone was busy, especially Joe."

Uncomfortable silence knitted a wall between them. Nate shifted on the couch. Ruth rubbed one of the yarn knots on a pillow, wishing Nate would leave her to her thoughts.

"I didn't know he was a congressman until today," Nate said.

For the first time, Ruth doubted Nate's honesty. How could he not know? He and Joe were family. Cousins know about each other.

Nate cleared his throat. "This might be none of my business, and tell me if it is, but you didn't seem happy to see him."

"I was surprised."

Nate ran his hands through his hair, creating furrows in the soft blond strands. "I guess I'll have to accept that, but just so you know, I don't believe that's all there is to it." The pause stretched long. "If he tries to hurt you—in any way—I'm here for you."

"Why would he want to hurt me?" She licked a dot of blood from her lip.

"When we were kids, he always had to win: board games, swimming, favors from our parents. It didn't matter. But nothing made him happy." Nate rested his arm on the back of the couch. "Man, if I lived like he did, I'd never complain. I dreaded the times we would get together, wondering what fancy new possession he would rub under my nose, what castoffs he would bring that I was supposed to be grateful for."

"I never had a cousin. There was just Mom and me."

"What I'm trying to tell you," Nate said, staring hard into her face, "is that whatever is between the two of you, if he thinks you came out on top, well, he'll try to even the score."

The fact that Joe had called her his girlfriend wiggled in the back of her mind. Did he have intentions that she was unaware of? No, Joe was now a professional man, a congressman, and he was in Logan on important business. The fact that she lived in Logan was coincidental. He was a big man and she a tiny fish. And Nate…she wasn't sure anymore.

Nate stood. "One more thing before I go. Joe saw us together, and that could be a problem. He may assume things, and I doubt his competitive nature has changed."

Ruth locked the door. Nothing would entice her to date Joe again, but where did that leave her and Nate? She had hoped a relationship might grow between them. But if Joe mentioned to Nate why she had twelve hundred dollars of his money, Nate may decide to never look at her again.

10

Monday, June 3

Monday morning. Clouds touched the rooftops as though heaven refused to hold them up. Nate prayed for rain, for a break from the oppressive humidity. Maybe a good storm would scare some of the crows back to where they came from.

Inside the house and perched on top of a ladder, he filled his spatula with mud from the red plastic container hanging from his belt and scraped the compound across the seam in the drywall, leaving behind grooves that would need sanded later. He stared at the wall. Just like his life. Do your best, but God comes along and buffs up the edges.

Chet sat on a stool beside Nate's ladder, his plaster-encased leg extended to the side as he pressed mud into lower seams. "Hey man," Chet said. "You going to finish, or do you want to keep on daydreaming?"

Nate dug deep into the bucket of mud. "Good to have you back, buddy."

"What did you think about the church service yesterday?" Chet ran his spatula across the drywall.

"It felt strange. You know, as if I wasn't really in church." Nate scraped his empty pail, swiped the mud on the wall, and then climbed down the ladder.

"Reminded me of church camp when I was younger." Chet looked at Nate. "Hey, maybe you can build us a fire on Sundays. We can sit around it while we sing in the heat. Hmm. Bad idea. We don't need more heat. How hot do you think Hell will be?"

"Hot. If no more show up than yesterday, Hell might be a crowded place." Nate scooped mud from the five-gallon bucket and smeared it into the red container.

"Give folks a chance. It's a big change, coming to the wilderness instead of sitting in an air-conditioned building."

"We should be in a building."

Chet leaned back against the wall. "Not really. I liked it. It reminded me of the early Christians and how they met in homes. It felt neat."

Nate grimaced. It was fine and dandy to sit in his yard and watch the sheriff drive by, but that wasn't church. They needed to be in God's house.

Chet repositioned his leg, the sound of the cast sliding across wood mimicking the plaster skimming the wall. "I hear the mayor's got a plan to get rid of the crows."

Nate worked his jaw. He really didn't care what the mayor did. Most likely, the plan belonged to Joe anyway. Of all the times for his cousin to show up. Gone for years and then on the very day Nate was with someone who might become important to him, there he was. Joe never did anything without a reason, and Nate suspected the reason he was in Logan had more to do with Ruth than the mayor. The thought twisted as he slid the spatula across a seam. "Did you know Joe's in town?"

"No kidding. Cousin Joe? What for?"

"Apparently he's helping the mayor spend the new tax money."

Chet laughed. "Should be an easy job."

"He saw Ruth and me at the Main Street Café."

"And?"

Nate sat on the top of the ladder and dangled the empty trowel between his knees. "You remember how jealous Joe was of everything; well, I'm afraid he'll think Ruth and I are a couple and hit on her."

"Are you?"

"Am I what?"

"A couple, doofus."

There wasn't anything special between Ruth and him. At least, not yet, but Joe didn't deserve her. His jaw tightened as he remembered how huge her eyes had grown when Joe had shown up. A deer in the woods would be happier to see a hunter with a gun than she had been to see Joe. With Ruth's gentleness, the brute would eat her alive.

"Earth to Nate…you didn't answer my question."

"No, we're not a couple. There, you happy?"

Chet held up his hands. "Hey, I just asked." He scraped his loaded trowel along the seam. "I think Ruth's tougher than you give her credit for. She didn't seem afraid of those crows Friday night."

She hadn't, had she? That crow in her house—it must have been the surprise that scared her more than the crow.

"Betsy wants the two of you to come to supper some night next week. Any preference?"

"I don't know." Nate rubbed a hand across the top of his head, tipping his hair with spackle. "Things are weird right now."

"Well, let me know. Unless you tell me some other time, Bets will expect the two of you next Thursday night."

Swell. Nate slapped mud on the wall, trying to shove his thoughts into the small seam. They had a dinner date, and he didn't even know if Ruth was still interested or if Cousin Joe now held her attention.

~*~

"No, Mr. Charlie, it isn't like that at all." Ruth blew out a breath. She needed him to understand. This wasn't how she expected the Monday conversation with her friend to go.

"You aren't afraid of Mr. Joseph, but you want to avoid him. I'm just an old man, but it seems someone you dated should bring better memories than the ones you want to forget." His eyebrows rose. "And what of Mr. Nate, the cousin?"

"Did you know all along?"

"That Mr. Nate had a cousin? Of course I did. Most folks in town know."

"Why didn't you tell me?"

"It wouldn't have made a difference. Some things are destined to happen."

The crows sat in thick groups on the courthouse lawn as well as dotting the tall grass in the churchyard across the street. Nate's church. After a couple of weeks of neglect, already the place looked deserted and empty. Would the city eventually mow the lot or would the grass simply grow until it became a field more suitable for cows than the middle of town?

"You think you chose Logan, but that's not the case." Mr. Charlie had lowered his voice. "Logan was your destination long before your car ran out of gas." He turned sightless eyes toward her. "Long before you left the safety of your mama's home, before running to

Wilmington to keep the secrets you were hiding, your destiny was Logan."

Mr. Charlie's philosophical thoughts felt like fingernails on a chalkboard. This talk of her destiny had started when the crows came, and the feathered blight was still growing, more every day. Her words came out hard. "I told you why I was in Wilmington." She fingered the chain around her neck.

"I know what you told me."

A man rushed up the stairs; another followed. Cars backed up at the light. It was closing time for local businesses. For the first time Mr. Charlie's empty eyes unnerved her.

"And what did you tell your mama?" he finally asked.

Ruth didn't want to talk about it. "I told her what I told you."

"That you moved to Wilmington for a job, and the job ended, so you headed home only to run out of gas."

"Yes."

"And now Mr. Joseph has shown up and can destroy your well-rehearsed story." It wasn't a question.

"Please, can we just forget it?"

"Of course."

A man and woman walked down the sidewalk toward the crosswalk. Deep worry lines etched their faces. The same couple passed every day, usually laughing, heads tipped together. The change from upbeat to worry unnerved Ruth. She had seen too much of it in the past few days, including the shift in her personal life.

"How many birds are there now?" Mr. Charlie asked.

She sighed. "Same as Friday. They're all over the place. I'm surprised you don't trip over them when you walk." She turned sharply, searched his face, and glanced at his elbows and the worn fabric over the top of his knees. "You don't, do you?"

"No, the birds let me alone. For the most part."

She wondered what he meant by that but was too drained to ask. "When will people stop expecting Attorney Dunlap to fix the town's problems? A couple stopped by this afternoon angry because their road hasn't been paved yet, and the dust is getting on the wash she hangs on the line. They want to sue the churches. Who hangs clothes on the line anymore? And earlier a man, he didn't have an appointment or anything, I was straightening the waiting room, and he just barged in and expected Mr. Dunlap to see him. I thought Kathleen might call the police, but finally, the man stormed back out, as mad as when he came in."

"It will get worse."

"I don't know how it can. People are at each other's throats all the time. No one is happy. Surely, you've noticed it, sitting here. Well, the anger, at least." She wiped sweat off her forehead. "Why don't you sit somewhere else in the summer? It's so hot here."

"I need to be here." He smiled. "It feels nice to be worried about, little one. It's been a long time since that has happened."

For once, Ruth felt grateful for Mr. Charlie's blindness. He could not see the tears that puddled in the corners of her eyes. She left Mr. Charlie sitting alone on the step, just as she did every Monday through Friday. But today, instead of turning right she turned left. She wasn't going home just yet.

~*~

"I'm coming. I'm coming." Stewart Gleason folded the evening paper and placed it on the footstool. As he opened the front door of his sprawling ranch house, his face hardened. "Why aren't you at the golf course or sitting on a fancy yacht somewhere in the Mediterranean?"

Joseph Ackerman stood in front of him, smiling as though the two were best friends rather than living on opposite sides of the moral train track. Joseph didn't ask to come in, and Stewart didn't offer. "This is a courtesy call. I thought it would be polite of me, as a fellow legislator, to let you know I'm working with your mayor."

Stewart scowled. "This is my town. If Mayor Bloom needs help, all he has to do is call me."

Joseph flipped his hand; a heavy gold ring sparkled in the light. "It's nothing political." He picked a piece of invisible dirt from beneath manicured fingernails. "This is business. Your mayor wants help structuring a plan to utilize the revenue from the new tax. I'm his man."

"As far as I know, there hasn't been any revenue to utilize." Stewart wondered about Ackerman's real game. The rich, young playboy didn't need the work. Any dollars he earned in Logan would be piddling compared to what he was worth. "Doesn't your own district need help?"

Joseph grinned. "They decided to delay implementation."

Stewart didn't miss the irony. "Well, thanks for informing me." He turned to close the door.

"This isn't personal, Stewart. There's more going

on than you can see, power that shapes the future. You have to know where to look, my friend."

"I have no idea what you're talking about."

"Too bad about these crows; they're making a mess of your town."

Stewart Gleason shoved the door, blocking the face of the man he hated most. Rumbling sounds came from his stomach. He thrust a hand into the pocket of his shorts in search of antacids.

~*~

Ruth hadn't expected it to be this dark, but thick clouds hid the stars and moon. She caught the toe of her sandal on a broken edge of the sidewalk and flung her arms outward to regain her balance. She settled the satchel of books back on her shoulder and continued walking.

Already upset from the horrific day of work, Ruth had felt worse when Mr. Charlie second-guessed her story about arriving in Logan. Well, it was true—at least part of it.

Stupidity kept her at the library too long, but she wanted to stay until after dark to avoid being seen by Joe—if he was watching. He didn't know where she lived, and she wanted to keep it that way.

Her footsteps sounded too loud in the semi-quiet. A few cars remained in the parking lot at Jerry's Diner, their owners most likely lingering over dessert and coffee. The smell of grilled meat spilled out the vent, and memories of the burger she had eaten with Nate only a week ago made her mouth water. Peanut butter didn't taste as good as it used to, even if she toasted the bread.

Darkness became more complete as she rounded the corner, leaving behind the lights of the business district. The first residential streetlight lay a block ahead, and it was the last before she reached her house. Fishing in her purse, she touched the hardness of her house key and held the point poking out between clenched fingers. Why did she keep forgetting to check about a cellphone?

Disembodied sounds that normally would not have bothered her developed ominous overtones. A barking dog, banging doors, someone's television. Her own breathing was too fast and too hard.

Footsteps tapped behind her. She glanced over her shoulder. A breath of air disturbed the shadows from their sleep causing motion all around her. Surely, the sound had been nothing more than the bend of limbs. She stepped into a puddle of light that lay beneath the tall pole and lingered, hesitant to return to the dark. "There's nothing in the dark that isn't in the light." Her mother's voice. Ruth wasn't sure she believed it.

Her house waited only a block away. Most of the windows she passed were covered with dark cloth. About a year ago, after Mrs. Walters was attacked, Ruth learned to keep her eyes straight ahead, her mouth closed and her thoughts to herself. The woman called the police on a neighbor having a pot party. Someone else lived in Mrs. Walter's house now.

There was no mistake. Rhythmic sound of footsteps followed her. She tensed, ready to run. Her fist grew clammy around the house key, but she gripped it tighter. Hair swirled around her head as she turned right and left, panic seeping into her core as she searched for a place to hide: a house with a lit window, a thick-trunked tree, anything. The footsteps drew closer. Her house was next, dark and quiet. She never let a light burn when she was gone.

Overcome by fear, she ran.

~*~

Ruth shoved the door closed behind her. Her lungs struggled for air. She slid to the floor, never hearing the footsteps pass. But with her heart thundering so loudly, the person could have stomped by and she would have missed him.

She waited. When no sound penetrated the door, she hastened through the living room, into her bedroom, and then the kitchen, turning on lights as she went. Finally, with every light burning, she slumped into a folding chair at the kitchen table. She had missed dinner, but the thought of food made her queasy.

Something hit the kitchen window and she jumped. Not a rock; the sound was too soft. The window over the sink glared, black and faceless. Anyone in the neighbor's driveway could see her sitting inside. She reached behind her and switched off the overhead light. The room filled with misshapen shadows.

She remembered the crow. Most likely she could explain the sound if she tried. She thought about the day. Mr. Charlie had upset her; she had come home late, walked in the dark, imagined footsteps. Her heart rate began to slow.

Another sound against glass: this time from the living room window. Ruth darted toward the refrigerator. She crouched beside the humming behemoth and pressed her back to the wall.

After a few seconds of silence, Ruth crept across

the cracked linoleum floor and pulled open the drawer. Not wanting to stand and be seen through the window, she walked her fingers blindly among the contents. Her breathe wheezed in the silence as she searched. Finding the knife, she wrapped her hand firmly around the worn handle.

She distinctly remembered locking the front door, but the latches that held the windows were rusty. Squirreled back beside the refrigerator, she watched the beam of light coming from the bedroom. Anyone walking across it would leave a shadow. She stared at the light and waited. The plastic clock above the stove ticked off the seconds.

Pounding erupted all around. Horrifying sounds, hitting every window over and over.

With hands clamped over her ears she pulled herself into a ball. The urgency of the pounding increased. Her body would soon explode from the terror. She waited for the glass to break. Pounding. Pounding.

Screams pierced the kitchen and ricocheted off the walls. Her screams; her terror. The horror continued until her strength was gone.

11

Thursday, June 6

If the rowdies who had tried to frighten her the night before were watching as Ruth walked to work, she refused to give them the satisfaction of showing fear. With her head high and her back stiff, she walked down her street, all the while anticipating what might await around the next corner, behind the shadow created by the overgrown bushes or in the car that moved a bit too slowly toward her. Logan had become her home, and she would not succumb to pranks. She would not be driven out by someone else's cruelty.

She should call the police and make a report. She could use the office phone, but what would the police do? The windows weren't broken; they had left no footprints. The only oddity had been the number of black feathers lying around the house. But then, crows were everywhere.

Exhausted from the lack of sleep, she wondered how she would get through the day. More than that, what would she do when the sun finally set? Every attempt to shake off the feeling of evil met with defeat, and the tightness in her chest remained.

Reaching downtown, Ruth stopped.

Across the street, the two stained-glass windows that flanked the front doors of the church stared like vacant eyes, black and sightless, their red, gold, and blue colors gone. The doors that had been chained for two weeks stood open.

Ruth crossed the empty street and moved up the cement walkway that led to a wide covered porch. She stopped outside the open door. Should she walk in? Was there a procedure to gain entry? Someone had taken the time to use red spray paint on the cement floor. Wrinkling her brow, she tried to focus on the graffiti.

"Pay to Caesar what is Caesar's."

Ruth jumped at the sound of Nate's voice.

His tight mouth showed the anger that his empty eyes denied.

She pointed to the floor. "Who did this?"

"No idea."

"The windows?"

He grimaced. "Black spray paint."

"I'm so sorry." She ached to comfort him.

"There's more," Nate said.

He led her through the unlocked doors and across the vestibule. Beyond was a large room with splintered wood and shredded royal blue fabric thrown into three large piles.

"They used to be our pews," Nate said.

Streaks of red paint scarred the pale blue walls. Books lay bent among the rubble. Ruth put a hand to her throat and turned her head, needing to hide her horror. Only then did she realize that their hands were clutched in a tight grip, a refuge among the confusion.

She met his eyes, her shock contrasting with his pain.

Nate loved his church. He had talked about it the first time they were together—the night he bought her a hamburger at Jerry's Diner and then again at the picnic in his yard. Many of those attending told her how Nate spent hours at the church painting, replacing broken posts, mowing the grass. Whatever needed done, Nate was the go-to man. And now, the center of his life looked as if the devil himself had destroyed it. No one would be more hurt by the vile actions than Nate.

Pastor Clark and Police Chief Bill Stafford walked through a door in the front of the sanctuary. Pastor Clark rubbed the back of his neck. "I haven't seen such aggression toward Christianity or houses of worship since I was in Haiti."

"You were in Haiti?" the Police Chief asked.

"A long time ago. My parents were missionaries in Haiti when I was a kid."

"Bet you saw an eyeful."

"A lot like this but with chicken feet and splattered blood." The pastor shared a narrow smile. "No, this isn't voodoo. This mess belongs to angry men."

The chief eyed Ruth and then turned to Nate. "Anything missing?"

Nate pulled a sheet of paper from his jeans pocket. "Most everything electronic that could be carried out is gone."

"How in the world did they do this right in the middle of town?" The chief rubbed his jaw and stared at the mangled pews. "We have a cruiser passing through this area at least every hour." He shook his head and turned to Pastor Clark. "You have insurance?"

Pastor Clark nodded.

"That's good."

A deep sadness settled over Ruth. Everything came down to money. Had it always been this way and she had never noticed?

"I'll make a report," the chief said. "In the meantime, let's get this place locked up again."

Pastor Clark turned a heavy gaze to the chief. "Thanks for notifying me. I appreciate it."

"Soon as I got the call, I headed over. When I saw the mess, I phoned you."

"Who called it in?" Pastor Clark asked.

"Some man at the courthouse. Said he was going to work early and noticed a couple guys creeping behind the hedges. He yelled, and they ran. By the time we got here, well, this is what we found."

Ruth felt Nate stiffen. "Man have a name?" he asked.

"Yeah, Joseph something."

Ruth and Nate shared a quick glance. Please let this be a coincidence. Nate said Joe would seek revenge any way he could. Was this her fault? Too much had happened too quickly. She was drowning in its immensity.

12

Thursday, June 13

Ruth settled into the seat of Nate's truck with a comfort she would not have expected three weeks ago. She wore her best summer dress, the yellow sleeveless one with white flowers running the length of the fabric. She had pulled her fine hair into a knot.

Exactly a week ago today, Nate's church had been vandalized. He had invited her to the dinner at Chet and Betsy's as she'd left him that morning to continue to work. She had agreed but had believed the dinner would be cancelled when Chet and Betsy found out about the trouble. But Betsy made Nate promise to come, and Nate said if he had to go, so did she. The trip to the Ross's took less than five minutes. Ruth smelled the pasta sauce as soon as she stepped onto the front porch.

Nate told her she would love Betsy's house, and he was right. As she looked around the living room, it was hard not to feel at home when the décor looked a lot like hers. The upholstered furniture was draped in pale blue fabric. Two end tables had their origins as boxes and crates. She grinned when she spied the lamp Betsy had obviously created from a castoff ceramic vase.

"Welcome to the Ross's," Chet said, giving her a

gentle lopsided hug as he leaned slightly toward the heavy cast. He smelled like soap and aftershave.

A small wiggling bundle of boy streaked through the room, pulling behind him a green balloon tied to a string.

Nate caught Chip around the middle and spun him off the floor. Amid giggles, Nate hugged the child and set him back on the floor. "Say hi to Ruth before you run off. You remember her from the picnic at my house, don't you?"

Chip looked a lot like his dad, with lanky limbs he needed to grow into and fine hair that had a mind of its own. Deep brown eyes looked up at her as he formally held out a hand. Then he ran from the room, green balloon flying behind him.

Ruth stared after him. "Is he always so full of energy?"

"Always." Betsy entered the room carrying two glasses of iced tea. She handed one to Ruth and the other to Nate.

"What about me?" Chet glanced at his cast. "I'm wounded."

"You know the way to the kitchen, and this scullery maid only has two hands." She gave him a quick kiss on the cheek and turned to Ruth. "Feel free to sit if you want or join me in the kitchen."

The preparations for supper were quickly finished, and Chip was rounded up, hands washed, and settled on his stool at the table. Before the others had time to sit, Chip announced in a grown-up voice, "I pray." He folded his fingers together. "God thank You for food, even salad."

Chet quickly dropped into his chair.

Betsy winked at Ruth and closed her eyes.

"Thank You for Mommy and Daddy and Uncle Nate and his girlfriend. Thank You for cake and for television and—"

Chet cleared his throat.

"Amen."

Ruth and Nate sat across the table from Chip. The boy had the whole side to himself, and Ruth soon appreciated the wisdom of the seating arrangement as spaghetti landed beside Chip's cartoon cup, in front of his matching plastic plate, and on the floor. Betsy sat on the end closest to Ruth while Chet stretched out on the opposite side.

They passed the food from person to person: family-style, Betsy called it. Conversation about the guys' work was interspersed with comfortable silence.

"Hope you like chocolate," Betsy said, handing Ruth a slice of chocolate cake with a scoop of ice cream on the side. "I guess I should have asked before I served you."

Ruth licked icing from the tip of a finger. "I love it."

Betsy put her elbows on the table and leaned toward Ruth. "You remind me of someone."

"The drug store, remember?"

"No, from somewhere else. The more I look at you, the more convinced I am that I've seen you before."

"Well, I was raised in Atlanta."

"I've lived my whole life in Logan."

"I spent a year and a half in Wilmington, North Carolina."

Betsy shook her head. "That's not it. Oh, well. It'll come to me."

Chip wiggled out of his booster seat only to be

caught by Betsy. "Is that how we leave the table?" Betsy's mother-expression loosened a soft chuckle from Ruth, remembering her own early childhood, back when life was normal.

Chip returned to his chair. "May I be 'scused?"

"Yes, you may. Get the dishcloth and let me wipe your face and hands before you go off to play."

"He's such a good boy." Ruth watched him run toward the kitchen.

Chet laughed. "He's on his best behavior for you."

A knock sounded.

While Betsy wiped Chip's face, Chet made his way to the door, his cast thump announcing each step. "Someone probably selling something," he said over his shoulder. "I'm the master of chasing them away."

"And he is," Betsy said. "We had the cutest little girls stop by and—"

"Nate, you need to come to the door, buddy."

Nate wrinkled his forehead and mumbled, "Who can want me here?"

Awkwardness seeped under Ruth's skin as she sat alone with Betsy. "I like your house," she said, desperate to talk about something.

"We bought the place but had little money left over to fix it up. Thankfully, it was solid and didn't need any structural work. Chet added the front porch last year."

"I noticed the porch." Ruth glanced toward the sound of mumbled voices at the front of the house.

"I hope you don't mind all the homemade touches."

Ruth smiled, this time with sincerity. "Your house looks a lot like mine except the stairs to the second floor at my house have been blocked off. The dining room is my bedroom."

"So what about the upstairs?"

"The owner said he wanted to renovate the second floor and rent it out, but I've been there two years, and he hasn't done anything yet. Actually, I'm just as glad. It gives me a sense of privacy."

The two men returned with Nate clutching an official-looking envelope. He turned the envelope over and examined the front.

"You going to open it?" Chet asked.

"Chet." Betsy frowned. "Maybe Nate needs some privacy."

Nate resumed his place at the table and opened the envelope.

More trouble; it had to be, or Nate wouldn't look as if someone had just cut off his head. The vandalism at the church had caused him a lot of stress. How could peaceful Logan suddenly offer up so much pain? Nate slipped a sheet of paper from the envelope.

Ice clinked in Chet's glass as he drank.

Betsy rose to clear the table, but Nate motioned her to stay. "It seems I am to be assessed extra tax at the home place."

The paper shook slightly as he handed it to Chet. "There's an item in the Salvation Law that defines a church as any place that is occupied more than twice in one month for the purpose of worship. Sunday was the second time. Any more and my home will be declared a church, and I will have thirty days to pay the tax or be locked out of my home."

Chet passed the letter to Betsy.

Nate swallowed. "No wonder Joe wanted this delivered."

Ruth stiffened. "Joe?"

"Yeah," Nate said. "Apparently my dear cousin intercepted the letter and paid to have it hand delivered. The poor guy had a heck of a time tracking me down tonight and finally saw my truck out front. Joe somehow managed to provide him with a description, and the license number."

"We'll hold worship somewhere else," Chet said.

"But we'll have to change locations every two weeks. Life is confusing enough without keeping track of where you're supposed to be for church each Sunday morning." Nate slumped back into his chair. "My church, now my house. What's next?" He glanced at Ruth.

Cold fingers ran up Ruth's back. Was she in the middle of a battle between two cousins?

~*~

It was after midnight when Nate and Ruth left for home. Ruth agreed to attend church with Nate on Sunday, now to be held at the Ross's home. Chet and Betsy's house felt comfortable to her; it would be a good introduction to Nate's religious world. Nate remained on the stoop until she'd locked the door from the inside then waved to her through the living room window. His truck disappeared down the street.

Ruth made it as far as the bedroom before a knock came on the door. Nate must have come back! While her heart did a dance, she ran back to the living room. As she unlocked the door, she realized she had not heard the diesel engine of Nate's truck. Too late.

Joe grabbed the edge of the opening door. "Hello, Ruth. Keeping late hours, aren't you?"

"What do you want, Joe?" Suddenly she was tired;

it was late; she had to be at work in less than seven hours. Then she jerked awake. "Have you been watching my house?" She raised her chin. "This is my life, and I don't welcome your intrusion."

"Hey, Ruthie. I just stopped by to invite you to dinner tomorrow night." His words flowed smooth as silk.

Had the footsteps that followed her the other night belonged to Joe?

"I saw Nate leaving, so I knew you'd still be awake." Contempt filled his eyes. Contempt for whom—for her or Nate? It didn't matter.

"It's late. I need to get to bed."

"No problem. A girl needs her beauty sleep, especially the night before a big date."

Her face reddened. "There won't be a date tomorrow. Now, let go of the door."

"Oh Ruthie, Ruthie." He reached out and stroked her hair.

Ruth twisted her head away. She wanted to run from his touch, but leaving the door would allow him access to her apartment. "Don't touch me again." She squeezed the words through clenched teeth and tried to pull the door closed, but Joe held it tight.

"You didn't mind my attention before."

"That was a long time ago, Joe. Please go." Ruth felt his stare but refused to meet his eyes. She wasn't afraid of sinking under his sensual gaze—she had overcome any physical attraction long ago—but she knew if she allowed herself the intimacy of a direct look, the anger she held bottled up would ignite and nothing would stop it. She was too tired and too emotionally spent right now. If she fought with him tonight she would lose, and she swore to never again be defeated by Joseph Ackerman.

He stood with his fingers wrapped around the edge of the door.

Memories flowed of other times she had listened as he breathed in her ear. She bristled. "Get away from me."

"Promise you'll have supper with me. Just once and I'll never bother you again—if that's what you still want."

"No!" She tried to pull the door closed.

"I'll make it worth your while."

She froze at the suggestion in his tone. Did he really think she wanted him again, especially after what he did? The pain he'd caused her?

"I'll pick you up at six."

"No." Ruth's arms and legs shook. She clutched the door tighter.

"You didn't spend my money the way you were supposed to. What if I share that information with my cousin?" A look of victory spread across his face. "I'll see you at six."

She faltered. How could he know that? No one knew. No one.

Even after he disappeared down the sidewalk, after the sound of his shoes stilled in the darkness, Ruth clung to the stability of the door. "No. I won't go," she murmured to no one.

How could she build a new life when her old one kept haunting her?

13

Friday, June 14

Another hour passed. The dreaded date with Joe loomed closer with each jerky movement of the red second hand. Ruth wanted to pull the clock off her office wall and stomp the wood frame to bits; grind the mechanisms to shards. As the workday ended, she closed down her computer and settled the worn blue strap of her purse into the familiar groove over her shoulder. There was still time for her visit with Mr. Charlie.

Once outside, it took seconds for sweat to drip down her chest in little rivulets, soaking the fabric of her bra. The pink cotton shirt clung to her back. Cars passed, stirring the air enough to lift strands of her hair but failing to provide any respite from the June heat.

As usual, Mr. Charlie sat on the courthouse steps. She should have brought a bottle of water for him. Again, she wondered at his adamancy to remain in that spot.

"Ah, Miss Ruth." Mr. Charlie's smile welcomed her. "How was your day at work?"

She settled beside him on the hot cement. "Same ol', same ol'."

"Hmm."

She waited for more, but he stared toward the church, as he did every day lately. "I have a Gala apple today." Ruth placed half the slices into his hand.

"Gala's my favorite," he said, taking a bite of the flesh.

"I didn't know that." Ruth fingered her apple. "Why Gala?"

"I like the name."

Simple as that. They chewed in silence. She needed to ask him about Joe, but it could wait a bit longer.

Mr. Charlie coughed. The gagging, choking sounds kept coming. A man on the sidewalk stared but continued past them.

Spittle dribbled down Mr. Charlie's chin as he forced out one lung of air after another. The skin around his lips turned blue as Ruth stood in shock. She should know what to do. Should she pat his back or raise an arm? Which arm? Did it matter? As she debated, Mr. Charlie's cough subsided. He wiped his face with the edge of his shirt.

"Are you all right, Mr. Charlie? Do you need to go to the hospital? Or to the doctor?" Without thought, she grasped his hand.

He smiled. The tight lines in his face softened. For an instant, Mr. Charlie reminded Ruth of her father.

They sat holding hands until a shadow fell over them.

"What do you think you're doing?"

Her hand jerked from Mr. Charlie's. "Joe!" His expression sent daggers into her, the hardness of his eyes making her feel dirty, and that angered her even more. How easily she let others control her emotions. "What do you want, Joe?"

"What are you doing here...with him?" A sneer accompanied his words.

Ruth burned with anger. She took the blind man's hand in hers. This time he did not return her squeeze.

"Mr. Charlie is my friend. We visit together every day, and it's no business of yours." She wanted to tell Mr. Charlie how sorry she was for Joe's inappropriate behavior, but she sat with her teeth clenched tight.

"You have any trouble with the crows, young man?" Mr. Charlie asked.

"Ruth, go home. You're making a fool of yourself."

"You don't have the right to tell me—"

"Young man, what about the crows?"

Joe grabbed Ruth by the upper arm and pulled her to her feet. His lips curled in anger. "I said go home."

Ruth pulled away and rubbed her arm, the imprint of his fingers red on her pale skin.

Mr. Charlie slid toward her, his trousers scraping against the hard cement as he moved. "Ruth, perhaps you should go on home."

"But Mr. Charlie…"

"Do what the man says," Joe retorted. "I'll pick you up in an hour."

"I hate you. You know that, don't you?"

"Wear something pretty." Smiling, Joe strode back toward the courthouse.

Ruth stared, her mouth agape, her hands twitching.

"So that is Joseph Ackerman," Mr. Charlie said. "You have a date with him?"

"Not really. Well, sort of. He threatened to keep bugging me unless I went out with him one time." She sighed. "I just want to get it over with and never have to see him again."

"No one can force you to do something you don't want to do."

She glanced toward the courthouse door. "He can."

~*~

A formally dressed host greeted them at the door of the restaurant. "Welcome, Mr. Ackerman." Joe held Ruth's elbow possessively as the tuxedo-clad waiter escorted them to a table overlooking the bay. Twilight softened the reeds while the exterior lights sprinkled the tall grass in glitter. Off to the right, an island formed a small mound of green and brown in the dark blue. Spanish moss dripped from the trees that stood as sentinels for the small plot of sand and shells.

Once they were seated, Joe glanced around like a lord surveying his kingdom. "This is one of my favorite places. Makes the drive to Myrtle Beach worth it, wouldn't you say?" The room was packed with patrons clothed for a ball.

Ruth shifted uncomfortably in her cotton sundress and shoved her sandal-clad feet further under the table. "It took over an hour to get here." She refused to tell him she felt like the unwanted step-sister in this environment. He had to know she didn't have clothes for a place like this. Even if he didn't, any decent guy would have changed plans once he saw how she was dressed.

Looking through the window, Ruth imagined the smell of the salt air. In her mind, she could feel the evening breeze on her skin and its whispering sound as it moved across the marsh. Instead, she was trapped in a barely-lit room surrounded by the clank of china, murmuring voices, and jazz background music.

Without consulting her, Joe ordered for both of them. His smile told anyone watching that he was perfectly content with his life. Such arrogance.

Ruth seethed inside. She wondered if her clenched stomach would accept even one bite of food. What irony if all the money he was spending on crab and lobster ended up wasted. In spite of her reservation, the food tasted delicious.

When dessert arrived, Joe lifted his fork and smiled. "You disappeared from Atlanta. I called your mom. She said you had a job in Wilmington."

Ruth focused on her key lime pie.

"I know where you were in Wilmington." He settled back in his chair. "It wasn't a job that took you there."

The food in her stomach surged, and she fought her body for control. A glance at his face showed only hard lips and accusing eyes.

"You spent six months at a place that takes in unwed mothers. Who were you hiding from? Were you afraid perfect Ruthie would disappoint her mother?"

She didn't answer.

"What did you do with our baby? I gave you money for an abortion. You should have told me you changed your mind."

"If I changed my mind? I never wanted an abortion in the first place!" Her voice screeched like a shrieking bird trapped in someone's nightmare. "You were the one who said a baby did not fit in your career path."

The couple at the next table glanced her way.

Joe leaned forward. "Keep your voice down!"

She quieted her words, but not for Joe. She had to have her say, right now, or her courage would be gone. "I couldn't afford to raise her, and you made it clear you weren't helping. There was hardly enough money to feed my mom and me. I had no other choice."

"I paid for an abortion. Problem taken care of!" His flaring nostrils reminded Ruth of a raging bull. At least in this public place the bull was restrained.

She stared at him, wondering what had happened to the sweet person she knew that summer. Her mom had been skeptical about a rich boy dating a poor girl, but after half-a-dozen dates, it seemed his attentions were sincere. He shared his dream with her, his need to change the world. It was a good plan, full of noble acts. All summer they'd roamed Atlanta's parks, shared ice cream cones, and canoed. She went with his family to their beach house. By the middle of August, and as time neared for him to return to grad school, Ruth expected a commitment, a promise they would remain a couple, that he would come home to her on breaks. While he was gone, they would talk on the phone and listen to each other breathe, …just like they did when he finally convinced her to join him in bed. She agreed, believing he loved her and they would be together forever.

After staring at the blue plus-sign on the third pregnancy test, Ruth finally believed the results. She was pregnant. She told him while they were sitting on a bench in the park. The sky was turning from blue to cobalt as a huge orange ball rested on the horizon. "Look at the sun," Ruth said. "I don't think I've seen it that big before."

Joe pulled her closer. "Mom and Dad are gone for the weekend." He always smothered her with attention, making her feel like the most beautiful, sensual, amazing woman on the planet. No one had shown her much love since her dad died, and Joe's sentimentality fed a hunger she haddn't realized she'd had.

He pulled her from the bench and grabbed her around the waist, kissing her gently on the lips—a promise of more to come. She trembled in delight as they walked on a deserted path toward Joe's car. He would be overjoyed at her news.

"I'm pregnant."

His arm stiffened. "Are you sure? We can get a pregnancy test."

"I'm sure," Ruth said, a smile softening her lips.

His eyes turned cold. "Whose baby is it?"

"Whose baby?" The question shocked her. They had been dating for four months. She stared at the face of the man who'd said he loved her. "It's your baby."

"But we used condoms all the time."

"It happens. We talked about it before the first time, remember?" She looked into his tight face and stroked his arm, trying to smooth away his doubt. She wasn't seeing anyone else—as if she would.

He pulled her toward the car, his grip too tight and his step too quick. "We need to get this taken care of now, before I leave. I'll take the money out of the bank tomorrow."

Ruth pulled away, confused.

"Look, I can't be responsible for a kid right now." He stared up the path. "I have plans. You know, important things that will make life better for a lot of people. I don't need this hanging over my head."

Emotions that she had arranged so neatly in her head now became tangled like a writhing nest of snakes.

He'd taken her home. The next day an envelope arrived by courier. It contained twelve one-hundred dollar bills. No letter. No personal words. Ruth tried to call him. She even went to his house a week later, but he was gone. His mom said he'd left for law school early.

Ruth hid the money under her mattress, the same place it was now. The money equaled blood, and she refused to spend money that represented the life of their child.

And somehow, he'd found out.

The noise of the restaurant blurred. Ruth heard her beating heart, the same heart that Joseph Ackerman broke when he'd refused to acknowledge their pregnancy and left her alone to deal with the life-altering condition. The same heart that beat above that of their child.

How dare he question her motives?

She pushed herself from the table. "I want to go home."

He stood and faced her. "Wait until I tell your new lover that he wasn't your first."

With uncontrollable rage, she planted both of her palms on Joe's chest and pushed. He stumbled over the chair and crashed against the window.

Heads turned. The room quieted. The sharp crack of glass echoed loudly.

Ruth ran from the room, leaving Joe to deal with the situation.

14

Saturday, June 15

Heavy clouds promised rain before the day ended. Crows dotted the yard, balancing placidly on spindly legs or nestling in the grass. Ruth stared at nothing as she sat on her front stoop, an almost empty glass of iced tea gripped in her hand. The ride home from Myrtle Beach the previous night had been horrible at best: an hour of silence so loud it hurt her ears. Not a word, mile after mile. Joe's unspoken rage almost smothered her.

The restaurant window didn't break, but it did crack.

Ruth didn't know how Joe would retaliate, but he would.

The usual Saturday morning garage sales were forgotten. Ruth wanted to talk to Mr. Charlie, but he never came to the courthouse on weekends, and she had no idea where he lived.

On the edge of town, he had said. That could be anywhere.

Life suddenly had become very complicated. She tipped the glass to her lips and the last of the ice fell onto her tongue. She sucked the coolness until it was gone. Somewhere between pushing Joe into the plate-glass window and arriving home after midnight, she lost the remainder of her dream for a better life. She felt like an empty shell with a face attached. Out of options; out of hope. No matter what decision she made, happiness would elude her. She had failed her mother, who still didn't know about the pregnancy, failed to meet Joe's expectations, and now, her past would rob her of the best thing that had ever happened to her: Nate. He could never love a used woman who gave up her child. Mr. Charlie called her the light of Logan. What a joke. She wasn't the light of anything.

Her bad day turned worse when a truck pulled to the curb, scattering a dozen crows that lingered near the road. Nate was the last person she wanted to see right now. He would notice her mood. She didn't want to tell him she had accepted a date with Joe, even if the acceptance was under duress. No way could she admit the truth about her past with Joe.

Nate had shared the reason for his animosity toward his cousin, and Ruth didn't want to be perceived as another one of Joe's castoff's. She was not the pure woman Nate deserved. Why had she become involved with this churchy man? Oh, yeah. It started that day at the courthouse; it was Mr. Charlie's fault—and where was Mr. Charlie today when she needed him?

"Hey."

Worn athletic shoes, feet attached, stopped in front of her. "May I sit down?"

There wasn't much space on the stoop. Ruth shifted to the right until the edge of the cement dropped away. Even so, Nate's body heat reached her. She loved the feel and hated that she loved it.

"You OK?" He stroked the tops of her fingers.

His skin felt hard—a workman's touch. She shivered as she remembered Joe's hands from the night before. With effort, she looked straight ahead, her gaze settling on Nate's truck.

"I took the day off," Nate said. "I wondered if you might want to do something."

"You washed your truck."

"Yep. Taking a chance it'll hold together without the dirt."

The crows resettled in the grassy strip near the road. One of the crows, the one with a scar running from eye to wing, fluttered closer and hopped within inches of Ruth's sandaled foot. She fisted her hands into balls. "I hate that crow!" She jumped up and screamed, "I hate them; I hate them all!"

Nate ran to the yard and flailed an imaginary sword. "Be gone thou foul fowl or I shall smite thee, for thou dost frighten yon maiden fair!"

A beating sound. Birds flew skyward.

"There, all gone, milady." Nate bent in a bow.

In spite of herself, Ruth laughed. "That's more like it." Nate's eye softened. "You ought to smile more often."

"Look behind you."

In spite of the knightly threat, two crows had returned to the comfort of the shady lawn.

Nate shrugged his shoulders. "You can't blame a man for trying. So, how about it? Are you up for a road trip?"

Five minutes ago, she would have said no, but now, with smile lines crinkling around his dazzling blue eyes, the heaviness eased. Ruth had no illusions about her relationship with Nate. Sooner or later, he would find out about her past, and then it would be over. But today she would live in the land of pretend, a land where she was beautiful and wanted and where she could ride off into the sunset with the handsome prince. "What do you have in mind?"

"I have a picnic basket in the back of the truck."

"It looks like rain."

"Yes, it does, but has it ever rained when you've been on a picnic with me?"

"I've only been to one picnic."

"Did it rain?"

"No."

"Do you know how to fish?"

"Fish?" Ruth stared at him. "No."

"Prepare yourself for an adventure."

~*~

Nate's legs dangled over the edge of the dock; toes skimmed the top of the water. He loved this place. Loblolly pines tall enough to scrape the clouds and oak trees as old as South Carolina hid the road that stretched along the top of the hill. Gray clouds, now thickened to black in places, blocked the afternoon sun. Each gust of wind brought the promise of rain closer.

Ruth hadn't talked much, hadn't spoken more than three full sentences. The feeling that Joe had some responsibility for her depressed mood made his gut tighten. If Joe had hurt her in any way…but he hesitated to ask. It was none of his business, after all.

She stood on the dock, her attention on the pink and white bobber he had bought just for her that rode the ripples in the water. The tip of her tongue slipped between her lips as hair blew around her elfin face. "OK, OK, I think I have it this time!" Just as the bobber sank beneath the surface, she jerked the fishing pole.

"Nice and steady now. Don't bring him in too

fast."

Ruth reeled in the line. The bobber broke the surface and disappeared again beneath the brown river water. Her face beamed in delight. "I see it! I see my fish!"

Nate scooped the net into the water. "Nicest bream I've seen in ages." He worked the hook from the fish's mouth and glanced toward Ruth. Eager hands stretch toward him, and he laughed. "Hold it tight and I'll get a picture."

"Hurry!" She pranced around on the wood planks, fish held tight in an extended grip. "I think he wants back in the water!"

He wiped his hands on his shorts and pulled the phone from his pocket. No need to tell her to smile.

"Can I put him back now?"

"Unless you want to eat it."

She blinked. "I can't. Look at his sweet face."

Nate took the fish. "My granddaddy always said you have to lower the fish back into the water slowly to allow it to acclimate." The fish lay still in his hands as he placed it in the water, and then with a flip of its tail, it disappeared in the murky river.

Ruth leaned over his shoulder to watch. "So this is fishing." Ruth settled onto the dock and wiped her hands on a wet wipe. "It's beautiful here."

Nate joined her. "This is my favorite spot. I come here when I need time alone."

"I was beginning to think there were no fish in this river."

"I promised you fish."

"Do you always keep your promise?"

Nate felt Ruth's gaze and it warmed him. "Yes, I always keep my promises. Want to test me?"

"Well, you were right about the river."

"Come to church with me tomorrow. I promise you'll get some benefit from it."

"It's going to rain."

"Church is at the Millers' tomorrow. We'll be inside."

Ruth stared at the river.

Nate followed her gaze. Due to the dry weather, the bank that usually lay hidden beneath dark water showed sprouts of life, like green whiskers on a clay man. Unless it rained, the bank would soon be draped in a thick mangle of vines and weeds. Mid-river lay the sandbar where he had once seen a buck with a ten-point rack. The deer had stood majestic, his head high, master of his environment. Nate had not seen him since.

"So what do you think, Ruth? Are you willing to trust me and come to church tomorrow?" He wasn't sure why she resisted church. And he didn't like the black funk she was in when he'd arrived at her house earlier. Something was wrong, and he longed to be the one to fix it.

"Church is important to you; I know it is." She looked up at him. "What if we trade promises? You tell me three reasons why you go to church. If I like them, I promise to go with you."

His heart leaped. This would be easy; church was his life. "OK, here goes. First, you get to spend time with people who have similar values."

"Mom used to take me to the apartment council meetings. Everyone had the same complaints, but nothing changed. I can't say it was fun."

"Church is different, but let me give you number two." Nate paused. What did he get from Sunday that would be meaningful to Ruth? His identity was woven with the white church building on the corner. Time in worship eased his tension, put perspective back where it belonged. But would Ruth understand that? He sought her eyes to make sure she was listening. "OK, each Sunday Pastor Greg shares a sermon that helps us understand the Bible and how it applies to our lives."

"So your pastor tells you how you should live?"

"No, he tells us what the Bible says about how we should live. The Bible is the word of God. As Christians we try to...no, we want to live a life according to God's standards. Pastor Greg shares those standards with us."

"We all have rules we live by."

"Sure, and as a Christian, I follow God's rules."

"So, what about number three?"

Nate licked his lips. He was sinking. This should be easy, and yet here he was, struggling to express why he went to church. *Come on God, help me out here.* "There is power in singing and praying together. It's hard to explain, but during corporate worship—that's what we call group worship—God shows up. You can feel His presence."

"I'm confused."

"What's confusing you?"

"When I first met you, your church building had just been closed. You said that was the worst that could happen."

"I remember telling you that."

"What I don't understand is why. You don't need the building. You met in your backyard or at someone else's house."

"Yes, but—"

She held up her hands. "Let me finish. Your

second point was lectures by your pastor. Didn't he give one of his lectures at your house?"

"They're called sermons, but yes, he gave a great sermon."

"Then point three. That's the most confusing. God only shows up in the church building?"

Nate chuckled. "No, God is everywhere. Most likely He's here now groaning over my inept description of faith."

Thunder rumbled; the vibrating roll still far off.

Out of habit, Nate watched the sky for lightning.

"If you don't need the building to do any of the things that are important to you, why is your building such an issue?"

A crow landed on the end of the dock. Soon a second joined it, then a third, their black feathers jutting out in awkward angles by the growing wind.

Ruth looked at the crows. "Can we go?" She turned in the direction of the truck, hidden by trees bent in the growing gusts. She gathered the fishing pole with her pink bobber.

"So what about church tomorrow?"

"What about the crows? What does your God tell you about them?" She glanced toward the end of the dock, which now stood empty. She yelled to be heard over the rush of the wind. "If your God can tell me why we're being pestered by these crows, then I'll come just to get the answer!"

God, why the crows? The minute he was starting to convince Ruth to give church a try, the crows appeared and spoiled it all.

Lightening flashed. Rain followed. Nate grabbed Ruth's empty hand and ran for the cover of the truck.

15

Sunday, June 16

The morning air smelled freshly scrubbed from yesterday's storm. Even now, drops of water clung to leaves and sparkled in the early morning sun. The setting might look peaceful, but Ruth pushed against the jitters that bounced in her stomach as she settled into the truck beside Nate. Why had she agreed to attend church? It had been a moment of weakness at the end of a glorious day.

She picked at the seam in her floral skirt and inhaled the scent of Nate's aftershave. How did one behave in church? Of course, this wasn't really church since it was in a house, but still, according to Nate, God would be there, and Ruth had a few questions to ask Him. "So what are the Millers like?"

"I don't know for sure. I've just seen them around town." Nate turned the corner and several crows lazily flapped out of the way.

"Don't the Millers go to your church? I thought that's why we were going to their house."

Nate touched her arm. "You'll be fine. Wait and see. As for the Millers, we're going there because they live close to us. The pastors divided Logan into sections, and then families volunteered to host church for two Sundays at a time. If you want it, I have a schedule in my Bible."

Ruth took a deep breath and then let it out in a sigh. She was going to church. Dappled light from the overhead branches danced in her lap. She loved the trees.

Logan was carved out of part swamp, part forest, and many of the town's trees were ancient, their branches arching over the streets like graceful porticos.

At times, she imagined how Logan must have looked in another era, a quieter, slower time. "What do I have to do to prepare to meet God?" They were strangers, she and the Big Man. "I don't suppose I bend my head and say, 'here I am!'"

Nate's lips puckered like a small prune.

Ruth must have said something wrong, but it could be his attempt to hide laughter. Either way, she shrank into the seat. No one expected a traveler to India to know all the rules, so why expect everyone to know how to behave in the land of religion? She chewed on the edge of her nail, not sure how to fix her mistake.

"Just focus on God. You don't do anything special. Just talk to Him—like you talk to anyone else, except in your mind. He wants to be your friend."

Oh, yeah. God wants to be her friend. She wanted to ask why, but Nate would give her another look. After all, people in his world of religion knew things like that.

"You don't have to be nervous. I'm sure the Millers are nice people, and I know most of the others who will be there." He glanced across the seat at her. "Chet and Betsy—they'll be there."

It wasn't meeting strangers that had kept Ruth awake during the night. It was meeting God. The very thought made her throat grow thick. Nate talked about

God as though He was his best friend. But really—God—the creator of all. God!

They passed through a quiet, middle-class neighborhood. The house directly across was a split-level, the lower windows at ground level. The crows shimmered and rippled as they stood in the yard. First one bird turned, then like a wave, the other black heads cocked in their direction. The crows launched their glistening bodies into the air.

Ruth grabbed for Nate's arm. "The crows—"

Like a tsunami, the large birds swarmed the truck, blocking out most of the light. Wings beat on the hard surface as they surrounded the vehicle.

In a single motion, Ruth released the button on her seatbelt and shoved her body next to Nate. Warm arms wrapped around her.

Thick talons flew past the glass.

Nate's breathing sounded over the thump of wings, his chest rising and falling under her ear.

In a whoosh and flutter, the crows were gone, forming a dark crack in the blue sky as they winged away.

Ruth sat motionless in Nate's arms.

The first burst of laughter came from Nate, soon joined by Ruth. Tears ran down their faces.

"Why are we laughing?" Nate asked between jerky breaths.

"I'm not sure, but I feel a whole lot better."

"I'll feel better when surrounded by church friends." Nate scanned the sky.

Ruth scooted across the gearshift to her seat on the other side of the truck. She gave the split level one last look. Not a crow remained. The incident had escalated so quickly. But what had just happened?

As they turned the corner, Nate squinted out the front windshield. "What's going on down there?" he murmured. About a dozen people stood in the middle of the street. "They're in front of the Millers' place."

Nate found a spot a couple of houses from their destination, parked, and helped Ruth from the truck. His tension increased as he led her down the sidewalk.

One of the men separated from the crowd and approached them. "Pay your tax, you deadbeat!" His nostrils flared. "What makes you better than the rest of us?"

"Ignore him," Nate whispered in Ruth's ear. His arm tightened around her waist.

The crowd shifted toward them: all men, one still in his teens, while another looked to be a hunched-over, white-headed grandpa. A couple of the men held baseball bats. Some carried cardboard grocery boxes.

Ruth gasped as she realized what was about to happen.

An over-ripe tomato hit her in the chest, the stench of rot making her gag. Another tomato spattered on her shoulder. She raised her arm to shield her face, only to have an egg smash against her hand, yolk dripping off her skin like ooze from a weeping sore.

Nate pulled her against his chest as they raced toward the Millers'.

The front door opened and hands dragged them inside.

The pop and smack of tomatoes and eggs continued, hitting the siding of the house.

"Here's a couple of towels. Wipe up a bit, and I'll show you to the bathrooms." The stocky man stood red-faced.

"What's gotten into those people?" Nate wiped

egg from his ear. Shell dropped onto the ceramic tiled floor.

Ruth tried to blot the tomato that covered her best shirt, now most likely ruined. She never thought being pelted with garbage was part of attending church.

A middle-aged woman dressed in white linen slacks and an aqua-colored silk shirt with abalone buttons, unstained, smiled at Ruth. The charms on her bracelet bounced together pleasantly as she extended her hand. "I'm Jean Miller." She glanced toward the double doors, now tightly closed "I'd say welcome, but given the circumstances—"

"Jean, they're still welcome. They've come to worship, and no mob of angry good-for-nothings will keep us from it." Mr. Miller, dressed in a gray suit and blue tie, pulled back a corner of the curtain and peered at the street.

"Come on, honey," Mrs. Miller said to Ruth. "I'll show you where you can get cleaned up. Don't worry too much about your appearance though; everyone looks a little splattered right now."

Alone in the bathroom, Ruth stood with arms limp at her sides. Should she laugh or be afraid? As water ran into the porcelain sink, she gripped the washcloth Mrs. Miller had given her. Her fingers sank into the thick fibers. Such a shame to dirty it. Ruth leaned toward the mirror and picked at a bit of green under her chin. Pepper or cucumber? Had she just been pelted with salad? A grin slipped across her face. Poor Nate. This would probably ruin his day, and all the other people who insisted on having church in spite of the obstacles.

Ruth cleaned up as best she could and headed toward the voices in the back of the house. About twenty people sat in the large family room. Besides Nate, Ruth recognized only one other couple from the picnic.

Shuffling sounded from the front of the house followed by a strong male voice. "Man, what a welcoming committee!"

Nate turned to Ruth and grinned. "Chet's here."

Eventually, a cleaned-up Chet appeared, a guitar case dangling from his hand, the cast on his left leg bearing rosy blotches.

Chip, with his hair standing in wet wisps, ran around the corner and leaped into Nate's lap. "Guess what happened to me Uncle Nate."

"Umm...you forgot to eat breakfast, so all the neighbors got together and tossed food at you."

"They threw tomatoes at me!" The boy pinched his face into a tight pucker. "Ew. Tomatoes."

"I know buddy. Pretty bad, huh?"

Betsy strolled into the room, her forehead puckered in concern. When she saw Ruth, she smiled and gave her a hug. "I'm so happy to see you!"

"Come on, children," Mrs. Miller said. "I have a special church service planned just for you in the next room."

Betsy moved across the room to an empty chair, darting around half a dozen children who chased after Mrs. Miller.

A young woman who looked like she might be Mrs. Miller's daughter collected the last two stragglers and herded them toward the doorway.

The adults settled into what seemed to be a sense of familiar comfort. Faces lost the tension lines from moments earlier. Ruth's heart began to pound. For a while, she had forgotten why she was here. Time to meet God! A heavyset man Ruth remembered from the picnic as being one of the other pastors leaned forward in his chair.

Nate squeezed her hand and smiled.

The man began to speak. "For those of you who don't know me, I'm Zane Roberts, pastor of Calvary Baptist Church. The police promised the protesters will be removed before we leave."

"Removed to jail I hope. The nerve of them—" A middle-aged woman's face reddened. The man beside her patted her arm. "No need to stress, Mary Jane."

Mary Jane turned toward him and scowled.

"Can we file charges, like assault or something?" a younger woman asked. An especially large smear stained her yellow blouse. Drops of tomato speckled her white slacks.

Pastor Roberts ran a hand across his cheek. The weariness in his sigh caused Ruth to wonder about the stress of leadership since the closing of the church buildings. Although no big deal to her, it seemed gargantuan to the people sitting on the Miller's furniture and spilling onto the floor.

"We could, but let's put this morning's excitement behind us for now." The pastor sniffed a stain on the sleeve of his white shirt and shared a tight grin. "Kind of hard to do, but Satan wins only if we let him."

Chet picked up his guitar and the group sang for about a half hour. The voices blended in a harmony that swirled around Ruth like a summer breeze. They sang of love and appreciation for Jesus. When two of the ladies raised their hands, Ruth glanced nervously at Nate, who stood beside her, his eyes closed. Others looked toward the ceiling. Most faces held expressions of rapt wonder.

Ruth gulped back the lump that threatened to choke her. The expectancy of something about to happen heightened. More music. More swaying. God was coming. He was coming!

Just when her breath was reduced to tight threads and she thought she must either bolt from the room or pass out, Mr. Roberts opened his Bible. As they settled back into their chairs, some onto the floor, Mr. Roberts began to talk. He spoke of running the race.

Ruth understood his intent. If the people were committed to Jesus at the church building, they needed to remain committed to Him without it. Her breathing slowed. She understood this! She continued to steal surreal glances around the room. She had expected God to show up before this.

They prayed for the third time. And for the third time Ruth closed her eyes and held her breath in anticipation. She wasn't sure what to expect from prayer in a church that wasn't a church, but nothing happened. Shouldn't electricity be going through the room, or a soft wind, or a Voice?

They prayed, but for what good? Ruth understood the concept of commitment, but prayer? It seemed to serve no purpose. Maybe prayer had different results in a real church. That would explain why the people were so upset over losing their buildings.

When they opened the front door to leave, two police cruisers sat across the street. None of the menacing crowd remained, but the result of their work lay in rotted heaps around the house. Globs of red snaked down the siding; vegetables dangled from shrubbery and eggs lay smashed in the yard, their yellow yokes like smears of sunlight gone wrong. Crows lorded over the garbage as hordes of flies feasted.

With his lips pressed tightly together, Nate led Ruth to the truck. "Sorry, Ruth. This usually doesn't happen. I can't imagine what got into those people."

"They're angry that the tax isn't being paid. People expected the roads to get paved and salaries to go up. Nothing has happened."

"We can't give what we don't have."

As Ruth waited for Nate to unlock the truck door, she smashed a tomato with the toe of her shoe. She looked down in surprise. The tomato was hard under her foot. Sliding the rotting flesh, she exposed a small rock, big enough to cut the skin or leave a nasty bruise. Glancing around, Ruth noticed a number of rocks scattered within the remains of the tomatoes. No rocks had hit her. Even though they appeared stained and were definitely smelly, none of the church goers had been hurt. Even the children had been pelted. Little Mary Carpenter looked to be only a year old, and red ooze clung to her blond curls. A well-thrown rock could have blinded her or any of the little ones. With all the rock-laced tomatoes dotting the ground, why had no one been was hurt? More than coincidence?

Had God been outside protecting them? Did He do things like that?

She gave a shiver and looked around. This whole God-thing made her nervous.

16

Monday, June 17

Monday, the beginning of a week, and Ruth needed to ask Mr. Charlie about God. She watched the clock, willing the time to pass. Her new work space since being promoted to primarily research, was the first room after Mr. Dunlap's office. Having an office usually provided a sense of fulfillment, but today, she wanted to leave.

Had her date with Joe only been three days ago? The memory no longer ranked first place in her thoughts. Sure, the night had been a disaster; she expected nothing more. And Saturday started out lonely but ended with an amazing fishing trip with Nate. And then church on Sunday. Church was what she needed to talk to Mr. Charlie about. He would know the answers.

The minute hand slid to the hour. Ruth closed down her computer, rolled the chair under the desk, and grabbed her blue vinyl purse with the apple inside.

She made it as far as the front office door. "Ruth, if you have a minute before you leave..." Mr. Dunlap had never asked her to stay before. In fact, she seldom saw him. New requests in her work box verified his presence.

"Um, I, well..." She looked from the door to her

boss's face.

"This'll just take a second. There's a new form you need to have ready first thing tomorrow. I have court and won't be here if you have questions. The client is coming at ten to pick it up. Fred Murphy, remember him?"

She did remember Mr. Murphy. Mr. Dunlap had called her to his office to serve as a witness to the man's signature. Mr. Dunlap had placed a blank sheet of stationery over the written part of the document, which had been pure white with a navy blue gilded edge. It had struck her as odd to witness something written on such fancy paper. The man himself, Mr. Murphy, held nothing more than a wisp of memory in her mind, but the fleeting impression was of someone mousy and quiet.

Sighing, Ruth followed her boss into his office. The room was the same size as hers only in Attorney Dunlap's office red, gold, and brown Oriental rugs covered his polished wood floor, and a mahogany desk almost filled the small room. Matching bookshelves full of thick tomes flanked the inside wall.

Attorney Dunlap pulled a multi-paged form from one of the drab green folders in which he stored works in progress. He instructed her on how to fill out each blank line.

Ruth nodded and murmured, trying to focus, but her mind kept wandering to the stairs of the courthouse.

Her boss finally closed the folder, smiled, and wished Ruth a good night.

She sprinted down the hall like a school girl leaving the principal's office. As though walking into a steam-bath, the humidity engulfed her as soon as she stepped outside. The brick historic house next to the office still held a family, rather than a business. Potted geraniums lined the stairs leading to a front porch. Red blooms thrived in the hothouse environment. A fat crow sat so still beside the plant it could have been a decorative ornament. She slowed for twenty paces and enjoyed the shade from the overhanging branches of live oaks.

Traffic grew heavier as cars from the side streets dumped into Logan's main thoroughfare.

Mr. Charlie sat at his usual spot on the courthouse steps.

An unexpected tightness squeezed her chest. What would she do if she ever lost him? As she walked, Ruth watched the older man bend his head in one direction then shift it to another. She chuckled, the fear seeming silly.

"I thought you weren't coming today," Mr. Charlie said as Ruth settled beside him.

"Why would you think that?" She fished in her purse for the sliced apple, eager for the moisture to fill her dry mouth. "You should bring some water to drink on hot days like this," she added, noticing Mr. Charlie's cracked lips. She placed half the apple in his outstretched hand and then slipped a slice into her own mouth. Oh, the bliss of juice!

"How was the date with Mr. Ackerman?"

Of course, he would remember. Joe had made a fool of himself last Friday in front of Mr. Charlie. She swallowed her apple. "He drove all the way to Myrtle Beach to some fancy restaurant." She chewed another apple slice. Juice slipped from the corner of her mouth and she swiped it with her fingers. "It was just like him to want to make an impression. I wasn't dressed to go there, and of course, I felt out of place, like some poor relative being treated to the big-life."

"You're still angry."

"I'm not angry."

"Oh?" Mr. Charlie's eyebrows rose, deepening the dark lines forever carved into his forehead.

"It's just that...I kept a secret from him; from everyone, really. Somehow, he found out. I don't know how, and it bothers me."

Mr. Charlie faced the street, his jaw making clicking sounds as he chewed. "Knowledge is power."

"Joe wields power like a pro. I don't know what he'll do with the information, but I made him mad, and according to Nate, Joe will want revenge."

"Will this information send you to jail?"

Ruth snickered. "It's not like that. It's personal."

He bit down on the last slice of apple. "Have you seen Joe since the date?"

"No, thank goodness. But I was gone most of Saturday and part of Sunday, and this is only Monday."

A smile skimmed his face. "Full weekend. Busy social life?"

Her face reddened. "Nate took me fishing on Saturday, and he talked me into going to church with him on Sunday, even though I'm not sure the God Nate believes in exists."

"Men seem to be talking you into a lot of things lately, my friend."

"I don't know what to do, Mr. Charlie." Ruth stared mindlessly at the evening traffic, at the vandalized church, and at the crows. Everywhere crows, like a plague that had settled over Logan.

Mr. Charlie swallowed and cleared his throat.

"You want to avoid Mr. Joseph, and yet you get into a car with him. You don't have a relationship with God, but you go to church."

Ruth blinked. How easily Mr. Charlie summed up her life: shallow. "It's like, if I don't put something inside myself, then life does it for me." She turned toward him, a reflex more than anything else, and stared at his expressionless eyes. "I don't know who I am anymore."

"Time is short. You need to decide what you believe in and stop being what others expect. You do this with me, too. I enjoy your company more than I can tell you, but I know the Ruth you show me is only part of who you are. The rest of Ruth is still locked away—maybe in that purse you carry." He chuckled.

His words cut. She had expected sympathy. "Mr. Charlie—"

"Do you believe in God?"

"I think so." She did, didn't she? She fingered the chain around her neck, the symbol that represented the one time she had made a promise to God. "Not the same as Nate, but I believe there is a Creator."

"Then you must believe in the devil as well."

"I haven't thought about it."

He shifted so that he faced her, his emotionless eyes contrasting with a face that held urgency. He reached for her hand, and she gave it to him. Usually his grip was just tight enough to show he cared, but today his fingers pressed painfully. "This is important. There is heaven where the spiritual beings live. And there is earth where we mortals reside."

"Mr. Charlie…" She tried to pull her hand away, but his grip tightened.

"You have to hear this. I need you to understand."

He eased his grip and rubbed his thumb across her knuckles. His voice quieted even as her heart raced. "Between heaven and earth there is a thinly veiled battle for the souls of man."

Her mind muddled. Heaven, and earth, and battle. "Mr. Charlie—"

"When the crows started coming, the battle sank right into Logan. You know what Logan means, don't you?"

"It's the name of this town." She clenched her teeth to keep from snapping at him. None of their conversations had ever bothered her, or even frustrated her. Over the past two years, they had talked about everything. But this heaven and earth stuff, it frightened her.

"Logan is Gaelic for hollow," he said.

How did he know these things? She slipped her hand from his and twined her fingers together. Sweaty palms. Her sweat and his. Together. She remembered thinking that they had become a kindred spirit, able to read each other's thoughts. At the time, it had comforted her, but not today.

He leaned against the step. "You wondered why you came to Logan." He gave a big sigh and turned his eyes toward the empty church. Did he even know he was looking at the church? "Back in the late 1700s the Scots settled this area and named the town Logan, a hollow that homesteaders could fill with religious freedom. Somewhere in time the evil spirits took note of Logan." He turned his face in her direction. "Why do you suppose Logan is the only town in all of South Carolina where the leaders chose to implement the church tax?"

"We need the money."

"So does every other town." Mr. Charlie leaned forward. "This is important, Ruth. I knew the time was near as soon as you showed up."

"Time is near for what?"

"The pieces started coming together. You are from Scottish blood. That was my sign."

"My mother's parents emigrated from Scotland. I never knew them."

"And then the crows came. The law was passed and Logan closed its churches. The shift happened." He shook his head slowly. "Logan is a battle zone. We are at war."

She felt cold in spite of the heat, the kind of cold that turns blood to frozen slush, that freezes the brain and fogs the mind. Raw fear laced with confusion. Mr. Charlie was her friend. She had nothing to be afraid of. Yet, coldness probed at all the tender spots.

"Look around you." Mr. Charlie's voice droned on.

She didn't want to listen but was unable to stop.

"Churches are closed. Crime is up. The mood is angry." He paused.

She panted for air.

"Why do you think the crows came at the same time all of this started happening?"

"I don't know."

"Because God's plan is taking place right in front of us."

"What plan? There is no plan."

"God takes His time. He uses situations and people to bring change."

"Yesterday I got pelted with rotten fruit and vegetables. From what I hear, the churches won't open anytime soon. And what about me?" The pain of abandonment, rejection, and loss cut to the very center of her being. Let Mr. Charlie talk about heritage and the fate of Logan. She couldn't care less about Logan. What about her? What about Ruth Cleveland, whose father dared to die when she was a child, whose mother became lost to work. She grew up alone, taking care of herself. And she was still alone. Close to screaming, she clenched her teeth until she thought they would shatter. "Why doesn't God care about me?"

"Ruth—"

Tears ran down her face, and she shoved them away. "My life is a mess, and God doesn't care!"

"Ruth, God cares."

"I hurt so bad."

She felt the soft touch of his hand against her arm. "God doesn't guarantee life without pain, but He gives us a way to make good come from our past. He wants us to live happy lives surrounded by His love."

"I don't see much love."

"God is here, and you are part of His plan. He loves you, child."

"Yeah, right."

"God brought you here for a reason."

She was tired and wanted to go home. Mr. Charlie was the only person in Logan she ever felt comfortable with, and he had just turned into a complete stranger. She wanted to talk to him about God, but not all this other nonsense...battles and demons and hollows. "You think I'm here because I'm Scottish. Sorry, but I'm here because my car ran out of gas." Her words snapped more than she intended.

"What do you believe, Ruth? Make your own decisions, not the ones others expect of you. Allow yourself to become the person God created you to be."

"It's too late for that."

"It's never too late."

How dare Mr. Charlie tell her God had good things for her? Mr. Charlie didn't know her at all. He did the same thing everyone else did—he imagined what he wanted to see in her. He imagined her to be good because she sat with him, shared a stupid apple with him. "You want to know what I'm really like? Joe and I had a child! Yes, I slept with Joe, and I got pregnant. I gave the baby up for adoption because I was too selfish to raise her." Bitter words flew. "And you think God brought me to Logan so He could give me something good? God is not going to reward a person like me."

Mr. Charlie reached for her.

She jumped up. "There, now you know what a pathetic person I really am. I deserve someone without feelings, like Joe." Choking on her emotions, she ran down the sidewalk toward home.

Crows stared as she passed.

~*~

As Ruth raced around the corner, tears blinding her eyes, a hand grabbed her arm and dragged her off the sidewalk. Sandwiched in a narrow alley between the courthouse and the adjacent building, the motionless air smelled of urine and crow droppings. Everything reeked of crows lately. Ruth flailed out her arms and met flesh.

"Stop that!" a male voice hissed as he twisted her arm.

In a heartbeat, fear turned to rage. "Joseph! How

dare you? Get your hands off me!"

"I could have met you on the courthouse steps while you were with your friend." His sarcasm rolled as smoothly off his tongue as the rivulets of water that slipped down the brick walls. "I told you to stop sitting in public like a gawking schoolgirl—or worse." He crossed his arms over his chest. "Grow up, for goodness sake."

She didn't have to stay and listen to Joe just because he wanted her to. Mr. Charlie said the choice was hers. The knowledge felt liberating. She pushed Joe aside and stepped toward the sidewalk.

"I found our baby."

~*~

Charlie eased himself into the worn recliner, his senses on high-alert. They were coming. He felt them. He knew all along it would happen, but who, why, and when had, for months, remained unknown. Ruth became who. And then God revealed why. He settled back to wait. When would soon arrive.

Back in the day, this dead-end street had been full of families working at the mill, trying to make an honest living. The families were gone. So were the houses. All but his.

The old, single-story house creaked around him. One main room with a living space and a kitchen. Folks called it open concept now. It used to be called efficient. Two small bedrooms and a bathroom along the side. Charlie had lived here all his life.

He struggled from his chair and stood in the opened door at the side of the house. The air smelled of rain soon to come. Cars seldom drove down the patched-up road with potholes the size of watermelons. There was little need for anyone to walk this way. The other houses fell into disrepair and collapsed as the occupants either passed on or moved to safer places. "Our time is coming." He patted the frame of the door. "But I have plans for you."

Tall grass moved in the shifting breeze. The rustling sound reminded him of his wife, long passed, and how her cotton skirts moved around her legs when she was in the kitchen. Crickets, chickadees, and frogs now competed for his attention.

Closing the weather-worn door, Charlie pulled an envelope out of his shirt pocket and placed it on the yellow Formica table. There used to be four matching chairs, but the chairs wore out long-ago and were replaced by two folding ones. Spanning the back wall, lower cupboards supported a cracked vinyl counter. A porcelain sink rested under the square window that overlooked the patch of weeds out back that ended in the swamp. No one went into the swamp.

His wife cooked many-a-meal on their old three-burner gas stove. The refrigerator stopped working about the time the crows started showing up. He hadn't replaced it. He pushed his tongue back and forth between the gap in his teeth. He tasted blood and realized he had worn a sore on his tongue. Had he done enough to prepare her?

The tapping started almost immediately.

Charlie closed his eyes. The 'when' was now. Another quick listen to the darkness outside, and he settled once again into the recliner.

The gong of the clock up town drifted through the night air. Twelve strikes.

God, help me.

17

Tuesday, June 18

A day later, Ruth once again sat across from Joe. This time she had insisted on choosing the location: Jerry's Diner—noisy, crowded, and impersonal. Checkered linoleum floor, Formica tabletops, and paper napkins. Sweet tea served in Mason jars, and hush puppies piled in a red plastic basket. Nothing like the posh eatery at the beach. They found a booth in the back of the long dining area.

Her hands jittered at her sides; her stomach quivered, and her muscles were like mush. Overall, she felt as if she had just stepped off of a tilt-a-whirl. She breathed deeply, trying to steady herself for what was to come. Joe's announcement that he had located their baby—given in traditional Ackerman aplomb the day before—had shaken her.

Until now, Ruth had refused to think about the baby. She gave up her parental rights even before the delivery, transferring guardianship to the State of North Carolina. But in the loneliness of night, Ruth couldn't help thinking about the infant she had birthed, what she might look like, what she was doing. Ruth ached to know that her child was happy, that the adoptive family loved her, and was providing the security of a two-parent home.

The social worker assured Ruth that all potential

parents were carefully screened. Even after placement, the home would be monitored for months before the adoption became final. Her child would be fine.

A lusty wail and a glimpse of a wet, glistening body being carried across the room by a green-garbed stranger were the only memories Ruth had of her baby daughter. A flash of pale arms and legs, a head smeared with birth fluids. And then she was gone. Forever.

Across the booth from Ruth, Joe tapped his fingers on the shiny tabletop. Blue eyes stared at her from the other side of the table. "So, aren't you curious?"

She stared back. Yes, she ached to know but was terrified. What if finding their child was a Pandora's Box, something they shouldn't open? One step and then another. Find an address, drive by just to look...when would enough be enough?

The voice of Buddy Holly, loud enough to drown out conversations, poured from speakers in the ceiling. The air smelled of grilled meat and hot oil. She rubbed a throbbing temple. "Joe, we need to let it alone. What is done is done."

Joe looked as out of place in his high-end clothes at Jerry's Diner as she had at his fancy restaurant. His navy dress shirt and tan jacket shouted money against the worn paisley cushions. Most likely aware of the impression he gave others, he relaxed against the booth. His back covered the green duct tape that sealed a tear. He crossed his arms and smiled. "I never signed away my rights."

Anger flared, burning to ash any thought of congeniality. "What rights? You didn't want anything to do with the baby."

"I didn't know there was a baby until recently.

You conveniently forgot to tell me."

"I told you—"

"You told me you were having an abortion."

Heat reddened Ruth's face. She gritted her teeth. "I never—"

"It doesn't matter. I have paternal rights, and I plan to use them."

She stared at his steely blue eyes and harsh mouth. Once she had found him appealing. Now she was repulsed by his presence. Had he changed, or had he always been self-seeking? Had she simply been blinded by his false affection and smooth words?

"Why are you doing this, Joe? You don't care about the baby. You're using her for some reason of your own."

"Am I?"

Laughter spilled from the adjacent booth while teens crowded six into each side.

Joe's head bounced as the back of his booth rocked with movement. Turning, he scowled at the teens.

"What you lookin' at, old man?" The metal ball on the teen's tongue flashed as he spoke. The others laughed.

The heavyset waitress approached the booth. "You kids behave, or you'll have to leave."

A thin rail of a girl batted her eyes. "We always behave, don't we, Donny?" Raven hair fell to her shoulders, anchored to her scalp by two inches of blond roots.

"Yeah, we always obey our mamas."

Music wailed, and voices rose to match it.

"We can't talk here." Joe pulled a legal-sized cream-colored envelope from his jacket pocket. He placed the envelope on the table in front of him and stroked the paper. Long, thin fingers. Tapered nails. She couldn't pull her gaze away even when two plates with burgers and fries were set in front of them.

Joe slid the envelope to her side of the table. "Eat up."

How could she eat? She wanted to know. Oh, she wanted to know so badly; and yet her daughter belonged to someone else. It was meant to be that way—a child growing up with a loving mother and father.

She pushed the plate away.

"You're the one who chose this place," Joe bit into Jerry's Special Half-Pounder. A new round of laughter came from behind them, and he scowled. "Tell you what." He again placed fingertips on the envelope, toying with her, trying to force a reaction.

She held her breath but tried to act like she didn't care.

"You take it," he said. "Open it now. Open it later if you want. Do as you please."

Ruth stared as he pulled his hand away and took another bite of burger. Mustard dripped onto the silk shirt.

"Oh, there are pictures inside, too."

Pictures of her child! The need to look was almost more than she could bear, yet she remained stiff in her booth, afraid to move for fear an avalanche of motion would follow.

He raised his eyebrows. "Take it. Go ahead." Sliding to the end of the bench, he stood. Pulling out a leather wallet, he tossed a stack of bills onto the table, leaned over, and kissed her cheek. "I'll talk to you later."

Her heart continued to beat. She could feel it.

Surely, air moved in and out of her lungs. Otherwise, she would be dead.

The envelope lay on the table. She could leave without it. There was no name on the front. If she spilled ketchup over it, the staff would most likely throw it away.

Or she could mail it back to Joe. Mail it to the courthouse in his name. Let him know she never opened it.

Her hands ached from being knotted together in her lap.

She grabbed the envelope and raced from the restaurant.

~*~

The pounding on the windows came again that night. This time she was in bed. She remained among the safety of her covers, wrapped in the comfort of her quilt, Joe's envelope hot beneath her, hidden beside the blood money. She rolled into a ball, her hands over her ears, and waited for the noise to stop.

Please, let it stop.

18

Sunday, June 23

Numb from Joe's revelation about finding their daughter, Ruth should not have been in the mood to attend church, but the pull to be with the tomato-strewn people from last Sunday tugged at her. Now, here she sat beside a man with whom she was growing too fond. Why had Nate entered her life now just as Joe resurfaced to ruin it?

No protestors stood in the street like last Sunday, but their work was already done. Azalea bushes lay in the yard, their cut stubs still lining the curving brick walkway from the street to the house. "Pay your tax," and "we don't want you here," written in what appeared to be red spray paint, stood starkly against the white brick house.

Ruth turned away, the dripping letters reminding her of blood.

The environment changed when she entered the house. The Sparks' living room looked as though it had been professionally decorated, with stiffly folded gray drapes, marble lamps, and matching dark-gray wing-backed chairs with dark-blue striped throw-pillows. Ruth glanced at the ceiling, at least nine feet overhead. The crown molding may have been real plaster; she wasn't sure.

Mrs. Sparks guided her and Nate to the light gray,

almost white, couch beneath the window. The fabric felt thick and expensive. The hardwood floors glowed beneath an oriental rug of blues and grays that looked elegantly worn. Ruth wondered if the Sparks' ever used the living room, or if it was for special occasions.

A card table, standing like the orphan child of the house, separated the living room and dining room. On it rested a Bible and a glass of water.

In contrast to the elegant room, almost everyone was dressed in less than their Sunday best. Ruth had chosen her cotton dress carefully, not wanting to have another outfit ruined by protestors. Everyone else must have had the same idea. Each Sunday, twenty houses were needed for worship. It was impossible for the police to keep a cruiser stationed at each site.

"Sit here." Nate rose, offering his spot to a middle-age woman.

Ruth expected Nate to move to the wall with Chet and Betsy; instead he slid to the floor, leaning gently against her legs. The familiarity brought color to her cheeks. To anyone looking, his behavior said, "she's mine."

"Hi, I'm Wilma Reynolds." The newcomer smiled at Ruth.

"Ruth Cleveland."

"Aren't those crows awful?" Wilma asked. "They about half cover the yard."

Ruth had noticed them, and their presence had given her shivers, but the bloody letters stole her attention as she'd walked to the front door. Now, glancing out the window behind her, a black and white cruiser slowly passed. The police had the addresses of all the day's host homes.

An older man made a clicking sound with his

tongue. "Always more of them crows around on church day, so it seems."

The door opened again and a well-dressed woman entered. Her spiked heels clicked on the wood floor as she walked into the living room.

"Beth Ann!" Wilma called to the woman.

"Hey, friend!"

"I'd offer you a seat, but..." she scrunched her shoulders together. The two women chatted, one sitting, the other standing.

Strange, this unfathomable desire to be with church people. Here, surrounded by those who shared a faith in a God Ruth didn't understand, the fear of her secret felt less intense. She tried not to think about her mistake but to simply move from day to day. That's what she did best—blindly push ahead. Since meeting Nate, something in her had awakened.

Jeb Hawthorn, the Road Man, as she'd thought of him since the day he dug out her pine trees on the swamp road, strolled into the room clutching his Bible and the hand of a skinny little boy about five. "Hey, folks. Nice sunny mornin' God's given us."

Ruth caught his eye, and they smiled the familiar acknowledgement of friends. Her seed of contentment grew another root.

"There's my pretty wanderer," Jeb said to Ruth. "Glad you aren't confused by having to change locations every week. Got to love the mayor and his definition of a church."

Before Ruth could reply, Nate interjected, "I keep her informed." Nate began to stand but Jeb waved him down.

"Stay put. Otherwise, you might lose your spot." Jeb gazed around the room. "We got us a crowd today."

A burly man and a petite woman entered. His booming voice sounded above the chatter in the room. "What happened to the front of the house?"

"I didn't hear a thing," Mr. Sparks said, throwing his hands up. "Clarence told me about it when he got here this morning. They cut the azaleas, too."

The burly man, introduced as Mark Fisher, laughed. "Wore my old clothes today just in case we had a re-match with the tomatoes." He snickered and a glint shone in his eyes. "Thought about bringing a box of my own; you know, give me a chance to return fire."

"Oh, Mark, stop it," the petite woman said.

He grinned at his wife and winked. "I brought something else." He pulled out a disposable plastic poncho.

"Honestly. Do I have to check your pockets when we leave the house like I did our son?"

The Fishers blended into the mix of the room.

When the pastor of the week, Thomas Crowley, minister of Grace Trinity Lutheran, stepped behind the card table, the room quieted. "Good morning to all of you."

Ruth's eyes widened, surprised at the deep baritone voice from the short, stout man.

The pastor scanned the room, his gaze settling on the hostess. "Velma, I think we have another guest. I heard the kitchen door."

Velma glanced at her husband. "You didn't lock the door?" She hurried toward the kitchen and soon returned. "The door wasn't latched. I closed it, and," she said with a glare toward her husband, "I locked it."

As Pastor Crowley began reading the scripture, Nate turned and lifted his Bible toward Ruth. His rough fingers moved gently over the thin pages, making scratching sounds on the paper as he traced each word.

The pastor read from I Kings 18.

To Ruth, the story sounded like a fable. A prophet named Elijah poured water over a meat sacrifice and prayed for God to consume it. Fire fell from the sky and all that remained of the meat was a pile of ashes. Even the rocks burned from the heat of God's fire. Then fire destroyed the idol, Baal.

Ruth didn't know the Bible contained stories like this. She thought the Bible held lists of rules, like the Ten Commandments, and the consequences of not following them.

Elijah sounded like a cool man who really trusted God. She believed in God, she was sure of that now, just not a God who took the time to notice her. Now that she knew God didn't actually make an appearance at church either, she didn't see much use in prayer. And yet, Elijah knew something about God that she didn't know. Another question for Mr. Charlie.

An offering was collected in a round metal plate. The pastor nodded to several of the men, including Nate, to take the money to the kitchen for an official count. Nate had explained that the churches had made some sort of arrangement for the offerings in order to pay utilities on the various buildings and meet the obligation of the pastors' salaries.

"Thank you all for coming." Pastor Crowley concluded. "Anyone who can stay, I'm sure the Sparks would appreciate help scrubbing the paint off the bricks in the front of the house."

"I hate to suggest this," a middle-aged gentleman said before the people began to head for rags and buckets, "I know we've gone from two weeks at one place to one week, but maybe we should keep our worship location a secret altogether. Look what happened today."

"But how will new people know where to go?" Betsy remained sitting on the floor beside Chet, who had his casted leg stretched out in front of him. "We've been posting the locations on social media—"

"And we have our printed schedules," a gray-haired woman said, waving a well-folded sheet of paper in the air.

"What if we post a note on the church doors telling people to contact one of the members?" Mr. Sparks asked.

"Then anyone can find out where we are." Chet rubbed his chin. "How about we pick up any new people who want to come?"

"It's so devious." Mrs. Sparks shook her head, her frown deepening. "I hate that we have to resort to hiding." She looked out the front window of her house. "What do they get out of taunting us?"

Old Miss Hannah sat queen-like on the overstuffed wing-backed chair across from the window. An old cameo brooch was pinned to the neck of her light blue dress. Thin gray hair was twisted in a bun at the base of her head. The scent of roses emanated from her. "How long before these hoodlums become violent?" The folds of skin under her chin quivered as she talked. "I mean, more than throwing tomatoes. What if they start shooting at us? I have an old shot gun the mister kept for stray dogs."

"I like your spirit, Miss Hannah!" Mark Fisher exclaimed.

Pastor Crowley's hands jerked up. Crinkles

formed around his eyes. "I don't think we need to pull out guns, Miss Hannah, but it's a good idea to be on guard."

Lydia Miller waved for attention. "What about our children?"

"I really don't—"

Movement in the doorway behind Pastor Crowley caught Ruth's attention. The man almost looked like a shadow. He was tall, dressed in black, with a ski mask covering his face. The figure tossed a burning cylindrical object into the room.

The pressure from the explosion shoved against Ruth's eardrums. For a few minutes, the ringing muffled the screams.

"Are you all right?" Nate's voice sounded hollow as he shook her by the shoulders.

Ruth nodded, unable to force words from her throat.

Wilma Reynolds lay slumped across Ruth's lap.

Nate turned his attention to the injured woman.

The marble-based lamps were broken on the floor; books that graced the mantel had flown across the room. Both of the wing-backed chairs lay on their backs. Fragments of the coffee table were scattered throughout the room, a large section covered the top of one of the chairs.

Lydia Miller lay against the side of Jeb Hawthorn. He stood, shook bits of wood and plaster from his hair, and helped Lydia to her feet.

Betsy picked her way toward Ruth. "Are you all right?" She clutched Ruth's arm.

Mrs. Fisher silently leaned against the wall, her right arm cradled in her left, her face ashen.

The windows had exploded and glass crunched

into the carpet and the hardwood beneath. In the background came the cries of children, followed by Mrs. Sparks' soothing voice.

Ruth glanced around for some way to help. At first, her foggy brain didn't make the connection. She thought of the Wizard of Oz, of the house, the witch...motionless legs stuck out from under a large section of the coffee table. She pulled in a gasp. "Nate! Help!" Ruth ran across the room, kicking past splintered wood and bits of fabric. "Miss Hannah!"

Nate reached the woman first and threw the wood off the old woman.

She didn't move. Red soaked the collar of her blue dress. Blood dripped from beneath the folds of her neck.

"I need help here!" Nate's tense voice carried over the noise.

Jeb Hawthorn ran to start CPR.

Nate yelled, "Someone call 9-1-1."

Ruth watched in stunned silence.

Chet clutched Chip in his arms.

A teenage girl tried to herd the kids back into one of the bedrooms.

The room grew silent as the church members became aware of the attempt going on to save a life. Betsy took Chip and left the room. Chet replaced Jeb at chest compressions. Nate continued to breathe air into Miss Hannah's lungs. The sounds of crying filtered through the room like background music.

Pastor Crowley began to pray. "God, please wrap protective arms around our sister Hannah. Protect her until help can come. We know You love her, and we love her, too...

People clung to each other and closed their eyes.

Mrs. Fisher took Ruth's hand and rubbed her thumb back and forth across Ruth's skin.

Numbness settled over Ruth. Needing to look away from the blood leaking onto the floor, the faces uttering hopeful prayer, she turned her head toward the front of the house. The window was gone. No one lurked in the yard, no rebels with masks stood watching. The responsible party most likely had fled soon after flinging the bomb.

At the sound of a siren, a collective sigh filled the room. Pastor Crowley guided the paramedics to Miss Hannah. Another squad arrived and then the police. The people were asked to move from the living room into the dining room and kitchen.

As Miss Hannah was wheeled out of the house with the paramedics still doing CPR, Nate buried his face in Ruth's neck. They clung together.

"I never imagined that anyone in Logan would do something like this." His words muffled as he pulled her even closer. "I just never thought."

The police officer's phone rang. He mumbled into the receiver then turned to the officer beside him. "Someone just broke into the Jewelry Box downtown."

~*~

Darkness settled over Logan. It had been well into the afternoon before the police released them to go home.

Ruth wondered if Hannah was alive. Did Mr. and Mrs. Sparks regretted opening their home as a substitute church? The showplace living room was totally destroyed. If she had beautiful things like that...she looked around her own living room, dressed in homemade slipcovers and nailed-together furniture. She loved her home as much as Mrs. Sparks probably loved hers, and knowing how quickly it could all be gone...her chest tightened. It wasn't the objects, as much as the work she'd put into them. The coffee table made of crates and a castoff cupboard door, the slipcovered chairs and the flowered curtains made by her hands and thus they became a part of her. She had not lived in a home filled with love in a long time. The destruction of her things would be paramount to a personal attack.

Pastor Crowley's message crawled through her brain all day. God used fire. Sure, Elijah's fire was from heaven, but still, it was fire that destroyed evil. The longer she thought about it, the more right it felt. Purged by fire.

She dug around in the kitchen drawer for a pack of matches. Then she moved to the bedroom. Searching beneath the mattress, she pulled out both envelopes: one given to her almost four years ago and aged to a soft cream, the second secured most recently, its sharp white color with a lingering scent of French fries.

The first envelope contained twelve one-hundred dollar bills. The second remained sealed. Her fingers brushed against the white paper of the newer envelope as though it were baby skin. Tears dripped down her face and for once, she gave freedom to her pain. Clutching both envelopes to her chest, she walked to the living room.

She imagined being someplace sacred with Elijah beside her. God would listen to Elijah; He would honor Elijah's plea. With a long sigh, she shredded the empty cream-colored envelope and arranged the shreds of paper on the cold brick floor of the fireplace. Then, one at a time, she crinkled the bills and placed them on top. Her kindling was ready. Now for the sacrifice.

She turned the second envelope over in her hand. It would be so easy to open it. No one need know. Her fears could be put to rest, her imagination calmed. But then Joe would win, wouldn't he? He knew she would look. That's why he'd left the envelope on the table. She placed the history of her child on top of the kindling.

The tip of the match sparked. She stared at the flickering glow until it burned her fingers. She lit the second match and held the fire to a piece of the shredded envelope. It smoldered, and then flames licked toward the money. She stared as her baby's blood money burned. When the hungry flames reached the second envelope, a deep sob heaved from deep within her. Her baby denied the second time. Lying on the rug she had woven from scraps and ingenuity, she watched the flames devour the temptation Joe provided.

The flames died and all that remained was gray ash that shifted as she breathed.

And her empty pain.

~*~

The yellow light from Ruth's back stoop penetrated most of the yard. But in the rear by the broken chain-link fence that masqueraded as protection, the darkness deepened. The salsa garden, in the middle of the yard where it got the most sun, laid half exposed in the yellow light, half hidden in the shadows. Tomatoes tucked within twisted branches looked like eyes keeping watch.

Ruth carried a spade to the far-right corner of the yard. She pressed a small box decorated with fabric and ribbon to her chest. With shadows for company, she buried the box of ashes, patting down the soil when done. The disturbed ground was indistinguishable from the sand and weeds of the remainder of the yard.

She returned to the house and turned off the light, leaving her sin alone in the darkness.

19

Monday, June 24

"How dare you call me at work?" Sizzling anger bounced across her nerves like fat in a hot skillet. Ruth glanced toward her office door, hoping neither Attorney Dunlap nor Kathleen were near enough to hear this conversation.

"You don't have a phone at that place you call home." Joe's sarcasm streamed through the receiver, the retort piercing Ruth's ears. "This is a courtesy call."

"Sure it is," Ruth said. Whatever he wanted, the results would benefit only one person—Joe. She fingered the chain hanging around her neck.

"That friend of yours, the bum that hangs out on the courthouse steps—"

Ruth gripped the black receiver, wishing it were Joe's neck. "Mr. Charlie is not a bum, and don't you—"

"Listen to me, will you?" She heard the hiss of his breath, satisfied that at least she'd frustrated him. "He's a nuisance, and people are starting to complain."

"That's a lie." Mr. Charlie had been sitting on the courthouse steps ever since she had arrived in Logan, and who knew how long before? "You're jealous of him. You can't believe I prefer to visit with Mr. Charlie than spend time with you." She needed to pace the floor but was tethered to the desk by the phone's cord.

"Think what you want, but I'm calling the police

first thing tomorrow morning and filing a complaint. This is your chance to warn him off."

So that was his game, using Mr. Charlie against her. He knew her weaknesses better than she knew them herself. Why did he bother with her after all this time?

She glanced at the clock, willing the black arms to twirl, to magically speed the time so she could bash Joe in the face. But the red second hand dragged as it moved in jerking tics around the white face. She sighed into the receiver. Who was she kidding? She could never hit Joe—it wasn't her nature. But there had been that night she had shoved him against the restaurant window in Myrtle Beach. Well, maybe now she could. How dare he take his vengeance out on an innocent blind man? Her rage felt stronger than her small frame could contain. "I get off work in an hour. We'll talk about this then."

Joe gave a low chuckle. "Sure, sweetheart. You know where I'll be."

Ruth slammed down the receiver and jerked the rubber band from her ponytail. She dropped her head in her hands and brown, silky hair streamed over her face. The harder she tried, the worse things got. The courthouse steps held a special significance that only Mr. Charlie understood. He had refused to move to get out of the sun. He wasn't about to move because Joe said so.

One of Mr. Dunlap's clients left a vase of roses from her garden and the yellow and pink blooms had ended up in Ruth's office. The odor, which seemed pleasant in the morning, now made her gag. She grabbed the stems from the clear glass vase, strode down the hall, and threw the flowers out the back door.

What happened to the sweet boy she used to know? Was she such a poor judge of character that she would befriend someone with a dark heart? Had she seen his hardness and ignored it, blinded by being the girlfriend of one of the most handsome guys she had ever met? No. Joe had changed. He had always been selfish but not the frightening person he was today. This man was a stranger, dark like the crows.

Back in the office, she didn't seem to be able to settle behind her desk. She glanced toward the hall, half expecting a bird to wander across the green carpet and stop in front of her. The crow with the scar turned up daily, sometimes outside of her house on the sidewalk, other times in the courthouse grass, and almost nightly sitting on a low tree branch on her way home, watching. The bird seemed bigger and blacker than the others. She knew her imagination made the bird more than it was, but the crow still unnerved her. The air felt tighter when he appeared, as though the sky pressed down on her. Mr. Charlie's explanation of battle made sense at those times, how the war was going on in Logan. She shook her head, trying to clear the confusion.

A half hour and she could leave. She settled behind the desk, thrummed her fingers on the surface, and waited. Finally, the dragging minute hand reached the twelve. Ruth grabbed her purse. Before she bothered with Joe, she needed to see Mr. Charlie, to touch him and reassure herself that he was all right. Joe wouldn't physically harm Mr. Charlie; violence wasn't his way any more than it was hers. No, he preferred mental manipulation. But still…

She rushed toward town, sucking in muggy air

laced with exhaust fumes. The rays of the sun stung her skin. Mr. Charlie had to get out of this heat. A lump the size of Texas clogged her throat. Losing him would be the worst thing that could happen, worse than Nate losing his church.

A diesel engine roared from behind, and she turned. It was a black Ford, not Nate. She pushed herself to a walker's jog. She hated Joe so much. By the time she reached the courthouse steps, her heart pounded from exertion and anger.

Mr. Charlie smiled as usual, unaware of the chaos Joe created.

"You sound out of breath. You run?"

She settled on the step, content for the moment to find her best friend in the world safe. "No. Yes. It's just hot out here."

Mr. Charlie wiped his forehead. "It's a dog day, that's fo' sure."

He stared ahead, as he often did, with sightless eyes seeing more than she imagined. The view was the same: the old church in front with large oaks offering unused shade, the courthouse to their backs radiating heat off the baked cement blocks, four lanes of asphalt between the buildings. Crows dotted the grass on both sides of the street. Two teens moseyed past, fingers flying over the keys of their cellphones. Cars smothered them in hot air.

"Mr. Charlie, can we sit somewhere out of the sun? We can cross the street and sit in the churchyard. It will be a lot cooler under the big trees."

"And how will I cross the street to go home?"

"I'll help you before I leave." She rose and tugged at his arm. He remained firmly on the step.

"Mr. Charlie, you have to sit somewhere else." Her

voice sounded edgy. "Joe is going to have the police come and force you to leave. Can't we just move before he embarrasses you?"

"Ah, it's the cousin, Mr. Joseph, that's got you all upset." Mr. Charlie turned toward her. A car raced by, making it through the intersection just as the light turned red. A wisp of coarse gray hair shivered on top of Mr. Charlie's head. "I thought perhaps Joseph was the reason for your temper." He reached out a weathered hand and sought her arm. "Don't give a thought to that young man. He can't harm me."

"But Mr. Charlie…"

"Not to worry, my friend."

Ruth gritted her teeth. She had to make him understand. He was an old man. Times were different now. People were less tolerant, less kind. Even when the police came, Ruth knew Mr. Charlie would refuse to leave. And then what? Would they haul him off to jail? Her stomach clenched.

"I have something to tell you." Mr. Charlie's voice took on the tone he used when he asked about the crows.

"There are lots of crows. I don't know how many, just lots. The same as yesterday." She wished he would quit asking about the birds.

"I don't want to talk about the birds." He turned blank eyes toward her. "I need to know that you understand, Ruth, just how special you are."

They had been through all this before. He really liked her, and she was grateful for that, but now was not the time to talk about her. She had to get him to move away from the courthouse. "I know, Mr. Charlie. You've told me that before." Then she jerked toward him. "The light of Logan! You can tell me what it is."

His thick lips formed a slight smile. "It is you. You are the light of Logan."

"But what is the light of Logan? What does it mean?"

He reached out a hand, and she placed hers in his, glancing back toward the courthouse as she did so. If Joe saw her sitting with Mr. Charlie, he would either call the police or head her way. She didn't have much time.

"When each of us was born, we had inside us all we needed to live happy and successful lives. God gives us that as a gift."

"It doesn't seem that way."

"That's because God also gave us free will. We have the right to do with our lives as we wish. Just because God gave us the tools for happiness doesn't mean we choose to use them. Sometimes, we let other influences change what we know to do."

"Mr. Charlie, please, I don't have time for this." Her mom used to say she had ants in her pants. That was how she felt now. She loved Mr. Charlie, but she felt almost crazy with the need to talk to Joe.

Mr. Charlie clutched her hand tighter. "Please, Ruth. Listen for just one moment longer." He released her hand and folded his together in the space between his knees.

Ruth sighed. "All right. I'm listening."

"Ruth, there will come a time very soon when you will be forced to make a stand. Even though it will seem like it is between men, the stand will be between the forces of good and evil. I know you won't like this part," he took a couple of breaths, "but you're the only one who can stop the spiral of evil. God has chosen you to be the light of Logan. God will help you when the time comes. You just have to ask Him."

How could she continue listening to this nonsense? "I have to go, Mr. Charlie. There's someone I need to meet."

"Ruth…you don't have to protect me."

"You don't understand."

"We're survivors, you and me. It takes a tough spirit to stand alone and do what's right." The wrinkles on his face deepened. "You are the light of Logan. You do understand, don't you?"

She didn't.

~*~

Ruth glanced around the cluttered space as she waited for the woman behind the counter to escort her five feet to Joe's private domain. The mayor had provided Joe with a makeshift office and reception area in an unused service section on the third floor. Joe's secretary had positioned her desk behind the counter with its swinging half-door, most likely to protect her from people like Ruth. Joe was in a room to the left, which probably had been a work-space or storage for this outer area in a past life.

The temperature inside the courthouse had to be thirty degrees colder than outside. Ruth rubbed the bumps that rose on her arms. Poor Mr. Charlie, still out in the heat. The air smelled like paper and stale tobacco smoke that had soaked deep into the wood like wax on a fine piece of furniture. Strange how the stench of tobacco lingered even though smoking had been banned in the building for years. The worn green and gray floor tiles bore testimony to the miles of people who had walked across them. Nate had been one. She squeezed her eyes, trying to push away thoughts of the man who was stealing her heart. This was not the time to think about Nate. She needed to focus her energy on Mr. Charlie.

The secretary answered the jangling phone, murmured a few words, and then replaced the receiver. "You can go back now." She nodded toward the door.

The difference was immediate. The air in the private space smelled like Joe: his aftershave, his sweat, his breath. A desk stood close to the back wall, minimized by a large table in the center of the room, covered with papers, black binders and notebooks of enough different colors to fill a crayon box. The wastebasket by the door overflowed with disposable cups stained brown. Two windows, tall and narrow, flanked the outer wall. Overall, the room was larger than she'd expected.

Joe leaned against the side of the desk. "Been watching you." He tipped his chin toward the window.

Heat flushed Ruth's icy cheeks. "You mean spying on me." She stomped across the worn carpet to the window and looked out. Four lanes of cars were lined up at the intersection. Mr. Charlie was gone. She hadn't even given him his apple.

"What do you want, Joe?"

"Have a seat." Joe nodded toward a leather chair beside his desk.

Ruth stared at him from the window, frowning.

Joe shrugged his shoulders. "Have it your way."

Ruth breathed in and out, trying to control her anger. A voice drifted through the door. The secretary was on the phone. Sharp sounding footsteps hurried down the hall. Metal ducts rattled as air passed through them. Traffic rumbled outside. Always the sound of traffic.

But between the room's two occupants: steely silence.

"I still love you, Ruth."

Her eyes widened. "You expect me to believe that?"

"Think what you will." He twirled a pen between his fingers. "What about the adoption papers I gave you?"

Her back stiffened. "I burned them."

He chuckled. "I'm surprised at you, Ruthie. I thought you had more curiosity than that."

"Curiosity, maybe, but my respect for our daughter's privacy is greater. Besides, it's not the baby I want to talk about. It's Mr. Charlie. Leave him alone, Joe. He isn't hurting anyone."

"He's hurting you."

"He has never hurt me! Do you think I would be friends with him if he did?"

"I don't like how he's messing with your mind."

"Messing with my mind?"

"He plants thoughts." Joe waved his fingers in the air. "You know. Ideas that shouldn't be there."

Ruth's jaw dropped as she stared at him. If there was anyone who messed with minds, it was Joe. Mr. Charlie—planting thoughts? She would laugh if the idea wasn't so preposterous.

"Get away from him, Ruthie. I told you once before, and you ignored me. Now I have to help you." His stare held a burning intensity. "It's for your own good."

"How do you know what's good for me? You have no idea what I need. You never have. It's always been about you!" She turned toward the door.

"Ruth, I will remove him from your life one way or another."

"Don't you dare lay a finger on him, Joseph Ackerman, so help me…"

His grin felt like a smack across her face. "So let's change the subject. You've lived in Logan a while now." Ruth didn't like the way Joe's eyes narrowed. "You ever hear the term 'light of Logan?'"

Ruth's eyes matched Joe's. What was he up to? Had he been doing more than watching her? Had he been listening somehow to her conversations with Mr. Charlie? "I have no idea what it means." Warning flags flew up. This had to do with more than Mr. Charlie. "How did you hear the term?"

"In passing. I didn't think anything about it until later. Thought it was something we can use in marketing."

He said it so casually, but he was lying. "Ask the mayor," she said. Joe had to have heard the term from Mr. Charlie.

"I asked the mayor." Joe's stare penetrated, but Ruth refused to yield and look away. "He doesn't know."

"Then it must not be important."

"You're probably right." Joe rubbed his hand across his jaw. "What if we trade favors?" he asked. "I won't act on the illegal adoption, and you quit seeing the old man."

"The adoption wasn't illegal."

"I wasn't consulted."

"I listed the father as unknown." Joe was using Mr. Charlie and their baby. Did he really know where the child was? Maybe Joe didn't have the right of parenthood he kept throwing out at her. In his fancy suit and shiny shoes, and slicked-back blond hair, Ruth couldn't imagine him wanting to raise their daughter.

"Why did you do that, Ruthie?"

"Forget it." She rushed out of the office, eager to get away from the man who used to make her feel like a million dollars. Now he made her seem lower than dirt. And why the questions about light of Logan? No way he heard it in passing.

She ran down the cement steps, aware that Joe was watching from the window above. The nerve of him, thinking she would give up her friendship with Mr. Charlie just because he told her to. As for his suggested trade…

A horn sounded, and she jumped. By the time she reached the sidewalk, her lip was bleeding; frustration and uncertainty built with each step. She had called Joe's bluff. Or had she?

~*~

"Hey, friend!" Betsy opened the screen door.

"I hope you don't mind that I stopped by. I was out walking and I…"

"Ruth, you are always welcome here. Come on in."

Even though the sun had dropped below the horizon, no lamps glowed to banish unwanted shadows in the living room. Even so, the room felt welcoming. Ruth took a deep breath and relaxed for the first time since Joe's phone call that afternoon. Tight muscles relaxed, she had been right to come here.

"I'll get some iced tea," Betsy said as she headed toward the kitchen. "And I'll tell Chet you're here."

"No, really I just…"

Betsy turned with a conspiratorial smile on her lips. "I have a better plan. Chet can be in charge of Chip, and I can have an evening off!" As she grinned, the end of her nose curled up like a girlfriend with a secret. "Have a seat. I'll be right back."

Betsy left in a whirl, taking Ruth's breath with her. The back door slammed, then voices. Chet laughed. The door banged again. Betsy pranced into the room. "Goodness, I left you standing in the dark."

Betsy turned on the lamp Ruth had admired during her last visit. With Nate. Her throat tightened. She needed to talk to Betsy about him. Maybe that was why her subconscious had led her here—but since when did her unconscious mind control her feet? Too many strange things were happening, too many conflicting thoughts.

"Come into the kitchen."

As they walked through the dining room, Ruth looked at the table where they had eaten. The surface was puddled in fabric and on the far side sat a portable sewing machine.

Ruth loved Betsy's kitchen, which was twice the size of hers. The table overlooking the yard was big enough to seat a family of six. A half-eaten cookie lay forgotten on the counter, while a broom with a wood handle stood against the wall, ready for duty. The room shouted love. Imperfect perfection. Betsy pointed Ruth to a chair at the table and pulled out a seat across from her.

From the window, Ruth watched father and son playing T-ball. Chip swung the red plastic bat, and the white ball with holes tumbled at least two yards.

"Good job!" Chet shouted as he hobbled after the

ball and placed it back on top of the T. He ruffled his son's hair and moved across the yard for the next round.

"They play ball almost every night," Betsy said, smiling. "Chip likes his daddy's attention."

The next ball went wide, and Chet lunged, missing it by inches.

"Yeah!" Chip yelled as he jumped up and down. "I get a point!"

"I'm surprised Chet's cast isn't all broken up," Ruth said.

Betsy chuckled. "Don't tell anyone, but this is already the second one. He's been warned by the orthopedic surgeon to go gentle with it, but you see how well he listens. The two of them will play until the mosquitoes drive them inside, which ought to be soon." Betsy focused her attention on Ruth. "So, you were out walking?"

Ruth squirmed in her chair, second guessing her decision to talk about Nate. "Big day. I needed to get rid of some stress, and walking is cheap."

"I admire your courage."

"What courage?" Ruth stared in surprise. There was nothing courageous in her behavior. In fact, most of the time she took the easy road, which led to another easy road, which led to nowhere, it seemed.

"I don't think I could move away from my family and launch out on a career of my own like you have. I would be scared to death."

Had she been brave or had she followed the easiest path? "At the time, it was the best for me to leave home, and when I tried to go back, I ran out of gas." Ruth forced a laugh. "So fate landed me in Logan. I wouldn't call cleaning and filing a career."

"Nate tells me your house looks like mine." Betsy chuckled. "I'm not sure that's a compliment, but I think he meant it to be."

Ruth glowed from the praise. "I love to make old things new again. People throw away so much that can be reused. I go to garage sales and find—" A sheepish smile crossing her face. "Sorry. Just get me going."

"My passion didn't start as noble as yours. Chet and I were living on little money, and the only way to get what I wanted was to make it myself. Chet bought me a sewing machine, and now I hunt for bargains and create as many things as I can."

"I've always wanted a sewing machine. What kind do you have?"

"Let me show you." Betsy led Ruth back to the dining room and switched on the ceiling light. The aged white glass cast a soft glow over the room's blue walls.

The two women leaned their heads together as Betsy explained the workings of her sewing machine.

"So what are you sewing now?" Ruth lifted a corner of the ivory fabric and ran her hand over the smooth texture.

"I got it at a yard sale. I thought I could make a sundress out of it, but the fabric wants to fray. Every time I try it on, a seam pulls out."

Ruth examined the material. "What if you made French seams?"

Betsy gave Ruth a confused look.

"Let me show you on a scrap."

When Ruth finished the seam, Betsy grinned. "Perfect!" She hugged Ruth. "You are a genius."

The two women worked on the dress until Chet entered, pulling Chip by the hand.

"There's no skeetas out there, Dad," Chip said as he scratched his arm.

"And the moon is made of cheese," Chet replied as he shepherded the boy through the dining room.

"Huh?"

"Forget it. Head to the bathroom."

The small boy put his hands on his hips. "You giving me my bath or is Mommy?"

"Mommy is having a well-deserved night off. Now march."

The two disappeared into the living room, followed by the sound of Chip's soft footsteps and the thumping of Chet's cast on the stairs.

Ruth stared after them. "You're lucky to have such a great family." The surge of longing came swiftly, her hungering gaze lingering on Betsy's husband and son. Would she ever have a family of her own? Sadness settled into the deep part of her heart.

"I'm not lucky; I'm blessed," Betsy said. "I thank God every day for Chet and Chip, and for Chip's birth mother."

Ruth stared at Betsy. "Chip's adopted?"

"We can't have children, and God provided Chip. I forget he's not my own flesh and blood."

"You pray for his birth mother?"

"I do. Can you imagine the courage it took to give such a precious gift? I pray that God will bless her and send her good things."

"Does Nate know Chip is adopted?" Nate seemed attached to Chip, as though the boy were from honest genes, and not created by lust and sin. But then, not all adopted children were conceived by deceit and lies as her daughter had been.

"Of course he does. Chet and Nate have been

friends forever. Nate was the best man at our wedding." Betsy laughed. "Nate adores Chip. I guess he sees Chip as the blessing he is. God makes good happen from bad."

"Would you ever want to meet the birth mother?" Ruth held her breath. Was there a chance that someday she would be able to see her daughter?

"I don't know." Betsy furrowed her brow. "I guess I haven't given it much thought. I suppose eventually Chip might want to meet his biological mother. I hope, when the time comes, I'll be gracious enough to accept that. But right now, I want him all to myself."

"What about the birth father?"

Betsy looked at Ruth. Finally, she reached across the table and gripped Ruth's hand. "Something you want to tell me?"

"No, I was curious...I just..." Betsy's expression was like an open door to soul-sharing. Tears welled in Ruth's eyes. She had never told anyone. "I had a daughter and gave her up for adoption."

Betsy slid closer to Ruth and wrapped an arm around her. "That must have been awful for you. And here I am blabbering away. I'm so sorry."

"If Nate finds out..."

"Nate is so in love with you."

Ruth stiffened. Betsy was wrong. "Nate is in love with who he thinks I am: the perfect virtuous woman. He loves his church and everything in his life has to meet that standard. I don't." Given time, even without her history, Nate would discover her imperfections and move on. Even so, Ruth's heart rate picked up when Betsy said Nate loved her. What had Nate told them about her?

Feet thumped down the stairs. "Chip's ready for a

good-night kiss from Mommy." Chet looked at the women. "Leave you two alone, and you look like you killed the dragon."

Betsy squeezed Ruth's shoulder. "Maybe we did. I'll be right back."

Ruth stood. "I need to go."

"It's dark. Let me get Chip settled and I'll drive you home."

"I can walk. It's not very far."

"Chet, make sure she doesn't leave before I get back downstairs."

"Aye, aye, matey." He turned to Ruth. "Want some water?"

"No, thanks." She stood. "Tell Betsy—"

"Oh, no, you don't!" Chet held up his hands. "You heard her. If you aren't here when she comes down those stairs, I'm in the doghouse, and we don't have one. It'll be me at the mercy of those mosquitoes out there." Chet headed to the kitchen.

Ruth sat back down at the dining room table. Her confession would pass from Betsy to Chet and then what? Would Chet tell Nate? Chet and Nate were best friends, after all. No way to undo what was done. But now she knew that her daughter would be better off if she kept her distance. She could only hope that Joe's threat of interfering was nothing but hot air steaming out of an angry head.

Betsy's footsteps were so light on the stairs that Ruth barely heard them. Betsy kissed Chet on the cheek before she turned to Ruth. "Ready?"

Their two houses were only six blocks apart, but the well-tended neighborhood gradually transformed into an area of silent neglect.

"Betsy, I hope you won't tell Nate."

"He needs to know, but I won't tell him."

Ruth stared ahead. "I'll tell him." And then their relationship would be over.

"Don't sell Nate short. He has high moral standards, but he is capable of great empathy."

Ruth wasn't sure this empathy would extend to her, but she kept silent.

"Nate has taken a beating lately with the closing of his church." Betsy looked both ways before turning left at the stop sign. "His church is his life, and now he feels like a man set adrift without a purpose."

"Is it so wrong to tax the churches?" Perhaps it was the darkness that made the question easier to ask. "People in Logan just want equality. Businesses are taxed, and families are taxed. Why not churches?"

"Churches are nonprofit. All the money collected goes back into the church's ministry. I suppose someone smarter than I figured out it was the right thing to do."

Ruth glanced at Betsy, unsure if she should share the minutia of information stored in her head. Maybe if Betsy understood the truth... "The tradition of exempting churches from tax isn't something new. It began centuries ago. Times have changed but our practices haven't."

"Centuries ago? I thought it was a more current law."

"Since Constantine, the emperor of Rome, became a Christian back in 300 AD or something."

Betsy chuckled. "You are a veritable encyclopedia of information."

"Sorry."

"Don't apologize. You learn all of that, while I learn nursery rhymes and the best way to potty train."

"You sell toothpaste and ant spray, too!" Ruth said, attempting to lighten the mood.

"True. And razors to handsome men." Betsy glanced across the seat to Ruth.

Not Nate again… "According to some Washington analyst, the government is losing between $300 and $500 billion dollars a year by not taxing property that belongs to churches."

"Ruth, you really don't want to tax churches, do you?"

"I don't see churches making that much difference in the world."

A choking laugh spit from Betsy's mouth. "You can't be serious?"

"I think I am." When had she become so confrontational?

Another stop sign and a left turn. "Since the churches have closed, looting is rampant, vandalism is a hobby, and I saw in the paper that contributions to United Way are seriously down for the year."

"What does crime and donations have to do with the church?"

"The church has been stripped of it's ministry to spread the Word. People look at the locks on the doors and equate that with putting limits on God." In the light from the dashboard, Betsy's eyes seemed to glow with energy. "God isn't in the building. The building is just where we go when we want to worship together. Remember how crowded it was last Sunday at the Sparks?"

Ruth did remember. Her mind clouded as she thought of the bloodbath that followed. All over taxes.

The car's headlights cut a cone of color in the darkness. They had left the streetlights behind, as well as the relative safety of the middle-class neighborhood. A couple of dark-clothed figures stood on the side of the road. Betsy pushed the door locks. The metallic click gave reassurance against the unknown, even though the figures were well behind them now.

"I read that Oklahoma gave a tax-exempt status to a satanic church," Ruth mumbled.

A dark basketball-sized mass smashed against the windshield.

Betsy jerked the steering wheel to the left.

Ruth threw her hand against the side of the car. Her head jerked forward. The beams from the headlights threw patterns across the moving landscape until Ruth wasn't sure what was solid and what was nothing more than air. Her teeth rattled.

The car's tires scraped against the left curb. With another twist of the wheel, they were flying across the road, over the right curb, and into a bush.

Betsy's hands remained fixed to the wheel. "What in the world?" With huge eyes, she looked at Ruth.

Ruth's heart pounded. "I think it was a bat." Her hand fell to her side. She shook all over.

"That was no bat. It was a crow!"

"At night?"

"Look," Betsy whispered.

The car's headlights illuminated the yard, and from the windshield, Ruth saw half a dozen crows lined up on the grass, like a group of warriors ready to attack. "What are they doing?" Chills ran up Ruth's spine. "Their echo-location must be really messed up."

"Crows don't have echo-location."

Ruth stared at the crows. Her brain reeled. There was something she was missing, but she couldn't think beyond the crows and their beady black eyes.

"Look where we are." Betsy's words were little more than a breath.

So intent on convincing Betsy of the error in her thinking, Ruth hadn't kept track of their progress. That and the darkness…

"Maybe I should call Chet." Betsy continued to stare out the window.

The car was in Ruth's own yard.

As one, the crows lifted into flight and were gone. Ruth swallowed. A couple moths flitted in the beam from the headlights. One hit against the window. The sound brought to mind the banging on her house. And the footsteps that followed her home from the library. She was a woman living alone, without a phone or car, in the least desirable section of town. Why, oh why, did she keep forgetting to buy that mace? And now, crows out after dark, lined up like warriors when they should be asleep in a tree somewhere.

Ruth fumbled for the door handle. "I'll be fine."

As she got out of the car, a shadow skittered between her house and the neighbor on the left. As quickly as she spotted the shadow, the darkness absorbed it. Ruth hesitated, afraid for the first time to enter her own home.

Ruth locked the front door. With no light, inside or out, the living room lay in darkness. She knew the space by heart, every inch familiar. Tonight, the comfy home felt off in a way she couldn't define.

A scraping sound came from the left side of the house. Ruth sprinted to the lamp beside the couch and fumbled for the switch. The 60-watt bulb blazed to life and a muffled cry escaped her lips. A figure with wild eyes stared at her from outside the window. In the instant it took to realize the reflection was hers, she had jerked the thin curtains across the glass.

The scraping came again, this time louder. Her mind screamed, telling her to hide. The sound of her labored breaths pounded against her ears.

A different noise this time, harsher. Ruth clutched her throat, remembering the nights of window tapping. Her fear went to overdrive. Hands gripped the sides of her head. The knock repeated. "Hello. Is anyone home? This is the police."

Ruth listened. Feet shuffled outside her door. Mumbled voices. Pulling aside the curtain just enough to peer out, she saw two uniformed men. With her hands shaking, she struggled to unlatch the lock and open the door.

What did the police want at her house? They should be next door busting a drug party or headed up the street where pimps kept their women. Ruth leaned against the wooden frame, struggling to keep from becoming part of the spinning floor.

"Miss Ruth Cleveland?"

"Yes."

"I'm Officer Gandy and this is Officer Hoover.

Officer Gandy stood over six feet tall and carried an extra fifty pounds around his belt. Officer Hoover, still bearing the acne of youth, kept his gaze focused on the yard. Their cruiser was parked along the curb where she and Betsy had crashed just minutes ago.

"Have you had any trouble here tonight?" Officer Gandy asked.

"I just got in. I've been at a friend's house." She thought of the shadow that had flitted across the side of the house.

"Mind if we look around outside?"

Internal alarms sounded. "Just outside, right?" No way would she let them inside, even if they were police.

The younger officer walked to the right, shining a flashlight into the bushes that reached toward the windows.

The light filtering through her thin curtains and the open door, combined with the officer's flashlight, lit the yard as far as the street. No feathered figures dotted the grass. Ruth squinted at the tree. Small branches crossed bigger ones; massive limbs blended with the trunk. Leaves hung limp in the still air, layering a lacy black pattern on the ones beneath. Everywhere: potential hiding places for crows waiting for the new day.

"Don't mean to scare you, ma'am, but we received a tip that some church members are targeted for a bit of vandalism tonight. You were on the list."

Ruth's eyes widened. "Me? I don't belong to any church." Everyone knew she wasn't a church member. The urge to laugh pressed hard on her already jangled nerves. She squeezed her lips tight. Only with effort did she keep from releasing hysterical laughter.

"You were in attendance both Sundays at the homes that were damaged."

Her brows puckered. "So?"

"Each Sunday, only one of the church houses has been attacked, and you were at both houses. In someone's mind, that makes you a member."

Officer Gandy rubbed his chin. "Do you live here alone?"

Should she answer?

Shouting voices, male and angry, drifted from down the street. Car tires squealed. The officer glanced that direction and then back to Ruth. "Anywhere you can stay tonight?"

A hard lump settled in her stomach. The officer was serious. "Not really."

A narrow beam of light appeared at the left side of the yard as the Officer Hoover rounded the corner. "Nothing," the officer said and walked toward the parked cruiser.

"Just stay inside and keep your doors locked. We'll be making rounds all night, but if you need help, give us a call." Officer Gandy touched the brim of his hat.

She locked the door, regretting not mentioning the fact that she didn't have a phone. If trouble came, well, it would just have to come. Disregarding the spinning electric use-meter outside, Ruth turned on every light. The sound of protesting wood reassured her as she pressed a kitchen chair under the front and back door knobs.

She sat in the middle of her bed, pulled out the chain that hung around her neck and clutched the ring attached to it. The ring was the closest thing to a talisman that she owned, and right now, she needed all the comfort she could muster. Thoughts of the day she received the ring filtered through her aching mind.

Something scraped on the side of the house. She jumped but recognized the sound as the branches from the overgrown shrubs rubbing the house. The wind must be picking up. Wrapped in the quilt, she tried to press her body into invisibility against the mattress.

And she waited for the enemy or dawn, whichever came first.

20

Friday, June 28

As Nate approached Ruth's stoop, he grinned, anticipating her surprise at his early morning visit. He thumped his knuckles against the wood, and the door seemed to absorb the knock. Must have rot inside it. He could probably bust through the thing with his hands. Maybe the landlord would spring for a new door.

The lock clicked and the door opened. Ruth, wet hair dangling around her shoulders, stood in front of him. "Nate, what are you doing here?"

"I came to walk you to work."

Ruth shielded her eyes against the sun. "Why?" She gave him a wary look.

"I don't get to see you enough. You don't have a phone or a computer. The only way I can be with you is if I show up. So here I am."

She looked him over, as though deciding on the credibility of his answer. She seemed wary of him, but he wasn't sure why. The tension in her face eased.

"Let me finish getting ready."

Five minutes later, they walked toward town.

"I have something I wanted to tell you." Nate grabbed her hand, and his heart warmed as he felt her fingers mold against his. With the sun at their backs, their bodies cast long shadows on the sidewalk, the silhouettes molding into one. Ruth remained strangely silent. A crow flittered from a tree, blinking in the morning sun.

"You all right?" he asked.

"A little sleep deprived, that's all."

He searched her face and tightened his fingers around her hand. Something had upset her. Her mouth resembled a line of hard marble. The last time they had been together was Sunday. Had Miss Hannah's death affected her more than he thought? Ruth didn't know the woman, but then, females tended to be more sensitive than guys. Or had he done something wrong? "Anything I can do to help?"

Her laugh lacked humor, and he glanced at her, his concern growing.

"Sorry, I didn't mean to do that. Black humor: that's what my mom calls it when I laugh at things that weren't funny."

He struggled to understand. "You know I'm here for you, don't you? If you ever need anything…"

His heart ached as she glanced at him. Her hair with its flecks of shimmering red swung across her back as she walked. And those light brown eyes melted his heart. Without a doubt, he was in love. His heart gave a double-beat. She wasn't a Christian yet, but she had a good heart, and given time…

"So what did you want to tell me?"

He tucked her hand under his arm and her body brushed against his. Joyous agony. "Remember I told you about wanting my own business?"

"Yes."

"My boss is retiring and wants to sell his company to me. It will take a lot of money, but I've been saving for a while, and the bank is willing to give me a business loan." Slowing his steps, he looked down at her. His voice turned husky. "My life is finally coming together. I only have one more thing to put in place."

They turned the corner toward the courthouse. He followed Ruth's gaze across the street to the deserted church. Tufts of crabgrass sprouted in the yard. Black spray-painted windows mocked. A crow flew across the sidewalk. He had seen it before—the one with the scar. Ruth stumbled, and he tightened his hold on her arm.

"Well, well. Look here." Joe stood on the courthouse stairs and leaned against the railing as though the world was at his command.

Ruth's arm tightened under Nate's forearm.

"Hey, Joe." His cousin meant trouble. "What are you doing out so early?" He glanced across the street.

Joe's chuckle mocked. "Still at it, aren't you, buddy?"

Nate tensed, wishing Ruth weren't with him to witness whatever Joe had in mind.

"Still making that old church building some sort of idol in your life."

Ruth stiffened and started to say something then must have decided otherwise. Nate glanced at her tight face as she glared at Joe. Nate pulled her tighter against his side. "Church is important to me. It might do you good to go now and then."

"Oh, I go when I need to."

Nate pulled Ruth down the sidewalk with him. He hardly dared to breathe, hoping the confrontation was over.

"Oh, Ruth." Nate heard the rustle of paper. "I got this for you—a second copy of the adoption papers for our child."

Nate's face blanched. He turned toward Joe. "Of all the low down—"

"Oh, she didn't tell you? She and I have a history together. Your little princess was my queen."

"Joe, how dare you…" Ruth's words were venomous.

Nate barely noticed. He couldn't get beyond what Joe had said. Their child? Adoption papers?

"It was a long time ago." The words seemed stuck in her throat. "I was finishing high school when I met Joe. He said he loved me…" Her expression begged for understanding.

Nate let go of her arm. He stared at her as though he had never seen her before. It wasn't the baby, even though that was bad enough. But Ruth and Joe.

"Nate, please. Let me explain."

"I thought…" Words choked in his throat.

"I know what you thought, Nate, and I should have told you. I should have. Please believe me." She reached for the chain around her neck. "You helped me change." She stretched her hand toward him.

He backed away and turned to his cousin. "You win," he said, "just like always."

Nate felt Ruth's gaze on his back as he walked away. There was no reason to expect Ruth to have lived by his standards, but a relationship with Joe…it was too much.

~*~

Nate rounded the corner. Out of Ruth's sight. Out of her life. Never had hate filled her with such vengeance. Somehow, someway, she would make Joe pay for his cruelty.

Joe remained standing on the stairs, the envelope dangling from his hand, a smirk on his face. Every blond hair on his head in place. Impeccably groomed. Perfect in every physical way and yet so horribly ugly. Never could she allow this cold person to raise their daughter. He and his family thought more about money and status than love. Joe had told her so many stories about being left with a nanny over a holiday while his parents went cruising, or skiing, or off on a tour at some far location. The strange thing was, he didn't see anything wrong with it. This was the life he knew. But it was not the life she wanted for her daughter.

"I'll pick you up at six. We have a lot to talk about. Wear something pretty." He wiggled his eyebrows as he walked toward the double front doors of the courthouse.

Filled with rage, filled with pain, Ruth stood in place, unsure what to do. She could chase Joe and give him a piece of her mind, but for what good? Or she could run after Nate and try to explain, and yet, what was left to say? She could pray, but she wasn't sure she believed in prayer.

Besides, the concept of Nate's God being a loving Creator felt like a lose bolt, clunking and jolting, but never fitting. Square-bolt, round-hole kind of thing. Nate said God cared about her. And Betsy—she had told her, too. Ruth squeezed her eyes shut, but no matter how hard she thought about it, God didn't fit into any sequence of her life. And what about her friend Lizzi? Where was God when Lizzi needed Him?

Lizzi had been her best friend in elementary school until the day Lizzi was stolen away by her mother. Ruth still thought of it that way. Lizzi was being raised by her grandmother. No one knew where Lizzi's mom was most of the time, but one day at Lizzi's ninth birthday party a strange woman was there. Lizzi said it was her mom who showed up unexpectedly. Ruth remembered Lizzi's grandmother's eyes were red. Ten days later, and Lizzi was gone, forced to live with her birth mother.

Ruth didn't see Lizzi for seven years and had mostly forgotten her. Then the rumors started at school. Lizzi was dead. She had swallowed a bottle of aspirin and went to bed. Her mom didn't find her for two days. The story came out, bit by bit, the way horrible things were revealed. Lizzi had not been loved. She had been better off with a grandmother who cared for her, but the law forced her to leave that love.

And Ruth had lost Nate, not because of the baby, but because of her relationship with Joe.

Several cars drove by. Groups of people stood across the street at the light, waiting to come to work, ready to start a normal day as part of a normal life.

Ruth straightened her back. She had to start acting like an adult. For whatever reason, Joe still wanted her. There was no sense trying to avoid him. She thought of a restraining order, but she needed to be near him in order to try to stop his interference in their daughter's life. Her dream of being with Nate might have ended, but she still needed to control her life. There was no way she would allow Joe to raise their daughter and end up like Lizzi. There was nothing she wouldn't do to protect the child.

She would keep that date with Joe and find out what he was up to. What did he hold against Mr. Charlie and why the interest in the light of Logan? And did he really know where their daughter was? One more date, but this time with her eyes open. He might spy on her, but tonight she would return the favor.

~*~

As Nate stumbled past the courthouse, he overheard Joe's plans to meet with Ruth that night. His cousin's intentions were clear, and it sickened him. Mindlessly he turned the corner, leaving Joe behind. The next side street approached, and he took it, hoping to leave behind thoughts of Ruth as easily as he had left Joe.

He hadn't given her a chance to explain, and after he had promised to be there for her…Sure, he made the promise, but that was before he knew her involvement with Joe. The fact that Ruth and Joe knew each other from years ago bothered him, sure, but she never gave a clue as to the level of their relationship. His cousin had one-upped him all their lives. If it had been anyone else but Joe…then, maybe.

A stiff vine projected toward the sidewalk. Nate grabbed the stalk and pulled the plant from the ground. He slammed the vine with its clinging dirt into the street. He was at the back of his church. The early morning sun had yet to stretch above the level of the oaks, and the nighttime shade had cooled the churchyard. Nate slumped against the brick and slid to the ground. *God, is it too much to ask for a wife who loves me? I have served You all my life. I mow this grass, and pull the weeds. I paint and scrub and fix, and all I want is a wife, not Joe's castoff.* Nate pounded his fist into the ground. He remembered the difficulty he had explaining to Ruth why he went to church. His answers had felt so superficial, his explanation had put God so far away, just as God felt right now. Where was God when he needed Him? He had worked…he had worked…

He leaned his head against the wall. It wasn't about work. It was about grace. He knew this, and yet he'd ignored it. Car engines roared. Distant voices.

Crows dropped from the large oak and settled on the grass. A dozen, then more.

With each crow that darkened the yard, Nate's anger grew. He raced across the grass. "Leave me alone!"

Crows scattered, many finding refuge back in the towering limbs above the reach of the flailing man.

Spent, Nate once again fell against the church building. He had always been a good judge of character, and everything about Ruth felt right. Chet liked her, and Betsy. How could they all have been wrong?

A shadow landed over him.

"Surprised to find you here," Pastor Greg Clark said. He lowered himself to the ground beside Nate. "Shouldn't you be at work?"

Nate pulled his legs up to his chest and grunted.

"I heard someone yelling. That you?"

Most days Nate enjoyed talking with Greg. But right now, he wanted to be left alone to lick his wounds. "Stupid crows."

"Actually, I heard they are quite smart."

"These aren't."

One crow returned to the grass, then a second. Nate jumped to his feet. "I can't stand these crows!"

"How about we go to my house?"

The two men walked the four blocks to the Clark home. The kitchen in the ranch house had the feel of the eighties with green laminate countertops and yellow appliances.

Greg popped a container in the fancy coffeemaker and motioned Nate toward the old wood table. When the second cup was filled, he carried them to the table.

"I might as well tell you." Nate leaned on his elbows. "Ruth had a child. She gave it up for adoption." He didn't mention the baby was Joe's. It sounded so petty, and yet the thought made his chest tighten to the point he could barely breathe.

"Was this recent?"

"Right after high school, I think."

"That's been awhile. So why the anger?"

Nate's face reddened. "She lied to me!" He wanted to punch something. If nothing else, give a swing. But there was nothing to punch in the pastor's house.

"She lied to you?"

"Well, not so much lied as deceived. She let me believe she was a moral woman."

Pastor Greg rubbed the back of his neck. "I seem to remember you telling me she didn't go to church but was warming to the idea." He shook his head up and down. "Yes, that's what you said. She was warming to the idea."

Nate didn't want a lecture. He needed a friend who would listen. Someone who would help him feel better. He had a right to his anger. "She's been coming to church every Sunday, even after the tomatoes, and the bomb…"

"But she didn't go to church before, right?"

"No."

"You can't expect a person without Christ to live a Christian life. Once we meet our Savior, our sins are washed away. We become new. I don't think Ruth's there yet, but…"

Nate knew all that, yet he couldn't share the real source of his anger.

"Have you talked to her about the baby?"

"No, I just found out this morning. Joe told me."

"Cousin Joe?"

"Yeah."

"Hmm." Pastor Clark leaned back in his chair. "That adds fuel to the fire."

"What do you mean?"

"Come on, Nate. I've known you most of your life, and there has never been much love between you and Joe, but there's been a whole lot of competition. And I've seen the way you look at Ruth. How did Joe know…oh. Oh. Wow."

Nate lowered his head.

The pastor leaned in. "Does she love him?"

"Who cares? I don't know." Nate swallowed. "They're going out somewhere tonight to talk. From the look on Joe's face, I don't think talk is what's on his mind."

"And Ruth?"

"I don't know." Nate thought of the frightened look on Ruth's face when Joe first appeared in town. And this morning, the pain in her eyes as she reached for his hand.

"So what are you doing about this date tonight?"

"Nothing. It's not my business." Nate pushed his empty cup toward the pastor. "Thanks for the coffee." Outside, Nate wandered the streets, his thoughts as confused as his footsteps. Why couldn't he shake the memory of her wounded look?

~*~

Ruth chose not to go to work, which meant she also missed seeing Mr. Charlie. Instead, she spent the day worrying about the evening's date with Joe. When he arrived, she stood ready on the stoop to avoid any chance of him coming into the house. Surprised that he would ask, Ruth chose the Red Rock Inn outside of town when Joe gave her the choice. It was casual dining within a reasonable distance of Logan, which she had insisted on, and private enough that they would be able to talk. She came armed with an agenda.

The Inn sat on a knoll facing a pond. Pine and elm trees created a backdrop behind the water and ducks provided the entertainment. A wooden bridge ended at a gazebo that jutted well out into the water. Benches placed strategically along the walk allowed couples to sit.

Joe chose a table across the room from the window, which left Ruth with nothing to look at except Joe. She couldn't even stare at other diners since the large room was divided into smaller, more intimate seating areas by half-walls arched at the top, the openings adorned with vines and potted plants.

An icy fist gripped her heart, an alert to the presence of danger even though the room appeared settled and the weather calm. Perhaps they should leave? Searching for an excuse to go home, she found none. The feeling of fear had to be a reaction to her lack of confidence in questioning Joe. After all, she rarely confronted anyone.

The approaching waitress's stiff black skirt rubbed against her thighs as she walked. She stood at the end of the table, pen poised over pad.

Joe looked at the menu then up at the waitress. "The lovely lady will have the grilled chicken with the mango chutney and sautéed asparagus." He paused. "They are still your favorites, aren't they, sweet?"

The server waited. Ruth started to nod in agreement, but stopped. She studied the menu. "Actually, I'll have the swordfish with lemon butter and broccoli."

The woman glanced at Joe, who nodded his head. She wrote on her small pad.

Ruth smirked. Ruth, one. Joe, zero.

Joe stared at Ruth for a second before turning to the waitress. "I'll have the ribeye, extra seasoning and make it medium rare, with a baked potato, butter and sour cream." Joe closed the menu. "Oh, and your best bottle of Pinot Noir."

The wine arrived and was found acceptable. Joe poured a generous amount into Ruth's glass. "Go ahead and drink it. It won't hurt you." He swirled the red liquid in his glass and took a sip. "It might even do you some good."

Her first sample of alcohol had been at his house years ago. It had also been her last. Now, with Joe watching, she took a tentative sip and found the sweet taste soothing. She took a second sip and decided she could breathe again.

Joe smiled and set down his glass. He stroked the top of her hand gently with fingers that felt too soft. Not like Nate's. "I'm glad you've come to your senses, Ruth. There's no reason for us to fight."

She took another sip of wine, anything to build up her resolve to do what needed done. Joe had an agenda and it wasn't working for the mayor. What really brought him to town? And why the sudden interest in her? Mr. Charlie knew about the light of Logan, but what was this light, and what did it have to do with

Joe? But most important was their child. She owed their daughter the stability of an adoptive family.

"So how is the work coming with the mayor?" Ruth did her best to smile.

"Not as well as planned, but you know that. The churches aren't paying so there isn't any money to budget."

"That must make for long days with nothing to do."

Joe lifted his wine glass and tipped it in her direction. "Oh, I have things to do."

She had never been one for small talk, and asking probing questions was so far out of her comfort zone she might as well be on the moon, but that was the reason she had agreed to this date. Ruth swallowed the lump in her throat. "Tell me more about this light of Logan."

Joe's expression turned icy. "Does the old man call himself the light?"

Ruth's hand trembled, and she set down her glass of wine

"You don't have any idea what you're dealing with, do you? Poor, innocent Ruth."

Dinner came. Her silverware hit too hard on the white china. Muted voices swirled from various parts of the room. Ruth knew she should slow down on the wine, but Joe kept filling her glass and it was hard to remember how much she had actually drank. Besides, the liquid pushed the food through her constricted esophagus.

Joe maintained a monolog, mostly about his prowess as a legislator. Either he didn't recognize her sudden silence, or he didn't care. Questions about Mr. Charlie stopped for the time being.

The room spun. Why she was here, in this restaurant, with Joe? She hated Joe, didn't she? There was something she needed to do; she remembered that. In a restaurant with Joe. She hid an unexpected grin behind her wine glass.

Chocolate cheesecake arrived, and she tried to smother another giggle. Dark dessert with a dark man. Dark room, dark mood…

Another mouthful of wine slipped down her throat. "You never told me about the light." Ruth's tongue felt thick in her mouth.

"You don't need to worry about it. I have it all figured out." Joe's gaze softened.

She knew how the night would end, and she didn't really care. The damage was done. The giggles hit once more. Joe beamed, probably thinking his conversation was the source of her humor. Little did he know. Mr. Charlie, the baby, all her issues seemed insignificant.

No sense denying it, she was having those feelings, the ones she thought she would never have again. How many times had she fantasized about it? But Nate had been in the bed with her, not Joe, and she had a slender wedding band around her left ring finger. She knew it wasn't funny, but the laughing wouldn't stop. Must be more of what her mother called black humor. Her mom said she got it from her dad. She missed her dad. Things would be different if he were here to protect her. But she could protect herself now. Mr. Charlie said so.

They stood to leave and the floor heaved under her feet.

Joe grabbed her arm and grinned.

"Need to get her some fresh air," he said as the

hostess opened the outer door for them.

She leaned against the side of Joe's car as he searched for his keys.

"I knew you would try something like this."

At the sound of Nate's voice, Ruth jerked her head up. The parking lot spun, and she leaned heavily against the car. Nate stood just feet from Joe, his hands balled into fists at his sides. The sight was too much. She started to giggle.

Joe's eyes were little more than slits. "What are you doing here, Nate?"

"She's too good for you."

Joe shrugged his shoulders, unlocked the car, and opened the passenger door. He nudged Ruth with his arm. "Get in the car." He turned to Nate. "What do you care? She's used goods, and you always hated my hand-me-downs."

"Ruth, get in my truck." Nate's eyes burned. "I'm taking you home."

Joe stiffened. "Ruth, get in the car. Now."

Why wouldn't her mind work? She had come with Joe, hadn't she? There were questions…she bent to slide into the car, only to be grabbed and pulled back out.

"I'm taking her home," Nate said, "so I know she'll be safe." Ruth felt him pull her, but her feet were stuck. "The shape she's in, it's hard to tell what you might do to her."

Joe swore and lunged.

Nate released her, and she fell to the ground.

The two men tumbled in the dirt, arms flailing around a hurricane of dust.

She watched until her eyes became too heavy to hold open.

21

Saturday, June 29

Ruth wished the pounding would stop. She eased open her eyes to discover she was in her own living room. Gripping the sides of her head, she slid off the couch, hit the coffee table, and landed on the floor, a stream of unwelcomed light cascading across her body.

She remembered going to dinner with Joe, but she came home with...Nate? Joe's snarling face filled the backdrop of her swirling memory. Sometime during the night, she had awakened on her bed with a blanket spread over her. Undulating shadows drove her to the kitchen for a knife. Holding the weapon in front of her, she crept to the living room to wait for Joe.

Joe! She sucked in a lungful of air and struggled off the floor. Digging within the folds of the blanket, she finally spotted what she was searching for: the knife. Grabbing the handle, she sat heavily on the couch and clutched the knife close to her chest.

The pounding continued. "Ruth, if you don't answer the door, I'll call the police. I'm worried about you."

Ruth pushed the knife beneath a couch cushion before answering the door.

"Are you all right?" Betsy burst into the room. "Chet wouldn't let me come until after lunch, and when you didn't answer the door..." She held Ruth at arms' length. "Well, all kinds of horrible things flew through my mind."

"Why are you here?" Nausea squeezed Ruth's stomach.

"Nate stopped by last night. I've never seen him so angry. He said you were drunk, and he drove you home."

Shame flushed Ruth's face. "I've never been drunk before, Betsy. I promise." She fell among the floral throw pillows on the couch. "I told Nate about the baby yesterday morning. Actually, Joe told him, and then things got really out of control."

"I know. He told us."

Ruth squeezed out a dry laugh. "I can imagine."

"He was worried about you. That's why he followed you last night. He figured Joe would try something."

Ruth shrugged her shoulders. "Why should Nate care?"

"He's trying to figure that out himself. Men are slow-witted sometimes."

Ruth pulled herself upright and her stomach heaved. She took a few shallow breaths.

Betsy walked toward the kitchen. "You need something to eat."

"I'm fine if you want to go home."

Cupboard doors opened and closed. Water splashed in the sink. Betsy returned, a red plastic tray in hand.

"I didn't see any greasy food or coffee, which is what you really need." Betsy placed the tray on the coffee table. "This is all I could find. A peanut butter sandwich, apple slices, and a glass of water."

Ruth nibbled the sandwich and was surprised her

stomach accepted the food. But then, her body was probably ninety percent peanut butter. She swallowed a mouthful of water and the weight pushed the glob of food into her stomach. Tears, so quick to come lately, filled her eyes. "I can't eat the apple."

"That's all right. Half a sandwich is good enough for now."

A Gala. Mr. Charlie's favorite. She had saved the apple for yesterday, Friday, but Friday never happened for the two of them. What did Mr. Charlie think when she didn't show up? She imagined his eager expression turning to disappointment as he listened for her footsteps. How long did he wait? The sandwich churned and she eased her head down on the pillows as the number of bad mistakes accumulated in her mind.

The cushions on the couch shifted as Betsy sat. "No matter what happens between you and Nate, you are still my friend, and I care about you." Betsy rubbed Ruth's back, a slow soothing movement like a mother comforting a child.

Ruth relaxed and wanted to sleep, to forget. Only problem was she would wake up again with her same life waiting for her. "I don't even know if I have a job anymore," she murmured. "I didn't go to work yesterday."

"Neither did Nate."

"Why do I make such bad choices, Betsy? How did you end up perfect?"

"I'm not perfect, Ruth."

"You've never made a mistake in your life."

Betsy's hands stilled on Ruth's back. "How do you think I know that fatty food and coffee cures a hangover?"

"You read it in a book somewhere. No, wait. Don't tell me…it's in the Bible?"

"It's not in the Bible. I used to be quite a little party girl in high school. I told my mom I was spending the night with a girlfriend. Instead I sneaked to parties I knew she wouldn't let me go to and then crashed somewhere until morning."

Ruth looked at Betsy. "And your parents never found out?"

"Nope."

"So how did you get from party girl to wife and mother?"

"You mean, how did I become a Christian?"

"I guess."

"A friend invited me to a youth meeting at her church."

"The friend you were supposed to be spending the night with?"

"Remember Sarah from Nate's picnic?"

"How could I forget her? She was the one with the strapless dress that clung to her perfect body like skin."

Betsy laughed. "That's the one. She's had a crush on Nate since high school."

A car door slammed.

Ruth stiffened. Laughing voices filtered through the thin walls and disappeared behind the neighbor's door. "Do you think Joe will come?"

"I don't know."

"Is the door locked?"

Betsy locked the door and returned to the couch. "Where was I?"

"You went to church."

"Oh, yeah. Sarah invited me to her youth meeting. I had fun so I kept going. Eventually, I started to listen.

I gave my life to Christ and haven't taken another drink since. The desire is still there, though, and I rely on God every day to lead me through it."

"God doesn't lead me anywhere." Ruth pulled the pillow tight against her face like a stubborn child wanting her own way.

Betsy's voice reached her covered ears. "I'll pick you up in the morning for church."

"I'm not going to church." The words puffed through fiberfill.

"Why not?" Betsy pulled away the pillow. "Please, Ruth, you need to be in church. God will show Himself to you in His time, just as He did for me. I'll pick you up at nine and, just a warning." She gave a low chuckle. "I'll have Chip with me, so behave. Now get up and lock the door behind me."

Ruth pulled herself upright as Betsy closed the front door behind her. A car engine started. The vehicle pulled away. Ruth flopped back down.

~*~

A leaf brushed against her sleeping face, awakening her. No, a feather. Crows! Ruth gave a choked cry and scrambled up the back of the couch, away from the face that loomed over her.

"How did you get in here?" The words scraped against her constricted throat.

"Quite a place you have here."

"You never answered my question." Ruth's heart pounded painfully against her ribs. "How did you get in?"

"Your door was unlocked. Not smart in this neighborhood." Joe settled beside her on the edge of the couch and chucked her under the chin with a finger.

She clenched her teeth. "Get out of here." The scent of his cologne made her stomach churn. She could feel the heat of his body, or was it her heat?

He leaned over and kissed the top of her head. Trapped against the back of the couch, she pushed against his chest. After breathing into her hair, he leaned back and sought her eyes. "Ruthie, it's been too long."

She twisted away, and he grabbed for her.

The chain around her neck slid out.

He stared. "That looks like a cheap wedding ring."

As Ruth struggled to her feet, she dropped the circle of gold back under her shirt and allowed the metal to settle between her breasts where it had served as a constant reminder for over two years.

"Do you have something to tell me?" His eyes turned dark.

"It's nothing."

"Oh, it must be something. You wouldn't keep nothing tucked away in such a soft and lovely place."

Renewed energy fed her spent muscles. The surge of strength released courage. "Get out of here!"

He moved toward her. She dropped to her knees and slid her hand between the cushions of the couch. She grabbed the knife and jumped to her feet, snarling. "Keep away from me! Get out of here, and don't you ever come into my house uninvited again."

"So the ring is important?" He lowered himself onto the chair by the fireplace. "You go and get married? Who's the lucky groom?" Joe looked around the room. "And where is he hiding?" He leaned back into the chair.

The knife felt heavy, but she held it upright, keeping the tip pointed at Joe. "It's a promise ring."

"Kind of like an engagement ring?"

The smirk again; she hated that look. "I made a promise to remain abstinent until marriage. The ring is a reminder for me."

Joe raised an eyebrow and draped an arm across the back of the chair. "A little late for that, isn't it?"

"It's called secondary virginity. You wouldn't understand." No, Joe would never understand the concept of waiting for anything. "I made a promise to God after I delivered our baby."

"A promise to God?" He chuckled as the words tumbled out. "Well, we can't disappoint God now, can we? No sex until marriage? Easy enough. We'll get married."

The knife slipped. The promise had been made with all the other women, but since then, the vow had grown in meaning. Still unsure if the God she'd promised really cared, but the promise was to herself as much as to Him. "We won't get married, Joe." Ruth's mind tumbled. What could he possibly want from her? She wasn't pretty. She had no money. Most likely, she would hurt his career rather than help it. She hefted the knife back up. "Get out, Joe."

"Oh, I'm going soon enough. But first, look at this place, Ruth. Really look at it." He scanned the room. "You live in a dump in the worst part of town."

"I may not live in a palace, but I earned it myself. I don't have a mommy and daddy handing me everything I want."

"How about I make your life better?" Hs expression softened. "Move in with me. We can be married by Wednesday." He leaned forward in the chair. "I'll bring your mom for the wedding. You'd like to see your mom, wouldn't you? How long has it been?"

It had been over three years since she had left home, three years of only telephone conversations. Her mom had never been demonstrative, but still, the thought of even a quick hug filled her aching heart with joy.

"And I'll make the deal sweeter. How about I toss our baby's papers?"

She stared at him with suspicion. "What do you mean?"

"I'll throw them out. Shred them, never contact the child. Whatever makes you happy." His smile held little warmth. "Marry me and give me another child. I want an heir."

Her mouth fell slack. Was he serious? She had to be crazy to even consider this. And yet, marriage would keep him from destroying her baby's secure life.

"Tell you what." He stood. "I'll give you some time. How about I pick you up for lunch tomorrow, and we can celebrate."

She knew she should say something or do something, but her brain seemed stuck on empty. "I promised to go to church tomorrow."

"Good. Fine. Church is over by noon." He walked to the door. "I'll pick you up at two."

"Joe, no—" The door closed against her unfinished sentence.

~*~

Coming downstairs from putting Chip to bed, Chet looked forward to some time alone with his wife.

It had been a long couple of days, with Nate not showing at work on Friday, his sudden appearance at their home late Friday night, and then trying to calm Betsy's concerns for Ruth today.

He heard the sound of popping corn, and soon Betsy entered carrying the red bowl, their largest, filled with white kernels. Smiling, he molded his body next to his wife's on the couch, grabbed a handful of popcorn, and prepared himself to watch an oldie movie, but one of their favorites.

The cosmic ring of his cellphone mingled with the movie's soundtrack. Chet grimaced. "It better not be Nate. I can't deal with any more drama."

"He's your best friend. Invite him over." She slid across the couch.

"Hello." Chet walked to the center of the room. "Who are you?" His face grew pale. He disconnected the phone. "We just got a death threat."

"Seriously?"

"It was a man's voice. He said anyone who shows up at the Kritchner house tomorrow will be dead."

"Call the police."

Chet dialed 9-1-1. "I just got a death threat…yes…" The muscles along his jaw tightened. "I will. Thank you." He scanned the room. The windows were closed. A soft click was followed by a cool breeze. He'd never noticed the sound of the air conditioner before. Even Betsy's breaths pushed against his eardrums.

"Chet, what is it?"

"Mine is the fifth call the police have received so far." Chet moved the popcorn and pulled Betsy to his chest. He rested his cheek against the top of her head and inhaled the strawberry scent. He loved his sweet

Betsy so much. It had to be a prank. God, let it be a prank.

Betsy looked up at him. "We can have church somewhere else."

"Mommy?"

Chip stood at the top of the stairs, his small face visible between the slats of the railing. Cartoon pajamas hung askew on his slight frame. A denuded monkey, most of its fur having been picked off one fluff at a time, dangled under his arm. "I had a bad dream."

Betsy walked to the stairs and held out her arms. "Come here, sweetheart."

Gripping the banister over his head, he came down the stairs.

Betsy carried him to the couch where they melted together, mother and son, one loving mass.

Chet's throat tightened. If anything happened to his family… "We need to pray." He wrapped them tightly in his arms, vowing to keep them safe.

~*~

Paul Kritchner lay in bed wondering what had caused him to go from sleep to awareness. He glanced at the illuminated dial of his clock and sighed. Three AM. Rolling over, hoping to go back to sleep, he heard a sound: a rattle and clunk. The noise came from outside.

His wife snored softly beside him. The family teased that even a hurricane would not awaken her when she was asleep. Curious, he shuffled across the rug to the window. Velma used blinds instead of curtains in the second-floor bedrooms, thinking the wooden slats blended better with the country look she was after. He didn't care. Let his wife decorate their old 40's house however she wanted.

In the dark, he groped for the string. As he separated the slats, he strangled a curse and ran for the stairs. Where was his phone? Forget the phone, get the shotgun. Thoughts flew so fast through his brain that they smashed into each other. Without phone or gun, he unlocked the front door and ran into the yard. "What do you think you're doing?" he bellowed.

A gray dump truck lumbered over the sidewalk and sped away, a plume of diesel smoke trailing behind.

Paul stared at the large mound in the middle of his yard. Manure. No doubt about it. He tightened his lips and tried not to breathe as he turned back to the house. Large spatters of paint on the front siding and bits of balloon clung to the hedges.

The neighbor's porch light flipped on. Cyrus Phillips, struggling to tie his plaid flannel housecoat around his thick middle, walked across the damp grass. "The noise woke me up."

"I'm gonna call the police."

"You might want to put on some clothes first."

Paul glanced down and grinned. He slipped back into the house for his shirt and pants.

~*~

Paul nodded to Cyrus. "Come on in." The police were gone and Velma was still upstairs sleeping.

"Coffee?" Paul flipped the button on the coffeemaker and pulled two mugs from the shelf.

"You got a bunch of people coming over in the

morning, don't you?" Cyrus asked.

"Yeah, ten o'clock. Church." He scratched the top of his head. Why was this happening? He and his wife were trying to do what God wanted them to do. In all of his sixty odd years, no one had ever bothered him. Now, all of a sudden, being a Christian came with a curse. He thought of the phone call Velma had taken earlier in the evening. Really—a death threat? He had told her the call was a prank. He glanced toward the front yard. What if it wasn't?

"So what you gonna do about all that—um—poo in your front yard?"

"Give everyone a shovel, I guess. Free fertilizer."

"The flies'll have a field-day come daylight."

"I suppose."

Cyrus rose from his chair. "Come on. You'll need help. I have a few plastic tarps we can use to cover the most of it. That should get you through church."

Paul stared at Cyrus. The man's robe had come untied, exposing powder blue pajamas. The top button was caught up in the second button hole. The whole row of buttons was off. Velma would have made him fix it before he went to bed.

Strange man, that Cyrus. They lived beside each other for six years and hardly said good morning. Now here the man was, like the Good Samaritan, offering his help at four in the morning. And without finishing their coffee.

"Sun'll be up in a couple of hours." Cyrus ambled toward the door. "We best get moving."

Velma shuffled into the kitchen, rubbing sleep from her eyes. "What's going on? Do I smell coffee...Oh, Cyrus, I didn't see you standing there."

"So the smell of coffee woke you up, did it?" Paul

shook his head and grinned. Coffee would wake her, but not weather, not voices, not poo in the yard. He looked at her sleepy face. "We have a problem."

22

Sunday, June 30

Fifty-two people and numerous flies crammed into the living and dining rooms of Paul and Velma Kritchner's home.

Mrs. Kritchner swatted the back of the couch and wiped the sticky mess with a tissue. "Oh, my," she mumbled before moving on.

Ruth raised a folded magazine and glanced at the fly on Chet's casted leg. "Go ahead," Chet said as he leaned against the wall. "Give it a smack."

"I don't want to hurt you." She didn't want to hurt anyone at the Kritchner's even though she ached to vent the rage that boiled in her gut. With all her being, she hated Joe. An involuntary shiver gripped her. She needed to forget, at least for the next hour, Joe's horrid desire to raise their daughter unless she married him. Seriously?

Chet raised an eyebrow. "You going to get this fly or admire him?"

Ruth swung the magazine. "Just finishing fly number six."

"Ha, I still have you beat." Jo Sparks' braces glinted between her wide smile.

Ruth attacked the wall behind Chet's head. Two dead flies remained, glued to the beige paint, and her anger grew. Joe's words replayed in her head. Marry me, and I will toss out the baby's papers...marry me...marry me.

Paul Kritchner's voice boomed across the room. "Hey, we got two new folks here. Some of you know them: Cyrus and Mary Phillips, our next-door neighbors."

Welcoming voices swelled and bodies shifted, making way for two more in the modest house.

"Brought y'all a gift," Cyrus said, handing a fistful of fly swatters to Paul. "Thought you could use 'em."

"Cyrus spent the early morning helping me get that blue tarp over the pile of manure out there, donated by some unknown individual."

"I figured it was farm byproduct," said Clara Blackstone, sitting on one of the white kitchen chairs called to duty in the living room. "The smell and all."

"It was a lot worse at three in the morning," Paul said.

Ruth stumbled around the room, magazine in hand. It gave her something to do, occupied her body if not her mind. Any sensible person in her position would have skipped church this morning. Ruth had tried to talk her way out of it when Betsy showed up. But Betsy had refused to let her stay home, and with Chip's huge eyes staring at her, she had grabbed her purse and locked the door even though her mind remained trapped in Joe's prison of words. "Marry me and I will throw the adoption papers away." If she refused, he would do his best to tear their child away from the only family she knew. Lizzi's scared face swam in front of her.

The Kritchners' front door opened, and her heart lurched. Sooner or later the person entering would be Nate. He wouldn't miss church. She would have to face his disappointment and anger.

"Hey there, Miss Sarah. Come on in and find yourself a seat," Mr. Kritchner said.

Ruth sighed. Cute Sarah with her blond hair hanging down her back and neatly creased white slacks and teal silk blouse—Nate was a fool not to grab her up. Sarah would be the classic southern wife, just what Nate needed as he tried to launch his own business. Sarah probably had connections that would help, too.

Betsy looked at Ruth and patted the couch beside her. "Come on, girlfriend. We can make room for one more."

Five ladies shifted and Ruth sank into the worn green cushion. Six women now squeezed into a space comfortable for four, a reminder of last week.

"It seems every Sunday the crowd grows," Betsy said to Ruth. "Chet mentioned that we may have to form another group soon. Not many of our houses will hold this many people."

The sun streamed into the room, adding heat to the already over-warm space.

Ruth glanced at the picture window behind her. "I wish Mrs. Kritchner would let us close the drapes." With the window against her back, at least she wasn't looking into the glare, but she felt exposed.

A woman wearing a trendy pair of slacks and a pink sleeveless top sat on the other side of Ruth. "I tried to talk her into closing them when I got here," the woman said. "But she wants to be able to see people as they come to the door."

"Let people ring the bell." Ruth wiped a bead of sweat from her brow.

Busy discussing the front window, Ruth almost

missed the door opening.

Nate sauntered into the room, bringing with him half a dozen more flies.

Betsy touched Ruth's arm, giving her a reassuring smile.

Nate ignored her and barely glanced at Sarah as he worked his way through the packed room. He smiled as folks greeted him, but his grin seemed stiff. His usual easy-loping gait had the stilted walk of a tin soldier as he shuffled past people sitting on the floor to secure a spot on the far wall next to Chet.

Ruth stopped breathing as his gaze almost reached her...just a little more to the left. She stared hard, hoping he would feel her looking and turn her way. She wanted to give him a smile, to let him know she understood his feeling of betrayal, even though her heart was broken beyond repair. But he never turned.

Chip grabbed onto Nate's leg, and Nate hoisted the boy into his arms.

A man Ruth didn't know entered, then a family with six kids: five sons and the youngest a daughter.

Chip slid from Nate's arms.

"Whoa there," Betsy said, grabbing the boy as he passed the couch. She settled him on her lap.

"Come on, children," Velma called from across the room. "Let's find a better place to hang out." She walked toward a hall that led to the kitchen. It seemed the hostess at each house provided the lesson for the young ones.

Chip scrambled from Betsy's lap and ran toward Mrs. Kritchner.

"He's quite a boy," Ruth whispered to Betsy. Ruth couldn't imagine anyone tearing Chip from his family. Her daughter would be about the same age. No matter the cost, she had to stop Joe.

The service remained the same: singing praise songs to God, prayer, and then the lesson. The minister of the day, Nate's pastor, positioned himself close to the front door.

Ruth hadn't seen him since she'd wandered into the church after the vandalism. His hair had turned grayer, and his slacks puckered beneath his belt. Ruth ventured another glance at Nate, sitting stiff against the wall, his attention fixed on the minister.

"I'm Pastor Greg Clark from the First Street Church." He winked at Nate, who returned an anemic smile.

Betsy shared her Bible as Pastor Clark read from Matthew, but Ruth's mind wandered. She shifted on the uncomfortable cushion, wishing church would end. This was a mistake she wouldn't make again. Church attendance for her was over.

A man sitting on the floor stood and leaned against the wall. He must have had enough of the hardwood. The spot he created filled with one of the standing men. Just like soft serve ice cream. Lick up, drip down. One of those horrible black giggles formed in the back of her throat, and she bit her lip to stop it.

The window behind the couch exploded. Something hard slammed against the side of Ruth's head.

Shards of glass sprayed into the room. Tires squealed. Footsteps ran to the door.

Women screamed.

Ruth put her hand over her ears, only to feel stickiness in her hair. It was happening all over again. Betsy's face appeared in front of hers. She seemed to be yelling, but Ruth couldn't hear her. The room spun and she grabbed for Betsy's arm.

"Get her on the floor!" someone shouted.

Ruth closed her eyes against the burning light.

~*~

She woke to a still room. Beige walls stood rigid, and the floor no longer rolled like the deck of a boat. A paramedic held an oxygen mask to her face.

Betsy loomed over her, Chet at Betsy's side. "How are you feeling," Betsy murmured.

"What happened?"

"Brick through the window," Chet said.

Ruth almost missed Betsy's glaring look and the shrug of Chet's shoulders. "That's all?" Ruth asked. It seemed anti-climactic after last week.

Betsy stroked her arm. "It's all right, Ruth. Don't worry about it."

Ruth struggled to sit only to be pushed back to the floor by the paramedic. "Let's not rush things," he said. "You have a nasty bump on your head, and a gash that's gonna need stitches."

"Stitches?" Ruth's eyes widened.

"We'll take you to Memorial General and–"

"I'm not going anywhere!" She closed her eyes, cold sweat covering her skin.

"Ruth, honey—"

"No, Betsy. I want to go home."

"We really need to take her to the emergency room," the paramedic said. "The doc will want some X-rays. Besides, she shouldn't be alone with that head injury."

"How long will she need someone with her?" Betsy asked.

"At least eight hours."

Betsy glanced at Chet, who nodded. "I'll stay with her," Betsy said.

"She really should go to the hospital…"

"I'll sign a paper that says I refuse." Ruth longed for her bed. The queasiness in her stomach was an inch from the point of no return. Betsy was kind, but Ruth could convince her to leave once she was settled at home.

~*~

Betsy helped Ruth into her pajamas.

"Let me check your head before you lie down."

"It's fine, Betsy. Really."

Betsy laughed. "You sound like Chet. Just turn around and let me take a look."

Ruth turned her head, exposing the wound to Betsy's critical eye. "Well, the paramedics didn't clean it up as well as I would have, but I don't want to make the cut bleed again."

Betsy's face softened as she pulled the covers up to Ruth's chin. "How are you doing, really?"

"I'm fine."

"Stop it, Ruth. I know better. You just got bashed in the head with a brick. We all expected the room to explode like last time, but it didn't." She paused. "Besides, I saw the look on your face when Nate walked into the room. You like him, don't you?"

"Of course I like him. Who wouldn't?" She turned away from Betsy's knowing eyes. What would Betsy think if she knew about the possible marriage on Wednesday? Would it be that bad married to Joe? She had loved him once. But that was before she knew what real love was like.

"What will you do about Nate?"

"Me? What will I do? Nothing. Nate made it clear that anything that might have happened between us is over. Besides, I have too many other things on my mind to worry about Mr. Perfect."

"Like what?"

She closed her eyes and focused on regular breathing.

"I'm not going away, Ruth, so you can stop pretending."

Ruth opened one eye. Seeing Betsy's grin, she opened the other. "You were just here yesterday taking care of me. This is getting to be a habit."

"I'm your friend. God sent you into my life for a reason, and I refuse to let you struggle alone with whatever's on your mind. So out with it."

"You sound like Mr. Charlie. God sent me…blah blah blah. Isn't it possible I just showed up in Logan because I ran out of gas?" Ruth was tired of being told she was part of some huge God plan. She sighed. "I don't understand all this God talk."

Betsy sat quietly.

"I don't understand how you can think God has a plan for me. I can see it maybe for you and Nate, but I've never gone to church in my life."

"Not true. You've gone every Sunday for the past month."

"You know what I mean."

"So let me see if I have this right." Betsy held up one finger. "You're upset because Nate over-reacted to the news that you had a life before him." She lifted the second finger. "And you think the church should be taxed, which goes against the crowd you're hanging with. And you're estranged from God." She wiggled three fingers in the air. "Is that it?"

"I guess." There was so much more, but how could she begin to explain?

"Ruth, have you ever prayed?"

"You mean to God?"

Betsy chuckled. "Yes, to God, the Big Man, the Creator of the Universe and everything in it."

Ruth had expected Betsy to give her a lecture of some kind, a list of reasons why she should change her mind about the tax, chase after Nate, and start believing that God directed her meaningless life. She never expected Betsy to ask her about prayer.

"Well, have you?" Betsy asked.

"I…on Sundays I close my eyes. You guys always pray."

"I'll take that as a no. Give me your hands."

Ruth narrowed her eyes. "What are you planning to do?"

"We're going to talk to God."

Betsy had a conduit to God that she didn't have. Elijah and the burning rocks flashed into her mind. What if Betsy upset God and He sent flames to consume her house? God had every right to be angry with her.

"You're shaking like a leaf. What's wrong?" Betsy lay an arm protectively over Ruth's shoulders. "Forget the hands. We don't need them, but you need God." Betsy began to pray.

Ruth watched her friend's face as it tensed and then softened. She called God her Father. One of the ministers had called God Father. Tears welled in Ruth's eyes as she thought of her father and how much she missed him. More than anything, she needed him now. Her heart began to squeeze. Something was happening, but that something frightened her.

Betsy kept on talking, pleading at times. "God, Ruth needs You, but she thinks You're far away. Please help her know You are always near for her. Let her know You care, and You have all her problems already worked out in Your master plan. Help her to trust You."

Mr. Charlie had said that she was part of a master plan, that's why she ended up in Logan. Did God have her life mapped out? Longing took root inside her. The feeling grew until her need outweighed her fear. "God, please help me!" The words tumbled out. Tears streamed down her face. "Father, I need You."

A fist pounded against the door.

"Ruth, let's get going. I made reservations for two o'clock."

Ruth's mouth flew open. How could she have forgotten Joe?

Betsy continued to pray, her eyes tightly closed, her lips moving, her words coming in whispers.

Ruth's heart raced as she wiped the tears from her face.

"Ruth, open the door!" Her hope in God faded. Who was she kidding? She was Ruth Cleveland, unimportant loner, not Ruth, Princess of the King. She slid off the bed.

Betsy continued to pray even as Ruth's future stood a rotting door away.

~*~

Pain shot through the side of her head as the vibrations of her footsteps jarred her brain. Ruth opened the door. Joe would never leave otherwise.

"Why aren't you ready? I told you I'd pick you up." He pushed past her into the house, leaving her standing at the open door. "Get dressed." Impatience flamed his words.

"I don't feel well, I—"

"You just need some food. You look a wreck."

Betsy walked into the room. "She was hit in the head with a brick this morning and may have a concussion."

Joe glanced at Betsy, and then back to Ruth. "What's she doing here?"

"Hello to you too, Joe," Betsy took another step forward. "Ruth's in no shape to go anywhere. In fact, she shouldn't even be out of bed." If words could snarl, then Betsy's would have roared over her curled lip.

"She needs to—"

Betsy focused on Ruth, her expression stern. "Ruth, get back in bed."

Joe's eyes narrowed. "I said—"

"And I said no." Betsy's arms stiffened at her sides. "The paramedics told me to keep her quiet for the rest of the day, and I plan to do just that. I suggest you leave."

Crows clustered on the stoop of the open door.

Ruth's head hurt. She couldn't think. Pressing her palms into her eyes, she knew she was overlooking something important. Joe and Betsy, arguing. Birds at her door. The sound of her heart...no, it was the flap of bird wings! The crows were inside of her! "Get out!" She scratched at her chest. "Get them out!"

The door banged.

"Come on, honey. Let's get back into bed."

"The birds!" Ruth shrieked.

"They're outside in the yard. You're safe. God has your back."

Joe's mouth thinned. "I don't know what game you're playing, Ruth, but I'll see you tomorrow." He strode to the door and turned. "Don't forget. We're getting married on Wednesday, so get this nonsense out of the way by then." He left the house much like a whirlwind in the desert.

So, she was getting married on Wednesday. Ruth didn't remember agreeing, and yet it was the right decision, her punishment for disobeying God's law. The God that didn't know she existed still threw thunderbolts when she stepped out of line. Her daughter didn't ask to be created. Just as Ruth had protected her baby's right to be born, Ruth had to protect her child's future. If it meant marrying Joe to keep him from stripping their daughter from the only home she knew, then Ruth would do it.

She was getting married on Wednesday. Without Betsy's support, Ruth would have collapsed to the floor.

23

Monday, July 1

Ruth fingered the gash on the side of her head. Pain had dulled over the course of the day. As the work day ended, she raced up the sidewalk toward the county courthouse. Joe's announcement of their upcoming marriage bounced back and forth in her aching head, as though unsure where, in the fabric of her brain, the information fit. There had to be another way to protect her child. Mr. Charlie would know.

She walked past the house where the pots of red geraniums graced the front door. The tabby cat sat inside the window watching the crows. There were too many crows to count today. Setting her pace at a slow jog, she didn't linger in the shade of the oak like usual. When she reached the point where she could see the courthouse, instead of Mr. Charlie, Joe leaned casually against the handrail. Ruth's gut writhed like a nest of snakes. "What have you done to Mr. Charlie?" she shouted from across the street. "Where is he?"

Joe stared at her through the traffic.

At the crosswalk, a woman gripping a stroller and a man with a briefcase both glanced at her.

She really didn't care what they thought. She flew across the street and up the steps, ready for a fight.

"I didn't do anything with your friend," Joe said, grabbing her raised fists. "He didn't show up."

"So why are you standing here?" She jerked from his grasp.

He smiled. "Waiting for you."

"Wait a minute." She shook her head, hoping to clear the fog. "Mr. Charlie never came?" What had Joe said that day in his office? Get rid of him or else. Mr. Charlie should be here...

"Come on." Joe tugged her arm. "I told you he didn't show up. We have an appointment inside."

Still confused over Mr. Charlie's absence, Ruth allowed Joe to guide her toward the courthouse door. She scanned the yard. Maybe he decided to sit somewhere else—she'd told him it was too hot to stay on the steps.

"Act like a civil person, for goodness sake," Joe mumbled, as he pulled her down the hall, their footsteps echoing on the terrazzo floor.

"Hey, Mr. Ackerman. Thanks for including me."

"Ted." Joe tipped his head as they passed the young professional. Ted reminded Ruth of a younger Joe when Joe was intent on pleasing and anxious to serve. No time to wonder what Joe had included the poor guy in. Now that Joe found his success, a crust had formed over his former kindness.

Ruth struggled to keep pace with her thoughts. "Where are we going?"

Joe tucked her arm under his. "I thought you would have figured it out by now. We're getting our marriage license."

"Joe, wait...I'm not ready..." She hadn't talked to Mr. Charlie. Mr. Charlie had the answer...

Joe stopped in front of a closed office door and pulled an envelope from his jacket pocket. He looked up and down the empty hall. The scent of mint clung to his breath as he pulled her close. "I want a child." His eyes darkened. "Either you give me another one, or I'll take the one I have." He held the envelope rigid in front of her. "It makes no difference to me."

The glass-fronted door opened. "Oh, Mr. Ackerman. I was just headed for a break, but I can wait."

"Our fault, Angela. We're early."

A woman, her hair cut in a bob, beamed at Joe. "No problem." She turned to Ruth. "You must be the lucky bride." Angela led them into a room similar to the reception area in Joe's office. They stood in front of the counter while Angela continued behind it. A smudge of red lipstick smeared her teeth. "I need your birth certificates."

Ruth wanted to scream, to run, to hide. Where was this God who was supposed to be protecting her? Maybe God expected her to protect herself, but how? What about the plan for her that Mr. Charlie was so certain of? She was in trouble, and this time Nate wouldn't rescue her. "Joe, I—"

Joe smiled at Angela and gripped Ruth closer to his side. He pulled two pieces of folded paper from his inner jacket pocket and passed the documents across the counter. "The birth certificates you need."

When did Joe get a copy of her birth certificate? Things were happening too fast. She didn't know how to fight the force that swept her along. She couldn't breathe. Mr. Charlie's voice in her head said, "Be strong. Be strong."

Angela slid the marriage application toward them. Joe signed and turned the paper toward Ruth. She could refuse, couldn't she? That's what she should do. The pen shook in her hand. She stared at the red pen.

Red. With black ink. The back of her throat burned. The room spun.

Joe guided her to a chair and push her head toward her knees. "She doesn't feel well."

The pressure of his hand increased, holding her head painfully against her knees. His fingers dug into her scalp.

"I told her we could do this another day, but she was insistent."

Smothering in her own skirt, she couldn't even defend herself. Lies! How could he? Gaining strength from her anger, she pushed against his hand and straightened in the seat.

Angela offered her a paper cup of water.

If she wasn't so thirsty, she'd throw it into the smirking male face that hovered inches from hers.

"Angela, how about you bring the form around here for Ruth to sign."

The hapless woman would do whatever Joe asked. Ruth could almost hear her twitter.

Angela guided the red pen into Ruth's hand as Joe stood stiffly to the side. Ruth poised the pen above the paper. What would her life be like with a man who had an agenda of his own? There was still time to refuse…

Down the hall a baby cried.

She signed the marriage license.

~*~

Nate slid the ladders inside the mobile shed while Chet stashed the toolbox in the bed of the truck.

"Man, I thought this day would never end." Chet wiped the sweat from his forehead.

Nate yanked open the driver's door and got

inside.

"You want to talk about it?" Chet asked as he hobbled around the truck.

"You want a ride or not?" Nate started the engine. When had Ruth Cleveland gotten so far under his skin that he couldn't scratch her out? And Chet honestly thought he wanted to talk about it?

Chet lifted his good foot onto the truck's floor. "You got to get this off your chest, buddy, or you'll explode."

"Get all the way in or get out."

"Hey, man, I'm your best friend. I just want to help."

Nate stared out the windshield. Why did Ruth bother him so? He had asked God that question a hundred times since last Friday. "I don't need your help."

Chet pulled his foot from the truck and slammed the door.

Nate leaned his head against the steering wheel. He twisted the key and the hum of the engine died.

The side door opened.

Nate fell back against the seat and pressed his eyes shut. "Hey, man, I'm sorry."

"No problem. What are best buds for?"

An occasional chirp from a sparrow and the rumble of passing cars filled the void in the cab. Crows stood in silence, their presence dusting everything in black.

"Disgusting," Chet said.

Nate lifted his head. A large green and white smear dripped down the windshield.

"I thought the mayor planned to do something about the crows," Chet mumbled.

"He put out some sort of contraptions built of metal pipe and chicken wire. Even with the traps baited, the birds were too smart to get into them."

"I've never seen the crows eat. Strange, but I guess that's good for the corn."

Nate stared at the white smear that already baked dry in the sun. "How do you keep your problems from messing with your mind?"

"Maybe my mind is smaller than yours." Chet grinned. "Seriously, you have a lot going on right now with the church and…everything."

"I can't stop thinking of her."

"You got Ruth going to church. That's a start."

"Yeah, but that doesn't change the past. I mean, I'm happy she's finding God, but I don't have to marry her."

"She's a nice girl. We all make mistakes."

Nate glared out the windshield. Why had God allowed him to fall in love with someone who belonged to his cousin? God owed him…after all the work he did around the church…

"Joe was a real jerk yesterday at Ruth's house, but Betsy put him in his place."

"Betsy can do that." A smile broke Nate's angry look. "How's Ruth doing? That brick left a nasty cut."

"Betsy said Ruth was feeling better, but the knot was still huge when she left."

"Who's behind all this? Only our host home had trouble." He turned to Chet. "Doesn't that seem strange?"

"Ruth mentioned that people are angry over the roads not getting fixed."

"But angry enough to kill Mrs. Hannah? And what if that brick yesterday had hit one of the kids? What if it had been Chip instead of Ruth? That brick could have killed him."

Chet picked at his nails. "We need to defuse this anger somehow."

"You think?"

"What about fixing the roads?" Chet's face brightened. "Let's see if we can put together a crew, rent some equipment, and fill some potholes."

"Turn the other cheek?"

"Exactly!"

Nate rolled the idea around in his mind. He liked it; it was the right thing to do, even if it didn't solve any of his problems. He took a cleansing breath, enjoying the release of thinking, of tension. "I'll call Mr. Evans and see if he's willing to donate the use of his equipment."

"I'll get a price on asphalt. How about you get in touch with Pastor Clark. See if he can call the other ministers. Between us, we should be able to get a crew together for Saturday."

"Sounds good. Pull a rag out of the glove compartment, will you. I need to get that bird deposit off my windshield."

Chet handed Nate the rag. "You know, bro, you need to go home and do some serious praying. You don't have much time. According to Joe, he and Ruth are getting married on Wednesday."

The woman who stole his heart was about to marry his cousin? God, what have I done to deserve this?

24

Tuesday, July 2

Mr. Charlie was not sitting on the courthouse steps. He had not come yesterday either. Ruth gripped the metal handrail as she scanned the usual traffic in the area. A mother pushed a stroller while tugging on one of those doggie leashes with a curly-headed toddler attached to the other end. No blind, elderly man. Acid rose in her throat. Where was he?

Not knowing what else to do, she waited. Counting Friday, this was the third day Mr. Charlie had not shown; five days missing if the weekend was included. What if he was sick? Or worse?

People passed her on the steps, dashing to do the government's bidding. Across the street, the chain that secured the church reflected the late sun. Nate had painted over the graffiti twice, only to have the vandalism reappear within a day or two. When she'd asked him about the inside of the building, he just shook his head.

She glanced up and down the sidewalk, anxiously searching for Mr. Charlie's bent frame. Trying to block out distractions, she closed her eyes, listening for the thump of his cane. If only she knew his address. All this time, and she had never once invited him to her house. She had never asked where he lived, if he needed anything, if he had enough to eat. Tears filmed across her eyes. She had been so self-absorbed, talking about her life, her goals, her problems. Always wanting his advice, his listening ear.

But this time she knew—she knew—Mr. Charlie needed her. And she only had today to find him. Tomorrow she would become Joe's wife.

Music drifted from a passing car, one of the songs from house church. She remembered it because the words were strange, all about dancing on streets of gold. And then Chet had prayed for dancing hearts, ones that leaped for joy over being children of the King. If that were true, then Mr. Charlie was a prince. Surely, God loved Mr. Charlie and would protect him wherever he was.

A crow lighted on the sidewalk was soon chased away by a jogger. Two crows replaced it. Birds on the grass, more on the rooftops. White smears baked on the sidewalk. Cars were dotted with droppings. The crows held a meaning for Mr. Charlie. Every day he asked how many there were, what they were doing, if they were bothering her. She looked around and found it; the bird with the scar stood in the courthouse grass.

"Get out of here!" She kicked a sandaled foot toward the large bird. The crows were like a thousand black bodies all playing a role in some drama. Was she an actor or a spectator in this strange saga? The scarred crow must have the lead.

The longer she waited, the more her panic swelled. The more she told herself not to worry, the more convinced she became that Mr. Charlie was in trouble. What if Joe had chased Mr. Charlie away? Or told Mr. Charlie about their engagement—

Ruth stomped up the stairs to the courthouse. She chewed her lip as she moved through the wide halls. Either Joe sent Mr. Charlie away, or he didn't. In the latter case, she needed to find someone who knew where Mr. Charlie lived, which wouldn't be easy since he seemed to be ignored by passersby.

The filtered air reminded her of the coldness of the law. Everything submitted to processing, and then spit out according to a formula. Did bureaucracy have a soul? Had kindness ever existed? Perhaps someone stamped humanity on a document and filed it away, the term and its meaning never to be seen again.

Joe's secretary sat behind her desk, protected by the chest-high counter identical to the one Angela stood behind yesterday. "He's not here," the secretary said.

"When will he be back?" Joe's office door was closed. "This is important."

"I don't know. He didn't tell me."

A plastic nameplate rested on the corner of the secretary's desk. Helen. A bitter laugh formed, squelched with great effort. Really? Helen? Delilah or Sheba fit the woman better than Helen. Joe's secretary was rude, cold, protective of her boss, but otherwise uncaring. Definitely not a Helen.

Discouraged by Joe's absence, Ruth tried to think. Her mom always said she'd failed to consider the consequences. She couldn't let that happen now. "He has a cellphone. Can you call him for me?" She should have made the request an order. Now Helen could refuse, which she did.

"Do you know Mr. Charlie?" It was a longshot, but she had to try. Helen gave her a blank look. "The man who sits on the courthouse steps every day. You must have seen him. Do you know where he lives?"

Helen curled her nose. "I don't share personal information with bums."

Ruth bit her lip, which was already chewed raw. "Will you give Joe a note from me as soon as he gets back?" Ruth scanned the counter. "Can I borrow a pen?"

Helen struggled from her chair, tugged down her tight pencil skirt, and handed Ruth a pen.

Ruth looked for paper. She raised her eyebrows, beyond frustrated at the lack of cooperation. Would it hurt Helen to help her? "I can write on the back of one of these forms, I guess."

Helen delivered a piece of scrap paper and watched as Ruth wrote. No need to ask for an envelope since Helen already knew what the note said. Ruth folded the paper in half and put Joe's name on the outside. "Please don't forget." She tried to make eye contact, but Helen seemed more interested in the man walking down the hall.

"Yeah, sure. But I can't promise he'll be back today. He keeps his own schedule." Helen sauntered back to her desk.

Feeling dismissed, Ruth retreated back outside. She had waited longer than she should have for Mr. Charlie, and now the evening shadows stretched almost to the street. Cars followed on each other's bumpers; crows fluttered from place to place. Surer than ever that something had happened to Mr. Charlie, Ruth spared her lip and chewed on her fingernail. Running in circles wouldn't accomplish anything, but she needed to act. Mr. Charlie mentioned once that he lived on the edge of town. OK, start there.

Attorney Dunlap's office sat on a corner near the edge of the city. She had never walked on the adjacent road, but going left would take her out of town, while right would direct her into some of Logan's nicer neighborhoods. She'd head back to the office and go left.

Already the sky looked more gray than blue; she had to move, or be caught in a strange place after dark. Sweat dampened her blouse as she jogged back toward the office. *Please, Mr. Charlie, please be all right. I'm coming.*

~*~

She reached Mr. Dunlap's building and turned left onto Grove Drive. Both sides were lined with four-square houses spaced only feet apart. No driveways and no garages separated them. Cars were parked in yards or along the edge of the road, one tire on pavement, one on sand.

Ruth swatted at the mosquitoes settling on her arms and legs. What were the chances of getting malaria in South Carolina? Or West Nile Virus? Or Zika? Weren't they caused by mosquitoes?

As dusk approached, most of the crows moved to the trees. A few, however, lingered and kept beady eyes pointed in her direction. "The least you could do is eat some of these bugs," she mumbled, returning their black stare.

Grove ended at High Street, which was wider but less populated. To the left and down away, two houses in need of repair were separated by an overgrown field. On the right, about half a block away, a tall pole held a sign reading Family Pharmacy. The sign was unlit, but then, it wasn't quite dark yet. A couple of one-level brick buildings stood between her and pharmacy. The parking spaces in front were empty and no light spilled from the windows.

The taste of blood seeped into her mouth. She pressed her tongue against her lip and felt the sting. To the right and left nothing but decline. Should she try the houses to the left? There were no cars parked in the weeds, and the windows looked like empty sockets staring at nothing.

A middle-aged man jogged toward her, a sweatband circling his forehead and a gray cuff secured around his upper arm. Ruth held out her hand, and he stopped running but continued jogging in place. "Do you know a man named Mr. Charlie?"

"No."

"He's the blind man that sits on the courthouse steps." Desperation crept into Ruth's voice.

"Oh, yeah. I've seen him there once or twice."

"Do you know where he lives?"

"Nope. Sorry." He waited a beat longer then resumed his run.

Ruth headed toward the drug store. The sidewalk ended on Grove, forcing her to walk in the sand along the edge of the road. A car passed; the driver tooted the horn. She looked up in time to see the male driver's smile.

Maybe this wasn't such a good idea. The car went on, and she ran to the drug store. Even before reaching the parking lot she spied the boarded windows and locked doors. Taped to the window was a sign advertised a going-out-of-business sale.

A vehicle pulled to a stop in the parking lot behind her. She tightened her slumped shoulders. Had the driver of the car come back? Thoughts of what happened to women who wandered alone raced through her mind. Her mom had been right. Again. But here she was, and no one could get her out of the situation except herself. The vehicle door opened. She gripped her purse tight by the handle, prepared to whip it against the driver's body.

"Ruth?"

Her knees weakened with relief. In spite of their differences, he wouldn't hurt her. Surprised that he'd stopped at all, she turned. "Nate." Her hand sought the chain around her neck.

"What are you doing here?" He frowned. "It's good I decided to go home from work this way. This isn't the best place to be hanging out, especially alone."

"I can't find Mr. Charlie."

"And you think he's here?"

"I'm looking for his house." In her preoccupation, she had failed to notice that darkness had crept in. No street lights illuminated High Street. Not even a lightening bug blinked cheer into the desolate place.

Nate sighed. "You can't go walking around alone. Do you have an address?"

Her shoulders slumped. She didn't. Some dead-end street on the edge of town.

Nate smacked his neck. "These mosquitoes are eating me alive. Get in the truck. There's a map of the city in the door."

~*~

Nate wasn't the least bit comfortable with Ruth sitting next to him in his truck. Their easy relationship ended when Joe revealed her past. And now, with her wedding tomorrow, what was he thinking, offering his help? He started the engine and let the cool air blow in his face. He breathed deeply and held the oxygen before releasing it.

The illuminated dashboard highlighted her face, making the hollows under her cheeks seem even deeper than on Sunday. He glanced at the side of her head, wondering if the cut had healed, and then turned away. Not his problem.

"Mr. Charlie told me he lived on a dead-end street. He said there used to be other houses, but they're abandoned or torn down. He hasn't been at the courthouse in two days, maybe longer." She stared at his face. "I know you don't believe me, but he needs my help."

He should take her home, tell her to call Joe for help. But then, she didn't have a phone. She could use his. But would Joe help her? Probably not. Most likely Mr. Charlie was fine, sleeping off a binge or something.

Nate put the truck in gear and pulled onto the road. "Ruth, I…" Even in the darkness he saw hope radiate from her face. A knife stabbed deep and hard into his heart. Why did she have to be so beautiful? "The map is in the pocket by your door, but I know a couple of places that fit his description."

On Green Lane the old abandoned houses had been razed, so Nate drove to County Road Ten, farther out of town. The ruts in the pavement caused their bodies to bounce against the seatbelts like popcorn in a hot skillet.

"Might be a good place to bring the work crew from the church," Nate said as he gripped the wheel tighter.

"I can't imagine Mr. Charlie walking on this road." Ruth's head jerked back and forth, and her words came out like disassembled parts.

Nate stared at her. He couldn't help himself. Seeing her hair fly and those huge eyes of hers bulge bigger with every bump set him crazy.

Ahead of them and off the road by about two-hundred yards stood an old farmhouse with a tin roof, a big barn, and a field with more beat-up tractors than Nate had ever seen in his life. Light glowed from the downstairs windows of the house. "Looks as if someone lives there." Nate searched for the driveway among the knee-high weeds.

As he drove up the path toward the house, a collie bounded off the porch and ran toward them, barking. The yellow porch light came on and a man walked as far as the first of three wooden steps.

"I recognize him," Nate said. "He was at the picnic at my house, remember?" He turned to Ruth. "He and his wife. I haven't seen him since."

"Maybe they go to one of the other groups." She stared out the windshield.

"Not the house you wanted, is it?" Nate sensed her disappointment. "Maybe he'll know where Mr. Charlie lives."

"Chief won't hurt ya," the man called as Nate eased himself out of the truck. "He's got more bark than bite now-a-days." The man whistled. "Come on, Chief, get on up here."

Walking up the driveway, Nate held out his hand and the man took it with the hard grip of a farmer. "I met you at the picnic at my house a few weeks ago."

"Me and the missus thought we'd hear what the preachers had to say. Have to tell you though, we support the tax. Name's Harry."

"I'm Nate. Good to see you again."

"Suppose you noticed those holes in the road."

Nate rubbed a hand along his backside. "Hard to miss them."

"Well, we were hoping to have them fixed with the tax money. The city's out of funds for road work. Been out of funds for years, if you want my opinion. You come to tell me your church is going to pay their tax?"

Nate squirmed under the stare of Mr. Harry's rheumy eyes. He glanced around for a shotgun and then felt embarrassed doing so. Did he think that everyone who disagreed with the church was out to get him? "Actually, I wonder if you know where a man named Mr. Charlie lives. He's the blind guy who sits on the courthouse steps most days."

Harry scratched the top of Chief's head. "No, don't recollect I've ever met him."

"Well, I won't take up any more of your time."

When Nate reached the truck, Harry called out to him. "Had a fella stop by here a few weeks back and wanted us to join a rally against the churches." He chuckled. "Glad we turned him down. Sounds like you folks were greeted with some hog slop."

Nate tightened his jaw. The situation had become less than funny. "Did you hear that someone threw a bomb inside the Sparks' place and killed an old lady, Miss Hannah? And just last week a brick was tossed through the window and hit one of the church ladies. The brick would have killed a kid."

Mr. Harry stared toward the left, as though he suddenly needed to check out his darkened field. "Things have gotten out of hand. More's comin', I'm afraid."

Nate jerked. "What do you mean?"

"Nothing in particular. Just rumblings, you know. The kind of things you hear when you listen."

"Do you know who's responsible?" Nate gritted

his teeth. God, calm me down. I'm no good if I go blowing off at this man. "What about my church, the one on First Street? Any idea who vandalized it?"

"Don't really know. And I never saw the man before, the one that came here. Said he lived in town, though. I don't want no trouble."

"There won't be any trouble. And if you decide to give God a try, there's a phone number posted on the door of each church."

Nate started the engine before turning to Ruth. He shook his head, and she fumbled with the map.

"The next street is Howard. It's also the last one."

Howard Street was on the opposite side of town from Attorney Dunlap's office. It would take a man like Mr. Charlie over an hour to walk to the courthouse, so it seemed unlikely he lived there.

"Thanks for helping me."

"I heard you're getting married tomorrow." The words spilled out.

She hung her head. "It's something I have to do."

When she finally looked at him, his heart broke all over again. "Getting married isn't a duty, Ruth. It's something you do out of love."

"I'm marrying Joe because of love; maybe not the kind of love you want, but my kind." A crystal tear slid down her cheek.

Kicking himself for upsetting her more, Nate drove through town, past the courthouse illuminated by strategically placed spotlights, a sharp contrast to his darkened church across the street. At the edge of town, he turned right onto Garfield. Houses became less frequent, replaced by fields of corn and cotton.

Ruth glanced out the window. "What's that building?"

"Used to be a cotton mill. The place caught fire fifty some years ago, I'm not sure when exactly. It was never rebuilt."

"Mr. Charlie said something about working in a factory."

"Well, he seems old enough." The burned-out hull of the three-story brick building stood as a testimony to the past. Patchy islands of lanky stems, shining silver in the moonlight, supported seeded caps. "Kids come here and hang out. The city boards up the place, but the kids find a way in."

"Why doesn't the city tear it down?"

"Money, most likely. It costs to pull something like this down and then dispose of the brick. Another notch for the church-bashers, I guess."

Ruth shifted in her seat to better look at Nate. "Tell me about the light of Logan."

"Light of Logan? You mean a lighthouse? We're too far from the coast to have one."

"Mr. Charlie mentioned the light of Logan and then Joe asked me about it. I thought you might know what it is."

The unexpected question seemed honest enough, and yet Nate found himself peering into the dark for some unexpected surprise. "If there is something around here called the light of Logan, I have never heard of it."

"Just wondered." Ruth continued looking out the front window.

A few hundred yards further, a disturbance in the weeds on the right showed in the headlights. Lacking pavement and heavy with weeds, it took tire tracks to identify the disturbance as a road. Nate turned and stopped. The headlights illuminated empty fields that backed up to the swamp on the left and several houses in various stages of decay.

Nate blew air from pursed lips, discouraged. He had wanted to be her hero one last time. "I don't think this is it either, Ruth."

"We're close. I can feel it." For the first time since he had picked her up at the pharmacy, energy sparked from her eyes like electricity in a storm. "Drive on up a little farther. Maybe there's a house we can't see from here." She sat on the edge of her seat, gripping the front dash.

Nate pulled the truck slowly down the path, looking at each decaying structure as the headlights hit it. Good timber going to waste. Mr. Evans received at least two phone calls a month from people looking for recycled wood.

Toward the end of the road on the left, set back about fifty yards, stood a small, single-story house. The windows were dark. Weeds stretched tall against the worn siding. Passing the house, Nate drove to the end of the path where the road formed a circle. A foundation and brick chimney were all that remained of the house that once stood there.

"I can't believe he isn't here." Ruth slumped against the back of the seat. "I feel like he's so close." She rubbed her arms.

Nate circled around and started back toward the highway.

"Stop!"

Nate punched the brake, forcing both of them forward.

Ruth stared at the intact dwelling. "It has to be his!"

"Ruth," Nate murmured, "the house is dark. No

one's there."

She gave him a look that he thought only mothers gave. "Mr. Charlie is blind."

"Oh. Oh!"

Ruth jumped from the truck. She ran toward a path of trodden weeds that led from the road to the side door of the house.

He had missed seeing it.

"Mr. Charlie! Mr. Charlie, it's me, Ruth!"

Nate followed behind her and shivered. The place felt secluded, dark, and quiet. Creepy. If he believed in haunting, it would be somewhere like this. As he came closer, he could make out details of the clapboard house. At night, everything took on the shades of black and white, the house darker, the roof lighter, the windows—

"Ruth, no!" She was already half way to the house. Sprinting, he caught her by the arm. "Look!" He pointed to the house. From the road, it had not been apparent. The windows were all broken. The house had been vandalized.

"Mr. Charlie!" her scream cut through the night air. She struggled to free herself from his hand.

"Ruth. Stop. This is not the place."

Tears pooled in her eyes. "Yes, it is." She pointed. Beyond the house and barely visible in the dark was a clothesline with a row of shirts.

Even in the dark, Nate recognized one of the shirts as Mr. Charlie's. His gut filled with dread.

Ruth pulled from his grip. "I've got to help him!"

A cloud drifted across the slice of moon, cutting off the little light it had given. The darkness felt blacker than night. A northern breeze shifted to the northwest, across the back of the house, through the vacant windows and toward the path on which Nate and Ruth stood.

Nate stiffened.

Ruth covered her nose. "That smell, what is it?" She turned toward the house. "Mr. Charlie!"

As her call echoed away, a bat flitted overhead. No cars. No voices. The air that just a moment ago had brushed across them, now held its breath.

Nate grabbed her arm and blurted out, "I think it's a bear." She did not need to see what was in the house.

She stared at the dark house and then turned to the yard behind it. "There are no bears around here." Her voice quivered.

"Yes, there are. Black bears. Big ones." He glanced toward the cypress trees at the back of the house. "It's mostly swamp beyond this, until you reach the river."

"It smells like something dead." The clouds drifted, allowing the moon to reflect off her frightened eyes.

"Most likely the bear came while Mr. Charlie was away. The smell is probably the bear's catch: a coon or some other animal he hauled into the house." The words sounded like the lie they were.

"What if Mr. Charlie is in there? He could be hurt, or…"

He dreaded what he would find behind those aging walls, but no way would he let Ruth go inside. "Stay here. I'll go check." He pulled out his cellphone and flicked on the flashlight. The small beam cast a thin light on the path to the door.

"I can't stay here alone!" Ruth clutched his arm with both of her hands.

"Listen, if the bear's inside, there's a good chance he'll chase me." Nate reached into his pocket. "Take the keys to the truck. Get in and get it started. If the bear runs, I'll jump in the passenger seat and you take off. Keep the bear from turning my truck to scrap."

"What if you need help? I won't be able to hear you over the truck's engine."

"I won't need help."

She looked as though she might cry.

"OK, don't start the truck. Just get inside it and stay there."

"What if the bear chases you?"

Frustration sapped his patience. "Then the bear will make one huge dent in the side of the truck, and we'll have a great story to tell." He hissed the words between his teeth, wanting to get to the house, confirm what he suspected, and get Ruth away from this place of death.

She gripped the keys, gave a final look at the house, and bolted toward the truck.

Nate waited until the door closed behind her before he moved. The odor grew worse as he approached the house. He pulled his shirt over his nose and mouth, but it did little to stop the stench. At the side door, he turned the knob. Inside, the smell overwhelmed him. Gagging, he turned his head, thinking he might not make it more than a step past the threshold.

The darkness was complete. The light from his phone spread a thin beam. There was a flashlight in his tool kit in the bed of the truck, but if he went to get it, he wouldn't have the nerve to come back. He stepped on something thin and his foot slipped.

Feathers. Lots of them.

His light caught the edge of a table. Under the dusting of feathers lay an envelope. Written in large, block letters was Ruth Cleveland. He shivered: there must be more to the relationship between Ruth and Mr. Charlie than he knew. He picked up the envelope and stuffed it into his hip pocket.

Turning from the table, the beam landed on a body slumped in a recliner. A quick glance was enough to recognize what was left of Mr. Charlie. He ran toward the door, the nightmare glued forever in his mind's eye.

~*~

Ruth remembered another time she waited as Nate entered a house. It was her house, and he had saved her from a crow. Now he searched for a bear.

There wasn't a dead catch in Mr. Charlie's house. It was Mr. Charlie. She had failed him. The ache in her heart was complete.

Nate darted out of the house, ran a few feet, and leaned over the grasses. He hunched his shoulders and heaved.

The shirts on the line hung limp. The gray silhouettes of grass remained motionless, perhaps in respect, perhaps from the pervasive death that clung to the air. The only motion was Nate's shoulders and the sweat that dripped from Ruth's body.

She should cry. Memories of her father's death mingled with the pain of losing Mr. Charlie: policemen at the door, her mother's moan, life out of control. She had not cried then, either.

The truck door slammed. "I'm sorry, Ruth."

She should respond. Acknowledge Nate's help. Thank him. Do something. But her life was locked in a house she had never been in, and now would never enter. All that she had been, all the good parts anyway, flew away on feathered wings into the house with Mr. Charlie, and would stay with him. What was left of her, the shell, sat empty in Nate's car, breathing the scent of death that clung to him.

"We have to call the police." His words registered but were meaningless. He made the call and gave the address.

He turned to Ruth and sighed. "I can't take you home. They want to talk to both of us."

~*~

He turned on the truck engine and ran the air conditioner. The air cooled, but the smell remained, an odor that would haunt him forever. He reached for her hand, but she pulled away.

Every shadow beckoned and every sound rang with evil portent.

He rubbed his arms, trying to push away the tingling nervousness.

Ruth shifted on the seat beside him. "How did he die?"

The room, the darkness and the stench. Feathers slipping under his feet. Mr. Charlie's body. He took a few deep breaths. "He died in his recliner."

Her eyes burned with hope. "So he died quickly, in his sleep?"

"Ruth, I'm no coroner…" Never had he been more reluctant to share the truth, to spare the pain that honesty would bring. He wished he had never driven by the empty pharmacy, never found Ruth standing alone. Maybe she would have gone home, and both of them would be better off.

But eventually someone else would find Mr. Charlie's body. If more time had passed, some of the evidence might be gone…

After a lifetime of waiting, headlights streaked down the narrow road as a patrol car made its way toward them, followed by a second car, and an ambulance.

"Stay in the truck if you want." Nate opened his door and jumped out.

As Nate moved toward the patrol cars, a spotlight hit the house.

"You the person who called?" the officer asked.

"Yes, sir. We were looking for Mr. Charlie, the old man who sits…used to sit on the courthouse steps. My friend," Nate nodded toward his truck, "hadn't seen him for few days and was worried."

They walked toward the house: two police officers, the coroner, and one male and one female paramedic pulling a cart and carrying a large, red medical box. The beam from flashlights fell through empty windows lined with shards of broken glass.

The group stopped outside the open door.

Nate felt a warm hand clutch his; Ruth stood at his side, her unblinking eyes staring at the house.

The police entered, then the coroner, leaving the two paramedics outside.

Mumbled voices slipped from the open door and through the broken windows.

An owl left the safety of a tree branch, probably searching for an unwary mouse.

The paramedics murmured between themselves.

The coroner exited, nodded for the paramedics to enter. The coroner glanced at Nate and Ruth and walked through the weeds toward his car.

Ruth sprinted after him. "Wait!" She stumbled through the overgrown ground.

Nate chased after her.

The coroner stood by his car.

"How did he die?" Even in the darkness the urgency of her need-to-know was visible in her tense face.

"Are you family?"

"No, I don't think—"

"I can only give information to the family."

"But he doesn't have any family. I'm all he has."

Nate put an arm around her trembling shoulders.

The coroner's mouth formed a hard line as he glanced toward the house. "It'll take an autopsy to confirm cause of death. The results will be released to the police when available."

Ruth stared hard at the coroner. "He was in his chair…"

"Yes, but…until the autopsy is available…."

Before Ruth could ask more questions, the man got in his car and drove to the turn-around, loose gravel dinging against the sides of his car. They were still standing by the side of the road when the car passed again, on its way out of the dead-end street. Dust swirled in the reflected taillights and settled on their moist skin.

"I need to see Mr. Charlie before they take him away." Ruth's voice shook.

Nate squeezed her hand. "I wouldn't. Mr. Charlie isn't there, you know. His soul is gone. That's just the shell." Oh, please God, she can't see him. Not like this.

She slipped from his arm and headed toward the house. The paramedics pushed the cart out the side door with Mr. Charlie's body zipped inside dark plastic. "I want to see him. Please."

The paramedics glanced at each other.

A police officer walked toward Ruth. "They can't open the body bag, not until the coroner is ready to do the autopsy."

Ruth stared at the shrouded form on the cart.

"We have to maintain integrity of evidence."

Ruth jerked her head his way. "Evidence? Was he murdered?"

Nate groaned. Great, the police suspected murder. So did he, but he had hoped it was his imagination. The broken windows, the feathers, the bites on the body. Empty eye sockets…

"I'm not saying he was murdered." The officer planted his feet in a wide stance. "When anyone dies without a witness, we have to investigate."

"What about the windows?" Ruth asked.

"That will be part of the investigation." The officer's face softened. "I know you're probably the only friend the old guy had. I've seen you at the courthouse steps with him. I'll do my best to help you. But now, the two of you need to go home. Lock up and stay in your houses. We'll be in touch."

25

Wednesday, July 3, Pre-Dawn

Mr. Charlie murdered! The police all but confirmed it. Ruth didn't know how he died, but Nate knew. Something besides the smell had shaken him enough to cause him to empty his stomach.

The sky was still black when Nate took her home. He offered to stay with her, or to call Betsy, but she had declined both. After warning her to keep her doors locked, he left.

What she needed more than company was time to think. She dropped her clothes on the bathroom floor and stood under the shower. She scrubbed until her skin hurt, trying to rid herself of the the smell that seeped into her pores. By the time the water turned cold, she looked red and chaffed. Wrapping in a towel, she stepped over the soiled clothes, knowing she would never be able to wear them again.

Tears dripped down her face as she pulled out a nightshirt from the bedroom drawer. She flopped flat on the bed. Water from her hair soon soaked her pillow. Minutes passed as she stared at nothing. Eventually, truth would push its way in, but right now Mr. Charlie was gone and she was alone.

She walked to the kitchen for a glass of water. Out the window, tree limbs stretched black across the moonlit sky, making the heavens appear fractured.

Water flowed over her hand. Turning off the faucet, she set the filled glass on the counter and walked to the living room.

The cotton drapes covered the windows but failed to provide her with the usual sense of security. She checked the doors, both of them, and closed the windows in spite of the heat. Even wearing her thinnest t-shirt, she still was covered with sweat. Maybe it would be best to open the windows and doors, let fate do its thing. Life held little value. Even the furniture, so lovingly repaired and repurposed, looked tired.

She sat on the stuffed chair and pulled up her legs. Picking at the loose skin along her thumbnail, she pressed the raw tissue against her chest. Had Mr. Charlie bled? Had he suffered? Her sob cracked the silence.

Needing to move, she paced toward the kitchen. Oh, yeah, the water she forgot to drink. She took a swallow but the water hit her stomach like the weight of a truck. She emptied the glass into the sink.

Roaming the house one more time, she turned off lights as she went. In bed in the darkness, she saw Mr. Charlie's house, the waving grass and shirts on the line. The broken windows. Nate's pale face.

Heading to the bathroom, the now familiar stench greeted her. The soiled clothes remained on the floor where she'd left them. Taking a bag from under the sink, she shoved the clothes inside it. Holding the bag in front of her, she went to the back door and paused.

The police officer said to stay in the house. The plastic trash barrel wasn't that far away at the corner of the house by the neighbor. His windows were dark.

Heat lightning flickered a silent show. A whiff of

Mr. Charlie's scent reached her, and she gagged in spite of herself. She couldn't keep this reminder in her house all night. Removing the chair, she unlocked the door and opened it slightly. No footsteps pounded her way, no unexplained shadows danced across the lawn. She pulled the door wider and a night breeze ruffled her hair. She lifted her face to the wind, a treat after the closeness of the house. Gathering her courage, she took a breath and ran down the steps and turned toward the trash barrel. As she pried the top off the barrel, a gust of wind caught the plastic lid, sending it flying. Ruth raced bare-footed across the yard, danced through the garden, and found the lid pressed against the fence.

A gust of wind pushed hard against her. A door slammed.

Startled, Ruth jerked to stare at her neighbor's house. The door was closed. The windows remained dark. She crept over the grass, glancing at each shadow, tensing at the sound of leaves skittering across the grass.

She approached the porch. Her door was closed. Either the wind had caught it, or someone had entered and planned to keep her out. Her throat tightened as she stood in the middle of her yard. She sprinted to the back of the house and hugged the wood siding still warm from the day's heat.

Was someone waiting inside? The source of Saturday night's death threat? She needed to creep onto the stoop and see if the door was unlocked. Even if the knob turned in her hand, should she enter? Her teeth started to chatter.

Heat lightning grew to thick jagged streaks of power. Thunder rumbled.

Wind whipped hair into her eyes. Just moments

ago, she had been enjoying the breeze, and now the temperature dropped enough to chill her bones. She sandwiched herself between the plastic lid and the warm siding of the house.

Most likely, the wind pushed the door closed. Taking a deep breath, she fastened the lid back on the trashcan. Glancing around and seeing no one, she crept to the door and turned the handle. The knob turned, but should she chance going inside? Fearful of being seen by whoever may be inside, she jumped off the stoop and leaned tight against the wall. The rain started, soft at first, and then hard drops that bit her skin.

The day's events crashed in on her. She had planned to see Joe and challenge him about Mr. Charlie's absence. But Joe was gone for the day, so she'd wandered alone until Nate showed up. Blinking against the onslaught of rain, she wondered at Nate's rescue. Was it too much to hope he might be driving by in the middle of the night? Poor Mr. Charlie. Joe's voice echoed in her head, stop seeing him or else…

Surely, he didn't…no. She couldn't let her mind go there. He might threaten Mr. Charlie into staying away from the courthouse, but murder? Even as she denied the possibility, she questioned her own answer. What did she know about this new Joe? Everything he did surprised her: the violence, the seduction, the alcohol. Was Joe inside her house right now? He would not raise their daughter, no matter the cost.

26

Wednesday, July 3, Daytime

Expensive leather shoes made a different sound than canvas or flip-flops on the hard courthouse floor. Murmured voices: Joe and Helen—probably discussing how she pushed the woman aside and demanded to wait in his office.

"Ruth…you look awful." Joe rushed to put an arm around her shoulders.

She shrugged him off. After her episode last night outside, then searching the house with a knife in her hand and finding no one, she had laid awake waiting for dawn. She had a right to look less than glamorous. But even heartless Joseph Ackerman had to feel the ice in her eyes. "Mr. Charlie's dead, but I suppose that's no surprise to you."

"The old man's dead? How do you know?"

"I found his body last night."

"You went to his house?"

"He'd been dead for a while." She stared at him. This was her time. She would avenge Mr. Charlie.

"Well, he was old. We all die sometime." Joe walked toward his desk.

Ruth was dismissed. It was eight in the morning. They were to be married at five, and already he ignored her. But she would leave when she was ready. And she wasn't ready. "I need to know what role you had in his murder." She spit the words out.

"You think I killed him?" His face paled as he sank into the chair behind his desk. "Why would I do that?"

"Because I refused to stop seeing him. Because he was my friend, so you hated him."

"Ruth, I don't know where this delusion is coming from."

"If I find out you had anything to do with his death, so help me Joseph Ackerman, I'll kill you with my own hands."

"Not a nice thing to say to your groom on our wedding day." He stared at her with narrowed eyes. "You're in no shape to be married today."

Ruth stared wide-eyed. Did he mean to postpone the wedding?

"Ruth." His smirk frightened her, along with the fact that he wasn't upset about delaying the wedding. And it hadn't bothered him that she accused him of murder. There was something she didn't know. Life seemed to be a game for Joe. He was getting his players in a row. But for what?

"You still seeing Nate?"

"Of all the nerve! You talk one minute about marrying me, and the next you want to know if I'm seeing someone else. You destroyed my chance with Nate." Her body burned with heat. She took a few deep breaths, trying to gain control. "What do you really want, Joe?" She gripped the back of the chair.

"I want to know where Nate's church is meeting."

She lifted an eyebrow, surprised. There had to be more. "Why? You want to come?"

He shot her the now-familiar smirk. "Hardly. But at the mayor's request, part of my job is to collect the church's Sunday locations for the police. You know, so cruisers can patrol the areas. All the other groups in Logan are reporting, but I don't have anyone from Nate's group. I know you're going."

Ruth tried to think what his motive could be. He wasn't telling her the truth. "Why can't the churches report to the police department?"

"Come on, Ruth. Even you know the number of calls they get. Someone has to help take the load off."

Ruth stared at him, guarded, cautious. But what harm would there be? "This is all I have to do?" This would delay the wedding she didn't want. "For how long?"

Joe moved to the front of his desk, and Ruth waited stiffly for his advance. Instead, he leaned against the wood frame. She could see the thoughts shuffling in a hypothetical deck of cards inside his mind. Would the ace land on top?

"Ruth, there's so much out there you don't understand." His face softened. He looked more like the old Joe: eyes sparkling with excitement, the worry lines smoothing. "There is so much power, if we open ourselves to it." He looked toward the window then back to her. "I'm going places. I'll be doing big things."

"You always said that, Joe."

"No, you don't understand." He settled a hip on the desk, one foot on the floor. He stared at her with intensity. "My dad's a neurosurgeon. He's saved lives no one thought could be saved. The awards for his work cover a wall in the den. My brother—his technology corporation has gone global. I can only guess his worth right now. And me. What have I done?"

A small part of Ruth ached for the boy she knew, the not quite grown man who may have only wanted love after all.

"And then I found the power. I don't understand it all yet, but I will. And the crows—" he smiled, and this new Joseph returned. "I won't tell you, not yet, but I will do things that will make this country stand up and take notice. I want you to be a part of it."

She had no idea what he was talking about, but she sensed that it would be better not to know.

He crossed his arms over his chest. "I won't force you to marry me as long as you report the weekly location of Nate's church."

"Why is Nate's church so important to you?"

"I have my reasons. It's all part of the big picture."

"I'm holding you to your word."

"Get some rest. You look like you could use it."

~*~

She got as far as the cement steps where she used to sit with Mr. Charlie. Joe never answered her question about his involvement in Mr. Charlie's death. A sudden longing for her dead friend gripped her, and she sat on the still-cool steps.

Traffic lined Main Street, more than in the evenings. It was not yet eight thirty. She wasn't due to work until nine. The air felt balmy this early in the day. She took a deep breath, feeling free and chained at the same time. Her meeting with Joe had bought her time but had strengthened her fear that he was involved in Mr. Charlie's death. Something about his behavior seemed off, even for the new Joseph.

She hadn't planned to take her wedding day off. Now she was glad she didn't. She headed toward the crosswalk and the office where she would wait for

Attorney Dunlap. He had the answers to her child's future.

~*~

Ruth sat across from Mr. Dunlap. His office smelled of leather and old books, and with the blinds drawn, the space felt like a safe haven.

"I had a baby and gave her up for adoption. I listed the father as 'unknown' on the birth certificate."

"But you know who the father is?" Mr. Dunlap asked.

She bristled. "Of course I do." After a pause, she continued. "I was trying to save his name. He's an important person."

Mr. Dunlap scribbled notes on his yellow legal pad. She had seen notes just like those many times and had created files for them that hung in his locked cabinet. Even though most attorneys put their notes in a computer file, Mr. Dunlap still liked to do things the old-fashioned way. Her cheeks reddened as she imagined her name suspended on one of the metal arms.

"That was almost four years ago. Now the father's angry that I gave the baby up for adoption without his permission. He says he has rights to the child and," she steadied her voice, "he plans to seek custody."

Mr. Dunlap tapped the eraser end of his pencil on the desk blotter.

She swallowed. "Does he have that right? Can he claim a child that's been legally adopted by another family?"

"First of all, I don't deal with child law, so take that into consideration. But my opinion, based on what

I know, is that unless he has proof of paternity, he doesn't have any legal basis to declare himself the father."

"Paternity. That would take a blood test?"

"Yes."

Ruth sighed. A blood test was easy, but the adoptive parents would have to agree. "And what if he could prove he was the father?"

Attorney Dunlap scratched a spot on top of his head. "At the least, he can cause a great deal of trouble."

She frowned. That was not the answer she wanted to hear.

"Now, can I ask you something?"

Ruth settled back into the chair.

"Where were you Friday?"

"I, uh…I got some bad news. I was dressed and everything, but then…I'm sorry." Her shoulders slumped, and then she stiffened and looked up. "I am sorry, but I would have been worthless to you."

"I really need you here at work."

"It won't happen again."

"You look as if you didn't get much sleep last night either."

"I found my friend's body last night. Another friend and I found him—the man who used to sit on the courthouse steps, Mr. Charlie. He was the person who died."

Attorney Dunlap straightened. "Charlie Swenson?"

"I don't know his last name. I always call him Mr. Charlie."

Attorney Dunlap's stare unnerved her. Had she said something wrong? If Mr. Swenson was her Mr.

Charlie, did her boss dislike him for some reason? But he didn't seem judgmental.

"There can only be one Mr. Charlie. I didn't know he passed away." Attorney Dunlap rested his arms on the desk and leaned forward.

"We just found him last night at his house." She gripped the sides of the chair as memories of the darkness, the blown-out windows, and the smell returned. "We called the police, and they came and took his body away." Tears threatened to spill. She turned toward the curtain covered window.

"You're sure it was Mr. Swenson?"

"I didn't see him myself, but his shirts were hanging outside on the line."

"The house on Howard?"

"I don't remember the name of the street. It was dark outside, but it was the dead-end right after an old abandoned factory."

Attorney Dunlap picked up his pencil and resumed tapping. He pinched the bridge of his nose and stared at her.

Acid rose in Ruth's throat.

"I have something I need to do." He rose from his chair. "Sounds as though you had a rough night. Go home and get some rest. I expect to see you first thing in the morning."

Before she could answer, he grabbed his suit-coat from the back of the chair and walked out of the office.

Ruth sat in stunned silence. Attorney Dunlap knew Mr. Charlie. He seemed upset, or at least surprised, over Mr. Charlie's death. Her heart thumped wildly. In spite of the exhaustion, thoughts churned faster than she could process them.

~*~

After a sleepless night, Nate finally made his decision. At nine in the morning when the county courthouse officially opened, he showed up unannounced at Joe's office. The swinging half door banged against the wall as he stomped past the startled Helen and pushed his way into Joe's domain.

Joe rose from behind his desk. "If you want a fight, this is not the place." He glared at Nate.

Nate stood just inside the door. He had promised himself he would not lose control. He would not punch Joe. He would not behave in a way unbecoming to a Christian. But one look at his smug cousin with his navy suit and silver tie, and Nate wanted to jump over the desk and take him on. He took a deep breath. "I want this sham of a wedding called off."

Joe raised his eyebrows and spit out a laugh. "So you want your girlfriend back?"

Nate took a couple of steps and stopped. Joe had always been a jerk, but now his behavior defied description. "You aren't in love with Ruth. You're using her to get to me."

"You don't think I love her? I had a child with her."

Nate balled his hands into fists. "And we both know that doesn't mean a thing."

"It seemed to mean something Friday. Or was it my part that bothered you?"

Nate wanted to knock the man into tomorrow and knew he could do it. In spite of his behavior lately, he believed fighting never solved anything. He rubbed his shoulder, remembering the scuffle just days ago. "I don't know what hold you have on Ruth, but she's not jaded enough for your kind of games. Be a man, and choose an opponent who can fight back."

The phone on the desk rang. "I already called the wedding off." Joe turned away. "Joseph Ackerman speaking."

The wedding was off? As easy as that?

Something wasn't right; Nate's gut churned. He strode out of the office and into the glaring stare of the receptionist. Back in his truck, he headed toward the worksite. Pain crept into his hands, and he eased his grip on the steering wheel. A car turned in front of him and he pushed on the horn, holding it longer than necessary. "Drive the car or get off the road," he yelled through his closed window.

At the work site, half a dozen cars occupied the shady spots. Nate parked in the sun and grabbed his tool belt from the back. He glanced at the other vehicles, all of them junk. He shook his head. Why the bad attitude? The cars belonged to good workers. He should be grateful, since he would inherit them before long.

Inside the house, the sound of pounding came from the second floor. The drywall crew. Chet and Andrew, on their knees, jostled long strips of hardwood in the living area. "Looks good, guys."

Chet grinned. "About time you got to work."

Nate rubbed his jaw. "I had an errand to run."

"We're about out of flooring. I'll go to the truck and get a few more bundles." Andrew moaned as he stood. "Glad to get off my knees."

Chet remained on the floor. "You look like something the dog dragged in."

"Bad night." Nate sat on the floor beside his friend. "I found Ruth wandering alone on the west end of town last evening."

"Not a good place to be, bro."

"Ended up, she was looking for Mr. Charlie's house."

"The man who sits at the courthouse?"

"That's the one. Seems he had not shown up for a couple days, and she went to look for him. Only thing, she didn't have a clue where he lived."

"So she was going to walk the whole town?" Chet shook his head. "She must have really wanted to find him."

"We found him on old Howard Court. He'd been dead awhile if smell is any clue."

Chet grimaced. "Bummer. I bet Ruth was upset. How'd you handle that?"

Dealing with women's emotions was not Nate's strength, but he had done the best he could. He went on the wild goose chase, never expecting to find the man. But when they did, he had manned up and handled it. "I went home and showered forever. I tossed out the clothes I wore."

"What about Ruth?"

"I took her home. She was dealing better than I was. She didn't see his body."

"How's she this morning?"

Nate stiffened. "How should I know?"

"Just thought she might have been your urgent appointment."

Nate looked out the window, the view blocked by more houses. Not where he would build, but folks seemed to like it, living all bunched up together in a hive. He wasn't sure why he avoided telling Chet about his visit to Joe, getting the wedding stopped and all. But the words didn't come, and then Andrew dropped three bundles of flooring at their feet and started tearing off the paper cover.

"Back to work," Chet said.

Nate headed toward the roughed-in stairs to the upper level.

"You might want to think about why you feel so bummed, and do something about it," Chet said to Nate's retreating back. "The world isn't a perfect place."

Andrew looked at Nate. "You think the world is perfect? Want to trade trucks?"

Nate didn't bother to reply. As for his mood, if Chet had as much on his mind as he did, Chet would be bummed, too. He slammed his feet on the risers. People needed to get off his case.

The drywall crew had the task well in hand, so Nate took out his check-list. Best thing to do was keep busy. But instead of seeing his list of tasks, his mind resurrected the image of Ruth as he'd left her at her door last night. She needed a friend, and he had dumped her. His actions didn't sit well in the light of day.

27

Friday, July 5

No one worked on Thursday, since it was a holiday. Ruth refused the offer of a picnic with the Rosses and spent the time alone.

On Friday, she chose a new route to the law office, avoiding the courthouse. The walk took about ten minutes longer. She passed the newspaper office, free medical clinic, and a Hispanic market. The additional time paid off in peace of mind. Keeping track of her movements would be harder for Joe now that she didn't stop at the courthouse every day.

Since it was expected, she made her usual call to her mother but cut the conversation short. Her mom probably wondered what was wrong and most likely would worry until next month's call. But Ruth couldn't talk about Mr. Charlie or about Joe. Or Nate. The silent gaps grew uncomfortably long.

After work, she changed into old shorts and a paint-stained t-shirt, chucked her shoes, and wandered to the garden. Loneliness felt more acute today than it had over the holiday, perhaps due to the empty weekend that stretched ahead. But now, tomatoes needed to be picked and a couple of green peppers were ready. On impulse, she gathered the produce and arranged the vegetables, along with a bundle of cilantro, into a wicker basket. She dug through the bottom drawer in the bedroom, in what probably had been a dish cupboard once upon a time, and found a yellow ribbon and tied it to the base of the handle. Looping the handle over her arm, she slipped on her sandals and locked the door.

She enjoyed the walk to the Ross home, with the exception of the crows that constantly darted across the sidewalk as if intentionally irritating her. Ruth rang the bell on the front porch.

Betsy's eyes widened. "Hi," she said, clutching the door. "What are you doing here?"

Confused over the unusual welcome, Ruth held out the basket. "I thought you could use some fresh produce for supper."

Betsy continued to stare. "I'm sorry." She pulled open the door. "Come in. I'm just surprised to see you. Didn't you get married two days ago? I figured you'd be on your honeymoon."

Ruth grimaced. "Joe's announcement surprised you and me both." She followed Betsy to the kitchen, where she sat at the table.

Betsy stirred a simmering pot of spaghetti sauce. "You didn't know you were getting married on Wednesday?"

"I had no idea, and we did not get married."

Betsy dangled the spoon over the pot. "I bet that was a scene."

"Did you know Mr. Charlie died?"

"Chet told me. I'm sorry. I know the two of you were friends. You and Nate found his body?" She shook her head. "That must have been awful." Betsy brought two glasses of tea to the table.

They sat in silence.

"I always feel so comfortable here," Ruth said.

"Your house feels welcoming."

"That's funny. Nate says the same thing. Both of you are lonely, and my house probably represents home. Come as often as you like."

"Betsy, I never really thanked you for staying with me—what, twice now? I'm starting to become needy, and I don't want that."

"Forget it. Anything for a dear friend."

Footsteps patted across the floor. Chip, dressed in cartoon underwear and a green t-shirt, wandered through the kitchen door and pulled himself up on Betsy's lap. He settled against her, his sleep-filled eyes half-closed.

Betsy kissed the top of his head and brushed soft brown hair off his face. "Have a good rest, buddy?"

Chip snuggled closer.

"Miss Ruth is here. Want to say hi?"

"Is Daddy home?"

"Not yet. Uncle Nate is coming for supper, remember?"

Chip shared a lopsided smile.

Ruth gulped in surprise. She needed to leave before Nate showed up. She hadn't seen him since Tuesday night. He most likely assumed she was married, not that it mattered to him. "Thanks for the tea, and enjoy the vegetables." She hugged Betsy and gave Chip a quick kiss on his cheek. "Have fun tonight with Uncle Nate."

Chip scooted in his mother's lap. "Won't you be here, too?"

"Not this time."

"Stay," Betsy said. "I have plenty."

Memories of the last time they ate together mingled with the tempting scent of pasta sauce. She and Nate had been a couple then, sort of. Now Nate made it clear he had no romantic interest in her. Joe had said it—she was used goods. Nate had driven her all over town on Tuesday night, but every time she looked into his face, she saw pain. As much as she would love to stay, her presence would make him uncomfortable. Her absence would be payment for his kindness on Tuesday. "I have things to do tonight, but thanks anyway."

Remembering her promise, the reason she remained unmarried, Ruth forced a smile. "Betsy, where is church on Sunday? I can manage to get there if you tell me where to go." She felt like a traitor to the people who had shown her nothing but kindness. As she struggled with her guilt, she told herself there was no real harm being done. Maybe, just maybe, Joe really did have to report to the police. Either way, the promise bought her time to discover Joe's interest in Logan and his insistence on finding the light of Logan. Mr. Charlie's revelation the last time they met burned in her mind. She was the light.

Betsy hefted Chip onto her hip. "I'll pick you up for church. Nine OK?"

"Sure, but where are we headed?"

"The Carsons are hosting this week."

"Great. And where do they live?"

"Out on Patterson Street, too far for you to walk."

Ruth grinned. "All right, Mama. I'll see you at nine."

"You can't avoid Nate forever, you know."

Ruth gave her bravest smile. "Yes I can."

~*~

His knock came about eight that night. It wasn't quite dark, and the neighborhood hadn't begun its weekend revelry. Ruth opened the door and handed out a slip of paper. "You'll understand if I don't invite you in."

He took the paper and read it. "Thanks," he said as he slipped his hand inside the door. "I just want to talk."

"Joe, you promised." Her gut tightened.

Joe sighed and removed his hand. "You need to get yourself a security chain. This isn't the best neighborhood." He glanced toward the next house. "I heard some of the church people got death threats last week."

Was he probing? "The police stopped here, but nothing happened."

"I'm serious about the security chain. I can install it for you. I'll put one on the back door, too."

Did she trust him to enter her house? The bigger question, would she be able to get him out? She shifted from foot to foot, uncomfortable with the conversation. "I'm handy with tools. If you think it's that important, I can have it done before lunch."

"Ruth, I do care about you. I know our times together haven't gone well. Things are happening that you don't know about—pressures that are driving me mad."

For an instant, she stared into the face of the boy she had given her heart to, and much more.

The neighbor chose that moment to stomp out his side door and share a stream of words her mother would have used a whole bar of soap to wash out of his mouth.

"I can't stand the thought of you living nextdoor

to someone like that. Ruth, come live with me."

"And would I be any safer?" She didn't realize she was fingering the chain around her neck until Joe stared at it.

His eyes turned icy as he held up the slip of paper. "Well, thanks for the information."

"Pass it on to the police."

"It will get where it needs to go."

Ruth's hand trembled as she shut the door. Next week, she would find a way to give Joe the information over the phone, if she gave it to him at all.

28

Monday, July 8

Ruth felt more lighthearted than she had in a long time. Church had gone well yesterday, with not a hint of a problem. No vandalism. No hecklers. And with such a large house, avoiding Nate had been easy. She was getting to know some of the regulars and had a lot in common with a few of them. She actually felt a part of the group. Some parts of the sermon made more sense to her than others. She would have enjoyed discussing it with Nate. As it was, she would work through this God is Father thing on her own.

Her boss was waiting for her when she arrived at work. "Ruth, I need to see you." His stern expression was out of character.

Ruth's heart lurched. He motioned for her to sit, and he picked a half-sized sheet of blue paper off his desk. "This is a copy of Mr. Swenson's death certificate."

Mr. Swenson. It felt strange to think of Mr. Charlie as anyone other than Mr. Charlie. He probably hadn't known her last name, either. Their relationship wasn't based on personal facts but on enjoying the moment, and those moments had become precious to both of them.

Attorney Dunlap placed the document back on his desk. "The coroner has certified that Mr. Swenson did not die of natural causes."

She swallowed hard. "So someone killed Mr. Charlie?" Anger flooded her body. "The police—do they have leads?"

"Just because it isn't natural causes doesn't make it homicide."

Ruth sat, numb.

He picked up a pencil and tapped. "You may not like this. I have permission to tell you since you are as close to next of kin as we can get."

She was all Mr. Charlie had. He told her once that she was the daughter he'd never had. She steadied herself, owing it to her friend to listen to how he died.

"According to the coroner, Mr. Charlie bled to death as a result of multiple bites."

"Bites?" Had there been a bear after all? Attorney Dunlap was right; she didn't like it.

"According to the police report, the windows at the house were broken," he continued.

She knew that.

"Broken from the outside."

"How can I hate a bear?" Her voice turned sharp. "I have to hate someone!"

"A bear? Mr. Charlie was killed by the crows."

His words slammed Ruth in the chest as Mr. Charlie's death swirled around her. Images of windows shattering, the sound of bird wings, beaks he'd tried to fend off. Her throat closed. She couldn't breathe. Ruth ran from the office and out the back door. She leaned against the brick building, gulping in air as she sobbed.

Hands touched her shoulder. Kathleen Martin, Attorney Dunlap's secretary, pressed a tissue into Ruth's hand.

Mr. Dunlap stood behind Kathleen. "Does she need anything?" he murmured.

"Come back inside," Kathleen said. Kathleen's arm went around her shoulders as the woman led her through the door and into the workroom, where she settled her in a chair at the table.

Attorney Dunlap sat in the adjacent chair. He leaned across the table. "Ruth, when you're ready, I have Mr. Charlie's will. There's no rush."

"Mr. Charlie has a will?" He didn't have anything to put in the will except his dilapidated house with broken windows. It would be just like him, so on top of things, to make a will for nothing, just in case they found oil on his land.

She dried her eyes with the soggy tissue. "The crows. How could that happen?"

"The police don't know, but they're working on it. Something must have set the birds off."

"Poor Mr. Charlie." She looked at Mr. Dunlap. "I didn't know you knew him. I never saw him here." She looked out into the hall. "He never mentioned that he was here."

"He called me about a year ago. He wanted a will made but didn't think he could get to the office because of his blindness." Mr. Dunlap grinned. "Said he was afraid to cross the street. Anyway, I drove to his house one morning and took care of business. It became apparent he knew you."

Strange how an acknowledgement of their friendship made it more real. Her heart swelled with love.

"He said you glow in the dark."

She gave a blank look, and Mr. Dunlap shrugged his shoulders. "I was hoping you could explain it to me."

"Mr. Charlie said strange things sometimes."

"I have a graveside service set up for tomorrow at 10:00 AM. We'll close the office in the morning. Invite anyone who's special to you or who was a friend of Mr. Charlie's. I'm afraid I didn't know him beyond what I've told you." He paused. "About his will? I need to give you a copy."

"Maybe tomorrow?"

"Tomorrow's fine."

After he left the workroom, Ruth sat alone dabbing swollen eyes and blowing a nose that wouldn't stop dripping. She laid her head in her arms and cried for her losses: for her baby, for Nate, and for Mr. Charlie.

29

Tuesday, July 9

Myers Memorial Park once sat on the edge of town, but as Logan grew, neighborhoods expanded around it. Tombstones dotted the flat landscape. Surrounded by a black metal fence, the place of rest became a sanctuary for those who wanted to be alone with their grief. Benches waited along the narrow road that wound through the park.

A burgundy canopy shaded the site of Mr. Charlie's final home. Six folding chairs lined the front of the open grave. Betsy sat beside Ruth with Chet on the end. Kathleen sat on Ruth's other side with Mr. Dunlap beside her. One chair remained empty.

About a dozen people gathered behind the chairs, standing in silence. Most were church people. As each one gripped her hand or squeezed her shoulder, she marveled again at their love. They barely knew her, and none of them had known Mr. Charlie, yet here they were, sharing their Tuesday morning so she wouldn't have to face the day alone.

Ruth didn't hear much of Pastor Johnson's short message and prayer, and then the service was over. As Betsy led her toward their car, she noticed Nate among those still mingling. He tipped his head her way. She ached for his touch, just a hug, a chance to inhale his scent one more time, an opportunity to confirm her friendship. But he strode off toward his truck without a second glance in her direction.

"Come to the house, Ruth," Betsy murmured. "The ladies in our church group fixed some food. I thought it might be easier to have the mess at my house rather than yours."

Ruth went where the car took her, glad not to be alone. Mr. Dunlap had tried to reach her mom, but no one answered the phone at the Ackerman house.

Joe was no help, stating he didn't keep track of his parents' frequent trips.

Platters of ham and fried chicken, bowls of rice and gravy, greens, and macaroni and cheese covered the dining room table. Off to the side, Betsy set up a card table now loaded with fresh pie, bundt cakes, and banana pudding.

People milled about, chatting and laughing, pushing away the somber mood.

Betsy took Ruth's hand. "I want you to meet my mom." In the kitchen, an older replica of Betsy stood by the sink. The woman's dark brown hair and sparkling eyes matched those of her daughter. She handed Chip a glass of water. "There you go sweetheart. Drink it right here."

The boy took a couple small sips, gave the cup back to his grandma, and ran from the kitchen.

"Mom, I want you to meet my friend, Ruth. Ruth, this is my mom, Hazel Simmons."

Betsy called her a friend. Ruth's deflated heart fluttered to life.

Mrs. Simmons wiped her hands on her apron. Her hug was tight and warm, and Ruth allowed herself to be smothered by the embrace. "Betsy has told me so much about you, how you're so creative and clever."

Mrs. Simmons smiled. "I'm glad you and Betsy are friends." Her expression turned serious. "I am sorry about the death of Mr. Charlie. I didn't know him, but he must have been someone special." Hazel Simmons' hand tightened around hers in a final touch of love.

Betsy led Ruth to the table, handed her an empty paper plate, and pointed to the table. "You better eat something," she whispered, "or the ladies will be offended."

"How you holding up, Ruth?" Attorney Dunlap balanced his plate with one hand and a plastic cup of iced tea in the other.

"I'm fine. Thank you for coming. I know you made the arrangements and all, but I appreciate you and Kathleen being there with me."

"Wouldn't have felt right, otherwise. You're a valuable member of our team, you know."

Was she? It seemed strange to have him say so. Why did death cause people to share feelings that otherwise went unsaid? Maybe the reality of mortality became apparent or perhaps human frailty? Ruth offered him a thin smile.

"How about we meet at 10:00 AM on Monday morning and discuss Mr. Charlie's will? Take a few days off. You have some paid time coming."

"I'm grateful to still have a job."

"Under the circumstances, all is forgiven." He smiled and moved toward the living room.

Ruth felt a familiar touch on her shoulder, and she stiffened. She blinked away tears before turning. "I didn't know you were here." Her heart shuddered.

Nate gave a crooked grin. "Betsy would have beat me up if I didn't come."

Her shoulders slumped. It wasn't about her at all,

but fear of his best friend's wife. What did she expect of him? Here she was, for all practical purposes engaged to his cousin, and still forcing her feelings on him. Her decision had been purposefully made, but her heart still fought for the right to feel love.

Ruth dropped food on her plate, anything to fill the empty space. When she turned, Nate was gone. Chip's voice drifted from outside, so she sauntered through the back door and settled in a wicker chair under the elm tree. Chip and Chet tossed a ball back and forth. The air smelled of cut grass. Above her head, leaves shifted in the lazy breeze. Heavy with pollen, a large honeybee almost skimmed her face. She began to relax.

~*~

"Ruth?"

She jerked awake. Her heart pounded with urgency as she scanned the yard.

"Hey, it's OK," Betsy said. "I didn't mean to scare you. Everyone's gone. Do you wanted to stay awhile, or do you want me to take you home?"

"Everyone's gone?' Ruth rubbed her eyes. "I'm a poor hostess."

"You did exactly what you should have done. No one minded. They understood."

"Betsy, I can't believe the church people cooked all that food and came to the cemetery today."

"That's what friends do."

"I don't remember all this food when my dad died. I was young, so there might have been, and I don't remember."

"You didn't go to church then, did you?"

"No."

"Around here, a church cares for each other like family."

"But I'm not a member of your church."

"I'm talking about God's church."

"There's a difference?"

Betsy settled on the grass. "Some people get so busy doing for God that they forget to be quiet and love Him. Without love, church becomes more of a club." She sighed. "God wants our love. That's God's church."

"I appreciate the doing part today, but I'm ready to go home." In spite of the nap, Ruth's arms and legs felt heavy. She wanted to curl up with her blanket and stare at the ballet of shadows cast from the trees onto the living room floor.

"I'll get my car keys."

"You're the best friend I've ever had."

Betsy enveloped her in a hug. "I love you like a sister."

30

Monday, July 15

Ruth spent most of the week thinking. She thought about Mr. Charlie and what he'd meant to her. He'd said that God brought her to Logan, that she was the light of Logan and had a specific job that only she could do. Maybe Mr. Charlie was right. He'd taught her so much about being her own person. If only she could master the skill and quit letting people make decisions for her.

She thought about her baby and rested her face in the blanket she had made from pieces of her maternity clothes. Could she have raised their daughter alone? Had she been wrong to give her up for adoption? Maybe selfishness had been the real reason she had given her up after all and not lack of money.

And she thought about Nate, but she knew she needed to stop those thoughts from coming. The strength to do it resided within her. After the birth, she had denied thoughts of her baby. The loss remained acute, but time smoothed it away. If she tried, the same would happen with her memories of Nate.

But mostly she thought about Joe. He had stopped by twice to check on her, short visits to remind her of her promise to find out where church would be held. The promise was the only thing keeping her from standing in front of the justice of peace.

Church took place at the second secret location. It felt strange to be so clandestine, but then, no tomatoes or bricks were thrown at her. No manure, no flies, just blue sky and empty sidewalks. A cruiser had passed by as she'd walked to Betsy's car.

Joe had been telling the truth after all about reporting to the police department.

At seven on Monday morning, Ruth locked the house door behind her. Mr. Dunlap planned to share Mr. Charlie's will with her today. She chuckled at the thought. Mr. Charlie had a will. That was as good as Joe's secretary having the humble name of Helen.

Getting back to a normal routine gave purpose to Ruth's life that had been missing during her days off. In spite of this, a sense of impending doom seemed to walk with her. Gray clouds partially obscured the higher puffs of white. Maybe rain? The weather had been dry. The green peppers got a good soaking every night, but in spite of watering, the tomato plants leaned toward the ground, the stems bent and withered like old grannies, their productive time over. The cilantro died from heatstroke a week ago. Ruth rubbed her arms, trying to remove the tingling feeling zipping through her body. Most likely, the barometric pressure was changing.

Ruth approached Oak Street and the free clinic. As she turned the corner, a large crow flew into her; its stiff wings hit her face. She screamed. Breath hitched as she held her arms around her head. Waiting an eternity, she looked between layered arms. Crows sat thick around the closed businesses. Beady black eyes stared at her. At any moment, they could fly toward her like a swarm of angry hornets. What if they pecked her to death like they had done to poor Mr. Charlie?

The hour was early. There were no cars or people around to help her. Oak Street existed mostly as a short pass through for those going somewhere else. Besides the clinic, the street held the Hispanic Market, and a thrift shop. Several lots lay empty, weeds growing thigh-high.

Giving a moan, Ruth raced down broken sidewalks and sprinted around corners, only slowing when she reached the house with the cat. Leaning over, she clutched her aching sides. A few crows dotted the yards. One sat on the fence and cocked his head toward her. Too winded to move, she willed the crow to stay put.

As her breathing slowed, Ruth walked the remaining one hundred feet to work. No good would come of showing up in a panic. She forced a calm face, even as her insides churned.

"Hey, Ruth, it's good to have you back." Kathleen sat at her usual spot at the front desk. "It's been lonely without you."

"It's good to be back." The inbox on her desk towered with work. Sighing, she flipped the stack upside down and grabbed the first assignment.

Mr. Dunlap appeared at her door. "This a good time for you?"

Her stomach fluttered as she walked to Mr. Dunlap's office. The smell of leather reminded her of rich men, but Mr. Dunlap donated more work than he received payment for. God must be blessing him. Startled, she almost laughed. She'd thought of God! That had to be the first time she had considered God as kind.

When Mr. Dunlap pulled a paper from a manila file and handed it to her, she fought tears. Mr. Charlie's will.

"I made a copy for you. I'll retain the original for now."

Her hands shook. The knowledge that Mr. Charlie had a will surprised her, but mentioning her in it solidified their bond.

"As you can see, the will is short. Mr. Charles Swenson," he looked up and smiled. "Mr. Charlie to you and me, left his estate to you."

His estate: the house with the broken windows, weeds knee-high and worn shirts hanging on the line. The ache in her chest grew. The inheritance might amount to nothing, but Mr. Charlie cared enough to leave her everything he had.

"The estate consists of his house and any other assets he may have, and whatever remains of his small life insurance policy after paying for his burial." He shuffled papers. "At this time, that amount is $12.16." Mr. Dunlap cleared his throat and gave her a half smile. "You can buy lunch."

She swallowed hard and sought the chain around her neck. Twelve dollars wouldn't replace the windows, but she owned a house. Would she ever be able to live there, knowing what happened? "So what do I do now?"

"I'll take care of transferring the deed if you like."

"Thank you."

"You need to decide what you want to do with the place. The house won't be worth anything, but you might be able to sell the land."

Her mind stalled with indecision. She wanted to go back to the house in the daylight this time. The drive had seemed long that night with Nate, but Mr. Charlie walked it every day. Maybe after work she could make the trip. Or on Saturday.

She stood. "Thank you for everything you've done for me and for Mr. Charlie."

"I liked the old man. He had a way about him."

"Yes, he did."

Heading back to her office, she thought about Mr. Charlie's house on the dead-end road. Was it wise for her to go alone? Mr. Charlie had been killed by the crows. More than once the birds seemed aggressive when she was around. What if they attacked her?

She chewed on her lower lip. Mr. Charlie may have left her more than $12.16 and a broken-down house. He may have left her death.

~*~

"Joe, please."

Joe scowled as he sat behind his desk, his white shirtsleeves turned up to his elbows. "I just don't have time right now. The attorney said the place wasn't worth anything. Have the house pulled down and be done with it."

Ruth stiffened. "I'm going tomorrow after work, with or without you."

As Joe focused on the papers laying on his desk, Ruth gritted her teeth. What would it take to get his attention? "The crows killed Mr. Charlie. What if they kill me?"

"And your point?" He looked up and sighed.

"If I'm dead, who will tell you where church is being held?" If she didn't need help, she wouldn't have braved the horrible Ms. Helen or lowered herself to ask Joe to go with her. But the thought of being at the house alone frightened her more than either human.

"Tomorrow at 5:00 PM. Be here." He returned to his work.

Ruth left the office smiling. In twenty-four hours she would tour her house! Mr. Charlie's home. She sighed with anticipation.

~*~

Nate pulled his truck from the worksite and turned the vehicle toward town. The humidity of summer hung like a bowl over the state, and he wiped sweat off his face. At the stop sign, a passing driver sent a rude gesture in Nate's direction, and Nate ground his teeth. He knew the driver, a past employee who claimed he couldn't work with Christians. In spite of the successful workday on Saturday, the townsfolks still harbored anger toward the church. Last Friday a woman hurled insults at him while he was in the grocery store. He was wearing a t-shirt with a Christian slogan, and it made the woman raging mad. It took a call to the police to get the lady to stop cursing at him.

As he drove, at least one house on every block bore marks of vandalism. Spray paint, mangled landscaping, boarded up windows in the process of repair. Lately, Christians were fair game. And yet, the numbers on Sunday mornings continued to grow. Even with the torment, the spirit of God remained alive.

Nate's truck thumped over a hole in the road. Better focus on his driving or he'd be paying to realign the tires. He thought of the potholes they'd filled on Saturday. About halfway through the job, Mr. Harry arrived in his rusty Chevy. Uneasy, Nate watched him, not sure what the man might be up to. The old guy delivered a plate of fresh cookies from his wife and thanked them. Another workday was planned for the coming Saturday. It had taken some work to convince the maintenance folks to let them do the work, but they had finally relented, so it wasn't all bad.

Finding a parking spot downtown was easier than earlier in the summer. People avoided the heat—as well as the threat of being mugged. As he walked up the courthouse steps, his thoughts wandered to Mr. Charlie. Then he glanced at the crows gathered in the grass. Since finding Mr. Charlie's body, the birds had taken on a more sinister appearance. Was Ruth still walking to work? Maybe Joe had convinced her to quit and had offered to pay her bills. She couldn't have many expenses, living as she did, and not owning a car or a cellphone. He buried his thoughts of Ruth and entered the courthouse.

As he rounded the corner, Joe exited his office door. With no way to avoid him, Nate tipped his head toward his cousin. "Joe."

"Nate, I need to talk to you. Got a minute? We can go back into my office."

"Look, Joe, I'm kind of busy right now." Nate felt like the country cousin dressed in his t-shirt and blue jeans, dust on his work boots. Most likely, a cobweb or two clung to his hair. He didn't want to be pulled into his cousin's shiny office. Joe's looks and money never used to bother him. Suddenly he compared everything to Joe.

"I'll just take a minute. It's about Ruth."

Nate released a breath. "I can give you one minute."

Inside the privacy of his office, Joe pointed to the

large table.

The men positioned themselves across from each other.

"Want anything to drink? Water? A soda?"

"One minute, Joe. That's all you have." He tapped the toe of his boot on the floor, trying to imagine what Joe wanted to manipulate this time. As far as Ruth was concerned, the damage was done.

Joe tented his fingers. "Ruth and I have decided to postpone our marriage."

"Fine. You already told me that." Nate rose from his chair.

"Sit down. I still have thirty seconds. Ruth doesn't love me, even though I adore her. It is apparent that her heart lies somewhere else."

Nate narrowed his eyes.

"I want her to be happy, so if you have feelings for her…"

"And what do you want in return, Joe?"

Joe's eyes widened. "Me? Nothing."

"You never do anything for nothing."

"We're cousins. In spite of our differences, blood runs deep. I believe I can convince her to cancel the engagement altogether."

"What are you getting at?"

"Nothing, and my time is up. Have a good day, cousin." Joe leaned back in his chair and smiled, but the goodwill never reached his eyes.

Nate walked from the office knowing Joe was planting seeds, but for what crop? Since when did his cousin care about blood relations? It was just like Joe to toss aside his unwanted goods to the poor relatives. Did Joe really think Nate was so desperate that he would grab Ruth when Joe let her go? Nate's mind filled with thoughts, mostly about his cousin, how much he hated him, and how he needed to show Joe what he was made of.

31

Tuesday, July 16

At 4:45 PM, Ruth walked into Joe's office.

Helen planted herself behind the swinging half door and demanded she wait in the reception area. Helen left at five, after giving Ruth one final glare.

At 5:15 PM, Ruth knocked on the inner office door.

At 5:30 PM, Joe emerged, scowled, and walked toward the hall. In the car, he asked for directions to the house. "I told you to tear the place down. We'll be lucky to not get bitten by a rat." The muscles in his jaw tightened as he drove.

"I'd be more worried about crows." She never should have asked him to take her. Facing the crows alone would be better than putting up with his mood. She settled back into the white leather seat. He could only steal the pleasure of seeing her house if she allowed him to.

Maybe there would be something small she could bring home with her from Mr. Charlie's: a mug or a dish. The house and all its contents legally belonged to her. Mr. Charlie would be happy if she found something she wanted.

"I don't know why you fuss about the birds. Yes, there are a lot of them, and they make a mess, but they're just birds. It's not like they're out to destroy humanity." Joe shot a sideways glance at Ruth. "I haven't had trouble with them because I don't expect to."

"You come to work before the birds wake up in the morning, and you leave most days after most of the crows have headed back to the trees. And Mr. Charlie was killed by the crows."

"So they say. Did anyone see it happen?" Joe slowed the car. "Is this the road?" The rusted green sign still bore traces of Howard Court in white letters. Joe turned off the highway and stopped. "You expect me to take my car down there? You didn't tell me we'd need a four-wheel drive."

"It's just weeds, Joe. I've been back there. It's OK."

He inched forward. Grass scraped the underbelly of the car like fingers on the lid of a coffin.

"There it is!" The house looked worse in the daylight. She chewed on her lip. The wood siding was gray and weathered and the roof sagged more to the left than she had noticed in the dark. Still clipped to the line were the shirts.

"Do you plan on getting out?" Joe asked.

"Stay in the car. I won't be long." Suddenly, she needed to explore Mr. Charlie's home without Joe. Thankfully, Joe made no attempt to follow her.

Her pulse quickened as she walked down the weeded path. She dreaded the smell but wouldn't shy away from it. After all, the odor was part of Mr. Charlie. But as she approached the door, she smelled only pine and flowers, perhaps gardenia.

Passing the house, she walked to the back and removed the shirts from the line, folding the worn garments the best she could. Clutching the soft pile to her chest, she turned. It was time to go inside.

Neighbors in Atlanta used to tell her stories about

haunted houses—houses where someone had died inside. Ruth sensed no ill will as she stepped across the light filled doorway. Tears flooded her eyes; this was Mr. Charlie's home.

Scattered everywhere were black feathers. The sight of them angered her. Why would birds kill a man? A sudden breeze streamed through the broken windows causing the feathers to fly as though still connected to life.

Then she noticed the recliner. Sitting in the middle of the open room, the chair remained tipped back as though he still rested there. The odor of decay emanated from the stained fabric. Ignoring the smell, she rubbed her fingers across the arm before moving on.

Joe wouldn't wait forever.

Kitchen cupboards lined the back wall, the white paint worn thin. Open doors revealed empty shelves, with the exception of a small pan, a chipped white ceramic bowl and plate, and half a dozen cans of soup. A mouse-eaten bread wrapper lay on the floor. One chair stood by the metal table. A wall ran perpendicular to the kitchen and living area and formed a hall for the two small bedrooms and center bathroom. Ruth started to lay the shirts on the bed, but held them against her face instead.

Having seen enough, she pulled the door closed behind her. The wind, which had been more breeze-like when she'd entered the house, now blew in gusts. The dry grass whipped her legs. Tree limbs bent as black clouds rolled across the sky.

Joe stood along the side of the road. "Did you see this place." His suit jacket flapped around his trim body. "This is a goldmine!"

The first drops of rain fell as she reached the car.

Joe stood in the downpour, scanning the side of the road. When lightning streaked across the sky, he ran to the car, laughing as he slammed the door behind him. Water ran down his face; his navy suit soaked black. "You didn't tell me this was here. Who owns all of this land?"

"Probably the families that lived there, or maybe the city."

He grinned and thumped the steering wheel with the palm of his hand. "You're right. I bet it belongs to the city by default."

Her eyes widened. What happened in the short time she had been in Mr. Charlie's house?

"What did you drag out?" Joe asked as he started the engine.

"Mr. Charlie's shirts."

"Looks like rags."

She hugged the memories to her chest, glad she had rescued them from the line before the rain.

"I'd offer to take you to supper, but I'm not presentable."

She looked straight ahead. "I appreciate you bringing me out here."

He chuckled. "No problem with the horrible crows?"

"No problem."

They rode in silence. By the time they stopped in front of her house, the rain had slowed to a drizzle. The low sun peeked from behind parting clouds for a final farewell.

Joe put the car in park and turned toward Ruth. "I saw Nate yesterday at the courthouse."

She hid her interest as best she could. "Oh? What

is Nate up to?" And why did Joe feel it necessary to tell her this and at the end of the trip? She bit a hangnail from her thumb.

"We agreed that you should be free to date whomever you want."

She frowned and stared at him, her suspicion shouting louder than his words.

"I thought you would be more excited."

"So what about the adoption?"

"I still need to know the location of church. You keep your word, and I'll keep mine."

As easy as that? The wedding was off? Her daughter was safe? Why didn't she believe him? Joe's word was good only as long as it served his purpose. Giving him the location of Sunday services was easy enough, and she wasn't breaking a promise to the church group, not really. They needed the police protection. Something felt very wrong. The Joe she knew would never change his mind. Something had changed in his game, and she didn't have a clue what it could be.

~*~

Nate roamed his house, unsettled but not sure why. Sure, Joe's announcement yesterday that he no longer planned to marry Ruth had stuck with him. He'd almost shared the conversation with Chet but then decided not to. He loved Ruth but could never marry his cousin's castoff.

At his country home, darkness came quickly when the sun dropped behind the woods. The night hours belonged to crickets and frogs. As the rain ended, and even with the windows closed and the air conditioner running, the creatures' voices filtered through the house.

Nate stretched his arms over his head, trying to loosen the tight muscles in his neck and back. He checked to make sure lights were out and doors locked. Recently, he had taken to closing the curtains after dark even though very few cars came down his backwoods road. Before switching off the outside light, he scanned for crows. The birds should have gone to the trees hours ago, but he checked anyway.

In the darkened hallway, he tripped over the plastic bag of clothes he'd worn the night he found Mr. Charlie. Groaning, he lifted the bag and carried it to the washing machine in the nook behind the kitchen. As soon as he opened the bag, he gagged. Quickly, he loaded the clothes into the stainless steel drum. Paper crinkled as he shoved in his jeans. The envelope he had picked up off Mr. Charlie's table slid out of a pocket. He had forgotten it.

He pulled the envelope out and started the washer. He looked around for a can of room deodorizer. The envelope felt thick enough to hold a couple of pages of paper. There was something hard inside, like a key. Maybe Mr. Charlie planned to give Ruth a key to his house, but fate had interfered.

He grimaced. He credited fate for Mr. Charlie's death when God controlled all. Since childhood, he'd believed that. This slip of attitude added to his disquieting mood.

Finding an aerosol can with claims of smelling like April rain, he sprayed the letter. She had no need for a key now. The envelope might upset her, yet it belonged to her. He put the damp paper on the kitchen floor beside the door. Let it air out and he'd give it to her on Sunday.

The dip in his mattress didn't fit like it usually did; he had trouble finding sleep. During the night, he dreamed birds were pounding on his windows. Soft thumps. Crows trying to reach him.

32

Sunday, July 21

Church was at the Carters, and like the previous two Sundays, no unwanted bystanders greeted them, and the house had not been vandalized.

Ruth sighed, glad the policemen did their jobs protecting this magnificent home.

Sylvia Carter, tall, thin, and middle aged, greeted Ruth and Betsy. She led the two women through an entry that was as big as Ruth's living room, down a hall to the kitchen that looked as though it belonged in a restaurant, and finally into the family room. Each of the spaces had its own unique scent, one floral, the next more fruity, wall plug-ins wafting scent.

"I'm sorry about Mr. Charlie," Mrs. Carter said. "He must have been a special man."

Ruth tried to remember if Mrs. Carter was one of the church members who had attended the funeral, but her memory of the day remained fuzzy. "He was a good friend to me. I enjoyed his company."

Mrs. Carter moved on, and Betsy turned to Ruth. "Look at this place! Have you ever?"

The huge room held four dozen folding chairs and still felt spacious. About a dozen were already occupied.

"Look outside." Ruth stared out the floor-to-ceiling wall of glass at the back of the room where lush grass sloped downward to a small pond. Trees, carefully planted so as not to block the view, created shade against the intense South Carolina sun. Geese pruned their feathers.

"Chip will enjoy this when he gets here." Betsy glanced at her watch. "I should never have left those two men on their own." She giggled. "Every now and then Chet gets this urge to take Chip out to breakfast. His dad used to do that. I hate to guess what Chet is feeding that poor kid."

"Hey, ladies!" Mrs. Sparks entered the room. "Look at that view! I could live here." She strode to the side of the room and sat by Mrs. Miller.

"You get that yard cleaned up?" Mrs. Miller asked.

"Yes, thanks to all you folks."

Ruth and Betsy decided on two of the folding chairs—the fancy kind with padded seats—away from the window. Still able to see the view, Ruth gazed at the pond and flower beds and rose gardens. So much beauty in one place. The stress of the past few weeks began to fade.

"Chet's on his way," Betsy said, sliding her cellphone back into her purse. "So how was your week? I haven't had a chance to talk to you since last Sunday."

"Same old, which is good. Too many people still showing up at Attorney Dunlap's claiming the church caused them some calamity which they want Mr. Dunlap to fix. I'm really tired of it." Ruth stared at the serenity outside the window. "If one more person says Christians should be lynched, I think I'll do some lynching of my own!"

"Ruth!" Betsy's face scrunched in mock horror.

"I know. Mostly I keep busy typing and minding

my own business. "

Chip leaped into Betsy's lap. "Daddy gave me sugar for breakfast."

"Tattletale." Chet clumped toward them. "Get this cast off tomorrow."

"Good for you," Ruth said.

When Nate entered, Ruth hid her gasp. He looked as if he hadn't slept in days. Clean shaven, but his face was nicked along his chin and neck. To her surprise, he walked toward her.

He pulled an envelope from his jeans pocket and handed it to her. "I forgot to give this to you the other night. I found it on Mr. Charlie's table."

By the time she gathered her senses enough to thank him, he was across the room.

Another gift from Mr. Charlie. Her eyes misted and she dabbed them with a tissue. The envelope smelled of old perfume and Mr. Charlie as he had become. She ran her finger against the large block letters that spelled her name, and she imagined Mr. Charlie struggling in his blindness to write them. She tucked the envelope in her purse.

Loud music, wild and violent, with words too racy for children, blasted into the room. The volume throbbed against Ruth's body. Pictures vibrated on the walls.

Nate ran to the front of the house then returned to nod at Chet. "There's a white van in the driveway, a speaker mounted on to," he yelled. "Let's see if we can get this stopped."

Several of the men followed Nate and Chet toward the hall.

Chip slid to the floor behind Betsy's feet, one arm wound around each of her legs. Any other time, Ruth may have laughed, but fear etched his tiny face. Betsy scooped him back into her lap and pressed her hands over his ears.

Three pops, muffed by the loud drone of music.

Wanting to shove fingers in her ears, Ruth looked out the back window instead, hoping to rekindle the serenity she had found there, only to sense isolation. How close was the nearest neighbor? She couldn't remember.

The music stopped and tires squealed.

Mr. Carter ran into the family room, his shirt torn and blood dripping from his nose. "Call an ambulance!"

Betsy lifted Chip into her arms and ran toward the front of the house.

Others followed.

Ruth reached the entry and the open door.

Drops of red smeared the concrete driveway.

"Get the kids out of here!" someone shouted.

"Come on, children," Mrs. Carter called.

A dozen children drifted toward the house, faces turned to the scene in the front yard.

A man sat propped against a tree sobbing, while another tried to comfort him even as he clutched his own bleeding arm.

A loud groan came from behind Ruth, and one of the ladies pushed her way out the door.

Nate and Chet were doing CPR on a man's bloody chest.

Ruth ran toward Chet and Nate. "I know CPR. Do you need help?"

Nate, doing rescue breathing, nodded. His face was the color of cement, his shirt sleeve wet with blood.

Ruth remembered hearing the pops. "You've been shot!"

Nate slumped backward onto the grass.

Ruth assumed rescue breathing as a group of church members swarmed around Nate.

Paul Kritchner replaced Chet. Ruth watched the victim's chest rise with each rescue breath and fall when Paul compressed the man's sternum. The victim's skin was pale, but not blue. They must be getting some oxygen to his tissues.

The emergency squad pulled into the driveway. Two paramedics jumped out, the same two who had attended Mr. Charlie. They ran to where Ruth and Paul were doing CPR. The female paramedic knelt in front of Ruth and covered the man's face with a clear plastic mask, while the second paramedic checked vital signs and inserted a needle into the man's arm. While continuing CPR, they loaded the unresponsive man onto the gurney and the vehicle sped away.

Three police cruisers arrived. Another emergency squad raced into the drive.

Mr. Carter stomped toward the first officer. "What took you so long? We had young punks shooting at us. We called you an hour ago!"

Vera Kritchner touched his arm. "It was only six minutes ago, Alan. I called myself."

Alan Carter rubbed a bloody hand across the top of his head. "I'm sorry," he mumbled. "I'm sorry." He wandered away, his face downcast.

Relieved of her duties, Ruth turned toward Nate. He sat shirtless as Sarah Gardener wound gauze around his upper arm.

Ruth crouched beside them.

"He's fine," Sarah said. "He needs to go to the

emergency room and have this gash checked out."

Ruth cringed at Sarah's domineering attitude. Ownership belonged to the one who said so, apparently.

"It's just a superficial knife wound." Nate grimaced as Sarah secured the end of the gauze. "A stitch or two and some antibiotics and I'll be fine."

Chet walked from the police officers and headed to Nate. "Ready to roll, buddy?" Chet, with Betsy's help, walked Nate to the car.

Paul Kritchner's voice rumbled through the crowd. "How did those guys know where we were having church? We kept it a secret. I sure as the dickens didn't tell anyone."

Ruth's stomach tightened. She had, but then, the information went to the police. Doubt pushed her forward. She stopped in front of the police officers. "I thought you were patrolling the streets while we were having church."

The patrolman glanced up from making notes. "We were until last week when you guys decided to go underground. Now we have no idea where you all are meeting."

~*~

The last of the day's heat remained trapped inside Ruth's house. The tiny bit of breeze that blew in through the screens also brought humidity, making her even hotter. For a while, she sat on the stoop, but the mosquitoes drove her back inside.

She spread peanut butter on toasted bread and poured a glass of iced tea. Thoughts of the morning intruded. The beautiful setting and then blaring music.

Gunshots. Screams and confusion. Ruth let the memories come.

Nate, bloody and still trying to save another life until he passed out.

And Sarah Gardener leaning over Nate, bandaging his wound as though she were Florence Nightingale. The woman had her claws all over him. Ruth might not be able to have him, but Nate deserved someone better than the likes of Sarah Gardener.

Joe didn't send the church's location to law enforcement. He'd lied to her. Her mind twisted with thoughts of what he might be doing with her information, and those thoughts frightened her.

A knock sounded at the door and Ruth rushed to answer it. "Hey, Betsy. How's Nate?"

"Ten stitches and a ton of antibiotics. Grouchy, but fine." Inside, Betsy sank onto the stuffed chair. "How did you get home?"

Ruth chuckled as she called over her shoulder, "I rode in the truck between Mr. and Mrs. Kritchner. They argued the whole way about what time she called the police."

"That must have been fun."

Ruth brought two glasses of iced tea back to the living room.

"Mm. This is good." Betsy leaned her head against the back of the chair.

"How's the other man?" Ruth asked.

"Thomas Freeman. He was in surgery when I left. He isn't doing too well. His wife is there and their pastor."

They sat in silence for a moment and then Betsy pulled herself upright in the chair. "You haven't had a chance to tell me about Mr. Charlie's house. I would have gone with you."

Ruth shrugged. "I know, but it worked out. Joe drove me, and it wasn't that bad." She described the trip. "I brought home the shirts that were on the line. I can make pillows or a small blanket from them." She remembered the envelope Nate had given her that morning. With the emergency, she had forgotten it. Betsy was a friend, but even so, Ruth wanted to be alone when she read Mr. Charlie's words.

As soon as Betsy left, Ruth pulled the envelope from her purse, closed her eyes, and sighed. She ached all over again for Mr. Charlie.

Settling into the chair, Betsy had just vacated, Ruth ran her fingers under the seal and carefully pulled out three sheets of lined paper, yellowed with age, and a key. Ruth turned each page over several times, hoping to find writing. Disappointed, she turned to the key, which was smaller than a house key and had number, 112, stamped on the top. A safety deposit box, perhaps? The metal felt warm to her touch. She wiped her eyes with the back of her hand and pressed the key to her heart. Mr. Charlie had held this key. Reluctantly, she replaced the blank paper and the key in the envelope. She would show it to Mr. Dunlap in the morning.

33

Monday, July 22

Monday morning, Ruth sat behind her desk as usual but accomplished little work. Joe had lied to her, and each time she thought of his deceit, her fingers stuttered on the keyboard. Why did he need to know where the church was meeting if he never intended to report the information to the police?

Sunday night, Chet had stopped by with a fan, saying Betsy had ordered him to deliver it. He told her that the police had found the van. The driver and two passengers were in jail pending a bond hearing. Thomas Freeman was out of surgery after the surgeon removed two bullets from his chest, but he was in critical condition.

Ruth worked at the keyboard until 11:00 AM when she heard Mr. Dunlap's footsteps in the hall. Mr. Charlie's envelope felt cool in her hand as she grabbed it from her desk drawer and walked to the office next door. "May I bother you for a minute?" She held up the key and told him how she had come to have it.

Mr. Dunlap rolled it over in his hand. "It goes to a bank security box. Let me make a call for you." He settled behind his desk and pulled out the phone book. There were four banks in Logan, and on the third try, he smiled. "Yes, I'll send her over."

"Mr. Charlie has a safety deposit box at the City

Bank on Pine Street."

"Did you know about it?"

"He never mentioned it, but whatever's in it, if anything, belongs to you." Mr. Dunlap pulled out a set of keys. "I'll drive you over."

"I can walk to the bank during my lunch."

"You may have trouble gaining access since you're not technically next of kin. I'll ride shotgun for you, unless you would rather go alone?"

It took less than five minutes to reach Pine Street.

Inside the bank, Ruth showed the key to the buxom clerk named Ruby.

"Mr. Charlie passed away last week," Attorney Dunlap said, holding out the death certificate and Mr. Charlie's will. "This is Ruth Cleveland, his legal heir."

The woman's eyes widened. "Mr. Charlie died? He came in here regular, the first of every month, cashed his check and asked to see his safety deposit box. Every month, mind you." Ruby shook her head. "Mr. Charlie's gone? I'll sure miss him."

After getting approval from the supervisor, Ruby led Ruth and Mr. Dunlap into the viewing area. After securing the box, Mr. Dunlap said, "I'll wait outside for you. Let me know if you need me."

Ruth barely heard him leave. She ran a hand over the oblong metal box; whatever lay inside was her last gift from Mr. Charlie. She lifted the lid off the narrow container and gasped. Inside the box lay hundred-dollar bills all folded in half.

"Mr. Dunlap!"

Mr. Dunlap came back in and lifted the stacks of money out of the box. Resting on the bottom were seven deeds, all for Howard Circle.

Attorney Dunlap furrowed his brow. "Mr. Charlie

must have been buying the property on Howard Circle each time a site became available. Most likely he got them cheap." The attorney looked at the dates. "Some of these go back twenty years."

"What about the money? Mr. Charlie didn't have any money." None of this fit with the image she had of her friend. He dressed in worn clothes; his house was falling down around him. Why save all this money, and where did it come from?

"Let's see what we can find out from the clerk. Slip these titles into your purse. Best you leave the money here for now."

Ruby was helping another customer. When she finished, Attorney Dunlap waved her over. "You said Mr. Charlie cashed a check here every month?"

"A pension from the mill; one of the last people in town to still have one." She pinched her lips together for a second. "I guess I can tell you, you being a lawyer and all, but he got $480 a month. Had me give it to him as four one-hundred dollar bills and four twenties. Same every month. He had me pay his water and electric bill for him, asked me to fold the remaining hundreds in half before he put the money in his pocket. It always made me nervous, a blind old man wandering around with all that cash on him."

~*~

If it weren't for the anger toward Joe that sucked up all her emotional energy, Ruth would have mourned all over again for the loss of Mr. Charlie. As quitting time approached, she gathered her purse and headed toward the door, determined to do what should have been done sooner. Joe never answered her question about his role in Mr. Charlie's death, and now she feared he could be involved in the violence on Sundays. She had to confront him. Entering the reception area, Ruth ignored Helen and marched through Joe's open door.

He glanced up from his desk.

"You lied to me," she said through bared teeth.

Helen's voice came from behind Ruth. "Mr. Ackerman, I tried to stop her."

Joe waved Helen away. "It's all right. Close the door behind you, please."

"Forget the niceties, Joe. I want to know what's going on. A man from my church is in intensive care from a gunshot wound." She narrowed her eyes and took a few breaths. Mr. Charlie said to be strong, and she would be. "The police didn't know where we were meeting yesterday; you lied about reporting to them." Her chest filled with self-actualization. This was the woman she was meant to be: assured and in control. Joe would not use her again. "Why do you want to know where we meet?"

Wariness darkened his eyes. He walked from behind his desk.

Ruth was in a game of cat and mouse, only this time she stood ready. She had become the cat.

"Sit down, Ruth. You aren't making any sense."

"I will not sit, and I am making sense. Listen to me for once!" She glared at him. "Profane music blasted from a van outside the house where we were having church. Someone in the van shot one of the church members. He may die, Joe. And Nate was stabbed with a knife and had to go to the hospital."

"How is my cousin?" Joe rubbed his chin.

"Ask him yourself. Then you can explain to him

how the men in the van knew where we were."

"I told you—"

"You lied to me—don't even think about doing it again." Every muscle trembled. Her breaths came in pants as her heart thundered against her ribs. She felt so alive—so ready to beat the truth out of someone. Just give her an excuse. She balled her hands into fists.

"Ruth, I report to the police. If the message isn't passed on—"

"That's it." She held her chin high. "Forget about me telling you anything. Get your information from someone else." She turned to leave.

Joe bolted to the door and blocked her exit. His eyes grew black. "Don't be foolish, Ruth."

"Get away from the door."

"Sure. You can leave any time you want, but you need to look at something first." Joe grabbed her wrist.

"Let go of me or I'll…"

His laugh made her shiver. "You'll what? Helen won't help you." He pulled her to the desk and grabbed a legal sized envelope from the top drawer before shoving her into the chair.

Ruth knew what he held: the adoption papers for their baby. She turned away from him.

"There are pictures, Ruth. Pictures of our child."

She stared at the envelope. Pictures. How often had she wondered…?

"Not baby pictures, Ruth, pictures taken just last week. Don't you want to see what we created together?" He tore open the envelope and shoved the photo in front of her. Before she could avoid it, she had seen what he wanted her to see. At first, she sat stunned. Then the caldron boiled in her stomach. She wanted to leave, but her legs wouldn't move. "This is another one of your lies! I delivered a girl."

"Did you Ruth? Do you know that for sure?"

She tried to remember. No one told her the gender, that was agreed upon. She had seen the legs, a nurse's hands wrapped around her baby's wet body, around the chest, around the baby's bottom…

"Look at the adoption papers, Ruth." He held out the signed document. She searched hungrily for signatures, dates, hoping to find a mistake, but there was none. Her signature written in her small, sketchy text. She remembered signing the papers, the line with gender covered. Then the lawyer's signature. Last, the adoptive parents, Chester and Betsy Ross. Baby boy Cleveland became baby boy Ross.

"Now, unless you report to me as you agreed to, I will pursue parental rights."

She gathered her strength and returned his smirk with a ploy of her own, but she could barely push out the words. "I have already talked to Attorney Dunlap. You have no legal rights."

"Maybe not but wouldn't it be fun to try? You know the boy, don't you, Ruth? Ironic that our son should be raised by kids I grew up with."

Suddenly the stakes grew larger. No longer was she protecting an image of her child. Now her decisions would determine the fate of a child she knew, a child much loved and wanted. Ruth squeezed her eyes tight. *God, what am I supposed to do?* "How long do I have to keep reporting to you?"

"One more week."

"And then what? What guarantee do I have that you won't seek custody, even if I do what you ask?"

"You have to trust me."

Trust! He must be joking. He didn't deserve her

loyalty and never had. When she'd needed him the most, he'd walked out on her. A snake didn't lose his venom just because he outgrew his skin. Two things she knew for sure, her son, Chip Ross, would never be taken from his adoptive parents and forced to live with Joseph Ackerman. Second, Joseph Ackerman never kept his word.

The answer came to her, and it seemed right, even though she had no idea why. She looked him directly in the face. "This Sunday, church is at my house, and then it's over, Joe. All of this is over."

34

Sunday, July 28

Ruth avoided Betsy all week. Without a phone it wasn't hard, but normally, she would have stopped by after an evening walk or taken the family a few green peppers that refused to stop growing in spite of the heat. Instead, she spent hours at the library, hidden away until after Chip's bedtime when she knew Betsy and Chet would both stay home.

No wonder Betsy thought she had seen her before. She had, in her own son's face. All anyone had to do was look at Chip, the similarities were there: the same thin brown hair, the same slight build.

Usually, Ruth looked forward to Sunday morning, but not today. Having church at her house was stressful enough. There wasn't space inside for everyone, so the group chose to meet in her backyard in spite of the danger. The whole scenario made her antsy. Too many things could go wrong.

But the biggest hurdle for her was the fact that she would see Chip for the first time since finding out he was her son. How would she react, with this new knowledge? She dare not let her love for the boy show. The noose around her neck pulled tighter. Joe had promised: this last week, and she could stop being his snitch. But Joe lied. Why should this be any different? All week, she had wondered why she had told Joe that church was at her house. The words felt different than those she often spoke impulsively. She had felt strong saying them, as though she were the spokesman, and not the creator of the sentences. She grimaced, wondering if she had taken the last leap into a world of delusion.

Awake at 6:00 AM, showered and dressed, she sat on the couch and watched the sun push hints of orange and then pink through the mounding clouds. Wisps of hair fell into her eyes, and she flipped the stubborn strands back, only to have them slide across her face again. She got up and pulled her hair into a tight ponytail. While standing in front of the mirror, the chain around her neck caught the light. She pulled out the ring and clutched its warmth in her hand, gaining strength from knowing she had been strong once and could be again.

Dragging the kitchen table to the side yard opposite the trashcans and away from the nosy male neighbor, she then covered the grassy areas around it with blankets and finally arranged paper bags, crayons and paste on top of the table. All was ready for her children's lesson on Jacob's coat.

The Rosses arrived first. Ruth tried not to stare.

Chip held tight to his mother's hand and clutched his monkey under the other arm.

Ruth held back the whimpers that pushed from her heart. Her son!

"Ruth, you look pale," Betsy said. "Are you sick, too?" She put a motherly hand on Ruth's forehead. "I almost didn't bring Chip, but at the last minute we decided to come.

"Forcing a smile, Ruth shook her head. "I'm not sick, just hot."

"Hope the fan helped."

"Yes, thank you." Ruth gave a deep sigh. She wasn't sure how long she would be able to keep the truth of Chip's birth to herself, but the story would come out in her time and in her way, not Joe's. Now, if Logan's crazies stayed away until after church, she might live through the day.

"Sorry about making you sit outside," Ruth said to Mr. and Mrs. Dillon as they stood at the front door, gripping the frame of their folding lawn chairs.

"Not a problem," said Mrs. Dillon, a petite woman in her forties. "We'll have to do the same thing when our turn comes around." As Ruth led them through the living room, Mrs. Dillon stopped. "This is lovely. Look at this room, George—and the coffee table. It's just what I've been hunting for." She turned to Ruth. "Mind if I ask where you got it?"

Ruth gave a shy smile. "Actually, I made it."

Mrs. Dillon walked closer to the table. "Really? You made this?"

Ruth shrugged her shoulders. "It's my hobby, I guess."

"Will you make me a coffee table?"

A rotund Mr. Dillon grabbed his wife's arm. "Come on, dear. You can discuss furniture later."

In Ruth's backyard, people arranged themselves in close groups, some on chairs, some on blankets. Church had become very informal, and no one minded.

Just over the tops of the trees, the dense clouds pulled apart, forming tails at the end of their full bodies. Even if the sky cleared, the sun wouldn't reach the backyard until the afternoon. By then church would be over.

Ruth bit at her nail, jerked at every strange sound, and prepared to fend off whatever the anti-Christians planned for the day. She hoped nothing would happen. She hoped it for the people who came to worship God, and she hoped it for herself.

Mr. Freeman passed away the previous morning. Perhaps a murder charge would put fear into the troublemakers. Two dead as a result of radical behavior.

Nate walked around the side of the house just as Pastor Clark approached. "May I start?"

"Sure." A couple of months ago this would have been inconceivable—church at her house.

Nate barely glanced her way as he sat at the edge of the yard.

Betsy stood with a sleeping Chip draped over her shoulder, his brown lashes reaching pale cheeks. "Do you care if I lay him down on your bed? He didn't sleep well last night so I think he might be out for a while."

With a hesitant hand, Ruth touched Chip's back. So soft and warm. Her son, soon to be sleeping in her bed. She felt pressure in her chest as her heart swelled with love. Ruth sat down close to the craft area.

Betsy returned from the house and sat on a blanket in the grass.

Chet strummed a hymn, and people quieted.

Ruth's tension slowly began to dissolve as she anticipated the praise hymns and the peace the songs brought with them. A deep breath helped ease the tightness in her chest.

It happened fast. Six men, dressed in green camouflage and carrying rifles, rounded the opposite side of the house. Black lines ran down their faces.

They pointed their weapons at the guests.

Gasps and guttural cries came from the unsuspecting group. Then silence.

Ruth shrank in her seat, scanning each man, trying to recognize any of them.

"Hands where we can see them," one man shouted as he waved the muzzle of his gun back and forth. "Spread out," he yelled to his men.

The thin man closest to Ruth moved stiffly. He turned and faced her, his gun held at an awkward angle. Yes! Her heart leaped.

He was the young man who spoke to Joe at the courthouse the day they'd applied for their marriage license. He looked more comfortable dressed in a suit and tie than in the military garb and carrying a gun.

"I'm Pastor Clark and we are about to have a worship service." The pastor walked toward the lead gunman. "What do you want? At least let the children leave—let them go across the street. One of the ladies can—"

The blunt end of the riffle connected with the pastor's chest, followed by a loud huff. The pastor slid against the side of the house.

"I'll tell you when to talk."

Pastor Clark clutched his chest.

Horrified, Ruth grabbed tight to the sides of her chair. The plastic straps dug into her fingers.

Betsy made a mewing cry.

Ruth looked toward her and saw her friend staring at the screen door.

Chet's knuckles were white as he gripped the neck of the guitar.

Chip. He was in the bedroom, alone. So far, no one had entered the house. *Please God, keep Chip safe!*

Some of the worshippers sat with heads bowed, most likely in prayer. A toddler started to cry. The mother bounced the child in her arms as her own eyes grew round with fear. The man beside her leaned forward and placed a protective arm around them.

"Sit back or I'll sit you back."

The man gave his wife a silent look and slid his arm from her.

The sound of smashing glass came from the front. Another camouflaged man, his belly hanging out from under the olive-green t-shirt, moved along Ruth's side of the house, hitting each window with a baseball bat as he walked. The man swung the bat around the opening, removing shards of broken glass from the frame.

A primal scream rent itself from her body. "No! Stop! There's a little boy inside! Stop! Please!" She darted toward the house, and the thin young man caught her by her waist. She struggled and they fell hard onto the ground. A second man kicked her in the stomach. She doubled over, moaning.

"And now for the fun, ladies and gentlemen." The leader chuckled. Stacks of crates were carried to the backyard by another group of men. Black feathers stuck out from between the slats.

Crows!

Ruth watched in horror as the cages were held to the open windows and the crows were released into the house. There must have been six or more crows in each crate. When one crate was empty, another was brought to each broken window. How had they trapped all these birds when the mayor's plan to capture them failed?

With guns pointed their direction and smirks

lining the gunmen's faces, no one spoke.

Ruth sat in frozen silence listening to the sound of wings beating the air inside the house. She thought the birds would fly back out another window, but instead they seemed to be trapped inside, their wings thumping and beating.

Two soldiers stood with guns pointed at Chet and Betsy. Chet's face had gone white. Several women clung to Betsy, who struggled to stand.

Something crashed. A lamp perhaps? More crashes.

"Enough!"

In the haze of pain, Ruth heard his voice. She struggled to sit. "Joe, stop them! Chip is in the house!" He turned toward her, and she stared, horrified, at venomous eyes. *Find courage! Find courage!* "Joe! Listen to me! Our son is in the house with those crows! Our son, Joe, Chip Ross!"

Joe lifted his arms over his head. Crows flew from the trees and the sky turned black with their bodies.

People screamed, throwing arms over their heads or climbing under blankets and chairs.

Ruth stared, her breath caught in her throat. Was she to watch her friends be eaten to death? Her voice barely sounded through her constricted throat. "Joe, stop this!"

He turned to her. This time his expression was empty: empty of humanity.

Oh, dear God, help us!

Betsy began to scream. Faces turned her way.

Nate used the distraction to leap and pull Joe to the ground.

Joe grabbed Nate's neck.

Crows flapped overhead.

Screaming voices, chairs upturning. Gunshots.

The screen door opened and Chip walked out, monkey still clutched in his arms, Ruth's maternity-shirt blanket draped over his shoulders. "Mommy?"

Joe stared at Chip. Either by distraction or intention, he released Nate from his grip.

The crows took to the sky, leaving behind feathers, confusion and fear.

Ruth held her breath.

Joe's blank expression never changed. Not when he was about to kill his cousin, and not now, while staring down at his son.

Nate rolled to his side and clutched his neck with his hand.

Soldiers continued to stand, but guns slipped from position as they watched their boss.

Betsy and Chet bolted to their son.

Joe snapped his fingers. He and his men walked out of the yard.

Betsy wrapped her arms around Chip and sobbed loudly as Chet held them both.

People untangled themselves from twisted chairs and knotted blankets.

"Call the police!" someone finally yelled.

"Already done." The voice came from across the drive. The neighbor stood at his door, cellphone in hand. "They should be here any minute." He looked at Ruth and smiled. "Hey!" Then he walked back into his house.

"How dare you? Did you think this was a joke?"

Ruth turned.

"You're Chip's mother?" Heat streamed from Betsy's rigid body. Her nostrils flared as she held tight to Chip.

None of Ruth's past pain compared to the agony she felt as she stared into Betsy's face. She approached her friend, hands out. "I never meant for you to find out, especially not this way."

"Get away from me!" Betsy screamed. "I don't ever want to see you again!" Clutching Chip in her arms, Betsy ran toward the front of the house.

Chet gave a questioning glance and followed.

~*~

By now, the church people were familiar with the routine and they settled in chairs, knowing it would be awhile before the police would allow them to leave.

"Ma'am," one of the officers said to Ruth. "Is this your house?"

"Yes, it's my house. My messed-up life, my rotten luck. Yes, it's all mine." She had told Joe where church was to be held. The words that she'd believed had been given to her to speak, what a joke. Just when she had begun to believe in the goodness of God. God didn't care about her, or her town, or these people. She was to blame for all her own problems. Mr. Charlie might think some grand plan was directing her life, but he was wrong. She directed her own fate, and she was making her own mistakes. But this time, she had jeopardized the life of her own child.

"You need to come inside with me."

"And let the crows peck me to death like they did poor Mr. Charlie?" Her eyes widened.

The crows were still in her house, and they had been there when Chip was asleep on her bed. Chip walked out of the house, through the frenzy of birds just fine. Not a peck on him that she had seen. Not traumatized. He had behaved just like any kid waking up from a nap.

She rubbed her temples, trying to make sense of it. Her house must be a wreck. She heard the crashing herself. And yet, Chip survived. More than survived. Swallowing a huge lump, she followed the officer through her back door.

Dishes lay broken on the floor. The living room lamp was in three parts; gray stuffing from the chairs and couch covered the rug. She sobbed when she saw the coffee table, torn apart, slab clawed from slab.

Ruth expected the damage, but not the crows.

Dead birds lay everywhere. Everywhere except her bed with its boy-sized dent still visible in the middle. The window above the bed was broken the same as all the other windows, but not a shard of glass sparkled on the covers.

She walked back outside, homeless and confused, to find Nate waiting.

"Chip is your son?"

"Yes."

History repeated itself as he strode from the yard, leaving her alone in her misery.

~*~

Ruth stood where her garden had been, the remaining pepper plants trampled flat. Everyone had gone. All the first-floor windows were broken. Inside, dead crows lay thick. The police were finished—she could clean up now. That's what they'd told her. She could clean up now. Instead, she walked away.

She found herself at the First Street Church and slumped against the wall on the empty front porch.

Two cars drove down Main Street and then nothing. Across the street, the courthouse slept. No one disturbed the heavy glass doors. No one sat on the cement steps waiting for her. Joe's window remained dark. If he had gone there after destroying her life, he hadn't turned on any lights; but it was Sunday, after all.

A shadow covered her. "I went to your house, but you weren't there." Pastor Clark sat beside Ruth on the porch landing, red graffiti showing between them.

"You knew I would come here?" She hadn't known it herself, but it seemed like the place to be.

"I was on my way home."

"I've made a mess of everything." She squeezed her burning eyes.

"Want to tell me about it?"

The words rolled as if she had been waiting all her life for this moment. She talked about Joe in Atlanta, the pregnancy, the money for the abortion, and about the adoption. She shared her belief that the baby was a girl, and that she had just learned Chip's identity. She agreed to marry Joe to save Chip and then sold out the church to keep from marrying him.

Love had always been her problem. She refused to tell her mom about the pregnancy for fear of losing her mom's affection. Her ache for love as a teen ultimately cost the love she really wanted. More than that, love for a child that was never hers caused her to betray her church and lose Betsy's friendship.

As she stared across the street at the empty courthouse steps, she talked about Mr. Charlie, how he called her the light of Logan. She counted the crows for him. He had been her only friend and the crows had killed him. For some reason, it felt like her fault.

But the crows had not harmed Chip. In fact, all the crows in her house died. The birds could have flown out the windows, but they didn't. Instead, they'd died. Dropped all over her house. He could go see them if he wanted to. The birds could rot there for all she cared. She wasn't going back.

"What are you going to do?"

She thought of Mr. Charlie's place. There was the money, but she didn't know how much. She couldn't stay in Logan where everyone hated her. "I'll find work somewhere else."

"So you're running away?"

"No, I'm not running away. People who run away have something to run from. I have nothing. I'm just leaving."

"God brought you here for a reason, Ruth."

"I am so tired of hearing that!" She covered her head with her arms.

"Why did you come to the church?"

"No reason. I just ended up here." Her words rose, muffled between her arms.

"Maybe you wanted to be close to God and thought you could find Him here?"

She sniffed and nodded toward the locked doors. "I don't think God hangs out here anymore."

Pastor Clark's laugh surprised her. "You may be right about that. But do something for me before you leave town."

She eyed him cautiously.

"Tell Nate your story just as you told me."

She gave a loud huff. "He already knows my story."

"I don't think he knows all of it. Will you do that for me?"

A car drove by, slowed, and turned right. No one walked on the sidewalk.

No crows dotted the yard….no crows.

Her back stiffened. "Where are the crows?" They'd brought trouble and now their absence would bring more, she was sure of it. Her heart raced as she scanned for the black feathered birds that plagued the town.

"I wondered if you'd noticed the crows were gone. I have my own ideas."

She stared at him wide-eyed.

"Come to the house." He stood and reached out his hand to help her up. "You haven't had lunch and neither have I. We can eat while I talk. And then you can tell your story to Nate."

~*~

Pot roast and mashed potatoes. Ruth didn't think she could eat a bite but found herself stuffing food in as fast as she could move her fork. Jennifer Clark, Pastor Clark's wife, was exactly how Ruth imagined her: a delightful woman with big blue eyes and a tiny face. They had never met because Mrs. Clark attended a different group on Sundays rather than moving from house to house with her husband. All through the meal, she shared funny stories of growing up in Kansas, living on a farm, and raising animals. It sounded very foreign to Ruth. Maybe that's where she should go—to Kansas.

When the meal was over, Jennifer turned to her husband. "You two have things to discuss. I'll do the dishes." She kissed her husband on the cheek and carried the plates to the kitchen.

Pastor Clark stood. "Let's move to the living room. I want you to hear my story."

The living room looked as 1980s as the kitchen, with solid oak side tables and a green velour couch; old but sturdy, not put-together like hers. The room had been loved over time: worn in all the right places. The wide front windows let in dappled light that gave warmth to the space while the heavy oak door with its etched glass circular window lent a touch of elegance.

Now that the moment had come, Ruth felt hesitant to hear what Pastor Clark had to say about the crows.

Pastor Clark motioned for Ruth to sit on the couch. He settled in a leather recliner that held permanent indents of his body. Dishes rattled in the kitchen. The brass clock on the wall made ticking sounds that reminded Ruth of the tapping of fingernails.

"I grew up in Haiti where my parents were missionaries."

Nate had told her the story.

"In Haiti, the main religion is Vodou, or Voodoo as it is pronounced in the United States. Voodoo is a religious cult where the followers believe a spirit can move from one living thing to another living thing. In Voodoo, various services are performed for the gods in return for favors, such as wealth, long life, and so on."

Ruth squirmed, feeling uncomfortable. She wasn't sure why she felt fearful, and that made the tension worse.

"I had a chat with your Mr. Joseph shortly after he came to town. I knew him as a child; and when I spotted him a few weeks back at Jerry's Diner, I struck up a conversation. He was quite willing to talk, and I learned he had ambitions that were, in my opinion, beyond his abilities."

"Joe comes from a rich family."

"And therein lies the problem. He has a need to keep up with his parents, who are both overachievers. He created a vision for his life, and after graduate school, when he knew his vision was not happening, he became desperate."

"He's capable of doing anything. He's really smart."

"No, Ruth, he's average. But he's rich, and that confuses people. I don't know how he ended up in the occult; he didn't tell me that part. Simply in passing, he mentioned that he knew a source of power greater than the God I worshipped. I felt as though he was baiting me."

The doorbell rang.

"Excuse me for just a minute, Ruth." Pastor Clark walked to the front door.

"Hey, I got your message. What do you need?"

Nate! Ruth jumped from the couch. She needed to leave—now!

Nate's pleasant expression turned hard. "You didn't tell me she was here."

"I haven't finished telling Ruth my theory about the crows. You should hear this, too. And Ruth has some things to share as well."

Nate's eyes became bitter orbs. "Lying to me is bad enough. Deceiving my best friends is worse."

"Nate, you have it all wrong. Please—let me explain." How many times could her heart break before it stopped beating?

"I want both of you to sit down." Pastor Clark put a hand on Nate's shoulder and guided him to the couch.

After a stern stare from the pastor, Ruth returned

to her seat. She wanted to run as fast as she could, but the expression on the pastor's face told her she would never get out of the house.

"Jennifer!" he called over his shoulder.

Mrs. Clark walked into the living room, wiping her hands on a dishcloth. Unexpected guests with confrontational issues must not be unusual at their home as her expression remained soft even though tension blanketed the room.

"I want you to sit in on our discussion, Jenn. You might have something to add." A moment of eye contact passed between the two before Jennifer sat in the remaining chair.

Ruth positioned herself rigidly on the edge of the couch, too aware of Nate on the other end. Heat flamed from her body. She could still walk out—they weren't about to hold her prisoner. At least she didn't think so, but the day had been full of surprises. Emotionally, her tank sat on empty, just like her car when she'd entered Logan the first time. She had nothing to offer when the motor shuddered to a stop, and she had nothing to give now.

Pastor Clark cleared his throat and looked at Nate, who stared back with lips drawn tight. "I was in the process of sharing why I think Joe may be dabbling in the occult."

Nate blinked.

"I didn't give it any thought until this morning. But now, I believe Chip may be in danger."

Nate glared at Ruth.

"It's not her fault, Nate, but she is the answer. We can't save Chip without her."

Ruth's eyes widened. "I don't have any answers. I wish I did!" Nerves that were stretched beyond breaking pulled even tighter. Her son, in danger? She looked squarely at Nate. "I love Chip, please believe me. I would never do anything to hurt him. In fact, I've been trying to keep him safe!"

His sneer tore at her heart. "You love him so much you want to take him from the only parents he's ever known?"

"No! You have it wrong!"

Nate stomped toward the door, his heavy footsteps muffled in the brown carpet.

"Sit down!" The pastor's sharp voice cut into the tension.

Ruth jumped, and Nate stopped but didn't turn.

"I have known you all of your life, Nate Bishop, and a finer man can't be found. Nor can one more bull-headed. Now sit on the couch, and don't get up again."

Nate positioned himself as far from Ruth as the couch would permit.

"Now, then, do you want to do something to help Chip, or would the two of you rather fight and feel sorry for yourselves?"

Ruth stared at the carpet. Lunch churned in her stomach, and she regretted eating the second helping of mashed potatoes and gravy.

"We all love Chip," Pastor Clark said. "I remember the day Betsy and Chet got the call that a newborn was waiting for them at Social Services. They beamed ear-to-ear as they fumbled around, trying to figure out how to install the car seat. Then they packed enough diapers and outfits for a whole nursery of babies, and drove off."

Ruth listened, his story feeding the emptiness inside her. Every word stroked an ache that grew smaller. She drank in his voice and held out her cup for more.

"You remember, Nate. Chet took a week off work; and a good thing because I don't think he, nor Betsy, slept for several days.

"The whole church heard about Chip's first tooth," Jennifer said, smiling.

"What I remember most, though," Pastor Clark said, "was Betsy's first words to me when I went to visit a couple days after they brought Chip home." He looked hard at Ruth. "Betsy told me that she didn't know the circumstances that separated the birth-mother from her child, but God knew, and she would pray for that woman every day until she died."

Tears ran down Ruth's cheeks. A sob escaped. Betsy had told her the same thing. "I didn't mean to deceive her." She turned to Nate. "I thought my baby was a girl. I just found out a few days ago myself, and…"

He turned his head away from her.

"Wait," Jennifer said. "Ruth is Chip's biological mother?"

"Ruth, tell Nate and Jennifer your story."

"I don't want to hear it." Nate's jaw tightened.

"If you love Chip you will listen, because it may be the only thing that can save the boy."

Ruth stammered. She began to talk, and shared her thoughts as much as she had done with Pastor Clark at the church. She began with the death of her father, her mother's aloof behavior and need to work to support them, and the sudden attention of a handsome young man.

Nate stared at the wall, his face a hard mask of anger.

She shared how Joe gave her money for an

abortion and then rejected all her efforts to contact him. Nate's stern expression cracked when Ruth shared how she refused to abort the baby, and with no way to support a child, had made the tough decision to give the infant up for adoption. Her appearance in Logan was old news, as was Joe's arrival in town. When she shared Joe's intent to find the baby and seek custody, Nate looked at her for the first time.

"I believed my baby was with a loving family. It would be wrong to take her from parents who loved her, and give her to Joe, who only wanted a trophy." She hesitated before continuing. "I had a friend who killed herself because she was taken from the home she loved and forced to live with her mother, who didn't really want her. I couldn't let that happen to my baby.

"Joe wants a child. Either he'll take the one we had, or I can give him another." She pulled the ring out from under her shirt and held it up to Nate. "This ring represents the vow of secondary chastity I made after I delivered. The only way I can protect our first child is to give Joe another heir. I can only do that if I marry him and then raise the child myself." Every cell in her body cried for Nate to understand. "You told me no one should marry except for love, and I responded that I was marrying for love, just not how you thought. I love the baby I never got to hold. I love her enough to do everything in my power to protect her. Only now I find out my baby was a boy, and he is Chip. It becomes even more important to keep Joe from him."

"Joe told me you called the wedding off. That doesn't sound like you wanted to save Chip."

"We had the marriage license. And then, after Mr. Charlie died, Joe changed his mind. But instead of marrying him, he had a new condition to keep him away from our child. I had to tell him where the church was meeting. He swore that he needed to know so he could inform the police. The day I confronted him with his lie was the day he showed me Chip's picture and the signed adoption papers. He told me this Sunday would be the last I would have to report. I have no idea what happened today, why he acted so weird, why the crows died..."

"The crows died?" Mrs. Clark asked.

"They destroyed the inside of my house, but they never touched Chip."

The doorbell sounded over and over.

Jennifer glanced at her husband.

He shrugged his shoulders and again pulled himself out of the recliner.

Betsy, her face mottled and streaked with tears, raced to Ruth. "Where is he? Where did you take him?" She pounded on Ruth's chest, terror jetting out of her eyes.

Ruth stood in shock, trying to fend off her friend's attack without hitting back.

Chet entered behind Betsy. "Chip is missing." He groaned and put his hands over his face.

Pastor Clark pulled the distraught woman away from Ruth. "Calm down!" he commanded.

"She took my son!" Betsy's eyes were wide with hysteria.

"Chet, get hold of your wife."

Chet wrapped his arms around Betsy's shoulders.

Pastor Clark's voice calmed. "Why do you think Ruth took Chip?"

"We put him down for his nap," Chet said, his words tight, "and when he didn't get up at his usual time, I went to check on him. He wasn't in his bed."

"She took him!" Betsy flailed her arms toward Ruth, but Chet held her tight. "We searched the house and the yard. We can't find him anywhere!"

Pastor Clark rubbed the back of his neck. "So you came here?"

"She wasn't home," Chet said, nodding toward Ruth. "We thought you might know where we could find her."

"Please," Betsy said, "just give him back."

"Betsy, I don't have him!" Ruth turned toward the Clarks. "I didn't take him."

"I believe her," Nate said, his expression hard. "But I can guess who did." He glanced at Ruth.

"Joe." Fear mounted.

"The broken engagement. It all makes sense now." Pastor Clark looked at Nate. "Where would Joe take the boy that would hurt you the most?"

"The church!"

Pastor Clark moved toward the door. "It's faster to cut through yards than to drive."

Running through four backyards and across two streets, they staggered into the edge of the church's back property.

"Wait!" Pastor Clark hissed as Chet started to run across the overgrown yard. "If Joe's in the building, we don't want to confront him as a mass. Joe isn't himself. I think he's—"

Jennifer reached the group, holding her side and panting. "Shouldn't we call the police?"

"Let's see if we can find how he got in first," Nate said. "I'll circle around to the right. Ruth, you go around the building to the left. Check for broken windows or doors with the chains removed."

Ruth stood in surprise but grateful to be included.

"I should go," Chet said.

"No, I agree with Nate." Pastor Clark's expression was grim. "I need you here with Betsy."

Nate gave Ruth a nod, and she dashed across the yard to the left of the church.

"Anything?" Nate asked in a murmur as they met in the front.

"Nothing. All the windows are intact, and the doors are still chained."

They sprinted back to the waiting group. "The church is undisturbed. No windows or doors are broken," said Nate. "I don't know how else he could have gotten in."

As Betsy put her hands over her face and sobbed, Jennifer wrapped an arm around her. "We'll find him, Betsy. God knows where Chip is, and He'll protect him until we get there."

Betsy glared at Ruth, her face smeared with wetness. "You know where Joe took him. The two of you are in this together!"

"Betsy, Ruth tried to keep Joe from taking Chip away from you." Nate rubbed Betsy's hand. "She was willing to marry Joe to keep the boy safe. Why would she kidnap Chip when she tried to protect him?"

"I'm calling the police," Jennifer said, pulling her cellphone from her pocket.

"Where can he be?" Chet searched the grassy area as though expecting Chip to come flying around a corner dragging a T-ball bat and wearing a big grin.

Ruth tried to dig into Joe's mind, to think where he might hide a small boy. Not the office. Certainly not a hotel room. Chet had already checked her house, and Nate had been at his. It came to her as clearly as if she had known all along. "I know where he is!"

35

Sunday Evening, July 28

The late afternoon sun cast long shadows through the trees.

As soon as they turned onto Howard Court, Nate and Chet pulled to the side of the road and parked, the house not visible through the trees and weeds.

As the others tumbled onto the dusty road, Nate motioned for them to come closer. "I'll run and check the place out," he murmured.

Betsy grabbed Nate's arm. "No, I'm his mother. I need to go—"

"Betsy, think about it," Nate whispered. "If Joe is at Mr. Charlie's house, he isn't alone."

Jennifer remained close to Betsy, the place Ruth longed to be to comfort her friend and at the same time find comfort. But anger flowed so tightly around Betsy that Ruth could never reach her.

"Let Nate go alone," Jennifer murmured. "He's the fastest, and he's been to the house before. If he sees anything, he'll run back and tell us. And then I can update the police."

"I thought you called them?" Betsy asked.

"You all were running back to the house for cars. I told them I would call back. I didn't know where we were going."

The tall grasses along the edge of the road stood

like knives, hard and thick, protecting their right to exist. Nate slipped in among them, the sharp edges making scraping sounds on his jeans as he ran.

Ruth tried to remember the location of collapsed houses that might provide hiding places for Nate. Mr. Charlie's house stood in the middle of a clearing. The swamp lay behind it. From the road there was nothing to shield a person's approach.

Half a dozen black crows landed on the road.

"The crows are back."

Pastor Clark put an arm around Ruth's shoulders. "They never left, only moved to a different place. They're here with Joe. It will be all right. Wait and see."

His warmth comforted her. "I feel so helpless."

"That's how we're supposed to feel."

She choked out a laugh. "We're supposed to feel helpless? How will being helpless do Chip any good?"

"God already has it figured out."

Ruth admired his faith, but wasn't sure she liked his attitude. They should make plans, develop a strategy for getting into the house, or at least for getting close to it. Jennifer should be placing that call. She picked at the thumb that had already bled once that day. "Joe said something about finding power." Ruth continued to stare at the last point she had seen Nate. "Do you think Joe meant his soldiers?"

Pastor Clark stared down the deserted road. "Joe said the same thing to me. I thought he was baiting me, looking for a fight over religion. But after this morning, my thinking has changed."

"Do you know anything about the light of Logan? Mr. Charlie mentioned it."

Pastor Clark turned to her. "Unless I'm wrong, we will soon find out."

The way he searched her face made Ruth shiver. He said she was the answer, but she had a feeling she wasn't going to like the solution.

A cloud of crows swirled high overhead.

The grass rustled. Nate reappeared, breathing hard.

Chet raced to his side, and Ruth followed, unsure of her welcome but not caring. She had to know what they were up against at Mr. Charlie's.

"There are ten cars and twice that many trucks parked along the side of the house. I didn't see Joe or Chip, but a dozen or so guys, the same ones from this morning, were wandering around the yard in the front. I can only guess there are more in the back."

The situation was hopeless. There were too many men and no way to approach the house unseen.

Nate and Chet huddled until the tops of their heads touched. "They seem to expect us to show up," Nate murmured, "but they think we'll come by the road since there's nothing but swamp in the back. I can head through the swamp while you go down the road. Take a car; make some noise. Let them know you're there. See how many you can pull to the front. When I get a chance, I'll slip through a side window. I'll grab Chip and head for the woods. As soon as I get to my truck, I'll call your phone. When you hear your ring, get out of there."

"Shouldn't we wait for the police?" Pastor Clark stood beside Ruth. "Jennifer is calling them now."

"If Joe feels threatened, hard telling what he'll do," Nate said. "Best we find out if Chip is in the house and then sneak him out while we can."

Chet straightened. "They'll shoot you if they see you. I should go."

"You don't know the house. I do. You make the distraction, buddy." Nate squeezed Chet's arm and loped across the tangled grass toward the swamp.

Pastor Clark cleared his throat. "I think you women should stay here while Chet and I—"

Betsy stomped toward the car, tiny clouds of dust rising from her feet.

Jennifer followed.

Silently, Ruth crawled into the backseat.

Chet drove slowly, giving Nate time to push through the swamp.

Betsy sat beside him, gaze ahead, back stiff.

Dust billowed around the car, sending its own form of smoke signals toward the house.

Ruth leaned forward, aching for the short drive to be over, the rescue to be completed. What would Joe do when they showed up? She remembered the crazed look in his eyes earlier. Surely, he wouldn't hurt Chip.

The closer they got to the house, the more crows she saw. By the time they reached the house, crows numbered in the thousands.

Chet pulled to the left side of the road and killed the engine. The silence felt smothering. Fifty yards of knee-high field-grass separated the road from what was left of Mr. Charlie's house. As Ruth placed her hand on the door release, Chet motioned for her to stay in the car. He took a few steps into the field, the weeds making a swooshing sound with each advancing step.

"That's far enough."

Ten men in groups of two or three stood in the front of the house. Another two men wandered from the side door. Rifles hung from their hands.

Ruth looked for the skinny guy she had seen at the courthouse and spotted him standing alone by the door.

"I came for my son," Chet shouted, advancing another step.

The crack of a rifle. Dirt shot in the air about three feet from Chet.

"I said that's far enough," the man repeated.

In the front seat, Betsy whimpered.

Jennifer leaned forward and placed her head against Betsy's.

Beside Ruth, Pastor Clark sat with his eyes closed, lips moving. How could this possibly be God's plan? Though doubtful, Ruth still clung to the hope that the pastor was right.

"Where's Joe?" Chet called from the field.

"He ain't here." The man spit a dark stream into the grass. "Who else you got in the car?"

"It doesn't matter."

"It matters if I say it does. Tell them to git out."

Betsy sprang from the front car. "I want my son. Please, let him go. Please."

The man laughed; the sound stretched and pulled as it weaved across the open space. "Yeah, everyone wants the kid. I can give you a couple o' mine."

Jennifer and Pastor Clark huddled around Betsy at the car's front fender while Ruth lowered her feet out the back door, dry grass crunching under her sandals like brittle bones.

Chet moved forward. Another bullet punched into the ground.

Ruth slowly lowered her hand from the car door. Crows perched on the roof of the house. More occupied the path from the road, now worn from vehicle tires. Birds lined the branches of the small trees. Every black, unblinking eye seemed to stare at Ruth. It had to be her imagination, but even so, her stomach clenched. She told herself the birds weren't out to get her. But they had attacked Mr. Charlie.

Were these the same birds that killed her friend? Would the men protect Chip if the crows went crazy again? She imagined Joe's soldiers running for their cars, saving their own necks while forgetting the little kidnapped boy. A small moan slipped from her lips.

36

Sunday Evening, July 28

With each breath Ruth's resolve grew. This was her house, her land. Mr. Charlie had given it to her for a reason. Somehow, he had known. And Pastor Clark said it was up to her. She was the only one who could save Chip.

With legs that felt like they would buckle under her weight, Ruth stepped into the field. Crows scattered at her advance. "Joe, this is Ruth," she yelled across the open space. "Why are you doing this?" At first, she thought her words were lost in the distance, but then the men glanced toward the broken windows. They heard her, and Joe was inside!

Joe swaggered from the side door, the same door the paramedics had used to remove Mr. Charlie's dead body. Unlike the camouflaged men, Joe wore black jeans and a black long-sleeved shirt. Soft blond hair blew across his eyes as he stopped in the trail of tire-crushed grass. "Well, if it isn't the mother of my child. Hello, pretty one."

"Give Chip back to his parents."

"We are his parents." A single crow landed on Joe's shoulder. He reached up and stroked the black beast.

Bile filled Ruth's throat as she watched the unnatural display.

"Why are you doing this? I did everything you asked me to do." Ruth moved forward a few feet, cautiously, waiting for a bullet to displace the ground.

Chet stood a few feet in front of her.

"You will not be able to provide a second child."

"I told you I'd marry you." She moved again, passing Chet. She had to get close enough to see Joe's eyes; was this person Joe, or something else?

"You have that ring around your neck. If you're serious about providing me with an heir, throw the ring away."

She stood within twenty feet of him. "It won't matter, Joe. I don't need the ring to remember my promise to God. I'll sleep with you after I've married you. But to show good faith..." She lifted the chain over her head, clutched the ring for a second, and tossed it as far as she could. There should have been pain at the loss, but instead, Ruth felt a sense of empowerment

Joe sneered. "The ring doesn't matter, not now anyway."

Ruth took another step.

Where's my cousin?" Joe asked. "I expected to see him here."

"He's not with us."

"Do you love him?"

"It doesn't matter. I belong to you if you want me."

His face morphed into a rage. "You don't understand!"

"You made a deal, didn't you, Joe?" Pastor Clark's voice sounded from behind her where he now stood in the field beside Chet. "What is it you have to do?"

"Shoot him!" Joe shouted.

"No!" Ruth ran toward Chet and Pastor Clark, her arms stretched to provide as much protection as she could. "What's wrong with you?" she screamed.

"You don't know how much power is available in the world, Ruthie, until you go looking for it. But be careful. The cost will be high." He laughed and the sound flowed manic and wild. "Yes, Pastor, I made a deal. All I have to do is defeat the light of Logan to secure my future. I thought the light was the church, so I got myself a legislative seat, drafted the Salvation Law, and saw it passed. I had no idea you were in Logan, Ruth. You were never part of my plan."

"But you didn't hurt the church, did you?" Ruth said, the words coming unbidden. "The church isn't the building, it's the people. And the people, the true church, are still strong."

"I figured the light must be Nate. When I saw the two of you together, I knew how to stop him."

"So all of this is just a game?"

Men stood, guns forgotten at their sides.

Ruth prayed she was giving Nate enough time to find Chip. How many of Joe's goons were still inside the house?

"I offered you to Nate, but he turned you down. Such a shame, really. You have so much to offer a man, and no one wants you. Oh, my mistake. The old man who lived here wanted you. I figured he might be the light of Logan, the way he always talked about the crows and hung around like a prophet."

"You killed Mr. Charlie, didn't you?"

"I learned how to control the crows." Joe held up his index finger, and the large crow hopped onto his hand. Again, he stroked the feathered body before putting the bird back on his shoulder.

Ruth moved closer, one step at a time. He didn't object as she approached. When close enough to see his eyes, his venomous look tore the breath from her lungs.

"It is you, Ruth." Insanity softened his face. "You are the light of Logan. You are the one thing that keeps me from success."

The crow turned, and a distinct scar ran from head to wing.

Backing away, the wild grass tangled around her feet, and she fell backwards.

"You probably didn't notice, but the crows always go where you are." He smiled and waved his hands. "Look around, Ruth. What do you see?"

She struggled to her feet.

"The crows are here to watch, Ruthie. Oh, they're not just crows, but you know that, don't you, Pastor Clark? They want to see my destiny unfold."

"Joe, it's not too late!" Pastor Clark shouted across the field.

Joe was crazy. Surely, his men must see that. The urge to convince them crumbled her fear. "Why are you listening to Joe? He's talked you into hating. Look what hate has done to Logan! The streets aren't safe for your children. The moral barometer of the town, the church, is chained. While you're looting and fighting, the Christians that you've been brainwashed to hate are repairing the roads and fixing the houses of your grandparents.

"Open your eyes! What are you doing? And now you kidnapped a little boy? Is that how you want to be remembered—as murderers, and thieves, and kidnappers? I don't know what he promised you, but it won't happen. Put down your guns. You don't have to follow him!"

The men shifted, kicking up puffs of sand beneath their booted feet. Their doubt reached her and her voice strengthened. "Joe's obeying a god that you don't want to follow! Where do you think he gets his power?"

"I brought you here, Ruth, because you are the light I've been searching for." He raised his hands, lifted his head skyward and gave a bellowing yell.

The hair on the back of Ruth's neck stiffened.

Silence followed.

Then the sound started. Wings. The roof of the house seemed to lift as the black mass of crows took flight. From every direction, birds circled toward Ruth.

She would be killed just like Mr. Charlie.

God, help me!

37

Sunday Evening, July 28

Greg Clark stood in shock as the crows circled toward Ruth, all except the crow on Joe's shoulder. He was right. Only God could defeat Joe. Pastor Clark turned toward the car. "Pray!" he shouted across the field to Betsy and Jennifer. "Pray!"

"What's happening?" Chet shouted over the roar of wings.

"Pray for Satan to be defeated! Pray, boy, as you've never prayed before!" Pastor Clark fell to his knees among the weeds.

~*~

From the swamp, Nate spotted twenty or more camouflage-dressed men lingering in the yard. He didn't know how to reach the house without being seen. The men were bunched in groups. Mumbled words reached him, and now and then a bawdy laugh. Dozens of empty beer cans littered the ground.

A soldier flicked a cigarette and watched as a few blades of dry grass burned and then smoldered out.

The sound of rifle fire startled Nate. His gut clenched, and he said a silent prayer for his friends as the men run to the front. Needing to cross the hundred or so feet between him and the house, Nate sprinted over the now-empty yard.

Leaning flat against the back wall, he listened for approaching footsteps. He glanced around the corner. The side yard remained empty. Sticking close to the rotted siding, Nate edged his way to the first broken window and peered inside. A double bed almost filled the room. He remembered a cover on the bed when he had been there last, some sort of quilt. Now the mattress lay exposed.

He moved to the second window and raised his head slowly. Chip lay asleep on the twin bed pushed into the far left corner.

Nate's heart leaped. The boy was here. Between where he stood and the bed was the bedroom door—and a clear sightline into the living space. Six men lounged inside the house; six men who could turn his way at any second.

The sound of another gunshot slammed against Nate's ears, and he ducked below the window. Feet shuffled inside. Voices drifted from the front yard. Ruth's voice! Then Joe's. He needed to hurry.

He sneaked another peek into the bedroom and through the open door. The men had gathered around the broken front window. Taking a chance, Nate dropped inside. Broken glass ground beneath his shoes.

"What's that?"

"A rat. Saw them outside."

Nate bolted to the right, away from view. With nowhere to hide, he hugged the wall beside the door.

"Someone ought' a check on the kid."

"Let the rats have him for lunch."

A can tumbled across the floor. "I'll do it myself, you lazy…"

The sound of booted feet shuffled toward the room. Nate's mouth went dry. There was nowhere to hide. Taking several deep breaths, he prepared to fight.

As the footsteps came closer, Nate tightened his muscles. A shadow filled the doorway, and then a thick-set man moved into the room. He glanced at the bed, grunted, and walked out.

Nate sagged against the wall.

Screams and a vibrating roar came from outside.

"Come on!" yelled one of the men.

"What about the kid?"

"He's not going anywhere. Hasn't moved since Joe drugged him."

~*~

The winged bodies swarmed like an inverted bowl around Ruth. The birds bounced against each other as though pushing for position. The dome thickened until only the tiniest strip of light showed near the ground. Paralyzed with fear and helpless, she awaited her death.

~*~

Nate gathered the sleeping boy into his arms. As he ran out the bedroom door, he glimpsed through the front window and froze. A black cyclone of crows swirled in front of Joe. Chet and Pastor Clark were in the field on their knees; Betsy and Jennifer, out by the road, hugged each other. Where was Ruth?

Joe shifted his gaze from the sky to the window where Nate stood holding the sleeping Chip.

"It's over, Joe," Nate mumbled. Within Nate's

being he knew he would never fall prey to his cousin again.

Joe's arms quivered and then fell to his sides.

A handful of crows broke from the mass and streaked across the sky. Slowly, a few at a time, the crows broke free. And then more, until their bodies created a cloud of black as they flew over the swamp.

Nate walked from the side door carrying a drowsy Chip. As his gaze met Ruth's, he placed the boy in her arms. Chet and Betsy ran to her. His chest tightened with love as he watched Ruth kiss the boy's cheek and give him up, again.

One of the soldiers shouted, "Fire!"

Smoke billowed over the top of the house. Vehicles roared out of the field, only to be stopped by police cars racing up the road, lights flashing.

Sensing movement beside him, Nate turned in time to see Joe running toward the house. Flames licked across the roof.

"Joe! No, stop!"

With one foot already moving toward the house, Nate turned to Ruth, wanting to tell her all that was on his heart but only having seconds to do it. "Ruth, I have been such a fool. As soon as this is over..." He pulled himself away and sprinted toward the house, now fully engulfed in flames. As he ran, he glanced over his shoulder. "I love you, Ruth!"

38

Monday, July 29

The house was quiet as Ruth walked down the stairs from the Clarks' guest bedroom the next morning. The kitchen was empty, chairs slid in place, dishes washed. Ruth spied a note propped against the Rooster napkin holder on the table and she walked to it.

Ruth, we had an errand to run. Breakfast is in the refrigerator. Warm it up in the microwave. Call me when you get up. The house phone and my cell number are in the den.

Jennifer

Ruth had just put the eggs and pancakes in the microwave when someone knocked on the back door. A silhouette showed through the red and white checked curtain covering the small window. Thinking it might be one of the parishioners needing Pastor Clark, she opened the door.

Ruth's eyes widened, and she inhaled sharply. Shaking off her surprise, she pulled Nate inside. His clothes smelled of swamp and were half covered in dried mud. She led his slumped body into a chair, unsure what to say, or if she even had the right to question him. Instead of talking, she stared at his haggard face.

"Pastor Clark?" Nate asked as he sagged in the seat.

Ruth slid into a chair across from him. "He's not here. Jennifer left a note and said they had an errand to run." At his look of disappointment, she rose from her chair. "I have a phone number. Do you want me to—"

Nate wrapped warm fingers around her arm. "Just sit with me a minute."

With Nate's hand still holding her wrist and her heart pounding in her chest, Ruth lowered herself back into the chair. She ached to talk to him, to be with him, but part of her didn't want to hear what he might have to say about the past twelve hours. Should she still be afraid of Joe and what he might do?

"I chased Joe all night. One minute I saw him, the next he melted into a clump of cyprus. It was so dark..." Nate stared ahead, his expression blank. "I had my hands on him a couple of times, but he slipped away. Eventually I lost him, and in the dark, I had trouble finding my way out."

"So you spent the night in the swamp?" She swallowed the lump that had grown in her throat, amazed a water snake or alligator...or a bear...hadn't eaten him.

"I holed up in the crook of a tree. Not bad, really. When it got light I found my way out."

"You've got to be hungry." Ruth grabbed her breakfast from the microwave and placed it in front of him. She poured orange juice and watched as he devoured the food.

He sat back and sighed. And then he surprised her

with a smile. "I guess I should have washed my hands first."

She gave him a chuckle as her heart warmed even more. She wasn't sure how Nate felt about her. It had seemed infinitely clear yesterday, but today things seemed different. He seemed different. She wasn't sure why. "Nate, I never had the chance to thank you for rescuing Chip."

His gaze roamed her face. "You stood up to all those men."

"You weren't there."

"I heard you as I stood beside the house."

She listened to the sound of his breathing and hated that she loved everything about him. In spite of all she had been through, regardless of how many times things had gone wrong between them, she still loved him. A wedding no longer hung over her head or a need to protect her child. Still, her relationship with Joe erased any chance she had with Nate.

"Ruth." His eyes softened and her heart skipped a beat. "I need to tell you—"

The door opened. "Hey Ruth...Nate! What in the world?" Jennifer dropped her purse on the counter. "Are you all right?"

"Wondered if I could get my truck."

"That's right, we have your truck. I think Greg put your keys...here they are." She lifted a round plastic disc with attached keys from the counter. "Are you sure you're all right?"

"I'm fine. What time will Greg be home?"

"He may be gone all day."

"Have him call me, will you?" As Nate lifted himself from the chair, clumps of dirt dropped onto the floor. His mouth spread into a grimace. "Oh, man, I'm really sorry."

"I'll take care of it," Ruth said. She wished he wasn't going, leaving her questioning their relationship all over again. If only Jennifer hadn't arrived when she did.

He turned at the door. "Ah, Ruth...can we talk sometime?"

Her heart did cartwheels.

~*~

As Ruth swept the kitchen floor, Jennifer put Nate's dishes in the dishwasher. She turned to Ruth. "I promised to take you to the Ross home this morning."

Ruth felt pain in her stomach. Her best friend believed she had betrayed her. That was the last place she wanted to go; Betsy's anger was too fresh in her mind.

"Betsy's been asking for you."

"So she can make me feel bad all over again?" Ruth rubbed her arms. "You saw her reaction to me yesterday."

"Seeing her will never get easier, so come on."

The drive took less than ten minutes. As they parked, Ruth's gut began to twist. "I don't know. Are you sure she wants to see me?" She could peek inside, say hi, and express gratitude that Chip was safe. Then she could retreat. It was only a short walk to her house. After all, she had to deal with the mess there sometime.

Ruth turned her head sharply one direction and then another, scanning each yard as they passed. "There are no crows!"

"I haven't seen a crow since last night."

Ruth sat quietly for a minute. "Do you think all the

crows were at Mr. Charlie's?"

When Jennifer shrugged her shoulders, Ruth heaved a sigh. One more issue she would need to deal with. But for now, Betsy had to have her say. "Let's just get this over with." Arriving at her former friend's home, Ruth opened the car door and stepped out.

Betsy raced down the walkway. Her arms surrounded Ruth, and she pulled her close.

Ruth gripped hold of Betsy.

Tears streamed down both their faces.

"I am so sorry," Betsy mumbled into Ruth's neck. "How could I have said those things to you? Can you forgive me?"

"You're my best friend."

Betsy's gaze wandered to the door where Chip stood. Betsy took her hand. "Come and see our son."

Ruth looked at the small boy, shirtless and feet bare. He'd never looked more wonderful. She turned to Betsy, wiping tears from her eyes. "He's your son. Someday you may decide to share the story of his birth, but until then…I'm happy just to know him."

~*~

After an hour of visiting, Ruth and Jennifer left the Ross home.

"I appreciate you driving me, but I've walked between Betsy's house and mine a dozen times," Ruth said as Jennifer turned her car onto the road.

Jennifer stole a sideways glance. "You know you're welcome to stay with us as long as you want."

"I can pay for a hotel until I decide what I'll do."

"No way will I have you staying in a hotel when there's a perfectly good bed with your name on it."

They had already had this conversation.

Jennifer slowed as she approached Ruth's house.

Monday morning, and normally the neighborhood was deserted. Today, though, vehicles lined both sides of the street in front of her house.

She eased herself out of the car. A large pickup truck sat in the front yard. A couple of men Ruth recognized from the church hauled garbage bags out her front door and heaved them into the truck. A third man followed, the man who had tossed tomatoes at her that first Sunday.

"Hey there!" Paul Kritchner called to her. "Thought we'd fix your window."

Cyrus Phillips stood beside him holding a hammer.

Pastor Clark lugged a bag out the door.

Too surprised to think of an appropriate response, her "thank you for organizing all of this," sounded formal as she gazed in amazement.

"It wasn't us," Jennifer said. "We got a call last night to come and help today, along with all these other folks."

Ruth tried to think. Who else would care enough?

Her neighbor sauntered out of her front door, the man she had barely spoken to in almost two years. With his wild hair and crazy hours, she had figured it best to avoid him. "Hey there." He grinned at her. "I called Daryl, your landlord. He owns my house, too. Hope you don't mind."

Ruth stared. Her neighbor was helping? No way. She didn't even know his name.

He rubbed his chin. "Man, Daryl was flyin' hot over the busted windows. Said you were gonna have to replace them. So I called your friends."

"You called my friends? How did you know—"

"I saw the dudes in the backyard with you on Sunday. I know most of them from working at the auto body shop. Others just showed up."

"I can't believe you did this for me."

"Hey, we're neighbors."

"Your house needed some new windows, and some de-fowling." Paul Kritchner laughed at his joke. "Cyrus and I are trying to piece together your furniture as much as we can, but most of it got ruined. The birds are all bagged up and gone, though."

"But the windows?" Boxes of framed glass stood propped against the house.

"Donated by Stewart Gleason himself." Paul grinned.

39

Friday, August 2

Ruth waved good-bye to the last two workers, Paul and Velma Kritchner. At the beginning of the summer, she would never have thought the past week possible. Men and women, many she hardly knew, had been flowing through her house in a constant stream, repairing the damage created by Joe's soldiers and the crows. More than that, the workers had brought food, encouraged her, and many times apologized. Now new glass windows sparkled in the late afternoon sun, wood floors gleamed with a coat of wax, walls were re-painted, and all hints of birds and splintered wood were gone.

The few possessions that survived, her bed where Chip had slept, the blanket made from her maternity clothing, and one mug that had been protected by being in the sink, were now at the Clarks' house. Her clothes, cocooned within the heavy drawers of the built-in chest in the bedroom wall, had not been destroyed. The item she would have mourned for the most, Mr. Charlie's shirts, remained in the plastic bag where she had placed them.

Patsy Dillon had showed up on Tuesday with her husband, George. They took the day off work to help. It was Patsy who had sparked the idea of creating a furniture business. Patsy had approached her during their lunch break—club sandwiches, thanks to Chet and Betsy. Patsy sat beside Ruth under the front shade tree and pulled a hard scrap from the pocket of her shorts. "I found this in the corner and saved it." She fingered a small piece of wood with hints of yellow paint on one side.

"It's part of the coffee table." Ruth worked to push away the ache that came each time loss confronted her. Patsy had admired the table.

"I thought it might be." Patsy continued to stare at the broken bit of wood. "I wondered…when you feel able…can you make me a coffee table just like it?"

Ruth glanced up. "Seriously?" Did the woman realize she had made it from scraps no one wanted? Ruth had agreed. The possibility of her hobby becoming a job took root.

Later that same day, when the police contacted Mr. and Mrs. Ackerman about Joe's disappearance, Pastor Clark arranged for her to talk to her mom.

During the call, Ruth shared the truth about her move to Wilmington, about the baby, and about the past few months of agony. She told her mom about Mr. Charlie and about Nate. She shared with her about God. Hanging up had been hard to do.

With a deep sigh, she pulled the front door closed behind her and checked the lock one last time. This had been her first home and she was leaving it. She wasn't sure what the future held, but she knew she could face it. Having Mr. Charlie's money to fall back on helped a lot, but she felt different inside, stronger, more capable. Whatever she did—go back to Attorney Dunlap's office, start her own furniture business, or try something new—she would give it her all. And succeed or fail, it didn't matter as much as having the courage to try.

The roar of diesel filled her ears, and Nate pulled his truck to the curb and parked.

Ruth shivered, knowing what would come next.

He wrapped her in muscular arms and pulled her close. "How is my best girl?"

She snuggled into the hardness of his chest.

Every day this week, he had arrived to drive her to the Clarks', where they had dinner and talked. The past two nights, the Clarks had plans elsewhere. In fact, they had been gone overnight. First, she had cooked, and last night Nate had served her. This would be their last evening together for a while. Ruth held onto the man she loved a little longer.

"You ready for this?" Nate asked.

"As ready as I can be."

"I'll sleep better knowing you're in my house."

"And you'll be in the middle of the woods in a tent. How am I supposed to sleep?"

"I'll only be gone a couple of weeks."

"You can find God in two weeks?"

"You found Him in two minutes."

Ruth smiled. "I did, didn't I?"

Nate's phone chirped. As he read and responded to his text, she thought back to when black wings covered the sky. As she'd faced death, God came close and protected her.

Nate disconnected the call and smiled. Oh, that smile. Would she ever grow immune to its power? "Let's go," he said, still grinning.

They settled into the truck and Ruth took one last glance at her home.

The neighbor peered out his door.

She held up a hand in farewell. "Never judge a

book by the cover," her dad used to say. She should have remembered that sooner.

At the end of her street, Nate turned the truck left toward his house. "I want you to think of my house as yours. Use anything you want."

"And while you're off sojourning in the woods finding God, I need to find a place to live, decide on my job, and plan my future."

"Maybe I should stay for a while. I can—"

"No! I miss you already, but you have to go. You said it yourself. All your adult life you've been so busy working at the church that you never got to know God as Father. Thanks to you, I know Him. Now you need to find the Father; God is more than master."

"Look, isn't that Pastor Clark's car?" Ruth said as the truck pulled into Nate's gravel drive.

The front door of Nate's house opened and a figure stepped out.

A sob rose from Ruth's throat. "Mom!" Ruth jumped off the running board and ran across the stubbly grass. Two bodies collided in the yard forming a tower of arms around bodies. Through her sobs, Ruth looked at her mom. Her auburn hair was more gray and new wrinkles creased the thin face. But it was her gaze that held Ruth's attention—eyes that shined with love. "How did you get here?" Ruth asked.

Mrs. Cleveland glanced in the direction of the house where Pastor and Jennifer Clark stood on the porch. "They came to Atlanta and picked me up."

"We thought you might need company while you're here," Nate said.

"You knew!" Now the silly grins made sense.

"The phone call was to let me know your mom arrived, and I could bring you to my house."

Without letting go of her mom's hand, she hugged Nate. "I love you so much!"

A car pulled into the drive and car doors opened. "Uncle Nate! Aunt Ruth!" Chip wiggled from his mother's grasp and ran to Nate, who swung him into the air.

Mrs. Cleveland glanced at Ruth and raised her eyebrows.

Ruth smiled. "Mom, let me introduce you to Chip Ross, and his parents, Betsy and Chet."

"I have a fire going around back for hotdogs, if anyone is interested," Greg called from the front porch.

"And Mom, this is Nate Bishop." Ruth stared up at the man beside her.

Nate's cheeks colored as Mrs. Cleveland stared into his face the way mothers do.

Ruth chuckled. Her mom had already figured out what Nate Bishop meant to her.

Jennifer approached and wrapped an arm around Ruth's mom. "Will you help me carry out the picnic food?"

The women retreated to the house, and Ruth knew a friendship would blossom between the two.

Nate pulled her into a hug. She felt his lips softly brush against the top of her head and then he covered the spot with his cheek, as though to hold the kiss in place. "I love you, Ruth Cleveland, and it took almost losing you to make me realize it." His arms tightened around her. "When I get back home, I know a beautiful spot on the river where we need to spend some time."

The Light of Logan sparkled.

40

Monday, September 18

Stewart Gleason strode into the House of Representatives chamber. Same seat, new session. As he passed the pictures of Robert E. Lee and Thomas Jefferson, he tipped his chin in acknowledgement. He felt more in sync with their struggles than ever before. Assuming his seat, he removed the morning's folders from his briefcase.

As the chamber filled with new and returning representatives, laughter and banter bounced around the room.

Gleason heaved a sigh and settled back into his padded chair.

"How was your summer?" Todd Myers, now bronzed golden, smiled down at Stewart.

"Looks like you got in some of that beach time you wanted," Stewart Gleason responded.

"Took the wife and the girls for a few weeks to Hilton Head. Had to get away, you know?"

Gleason knew. He had spent the summer in Columbia, doing everything he could to get the Salvation Law declared illegal. In the end, he'd failed. No tan colored his skin. But a few wrinkles around his mouth and at the corner of his eyes had deepened.

Representative Myers took out identical files to Gleason's. He tapped them on the desk, aligning the corners. "You had a bit of excitement in Logan, I hear."

Stewart grimaced. He knew the questions would

come, and he had rehearsed his answers. He said what Todd already knew. "The mayor enacted the Salvation Law."

"I heard. We considered it but decided to pass."

"Smart move."

"I heard there aren't any churches in Logan anymore." Todd chuckled. "I can't imagine that's true."

Stewart faced Todd. He felt nothing but sympathy for the junior legislator who most likely would still be trying to do what was right long after Gleason finished this last term. "It was hard at first. The church buildings were locked. People didn't know what to do. Some folks believed all law was gone, and they had the freedom to do whatever they wanted."

"You had some looting."

"We had a lot of looting, harassment of Christians, and even a couple deaths. But you should be afraid, Todd. You know why?"

Representative Myers raised his eyebrows.

"The Salvation Law was repealed in Logan, but the law is still on the South Carolina books. Any county, at any time, can implement it. Are you a Christian, Todd?"

"I suppose so."

"You had better figure it out. When the law comes to your town, and it eventually will, your people better know the difference between attending church and following Christ. Too many people, good people, get so busy doing that they forget to develop a relationship with their Lord. When the church building closes, they have nothing. But in Logan, we learned and we grew."

"I heard Joseph Ackerman went crazy."

Yep, there it was, the part Stewart had been

waiting for, the part he had rehearsed. People wanted to hear the sensationalism, not the real story. "Todd, if you believe in God, you have to also believe in the power of Satan." Stewart scratched his chin. This was the tricky part. He didn't want Todd, or anyone else, to get the wrong idea, but the truth had to be told.

"Joseph was able to do things that he shouldn't have been able to do, like get a seat in the House, gather followers in Logan, and convince them to hate the church. In a matter of weeks, he became a cult-leader. He became his own law. Guys followed him: the unemployed, blue collar, even a junior attorney who worked with him at the courthouse. They did things for their leader they would not normally do. But Todd, here's the important part. It took one person to stand up to Ackerman, one girl, and his power collapsed."

Stewart knew his friend didn't understand. He didn't understand it himself and he had lived through it. It was unbelievable that a man could control crows. Or that the same man, singlehandedly, had closed the churches and turned honest townsfolk into an angry mob. But it happened and it would happen again. Joseph Ackerman had disappeared, along with the crows, but the power behind him remained.

Todd's laugh had a nervous lilt. "That's quite a story."

The gavel fell on the fall session of the House of Representatives.

Stewart Gleason opened his first folder. The greatness of the American political system—and he believed in this greatness—would never over-power the evil that fought against it. He would fight, and other legislators across the states would join him, but eventually they would lose. Satan would win for a season. But Stewart, along with other Christians, would do all they could to slow the decay of this great country one vote at a time. And in His perfect time, God would exact victory for eternity.

Thank you…

for purchasing this Harbourlight title. For other inspirational stories, please visit our on-line bookstore at www.pelicanbookgroup.com.

For questions or more information, contact us at customer@pelicanbookgroup.com.

Harbourlight Books
The Beacon in Christian Fiction™
an imprint of Pelican Book Group
www.pelicanbookgroup.com

Connect with Us
www.facebook.com/Pelicanbookgroup
www.twitter.com/pelicanbookgrp

To receive news and specials, subscribe to our bulletin
http://pelink.us/bulletin

May God's glory shine through
this inspirational work of fiction.

AMDG

You Can Help!

At Pelican Book Group it is our mission to entertain readers with fiction that uplifts the Gospel. It is our privilege to spend time with you awhile as you read our stories.

We believe you can help us to bring Christ into the lives of people across the globe. And you don't have to open your wallet or even leave your house!

Here are 3 simple things you can do to help us bring illuminating fiction™ to people everywhere.

1) If you enjoyed this book, write a positive review. Post it at online retailers and websites where readers gather. And share your review with us at reviews@pelicanbookgroup.com (this does give us permission to reprint your review in whole or in part.)

2) If you enjoyed this book, recommend it to a friend in person, at a book club or on social media.

3) If you have suggestions on how we can improve or expand our selection, let us know. We value your opinion. Use the contact form on our web site or e-mail us at customer@pelicanbookgroup.com

God Can Help!

Are you in need? The Almighty can do great things for you. Holy is His Name! He has mercy in every generation. He can lift up the lowly and accomplish all things. Reach out today.

Do not fear: I am with you; do not be anxious: I am your God. I will strengthen you, I will help you, I will uphold you with my victorious right hand.
~Isaiah 41:10 (NAB)

We pray daily, and we especially pray for everyone connected to Pelican Book Group—that includes you! If you have a specific need, we welcome the opportunity to pray for you. Share your needs or praise reports at http://pelink.us/pray4us

Free Book Offer

We're looking for booklovers like you to partner with us! Join our team of influencers today and periodically receive free eBooks and exclusive offers.

For more information
Visit http://pelicanbookgroup.com/booklovers

www.ingramcontent.com/pod-product-compliance
Lightning Source LLC
Chambersburg PA
CBHW031314280626
47169CB00019B/1531